Secret Chronicles of a Fashion Model

THE FUGITIVE'S GIRLFRIEND

Brooke Gantt

Secret Chronicles of a Fashion Model

THE FUGITIVE'S GIRLFRIEND

For Information, contact WBM Publishing

www.EverythingBrooke.com

ISBN-13: 978-0-615-68828-2

Table of Contents

Secret Chronicles of a Fashion Model:

The Fugitive's Girlfriend

"Stop! Please, stop! I won't do it again!" Elizabeth cried. She screamed in pain with terror in her eyes. The rage in Elizabeth's voice was not being used to fight for world peace but to persuade her boyfriend Casmir from choking her with a cord and sexually attacking her.

"Shut up!" he growled. A flood of tears gushed down her red flushed cheeks. Elizabeth screamed louder, as the phone cord wrapped tighter around her neck. Her boyfriend's one-eyed snake protruded deeper into her bruised anal cavity, face down, ass up. She dares not move, in fear of being slapped in the back of her head by his unforgiving hand.

Thus far, this was the most degrading abuse Elizabeth had endured by Casmir. The gun he once pointed at her or the pillow he suffocated her with until he decided Elizabeth could breathe again could not even compare. The feeling...the reckless pain at its best would be hard to describe, but Casmir knew having sex through the back door was the worst kind of intercourse for her, so he used it for punishment.

Even so, it still did not stop Elizabeth from rashly returning to Casmir's arms, shamefully happy they were still together.

"I love you," Casmir whispered by her ear.

"I – love – you, too," Elizabeth murmured slowly.

"Don't ever go to the store again without asking me, first," he said. Elizabeth and Casmir made love like nothing ever happened.

As the plot thickens, this shocking, unforgettable, and emotional rollercoaster ride of love will reveal a chain of events that no one should ever have to endure. Leave your comfort zone and get ready to enter the unbelievable and unreal wilderness of a manhunt with blood at the end, involving a lost but beautiful, biracial 15-year-old young lady. She goes by the name Elizabeth Tight...not Liz or Beth, just Elizabeth.

Her boyfriend, Casmir Nowak, was a 19-year-old polish gangster with a bad temper. The streets called him Richie, but he was as broke as a convict, which was odd, because everything Casmir puts his hands on was done with precision. He ran a clean shop, and he certainly had money before they met.

Casmir may be a loose cannon, but once upon a time he had a soft spot for Elizabeth. She remembered the day they met at the shopping center a year ago.

Elizabeth and her friend walked through their Philly hometown mall in their new outfits that Elizabeth designed herself, having much fun. Elizabeth loved life. She commanded a presence with her magnetic personality, "live by my own rules" unafraid attitude, and infectious giggle.

The interracial high school she attended helped her adapt to all cultural backgrounds, allowing her to easily make friends and adjust to any situation. Guys would leave love notes on her locker. Girls wanted to be her friend. She was one of those people you met and never forgot, which gave her first picks for valedictorian at her high school graduation the year she received her diploma.

Elizabeth did not know how to sing, but when she was not playing lacrosse or her favorite game UNO, she faithfully lip-sang on the youth choir at her church. She was always accused of being too nice and only living by her good morals and values, but that was her nature.

Elizabeth and her friend were full of joy and excited about going to their favorite snack shop to pick up some fresh, candy-coated popcorn. But when Elizabeth arrived, she saw more than flavorful popcorn at the stand. She saw something she had never seen before in her teenage life. She experienced something she had never experienced before in her teenage life.

Love at first sight.

Blood rushed in her veins. She felt dizzy as she panicked and motioned her girlfriend to keep walking. The cashier made eye contact with her loyal customer, Elizabeth. She even detected something unexpected just ensued.

Her girlfriend asked her if she wanted to go to the clothing store, but at this point, Elizabeth was not in the mood to think about shopping. Elizabeth did not mention to her friend that for the first time, she began to understand the taste and texture of love. Her friend also didn't know Elizabeth was on the verge of a meltdown because she figured she would never see her newfound love again.

Elizabeth sat on a nearby bench, slouching low, giving off an unpresentable image.

I do not know what is happening to me, she said to herself. *I came to the mall for popcorn, but the smell of pizza and buffalo wings we looked forward to as well was making me sick.*

Elizabeth fought off these feelings of despair.

As she gradually got up to enter the store her friend suggested, walking past her was the dreamy guy. His rich and radiant diamond like eyes made contact with hers, captivating every nerve in her body as if their spirits had known each other forever. Instantly her heart fluttered and all the passion and emotion she felt before returned. It didn't take long for her friend to figure out why she had been acting so somber.

Unexpectedly, he held up a familiar bag to hand to Elizabeth but instead she hesitated and glanced at it with an empty expression.

"Take it," her friend insisted. She accepted the gesture while taking a quick look inside; it was red coated popcorn, the only kind she ate. *How did he know?* Elizabeth asked herself.

He was undeniably a true gentleman with a pleasant and respectable persona. Between his shoulder-length curly blonde hair, his clean chin, and his unforgettable bright blue icy eyes he was utterly irresistible.

"What is your name?" the guy asked as he stood close to her.

"Elizabeth," she answered sweetly.

"Casmir," he replied. "And this is my boy Franky," as his friend walked over to them.

"Oh," Elizabeth momently blushed. "This is my girlfriend."

"Binga, her best friend," Elizabeth's girlfriend smiled widely.

Standing in the middle of the mall, having a conversation with Casmir as shoppers passed by, Elizabeth could tell he was easy to fall in love with and his hardcore attitude when needed made all the girls want him.

He looked intently at Elizabeth like he knew that he was excellent at seducing women; he never had trouble attracting them and out of all the girls Casmir had ever met, Elizabeth was the one he couldn't forget. He knew he would love her like his most precious jewel and he chose her from all the rest.

Instead of staying at the mall, Casmir invited Elizabeth to a local fair. As soon as they drove off in a fully loaded black SUV, his selflessness and generosity went beyond a single offering. He asked her to his place. And with her unafraid, willing to take risk attitude she went with him.

They talked and laughed for a good part of the evening at his prolific condo; the two of them had instantaneous chemistry and Elizabeth felt like the luckiest girl in the world but she couldn't help but wonder where he had gotten the money to buy such expensive things at a young age.

They continued to talk and laugh; the sweet and soft music of Luther Vandross surrounded them as it played softly in the background. She could tell he had an old soul at heart. Elizabeth learned Casmir had several distant sisters by different mothers and one brother by the same mom who his father was currently married to. She also learned Casmir grew up in the part of town her parents wanted to keep Elizabeth away from, but so far in her eyes, he was perfect.

Casmir could tell Elizabeth was a good girl and his bad boy image fascinated her; she could not resist. He looked her directly in the eyes with a wicked but enduring spark.

"You are so pretty." Elizabeth's face softened and her heart sank. She was in love with him already. Was it possible...

As the bright room became dark and the music struck a different tune, she gave him a big juicy kiss and all of Elizabeth's good morals and values went out the window, as she gave Casmir her virginity that night.

After the brash act, she observed the small spot of blood on the sheets while covering her young bush. *I shouldn't have gone beyond kissing but there is nothing I can do about it now*, Elizabeth thought. As the music came to an end, Casmir embraced her and she embraced him back, and as the night became wet and windy she asked him to take her home.

Casmir and Elizabeth easily bonded and adored each other. They spend every single day together. One day she asked Casmir to meet her at her house to have dinner with her family. He accepted the invite, arriving on time.

They ate, after Casmir volunteered to say the grace. *Nice,* Elizabeth thought. *He must really want my parents to like him.*

Casmir had nothing but good things to say about Elizabeth. He told them how caring, loving, and giving she was.

"I'm a sucker for her love," Casmir said to her dad.

Elizabeth's parents knew their beautiful daughter was very driven, a hard worker, and an amazing shining star, which sometimes made her mom jealous. But her parents were delighted to hear someone else saying all of these great things about their daughter. They felt like they raised a special child and that made them feel good inside.

Her mom really liked the fact he was close to his parents and he went to church. She thought the grace he said was beautiful.

"Whose fish is this?" Casmir wondered.

"It's mine," Elizabeth said, smiling sweetly. "My dad gave it to me for my birthday. Her name is Freckles."

"Nice name," Casmir said genuinely.

"Yeah," Elizabeth agreed. "I was cleaning out the fish tank today so that's why she's on the kitchen counter. I hope she did not gross you out."

"No, not at all," Casmir said.

Her mom looked at Elizabeth.

"Please take it back to your room tonight."

"Yes, ma'am," Elizabeth muttered.

"You are a daddy's little girl, huh?" Casmir asked.

"Yes," Elizabeth answered as her mom rolled her eyes.

"Whatever my dad does or gives me is special," Elizabeth continued as her mom stood up at the head of the table to grab the plate of baked chicken.

"I will get that for you Mrs. Tight," Casmir said, handing her the plate.

"Thank you," her mom said gently.

"Speaking of daddy's little girl, you have a younger sister right, Elizabeth?" Casmir asked, though he knew the answer to that question.

"You will meet her soon," her mom replied. "She is with a girlfriend for the weekend."

As the night ended, Casmir was headed out the door. Elizabeth picked up Freckles to take her back to her bedroom. He said his goodbyes and gave Elizabeth a kiss on the cheek. She flushed, and lightly touched his stunningly rugged face.

He is absolutely beautiful. But then she saw her mom staring at her hand. Elizabeth giggled silently to herself as she moved her hand away from his face.

"I will talk to you later, babe."

Casmir also noticed her mom watching them so he ended the night by saying to her parents, "Your daughter is a spectacular lady with lots of class. She means the world to me."

Her dad arched his eyebrow.

"Treat her right."

"I will...I promise, Mr. Tight. Good night," Casmir said. He turned to Mrs. Tight, "Good night, Mother Tight." Elizabeth's face flickered to Casmir one last time, and she instantly flushed again while Casmir shut the door. Mrs. Tight smiled as her mom ate the last big piece of chicken.

She definitely wore the pants in that family.

Elizabeth's mom and dad seemed to like Casmir a lot. They thought he was a fine guy, especially since he validated there parenting. Elizabeth was just overjoyed that her parents got along the entire time during dinner.

My parents were married on Valentine's Day, and they are still together, Elizabeth said to herself, *but it was like war of the roses between those two.*

On the other hand, love was exciting and harmony was in Elizabeth's and Casmir's relationship. They shared the same activities and had deep and meaningful conversations. Family events hit a sweet spot. They were inseparable to a point that Casmir's life was wrapped around hers but like most relationships, they all start out wonderful but this fiery relationship eventually came crashing down like icicles hanging in the balance until the spring thaw.

Casmir went from Mr. Nice Guy to showing his insecurities and the bond became chaotic.

Elizabeth contemplated whether or not she should leave Casmir alone but Casmir guarded his chosen partner like a prized possession, becoming obsessive, jealous, violent, and controlling.

As time went on, the strangest things began to happen. This once - materialistic guy lost his SUV and his lavish condo. He let his mustache and beard grow in long and his hair stayed dirty. Casmir wore the same white nylon sweat suit every day, even in the summer time. The only beautiful feature left on him was his fit body.

His Polish father and Irish mother could not explain his out of control ways or his new beastly look.

Ah! Appearances were deceiving because this now raggedy-looking guy with a missing tooth was cruel but very smart, clever, and systematic. As a result, Casmir did not jump into situations. He was effective at every thing he desired, even if it meant plotting or scheming along the way.

His next plot was holding on to Elizabeth, at any cost.

But thank heavens, he did not have a cent to his name anymore because he definitely would not be using it for the good of the land; instead Casmir would be more vicious with money and power.

Despite his flaws, Elizabeth thought Casmir meant well and she stayed with her man. She thought back to his kind manner at the popcorn counter. Deep down inside she knew Casmir loved her and they were good together.

Dedications

I dedicate this book to all females who have been abused, either mentally, emotionally, or physically.

I also dedicate this book to inspiring models and family and friends who have stuck by my side through thick and thin. Bless you all! I love you.

Lastly, I would like to thank my Lord Jesus Christ for my talents, gifts, and purpose; and loving me no matter what.

Chapter 1

An urban jungle melody was heard in the distance, cutting through the damp night air, Philadelphia's waterless fog and remote meadows drawn by a rainstorm. This was Philly's country, where the isolated forest and humid rain provided a continual slow faucet drip serving as Fairmount Park's rugged wilderness in the middle of America's most populous city.

The park slipped in and out of the natural surrounding areas of Pennyback, Cobbs Creek, and Tacony Watersheds skimming the Schuylkill River - filling the atmosphere with the history of art and culture. They are as much a part of the landscape as the wildflowers or the dark colored garter snake. But something had come to disturb this evergreen paradise, something as black as the water's murky vigor; a ticking time bomb named Casmir. He loved to stroll through the park at night hoping someone would bother him.

Casmir threw his hands up in the air, mouthing the words to his favorite rap song as the tunes from his headphones filled his ears.

He paused to adjust the sound, allowing the music to blast while he shouted the chorus, "More bitches and bitches and bitches and hoes, yeah! Bitches and hoes, yeah! Bitches and hoes, yeah! More bitches and bitches and bitches and hoes, just suck my dick, yeah!"

Elizabeth slowly walked up to him and in her normal sweet tone said, "Casmir." Elizabeth realized she was not loud enough. She tapped his shoulder and the hot-tempered Casmir swung around, balled up his rock hard fist, knuckles positioned to strike his opponent.

"It's me Casmir!" Elizabeth cried, dunking low, her hands shielding her face in a defensive manner.

He lowered his deadly fist, yanked his headphones away from his ears.

"You should know better than to sneak up on me like that, especially when I'm listening to *Bitches and Hoes, Yeah!*"

"I'm sorry," Elizabeth replied.

"What are you doing here anyway? I told you to meet me at the house," Casmir said sternly.

"I was at your house, and your grandmother said you were here," Elizabeth responded.

"You don't listen!" Casmir said forcefully. "Go to the house, sit down, and wait for me there!"

"Why are you here so late listening to music? You look crazy," Elizabeth joked. His face darkened as he slapped Elizabeth. She gasped. It was obvious he did not get her joke as she held her cheek, feeling like it was smashed to the side of her face for life. "Why did you hit me?"

"Go! And shut the fuck up," Casmir commanded. He whammed his foot into a trashcan, knocking it over. "Go!"

"Okay," she cried. "I was coming to find you, that's all!"

"Yeah right, you were probably messing around with my cousin at my house?"

"What?!" Elizabeth said, truly confused. "Don't 'what' me you dirty slut!"

Elizabeth disagreed, "I was not messing around. I was at the house waiting for you!" Casmir jumped forward, his blonde hair fell over his face as he pushed Elizabeth to the ground, forcing her to crash on her side awkwardly.

A stranger with a bald head and spooky eyes shouted, "Leave her alone!"

"What? Who you think you talking to? This is between me and my girlfriend." Casmir's devilish glare in his blue eyes made the man rethink his heroism as he walked away.

Meanwhile, Elizabeth saw an opportunity to lift herself off the filthy cement, but suddenly Casmir kicked her in the stomach, her hands flying to her belly.

"See how much trouble you caused, all because you don't listen, Elizabeth. Why is that?!"

"I'm sorry," Elizabeth cried, holding her aching gut.

"You always sorry! Get out of here before I put my shoe print up that ass!" Elizabeth used a nearby railing to get up off the ground and stumbled to his grandmother's house.

When she arrived she wiped her eyes and ignored the stomach pain. She did not want Casmir's 87-year-old grandmother under any stress.

Elizabeth finally knocked on the door. No answer. She knocked again, but louder. No answer. She knocked again even louder.

"Wait a minute," Casmir's grandmother said on the other side of the evergreen painted door that matched her floral porch furniture. A frilly fair skinned grandmother answered the door with tight curls, styled off her face to showcase her reading glasses and dentures. She smiled.

"Back so soon? Come in."

She was a lovely petite lady.

"You look like you've been crying. Where is my beautiful grandson so he can give you a hug? Did you see him at the park?"

"Yes. He wants me to wait for him here," Elizabeth said, admiring his grandmother's cute pant set, perfect for her.

"Okay, but what is wrong with you?" Casmir's grandmother asked quizzically. "When you left here you was fine."

Elizabeth could not give her a satisfactory answer. She was told by her boyfriend to sit down and wait for him.

"I will get you some water. Everything is going to be okay," his grandmother continued. *She is still going strong, babysitting children and all,* Elizabeth said to herself. *Amazing.*

Elizabeth sat on the plastic covered couch and ate some chocolate candy she had stuffed in her coat pocket, while waiting and thinking about Casmir.

I know Casmir loves me, he tells me all the time. If I can only stop making him mad and learn how to listen, he will be the same guy my parents liked when he came over for dinner. The same guy I met at the mall with my best friend Binga. The same guy I made love to the first night we met.

But I can't even go to the store, call a friend, or visit him at the park without his permission and then if I don't get permission he hits me, leaving bruises.

The little boy Casmir's grandmother cares for ran up to Elizabeth and gave her a hug.

"Hi, Beth!"

Urg! He's the only one who can call me Beth, she said to herself, *until he learns how to pronounce my full name, of course,* as she giggled.

"Hey, cutie," Elizabeth said, offering him some of her candy.

"Yuck! I can't like that."

Elizabeth laughed.

"You can't like that or you don't like that."

"I can't like it!" he laughed.

"Have you even tasted 'it' before or know what 'it' is?" Elizabeth asked.

"No," the little boy smiled. He made Elizabeth laugh more as Casmir's grandmother gave her some water.

"Thank you," Elizabeth said.

The little boy pointed at the candy.

"I need that."

"I knew you wanted some," Elizabeth laughed. She gave him the candy and the grandmother and the little boy left the room, while Elizabeth was left there with her thoughts.

One of these times, Casmir's hot head is going to go too far, but if I try really really hard not to make him angry he will stop his violent, obsessive, and jealous rages.

Regardless of how Elizabeth rationalized Casmir's behavior, she had a feeling Casmir was on the verge of seriously harming her or even killing her. Elizabeth's friends kept warning her. Casmir himself kept warning her.

"I have many ways of killing you," he said dryly during one of their phone conversations.

He was not only clever and smart, but also violently creative, and he used it to harm others, especially Elizabeth.

Casmir told her, "First, I would break us up; then patiently wait two years later and send pit bulls after you; no one will suspect it was me."

The way he said it to Elizabeth was like a satanic monologue. She could feel the evilness and fearlessness in his voice.

Casmir was not playing.

Even still, Elizabeth had a hard time believing that this once wonderful guy who treated her so compassionately would have the guts to possibly kill her.

She waited and waited at his grandmother's house. An hour later Casmir entered the front door. He saw Elizabeth there on the couch as he walked over and took her hand. Casmir apologized to her and just like that, they made love on his grandmother's couch.

After sex and eating the chocolate, Elizabeth's stomach felt worst. She headed home to rest. When she arrived she went straight upstairs to her bedroom. Elizabeth did not want her parents to see what state she was in.

Her dad hollered from downstairs, "Hi, Elizabeth!"

"Hello!" Elizabeth's said with a distressed voice, stammering from the top of the stairway.

Her mom looked at her watch and sighed unpleasantly at the late time. She then disregarded it and asked her daughter, "You want some leftover spaghetti and meatballs sweetie?! It's your favorite!"

"No! I'm going to bed!" Elizabeth responded, now conversing from her bedroom.

Her parents could sense something bad was going on. Elizabeth was not her old bubbling outgoing self. She was always a straight "A" student, but now her grades were slipping from spending too much time with Casmir, and she was no longer first pick for valedictorian at her school.

Furthermore, she stopped shopping, hanging out with her friends, and instead of lip-singing on the youth choir at church she loudly and rudely, sang the wrong words. Her friends at church thought she was losing it. On top of that, Elizabeth had every nail polish color invented, like a typical teenage girl, but now she had no interest in any of the colors but black.

Every time her parents asked about the relationship, she would tell them everything was okay. Elizabeth did not want to put them in danger, so she kept the gangster side of Casmir a secret. Besides, Elizabeth thought she could handle the situation. But regardless of whether or not she could, protecting her family trumped protecting herself.

Elizabeth kept in mind the day Casmir came to her school after she told him a boy called her out of her name. Casmir and two of his thuggish friends, Franky and Trigger, arrived at Elizabeth's multicultural but predominately white school, looking like they were in a gang straight out of Compton. They confronted and beat the poor guy up in the school's parking lot. Little did Casmir know, the young guy was prepared - at least twenty-one guys showed up to defend their friend.

Casmir's body was firm like a knight with strong arms and shoulders. He was about a head taller than Elizabeth and physically powerful. Casmir wasn't afraid of anything and everyone feared him. He stayed out of jail for his crimes, even when he was charged for murder. The witness was too frightened to testify.

Casmir had that absurd effect on people, except for the guys who jumped Casmir and his boys.

Ten guys were on top of Casmir and the remainder of the pack was fighting Franky and Trigger. They kicked and punched Casmir over and over again. The guys stopped because they saw something that was not a normal reaction.

Casmir rose up from the rocks and gravel like a hungry lion prowling for human prey to devour. The punches and kicks didn't faze him at all. One brave guy took a piece of a wood 4x4 and hit Casmir across the back. Casmir simply turned around to see who hit him.

"Thank you for getting that crack out my back," Casmir said with a menacing smile. While the courageous guy was still holding on to the plywood board, Casmir took the other end of the wood and swung the boy over top of his head. The brave - but stupid - guy fell on his face in pain. The rest of the guys were not so heroic. They slowly backed up while Casmir looked for his hat.

"Let's get out of here," one of the guys said with a trembling stutter. The other group of guys who jumped Trigger did not notice what was happening because Trigger was beating them up. He had everything under control, but it was a different story for Franky. One of the guys rolled over Franky's head with a bicycle while two other guys kicked and stomped his body simultaneously.

Casmir ran over like a charging bear, knocking the guy off his bike while Trigger followed close by to help Casmir. The group of guys jetted while Casmir and Trigger picked Franky up off the ground. He could hardly walk so Franky put one arm over Trigger's far shoulder and did the same thing with

Casmir's shoulder. They carried him off before the teachers called the police.

"Did we get them Richie?" Franky muttered.

"Yea, man we beat those suckas up bro," he replied.

"Hang in there man," Trigger said. "Before you know it we will be driving around in my Escalade looking for big titties."

Franky was later sent to the hospital for his injuries.

Elizabeth was called into the principal's office the next day. She sat outside the office waiting for her turn. Elizabeth gathered her thoughts, biting her fingernails. An hour passed until finally, the principle asked her into his office. She got up from the bench outside, the nervousness growing stronger as she entered the office.

The livid principle sat in his daunting chestnut soft leather chair and mutely stared at Elizabeth's scared eyes.

"Close the door," the principal said with a deep raspy voice.

Elizabeth took a seat and he asked for the name of the guys who fought one of his students on school grounds while the other school officials watched Elizabeth. She could tell the principal did not know the entire story. He had no idea about the group of guys who fought her boyfriend and his friends.

Elizabeth would not give them any information until one of the officials standing two feet away from her said, "Don't worry, you can trust us. We just need to know who was involved and why."

After a few more words of support, the principal and his officials convinced Elizabeth that she and Casmir would not get in any trouble. *Little did they know, I was not concerned about getting in trouble through the school; I wanted to make sure Casmir was not punished*, Elizabeth thought. *If Casmir was in trouble, I was in trouble with him.* Thirty minutes later, Elizabeth believed their words of encouragement and told her side of the story.

"Now we just need to speak with Casmir," the principle said kindly. She happened to have her boyfriend's business card from the worthless retail store Casmir owned with his father and brother. Elizabeth figured she could trust them and this was the easiest way for them to retrieve his information.

Elizabeth was told to leave the office and return to class. She skipped and whistled all the way back to her classroom. Elizabeth was happy nothing really happened.

Later that day, she called her boyfriend to deliver the exciting news. She told Casmir she was not suspended and they wanted his number to talk to him. Elizabeth also told Casmir that she politely gave them his business card.

"How dumb can you be?!" Casmir shouted. "You better call them right now and tell them it's not my business card!" Elizabeth wasn't sure what she did wrong. Her boyfriend called the principal instead, with Elizabeth on the line. She tensed up but was sure the principal would have her back.

The secretary at the school answered the phone. After fifty million screening questions and being placed on hold a thousand times, she finally transferred the call to the principal. When the principal answered, Casmir worked his magic. Before finishing the conversation, he had the principal on his side. They were talking like home boys, cracking jokes and everything.

"Knock, knock! Who's there? Therma. Therma who? Therma be a better knock-knock joke than this," Casmir said as they both laughed.

"I remember that one from back in the day," the principle replied. Not knowing Elizabeth was on the phone, the principal continued to say to her boyfriend, "What kind of girlfriend do you have? Do you know she gave us your business card with all of your contact information?" The principal laughed.

"Yeah, she is a little naïve," Casmir said with a chuckle.

Elizabeth could not believe her ears. Her principal had no idea Casmir was loco and could have jeopardized her safety. From that point on, Elizabeth never trusted or respected authority again and Casmir knew he could get over on anybody.

Chapter 2

Elizabeth couldn't articulate how dark and dangerous Casmir was. In the past, she broke up with him numerous times but she always came back. Every so often, he would break up with her for not calling him at a certain time or hanging out with friends without his consent. Instead of Elizabeth seeing that as an opportunity to let Casmir go, she would apologize and beg for him to stay with her.

After days of begging and expressing how sorry she was, Elizabeth would be devastated when Casmir said, "I do not want to be with you anymore."

The majority of the time, they would break up over the phone but there was one particular time he broke it off at her house. On his way out the door, Elizabeth grabbed hold of his ankles like she was holding for dear life from a raging river. She squealed like a baby and pleaded for him to stay.

"I love you!" Elizabeth cried. Still, Casmir walked out the door.

When Casmir walked out the door that day, Elizabeth thought her life was over. She was comfortable and use to Casmir. Elizabeth couldn't fathom not hearing his voice on the phone in the morning before going to school, during her lunch break, after-school, and before she went to bed.

Just to hear him say, 'hi babe,' or ask, 'what are you doing?' made her feel good inside, and she felt like she would never find another man to be with.

The only way he would take her back is if she allowed him to tie her naked body to the bedpost while he slashed and whipped her repeatedly with a thick leather belt to show him how sorry she was for making him mad once again. To punish her further, Casmir allowed his friends to watch for fun and later ran a sadistic sex train on her young, delicate body. This awful incident lasted for three hours non-stop.

He would say as he continued to slash her, "If I can't trust you with the little things, how am I going to trust you with the big things?" This was how Casmir would justify all of the unnecessary beatings he inflicted on Elizabeth.

"You are right! And I'm sorry for not asking you if I can meet my friend!" she exclaimed, tears hitting the ground.

The more she said she was sorry, the more he relentlessly whacked her. Several hours later, he would take her back with no remorse. Tears no longer hit the ground; they fell on his shoulder while he made passionate love to her.

"No one else loves you but me. Not your mom...dad...friends...no one," Casmir said. Elizabeth wiped her red teary eyes and rubbed ointment on her battered wrists.

One day in his grandmother's old sedan, Casmir and Elizabeth had a long conversation about him beating her. She broke down. Tears fled her face again as she implored him to stop the abuse. He took her head and softly put it down on his lap while she tightly held his thigh and continued to sob.

Casmir handed her a tissue from the compartment next to him. For the first time, she felt like Casmir may have a caring bone in his body until he rubbed the healing knot on the side of her face where he threw a heavy set of keys. This reminded her of the horror she had experienced with Casmir. He noticed she was uncomfortable about him touching the bruise, so instead he stroked her thick curly hair affectionately.

"I promise I will not hit you again," Casmir said.

Elizabeth continued to cry because she knew that was an empty promise. *How can he do any better? He watched his own dad break his baby mama's ribs.*

After all of the verbal and physical abuse Elizabeth received from this inhuman being, she still did not wake up until one day Casmir involved her immediate family. Although this was Elizabeth's biggest fear she still felt that Casmir meant well and he loved her in his own sick way.

Once again, Elizabeth sat and thought back to when Casmir treated her kindly. She deeply wanted that Casmir back, but deep down inside she knew that was not going to happen. *This is who he is.*

At the beginning, he put on a good front for me and my family and friends, but then he showed his true colors. I'm 17-years-old, now and I have to look at how he is treating me at this time, and I know he has the worst temper, I was definitely scared of him, and Casmir wanted my head on a stick.

Her task was to get rid of him some kind of way immediately; but this was easier said than done, especially because she still had feelings for him.

Elizabeth hovered and yearned deep within her soul.

The only thing she could think to do was to find a man that would take her mind off of Casmir. Could Elizabeth really pull this off? This was a big risk for her, but for a little over four years now she had been treated direly by Casmir. Elizabeth needed something new, someone who would grab her attention.

She constantly obsessed over the thought of being swept off her feet by a gorgeous man, but she knew she had to take control; waiting for this to happen was not an option. Elizabeth was desperate and desperate measures were in order to lift this dragon off her frantic heart that Casmir used as a chessboard ready to strike for his own guilty pleasures. *Checkmate.*

Her new neighbor across the street looked mighty fine to her. She did not know much about him other than that they both stood about the same height of five feet nine inches and his name was Matt Schneider. One thing she did know was that this sexy Jewish boy was just what the doctor ordered. Matt was going to replace her boyfriend.

Dating a Jewish guy was definitely something different for Elizabeth. She did not like to toot her own horn but she was sure it would be new for him to date a cat-eyed chick with full lips, high cheek bones, and porcelain skin, ethnically mixed with a little bit of everything. She inherited her mother's and father's best features and she was going to put it to use to break away from Casmir.

Elizabeth thought of ways she could capture Matt's attention.

Should I put on a sexy dress and go to my mailbox when he is leaving his house, ring his door bell, and ask for a cup of sugar? Or maybe the old' damsel in distress act, like I see in the movies? None of those would work but she knew what would.

One summer day, Elizabeth saw Matt coming out of his house. *Perfect timing.* Elizabeth had on the shortest shorts with a sizzling star printed bikini top to show off her boobs, strong jaw line, and beautifully formed long neck and collar bone. His expensive emerald green eyes caught up with hers. Elizabeth waved and by her surprise he waved back. There was an instant connection as she bent over to wet her sponge she used to wash her dad's car.

Ooops! Some water splashed on her. Silly Elizabeth. This would be the oldest trick in the book, but white boys like that kind of thing.

Not realizing how into it she was, her emotional mom yelled from the screen door, "Elizabeth, get into this house right now!" Elizabeth quickly stopped the enticing routine and smoothly looked over at Matt. Her mom noticed who the sensual show was for. She darted over to Elizabeth, promptly picked up the slippery, flimsy hose next to Elizabeth's bucket and beat her.

Her mom questioned Elizabeth, "What do you think you are doing? You have a boyfriend!"

She was so embarrassed, Elizabeth ran in the house as quickly as possible. Her mom did not understand that she could have ruined Elizabeth's chances of getting rid of her abusive boyfriend.

Elizabeth went to the front door to see if Matt was still there while her sister snickered in the background. As he was driving off in his black sports car, he glanced over at Elizabeth. His smile let her know she sealed the deal.

Shortly after Matt left, Elizabeth slipped her home phone number under his door on a card she purchased for him a few days ago. She had been waiting for the ideal moment to personally delivery it.

"I'm in love," Elizabeth said aloud in a playful and cheerful voice.

She impatiently waited and waited, hoping he would call even after that outrageous performance from her mom.

Elizabeth's house phone rang. Her heart pounded a hundred times at once, it seemed like as she picked up her phone.

"Hello babe," Casmir said.

It wasn't Matt but it was perhaps nice to hear a familiar voice calling me babe instead of cursing me out, Elizabeth thought.

"Oh hey," Elizabeth said shortly.

"Just calling to see what you up to," Casmir replied.

"Nothing," Elizabeth said.

"What...?!" Casmir hollered and then paused. "Alright...Elizabeth I gotta go."

"Is that your grandmother calling you?" Elizabeth questioned.

"Yeah," Casmir responded frustrated. "As soon as I get on the phone, she needs me to do something for her. I love you Elizabeth."

"Okay," Elizabeth said.

"You not going to say it back," Casmir said curtly.

"Love ya," she said weakly.

"Aight, bye," Casmir said unpleasantly. *So evil.* Elizabeth hung up the phone feeling as though Casmir knew she was up to something.

A couple of days later, the sound of her phone ringing woke Elizabeth out of her sleep. The first person she thought about was Matt. It had to be him. She was just dreaming about Matt.

Still half sleep and not paying attention to the time she answered the phone and said in a sexy sleepy voice, "Hello."

The guy on the other end replied, "Hello, how are you?" Elizabeth was still half asleep but so ecstatic.

"I'm good, Matt," Elizabeth said warmly. "Did you like my card?"

"What card?" the guy asked, curiously.

Elizabeth now noticed the time and it read 7:30 am. She wondered why Matt was calling so early, but she didn't care. Elizabeth was happy he called.

"I left a card under your door. I want to get to know..."

Before she could finish her sentence, a loud booming voice fiercely yelled, "Who the hell is Matt?! What card did you give him? Where does he live?! I'm on my way there!" He slammed the phone in her ear.

Elizabeth was beyond terrified. She crumpled inside as she dropped the phone, accidently tripping over her pink dresser. Elizabeth collected herself, put on what clothes she could find, and ran out the front door. Her crass boyfriend was playing on the phone and she fell right into it.

How can I be so stupid?

The unfiltered rage in his voice hit her like a body blow and after listening to the curse words that filled the air and the crashing objects in the background, like a cat with nine lives, she knew hers were up. Casmir was not going to just punish her...this guy was out to kill her.

Casmir made his way to Elizabeth's house but she had already departed to find safe shelter.

Before Elizabeth headed out the door she told her sister, "Whatever you do, don't show Casmir where Matt lives."

She ran to a relative's house close by.

Elizabeth's aunt already knew her boyfriend was a mad man so she did not need to explain anything to her. She told her aunt she needed to hide until her parents returned home and Casmir was gone. Her aunt understood, but was scared for her two little boys and her niece.

To calm Elizabeth down, her aunt offered her some fresh baked peanut butter cookies. Elizabeth told her no thank you, but helped herself to leftover cookie dough.

She then hugged her cousins and said to her aunt, "Has my uncle been by here to see his boys?"

"Sure, he has. He came by and picked them up, put them back down, and then said he will be back here next week to pick them up again." Elizabeth laughed.

"I know it's not funny, but my uncle is a comedian."

"Why are you asking questions about your uncle and laughing and shit? Forget about him! What is going on this time between you and Casmir?"

"You don't even wanna know."

Elizabeth's aunt observed her niece's demeanor.

"Yes, I do. You look more scared than normal. I'm concerned."

She explained what happened and twenty minutes later, there was a knock on her door. Elizabeth ran upstairs skipping every other step. She hid in the first room she saw. Elizabeth's aunt answered and acted like everything was cool.

"How you been?" Casmir asked in a calm manner.

"I'm good, what's going on?" Elizabeth's aunt answered stiffly.

Still with a pleasant manner he asked, "Have you seen Elizabeth?"

"No," Elizabeth's aunt lied. "But let me know when you find her because I need her to babysit."

This was a good technique to throw him off. The only problem was that Casmir was very observant – he could tell by her body language and the swaying of her eyes she was not telling the truth. He pushed his way into the house.

"Where are you Elizabeth?!" he yelled.

"Mommy!" the little boys cried.

Elizabeth's aunt was no timid woman. No longer holding her composure against the bully, she pushed back and threatened to call the police.

"I told you! I have not seen her...now leave," she demanded.

Casmir stopped shoving Elizabeth's aunt recognizing she was not the one he was after. As he walked back to his car Elizabeth's aunt saw a knife inside Casmir's sweat suit jacket. She reached for her telephone to call *9-1-1*, while Casmir opened his car door.

He looked towards Elizabeth's aunt.

"If you do see Elizabeth, tell her I said, 'if she does not call me ASAP, I will mail her parents the naked pictures I took of her.'" Casmir drove off like a bat out of hell.

Elizabeth snuck a vague peek from behind the curtain to make sure he was gone. At the end of the street, his car came to a screeching halt. He backed up. Elizabeth panicked and fell to the floor.

Did he see me?

Her aunt opened the door with a weapon in hand. Her stance was as malicious as any dangerous animal that walked on their paws. This time she was ready.

Casmir laughed and yelled out the car window, "You better put that away before you hurt yourself!"

Elizabeth's aunt ran towards Casmir's car with a butcher knife held high, her hair in disarray from him previously shoving her.

Casmir drove off and she shouted from the street, "Yeah! You are not so tough, are you now?" Then, she realized all of that huffing and puffing was for nothing, since Casmir was going the other way because of a dump truck holding up traffic.

Elizabeth was visible through the window. Her aunt looked up at her with stressed out eyes.

What have I done? Elizabeth asked herself. *Casmir's dick was good and all, but it's not worth all of this.*

One of the little boys ran to his mother, holding his arms out to reach for her.

"Mommy, let me hold you." She dropped the knife, picked up her son, raised him over her head, and with a motherly playful shake, she giggled with him and said, "I love you."

Elizabeth fell on her knees. She prayed to God her sister was okay back at home.

Her aunt shut the door only to be greeted by her other scared child.

"It's okay," she said.

Shortly after, Elizabeth ran downstairs to grab the phone from the couch and said to all of them, "I'm sorry for this."

Her aunt replied in a comforting tone, "As long as you are safe, Dew Drop." Dew Drop was her nickname for Elizabeth.

Elizabeth called her sister, and she said everything was fine, but Casmir had been looking for her for almost the whole day. Her sister paused and frowned.

"Sis, what is wrong?" Elizabeth questioned, sensing hesitation and sadness in her sister's voice.

Her sister struggled to say, "I had to tell him where Matt lived."

"Did Casmir threaten you?" Elizabeth asked with concern.

"No," her sister answered. "But I thought it would make him leave you alone. I'm sorry Elizabeth."

"Okay, don't worry about it," she said. "But please do not tell him where I am now."

Her sister also told Elizabeth he took everything out of her room.

"That little thief," Elizabeth murmured. "How would he like it if I raided his room in front of his brother and five sisters?" *Loser.*

"Did I just hear you say, 'brother and five sisters?'" her aunt repeated.

"Yes. He's the youngest of them. You would think he would be more sensitive, but that is impossible. Casmir is so screwed up because of his family."

"Why do you say that Dew Drop?" her aunt wondered as they both sat down on her lonely worn-out couch that sat against the wall. Elizabeth recounted highlights of the events while her aunt listened intently and the little boys played nearby.

"The story is when Casmir was in his early teens, his grandmother told him the truth about his father," Elizabeth said.

"What was that?" her aunt questioned.

"His father is gay," Elizabeth answered.

"Her son is gay?!" her aunt gasped and gave a puzzled look. "Wait a minute. His father is married to Casmir's mother, right?"

"The marriage is a cover up for business," Elizabeth said. "But anyway, let me finish telling you."

"Okay," she said.

"Casmir accepted it, but then his grandmother told him his father came out the closet after Casmir was born. It made him feel like it was his fault his father turned gay."

"Why would his grandmother say that to a young impressionable boy?" her aunt asked, anticipating her answer.

"His grandmother is 87-years-old. I don't think she knows what she is saying," Elizabeth answered. "One day, Casmir slapped me and I was very upset about it, and when I arrived at her house, she asked, 'where is my beautiful grandson?' and then said, 'so he can give you a hug.' Little did she know, he slapped me!"

"Yeah, but still that is devastating information for an innocent teenager growing into a man of character," Elizabeth's aunt said, "but it's no excuse for Casmir to lash out at other people. And although he had been exposed to a lot at a young age, Casmir has his whole life ahead of him to make things right. I hope he does."

"Yeah, I hope he does too," Elizabeth said.

"Forget about him Dew Drop."

"I am."

"No, I mean it Elizabeth."

"Mommy!" the little boy interrupted.

"Wait a minute," Elizabeth's aunt said.

Her little boy turned to his brother and said, "Mommy is stuck."

Elizabeth's aunt laughed.

"Mommy is not stuck. What is that you want little boy?"

"Can I have a popsicle and milk?" the little boy asked.

"What a combination," his mom answered. She stood up from the couch. "See, mommy is not stuck. I was talking to your cousin." Elizabeth's aunt grabbed both her boys a popsicle and saved the milk for later.

"As I was saying, Casmir is obsessive, jealous, and controlling, underlining signs of abuse. He came here to seriously harm you. I saw his knife, which means he is also violent," Elizabeth's aunt continued.

Elizabeth cried on her aunt's shoulder for a moment, and then scurried home. She was even more concerned about her family now.

When Elizabeth returned home and entered her bedroom, she felt like the air was being sucked out of her from pure evil; her whole body shook. Elizabeth's room looked like a scene from the cartoon *The Grinch Who Stole Christmas*. Everything was gone - her panties, clothes, shoes; EVERYTHING VANISHED!

He trespassed on my parent's property.

"How dare he!" she cried.

Though Elizabeth was very sociable, she also had an introverted personality and deep down inside, sometimes she liked to be alone. Her preference to be alone could come across as arrogance or conceited, but those suspicions weren't valid. She just needed time to recharge and gather her thoughts. Her favorite place to do this was in her room in the care of her dolls that made her feel safe.

Elizabeth felt ravaged and violated when Casmir took that from her. *What gave him the right to take my belongings?* Elizabeth asked herself. *My stay-in-bed-and-forget-the-world day haven is gone thanks to Casmir.*

Elizabeth lowered her head staring at the bare floor.

"Don't worry sis," Elizabeth's sister said lightly. "You can stay in my room."

Elizabeth hugged her sweet and loving sister and Elizabeth's sister hugged her back.

"Thank you. I'm sure me and Mickey Mouse will get along just fine," Elizabeth said jokingly. She and her sister laughed and continued to hold each other. Elizabeth looked up and saw the message her sister wrote on the back of her door a few years ago.

It said, "Never Give Up."

Elizabeth let her sister go, but had a stark realization. Casmir involved her entire family and like she said before, this was her biggest fear.

"He has crossed the line," Elizabeth continued as she dumped Freckles in the toilet.

"I can't believe he killed my fish. My birthday gift. Birthdays don't matter anyways. It just reminds me of the day I was born into this tragic situation."

Elizabeth and her sister said a prayer for Freckles while watching the toilet swallow her whole. She also cleaned up the shredded Valentine's Day card Casmir bought for her last year. A small note was lying next to it and it read, *You want to give out cards to men? Give him this.*

"Maybe now," Elizabeth said seriously. "Casmir can feel somewhat of how I have felt for years of being in this horrible relationship with him."

This would be the end of Casmir and Elizabeth indefinitely.

The next day, she saw movers in front of Matt's newly purchased home. Casmir intimidated him so badly that he feared for his life. She felt terrible, especially because they never officially met and he had no idea how he was mixed up in everything.

Elizabeth stood in her doorway watching Matt pack his last box. Moments later, there was a pitter-patter of feet belonging to the prettiest little toddler following along behind him.

"Come on Sally, come to daddy," Matt said. The little girl rushed forward into Matt's open arms with excitement. Elizabeth hadn't known Matt was a single father.

Matt put his daughter in her car seat and as he shut the door, he saw Elizabeth in her doorway. He stared at her with questions he could not get out. She could tell he was stressed from the bags under his eyes.

He walked towards her and Elizabeth shook her head side to side to sign to him, "No, stay away from me. I have caused enough trouble." Elizabeth's one tear confirmed he needed to listen. Sally and Matt drove off.

Matt will never know he secretly saved Elizabeth's life. He will continually be blessed.

After all of this, Casmir had the audacity to try an ample amount of times to get in contact with Elizabeth but this time, without a doubt in her mind, she never wanted to see him again and she meant it. Casmir knew he tremendously messed up, and he knew he no longer had a hold on Elizabeth; not even the nude pictures could coerce her. As a matter of fact, her family pressed charges against him for trespassing and stealing.

While they were at the courthouse, the judge ordered him to stay one hundred feet away from Elizabeth or he would be thrown in jail. He also had to return Elizabeth's things. On their way out the courtroom, Casmir became very emotional. He knew this was over for real.

"Elizabeth! Elizabeth!" he called. The guards and his parents held him back.

Elizabeth watched Casmir make a fool of himself, while rubbing her neck as she heard the same passion in his voice and saw the same terror in his eyes she had when he wrapped the phone cord around her neck, almost choking her to death. For the first time, he was scared.

"Come on, Elizabeth," her mom commanded urgently. "He is fooling no one with his phony self. I see you are clean cut again, eh Casmir? Wearing a nice conservative suit with a pair of reading glasses to make yourself appear respectful, more mature, and sane for the judge. But we all know who you are and in my eyes you just look like a well-dressed criminal."

He ignored her mom and continued to call Elizabeth's name as he broke away from the security and yelled, "I will love you forever, Elizabeth!" His voice echoed through the door cracks and walls of the courtroom halls.

Elizabeth left the building with no remorse.

Outside the courthouse, Elizabeth and her parents were headed towards their car. Casmir's parents were not too far behind. Elizabeth could sense the tension and she wanted to get her mom away from Casmir's parents.

My mom is a Christian but if you mess with her children it's a whole different story, Elizabeth thought. *She does not care if a person is three hundred pounds, she will fight. I have seen her do it!*

"You know," Casmir's mother said to Elizabeth, "You really should get to know a person before sleeping with them on the first night."

Too late!

"How dare you talk to my daughter that way!" Elizabeth's mom shouted. "Elizabeth is a decent young lady; your son even said so himself."

His mom laughed.

"My son said that?"

"He is mentally ill," Casmir's dad added.

"Mentally what?" Elizabeth said.

"Do you know he had to flee the country until his name was cleared in the States way before he met you?" his mom said.

"What?" Elizabeth's mom questioned. "What country? Clear his name? Why?"

"Don't worry about it," Casmir's dad answered. "We cannot discuss that right now."

"We thought he was back on the right path," his mom said, "so when we noticed his old ways coming back, we went into denial right, honey?"

"Yes, babe," Casmir's dad replied, hugging his wife.

"But now we know why he is acting up again," his mom said, letting go of her husband and turning towards Elizabeth. "You said you loved my son and then you slept with your neighbor. You did this to him!"

"I did not sleep with the neighbor!" Elizabeth exclaimed.

"Did your son tell you how he abused my daughter?" Elizabeth's mom asked. "That's why she wanted to get away from him."

"That is why we are in the courthouse today and the judge ordered your son to stay away from my child," Elizabeth's dad reminded.

"Bullocks! Your daughter caused everything!" Casmir's dad shouted.

"You see that bumper sticker right there on my car," Elizabeth's mom pointed out. "My child is a shining star. We raised Elizabeth in a good part of town to keep her away from hoodlums like your son."

"First of all, my son is not a hoodlum," Casmir's mom corrected. "Second of all, we come from the same place you come from."

"You know what," Elizabeth's dad said to his wife. "Don't waste your time."

"Oh, I'm not! Let's leave!" her mom shrugged.

Elizabeth's dad turned to Casmir's dad.

"Wait a minute, you are not fooling anyone. I remember you from the ole school. You ain't nothing but a pimp."

"Man, ain't nothing but a thang partner," Casmir's dad gritted angrily through his teeth.

"I'm not your partner," Elizabeth's dad said, equally angry. "Ain't nothing but a thang," Elizabeth's mom repeated. "Pimp? Partner? This is heathen talk; you all need Jesus."

"I got Jesus," Casmir's mom cried.

"I got Jesus too!" Casmir's dad corrected.

"You don't have Jesus, you fat rabbit," Elizabeth's mom said to Casmir's dad. Casmir's mom gasped as her husband rubbed his keg of a stomach.

"And you are definitely not from where we are from," Casmir's dad said brusquely. "You and your son are from the hood."

"A gay pimp from the hood?" Elizabeth blurted.

"Excuse me," Casmir's mom said.

"Who you calling gay," Casmir's dad replied. "Your mama," Elizabeth responded abruptly.

Casmir ran out the courthouse and hollered, "Mom and dad stay away from Elizabeth!"

"Elizabeth, you come with us right this second before I forget I got Jesus," her mom said.

"Mother Tight, I love her," Casmir said.

"I'm not your mother and you stay away from my daughter Casmir!" she cried.

"You damn skippy she is not your mother!" Casmir's mom screamed.

"You don't love me, Casmir," Elizabeth said. "You were going to stab me. My aunt saw the knife the day you took everything from my room."

"A knife?" her mom said sharply. "You failed to mention that to the judge. This man is dangerous!"

"I did not have a knife," he denied.

"Casmir, you are going to miss heaven, acting this way," Elizabeth's mom said, grabbing Elizabeth's hand to pull her away. "Go back to where ya'll come from."

"You promised me you were going to love my daughter," Elizabeth's dad growled, as Casmir walked away before the guards came after him. "I don't care where you are from. You had the opportunity to treat my daughter right!"

Elizabeth was still stuck on the mentally ill comment. *Was I dating a crazy person?*

"Does your son have a mental problem?" Elizabeth cried. "Is he crazy?!"

His mom smiled.

"You damn skippy!"

Chapter 3

Dumping her ex-boyfriend was a big accomplishment and although she eventually stopped thinking about Casmir, his threats, the scars from the beatings, and the fears he put in her head about him killing her in an unexpected way, she could never forget. She would always assume he was still capable of doing the unthinkable, but there was no land secluded enough for her to hide so she could not worry herself about Casmir. What Elizabeth *did* have to be concerned about was the pregnancy test she took. How would Elizabeth tell her parents she was pregnant with Casmir's child?

After wandering in Fairmount Park for hours, Elizabeth found a lone tree to sit under to reminisce. *I use to love when my parents brought me here as a little girl.* She then began to ponder about her four-month pregnancy. Elizabeth had a feeling long before now due to her swollen breasts and morning sickness there was a fetus holding court in her gut.

She kept the baby a secret from Casmir so she could raise it on her own. The dilemma was: whom could Elizabeth talk to about the pregnancy? Elizabeth's mom was a God fearing woman who instilled good morals and values in her, but her dad was her hero. Elizabeth did not want her father to be disappointed, but she had no other choice.

Elizabeth was visiting her grandmother's house when her dad arrived after a long day at work.

"Hi dad, how was your day?" Elizabeth asked.

"Challenging," her dad answered. "How was your day, Elizabeth?"

She ogled the ceiling, her fingers picking the worn hem of her jean jacket to bare threads. Her body feeling so scared.

"Good," she said.

"Are you sure?" he asked. "You look like something is on your mind Elizabeth."

She asked her dad to the guest room to speak with him privately. From the look on her face, her dad knew this was not good news.

Elizabeth turned to her dad, gawked down at the floor.

"Please don't be mad at me daddy."

"Mad about what?" her dad said. She simply spat it out, "I'm pregnant."

Her dad paused for a second.

"I hope it's not by Casmir," her dad groaned.

"Yes, I want to keep it," Elizabeth said.

"You are not having a child by that low-life," her dad replied. "Do I have to remind you of how he treated you? Does he even have an education?" Elizabeth's dad gave her no option and at age 17, she was to get an abortion.

Elizabeth then had to gather enough nerve to tell him she was too far along to have an abortion.

"Dad, I'm four months," she informed.

"What?! You're just telling me now?" her dad said.

"I'm sorry, I did not know how to tell you," Elizabeth said forlornly.

Her dad saw his daughter's face scrunched with sadness. Elizabeth and her dad weren't huggers but her dad would always make her feel like the world was hers no matter what the circumstance.

"Elizabeth, everything is going to be fine," her dad reassured. "Does your mom know?"

"No," Elizabeth said.

"Good. Keep it that way," her dad commanded. "No use in getting her all upset. I will take care of this."

Elizabeth's dad told her grandmother, and they called her aunt Iris, a doctor at the local hospital, who gave the okay to have the abortion despite Elizabeth's current condition. Elizabeth was still in the dark about how this process works but she was told by her dad to stay at her grandmother's house until the procedure was done.

The following week, Elizabeth was scheduled for an ultrasound.

She thought that was weird because she always figured ultrasounds were for women giving birth. Elizabeth followed her dad's lead and did not ask any questions; she had caused enough grief.

The quiet ride to the hospital was dreadful. Her dad was not mad, but he was not happy about the issue at hand either.

When they arrived, her aunt was waiting in the lobby with open arms. She comforted Elizabeth and told her everything would be fine. Iris then gave her brother and stepmom a hug.

As they walked to the ultrasound room, her aunt assured them that although she was not on duty for D&E that day, she made sure she set Elizabeth up with the best doctor, assistant nurses, and sonographer technician in the hospital. She then told them all they'd look out for Elizabeth and they did not have to worry about a thing.

Elizabeth entered the ultrasound room and moments after the sonographer came in to greet Elizabeth. In order to begin the ultrasound, she asked Elizabeth to drink plenty of water so they could see the baby clearly. She could tell by the look on Elizabeth's face that she was nervous.

"Everything will be fine," she said.

The sonographer technician left the room while Elizabeth drank glasses and glasses of water. Elizabeth noticed the sonographer was gone for almost a half hour and Elizabeth needed to release the fluids. She peeked out the door but there was no sign of the sonographer. Elizabeth closed her legs tightly, trying not to think about having to use the bathroom.

She paced the enclosed compacted room filled with frightening tools and machines.

"Where is that lady?!" she cried. Elizabeth was ready to burst. She knew that if she went to the bathroom she would have to start all over.

Finally after a few more minutes, the lady returned. She gave Elizabeth an uncomfortable look and took her seat as slow as molasses. It was as clear as a bell she was taking her time on purpose, perhaps to punish Elizabeth.

Having an abortion was not Elizabeth's idea but she felt like she was going to be the one to pay for this unbearable decision.

The lady proceeded to do the ultrasound and like a bull in a china shop she forcefully pressed on Elizabeth's stomach. Elizabeth's uncontrollable bladder relieved itself right on the examination table. The sonographer looked at her in disgust.

"This is your fault!" Elizabeth exclaimed. "You left me here on purpose! I ought to slap the taste out of your mouth!"

The sonographer became so emotional.

"Month one, the baby has organs and knows who you are. Every time the baby hears the sound of your voice, the baby waves his legs and arms...the baby's favorite lullaby is the sound of your heartbeat."

Elizabeth cried hysterically.

"You are sick! Don't you think I feel bad about this already?"

"Month two," the sonographer technician continued. "The baby learns she or he can suck their thumb."

"My aunt said you were the best and that you would look out for me! Why are you acting like this?! Who are you?! What are you?!" Elizabeth shouted. "Get away from me! Dad!"

"Month three!" the sonographer screamed. "The sex of the child is revealed. Do you want to know what you would have had, you baby killer!"

Her dad rushed in.

"I want to leave," Elizabeth said. "Forget the ultrasound."

"Month four," the sonographer continued in a normal tone. "The hair is starting to grow, and when the cold-hearted doctor intrudes the baby's warm and cozy home, the chemicals from the needle burn the baby."

"I don't know what kind of show you are running here, but you better leave my daughter alone," Elizabeth's dad commanded.

Elizabeth ran out the room and screamed, "That lady is right!"

Chapter 4

The next day at 7:00 am in the nicely heated hospital room Elizabeth changed into her gown to begin her abortion. Elizabeth folded her clothes in a neat pile while hearing a knock at the door.

"Come in," Elizabeth said.

The doctor walked in with the assistant nurse and he asked her some questions. They noticed she looked uneasy.

"Everything is going to be okay," the doctor reassured.

Too many people were saying, "Everything is going to be okay."

Elizabeth had a feeling everything was not going to be okay.

The doctor explained to Elizabeth they would have to induce the labor. She had no idea what that meant. The nurse handed the doctor a needle that was as long as a country mile. He stuck it in Elizabeth's stomach in order to insert a thick clear substance. The needle sliced through her like a hot knife through butter.

The doctor left the room while the nurse made notes on her chart.

"When is this going to be over?" Elizabeth asked the nurse. "It's going to be easy right?"

"You are going to go through a real delivery," the nurse answered.

"You are joking, right," Elizabeth said.

"Nope, you are too far along," the nurse said. "The doctor has to make you deliver the baby early which is a very rare and dangerous procedure. You will have to breathe and push."

"Breathe and push?" Elizabeth repeated.

"You, my dear, will experience contractions and labor pains just like a mother who is having a baby full term," the nurse explained.

Elizabeth could not believe her ears. Her father failed to mention that part. Well, it explained the ultrasound. They were treating Elizabeth as if she was having the child.

She appreciated the nurse's honesty. Finally, someone didn't sugar coat the procedure but needless to say there was nothing Elizabeth could do at this point, as she rubbed her stomach, thinking about her baby burning after what the sonographer rudely told her.

The nurse rolled Elizabeth into a delivery room. She did not know from one moment to the next what was happening. Elizabeth could only picture in her mind the women on television screaming while giving birth.

Her dad and grandmother helped Elizabeth to relax.

Three hours later, Elizabeth and her dad were watching the Price is Right while Elizabeth's grandmother was cracking nuts on top of one of the hospital gowns.

"These nuts are good and good for you," her grandmother said. Her dad looked like he was deep in thought.

"What's wrong dad?" Elizabeth asked.

"I'm just thinking about your mother. She can never find out about this," her dad answered.

"That's right," her grandmother agreed. "Your mother would hold this over your head for the rest of your life."

"But this was not my choice," Elizabeth reminded.

"It does not matter, she's a hard mother," her grandmother said.

Elizabeth's mom was a "Tell it like it is" type of woman and she couldn't take on too much at once. When her mom did, she felt overwhelmed and everyone had better run for cover.

"Don't ever tell your mother about this abortion," Elizabeth's dad said as the sonographer walked past the door, overhearing the conversation. "This does not leave this hospital room. It's our family secret."

The first contraction began and so did Elizabeth's high pitched screams. Her grandmother's nut shells went flying through the air as the nurse walked in; they rapidly plucked her head like a ping pong table.

"Where is the doctor?" Elizabeth's dad wondered. The nurse told Elizabeth to stay calm, wait for the contractions to become more frequent. Her grandmother attempted to collect her nut shells.

"It's okay," the nurse said politely. "We will have someone come in to clean that, ma'am." The nurse walked out and Elizabeth's grandmother gave up on the nut-cracking business. The three of them watched the end of Price is Right.

It was now 10:00 pm and the nurse went over to Elizabeth to help relax her through each contraction, allowing her body to do its work. At 1:30 am, Elizabeth was seven centimeters dilated and 85% effaced. Elizabeth was surprised to be so calm. She was halfway through labor and things did not seem that hard.

Elizabeth spoke too soon, the hard work started, with contractions becoming more intense, like really awful menstrual cramps. She had to really concentrate on her breathing. Elizabeth hollered for drugs, no longer being able to take the intolerable pain. The nurse gave her some prescribed pain killers. She was half way out, still feeling the pain.

After a while, her body had a really strong urge to push. Elizabeth screamed from the top of her lungs like a laughing hyena. Her grandmother walked out the door - she could not take it. Elizabeth grabbed her father's hand and squeezed so tightly he fell to his knees.

"My hand!" her dad yelled, eyes opened wide. One of the nurses pried Elizabeth's fingers out of her dad's hand.

"You're twelve centimeters dilated and completely effaced!" the nurse shouted. The doctor came rushing in and she was told to begin pushing.

"I need more drugs!" Elizabeth begged. But the doctor couldn't give her any more.

"Push Celina!" the doctor said. Elizabeth pushed like crazy for what seemed like a miserable eternity to later find out it was only for fifteen minutes. "Push, Celina!" the doctor continued. Elizabeth was under the spell of the drug, but she kept hearing the doctor call her Celina.

Although she was able to scream when the contractions took over her body, she was too drugged to tell the doctor her name was not Celina.

"Celina...Celina push!" the doctor said again and again. Elizabeth's body and hair was doused in sweat. "It's almost here. I see the head."

Elizabeth could feel the head within the walls of her sore happy trail. She still could not tell the doctor her name as she pushed and blared and pushed and blared.

Elizabeth felt something release but she did not know what it was. The feeling did not seem like it would be a baby but it was.

The baby is here.

This was the worst painful and emotional experience of Elizabeth's entire life. Her dad and grandmother were told to leave the room so that Elizabeth could begin her recovering process of fourteen hours and twenty minutes of earsplitting screaming and pushing.

On the way out the door, the nurse asked Elizabeth's dad to sign a one page hospital release form. He read over the form and signed it.

"Thank you, I just need to get your daughter's signature when she is up to it," the nurse said.

Shortly after, the assistant nurse returned to the room with papers while holding something wrapped in a blanket. Elizabeth looked up and it was actually the sonographer who gave her the ultrasound. The look on the technician's face was as dry as bone.

"I need you to sign your release papers," the sonographer said. Still under the drug and delirious, without reading the paperwork, Elizabeth signed a five page hospital release form opposed to her dad's one page form.

"Would you like to hold your baby?" the lady asked. Elizabeth gasped and did not reply. *She's holding my baby in her arms?* Elizabeth asked herself.

"Well, do you?" the lady said impatiently. Elizabeth just wanted the sonographer to leave as soon as possible, but she was curious to see what the sonographer was explaining to her in the ultrasound room; *maybe she was lying.*

"Yes, I would." *Why did I say that?* The deceased fetus that would have been a baby boy laid motionless in Elizabeth's arms, the image burned in her head like a laser knife.

From that day forward Elizabeth had nightmares; she dreamt her baby appeared walking towards her in a huge brimmed hat wearing a long tan trench coat.

Chapter 5

"Thank you, Aunt Iris, for everything," Elizabeth said. She gave her a hug.

"I heard everything went okay," Aunt Iris replied.

"I'm happy everything is finally over," Elizabeth said, still feeling a little weak.

"Good. Now don't be too hard on yourself over this. You will be okay if you stay away from that guy," her aunt urged.

"He is out of my life forever. I have a restraining order on him. He cannot come near me," Elizabeth said without a doubt.

"Okay, good," her aunt said. "Because you are too pretty and too nice of a girl to have someone mistreating you. Do you know how many men would love to be with you and treat you with kindness?" Elizabeth smiled.

"I will set my niece up with a nice guy - and good looking," her aunt continued. Elizabeth giggled.

"Casmir is good looking," Elizabeth reminded.

"I know I know I was just playing with you," her aunt smiled. "I love that name too. If he wasn't so crazy, I would have named my son Casmir. What kind of name is that anyway?"

"Polish, his dad is Polish," Elizabeth informed.

"Polish?" her aunt said. "But he does not have an accent."

"He was born and raised in Philly," Elizabeth replied.

"Well, born and raised in Philly or not, his parents should have named him Hitler Jr. as violent as Casmir is."

"Guess what Casmir means," Elizabeth said.

"What?" her aunt wondered.

"Destroyer of peace," Elizabeth laughed.

"Wow, now that is deep," her aunt said. "That is why it is very important what a parent names their child. The name should have a good meaning to represent the child well."

"Yeah, I tried to change him," Elizabeth said.

"That was your mistake right there baby," her aunt replied. "What you see is what you get. You cannot change anyone especially not a man. He has to want to change. Well, enough about him." Elizabeth's aunt gave her a goodbye hug.

"Come on dad and grandma, let's get out of this place," Elizabeth said. Her dad and grandmother were shortly behind her as Elizabeth stepped on the mat to automatically open the glass doors to lead her out into the cold afternoon air.

She bundled up her winter scarf and fastened the top button to her warm cream peacoat. Elizabeth turned her head to see how much further her dad and grandma were as she stepped off the curb. The wind was at her back while her hair brushed slightly across her fair skin. She stopped cautiously to watch a car in the middle of the street, parked directly in front of her.

Elizabeth moved her hair away from her freezing face, and she saw the craziest, wildest looking eyes staring back at her from the vehicle. At first Elizabeth thought she was seeing things, still under the drugs but then she realized she was not drugged.

"Casmir! I have a restraining order against you! Get out of here!" she screamed.

Elizabeth and her aunt must have talked him up and in a blink of an eye a bright shining white light appeared above Elizabeth's body, her coat once cream now, bloodshot red.

Chapter 6

"She is losing lots of blood doctor! Breathe Elizabeth!" the nurse cried. "Take her to the operating room, right now," the doctor commanded. "We are losing her!" another nurse warned.

Elizabeth was in critical condition, clinging on to dear life.

"Hang in there Elizabeth," the doctor said.

"Save my daughter!" Elizabeth's father pleaded to the doctor. Elizabeth's aunt held her dad back.

"I will make sure they do everything they can," Aunt Iris said. "Please save her, this is all my fault," Elizabeth's father said. Her aunt swiftly walked down the hallway to the operating room.

Twelve hours have passed. Her dad, grandma, and sister were in the waiting room.

"There's the doctor!" Elizabeth's sister announced as they all jumped up and ran to the doctor.

"How is she doctor?" Elizabeth's dad asked.

The doctor looked at them all and smiled.

"Elizabeth made it through the operation and miraculous she is in the recovering room."

Before anyone could respond; "Oh Lord Jesus! Is my baby okay, Jesus?" Elizabeth's mom said as she ran down the hallway, returning from the bathroom with rollers falling out of her hair.

"Yes, your daughter is in recovery," the doctor replied.

"Thank you Jesus!" her mom screamed.

"Why are you screaming?" Elizabeth's dad asked.

"Shut up frog," her mom snapped. "Can I see her now, doctor?"

"No, in about an hour we will allow visitors Ms. Tight," the doctor said. "She is sleeping at the moment but she cannot be under any stress." Her beleaguered mom was out of control, screaming Jesus through the hallways.

"This is why I cannot tell Elizabeth's mother anything," Elizabeth's dad said sternly.

"You had to call her didn't you," Elizabeth's grandmother said.

"Her daughter was dying," Elizabeth's dad reminded.

"She does not care about Elizabeth," her grandmother argued.

Her dad disagreed, "Yes, she does."

"Yeah. When she feels like it," her grandmother said.

"Mother, please, stop," Elizabeth's dad implored.

The sonographer approached Elizabeth's mom while she was talking to someone at the front desk about the Lord and said, "Well it's a good thing your daughter was already here."

"Excuse me," Elizabeth's mom cried. "Are you talking to me?"

"Your daughter was released from the hospital today," the sonographer informed.

"No she was brought here in the ambulance," her mom corrected.

"Is that what they told you?" the sonographer said.

"What is it that you want to tell me?" her mom asked.

"Let me show you. Follow me," the sonographer answered.

"Where are we going?" her mom wondered.

"Right this way," the sonographer replied. The technician took her into a room to show Elizabeth's mom something agonizing.

"This is your grandson," the sonographer pointed out. "Your daughter is a murderer."

"The devil is a liar," her mom responded. Elizabeth's mom had a very uncomfortable expression.

"She killed a perfectly healthy baby boy," the sonographer said.

"My daughter would never do anything like that and if she did, her dad probably put her up to it," her mom replied.

The sonographer showed her mom the paperwork.

"Well see for yourself. It is your daughter's signature, not her dad's." Elizabeth's mom's uncomfortable expression became angry while reviewing the release papers.

"Thank you. I will take it from here," Elizabeth's mom said. She handed back the forms.

In the face of what Elizabeth's mom just learned she kept her equanimity as she entered her daughter's room. Her peeved attitude turned into gratefulness as she saw that her daughter is still alive.

"Thank you Jesus," her mom said warmly. "How are you, baby? Mommy is here."

"I'm good, where am I?" Elizabeth wrote on a piece of paper. The doctor also informed the family that Elizabeth cannot speak right now.

"You are in the hospital," her mom said. Elizabeth had hazy memory at first, but then she remembered the abortion and she also remembered her dad saying not to tell her mother anything.

I thought I was released. What is going on here?

Elizabeth observed her injured leg that was bandaged up, swollen jaw, and an IV in her undamaged arm.

"Hey Elizabeth," her dad said. Her sister ran to give Elizabeth a hug.

"Hi dad," Elizabeth wrote. "Hey sis."

"I'm so glad you are okay," her sister smiled.

"It's okay sis. Why am I here?" Elizabeth wrote.

"How you feel?" her dad asked.

"I feel some pain but I'm fine. Why am I here?" She wrote in bigger writing.

Remembering what the doctor said about not putting Elizabeth under stress her father replied, "Well don't..."

"You were shot three times by that no-good man you brought in our lives because of your careless decision-making," Elizabeth's mom interrupted, ignoring the doctor's orders. "I taught you better than that! I raised you with morals and values."

"You need to leave," her dad said.

"No!" her mom cried. "She needs to hear this so she can see the consequences of her sins having sex without being married and dating an unsaved man."

"Leave," Elizabeth's dad demanded.

"Don't tell me what to do," her mom said angrily. "That's the problem you treat Elizabeth like a God and me like a peasant, you giraffe-looking imp. Elizabeth is spoiled and out of control because of you. You act like your other daughter does not exist!"

"Shut your face!" her dad shouted.

"The Lord says, you don't give dogs what is holy," her mom quoted to Elizabeth. "And do not throw your pearls before pigs; they will trample on you every time and turn to attack you. You are going to hell if you do not repent."

"Are you God," her dad said, sarcastically.

The room became quiet. Elizabeth's mom eyeballed everyone in the room, ending at her husband's.

"You all are going to hell!" Elizabeth's mom continued. Elizabeth rapidly shook while everyone argued and did not notice Elizabeth's state.

"You need to go take those silly rollers out your hair and leave Elizabeth alone, you demon," her dad sighed. Elizabeth continued to shake uncontrollably; spit falling down the side of her mouth as her grandmother added, "I told you to divorce her a long time ago."

"You stay out of this," Elizabeth's mom warned. "You are the problem too, you ugly looking woman." Her rollers were loosely hanging while some were falling all over the place.

"You are a phony Christian!" Elizabeth's grandmother cried. "And my son should have left your Black ass in the ghetto and married himself a nice white woman to keep our bloodline growing strong!"

"You evil bitter old woman!" Elizabeth's feisty mom exclaimed. She leaned forward to slap her mother-in-law. Elizabeth's dad held her back.

"Elizabeth!" her sister called. Her mom and dad ran towards Elizabeth while the doctor was called in. Before the doctor arrived, her heart monitor flat-lined, beeeeeeeeeep. Elizabeth passed out.

"Elizabeth! Stay with us!" the doctor shouted as he rushed in the room, followed by the nurses.

"She is not responding," the nurse said.

"Stand back," the doctor commanded. He sent electricity into Elizabeth's body from the defibrillator.

"Again...Clear!" the doctor cried. He rubbed the two panels together, sending denser electricity. Elizabeth had no reaction to the repeated bolts of electrical currents he used to coax life back into her body.

He slowly released the panels from Elizabeth. The air became stale as the doctor turned to the family and said something he could never get used to saying, "I'm sorry. We did everything we could."

"No! You did not do everything you could," her mom said, pushing past the crowd.

Elizabeth's mom laid her hands on Elizabeth's body. She wailed as she spoke a language no one understood. Her voice rose louder and louder like peals of thunder. The nurses, the family, and even spectators pacing the hallway stopped to watch. Elizabeth's mom was speaking in tongues.

"Ms. Tight, please stop. Elizabeth is gone," the doctor said. Her mom persistently spoke in tongues without letting go of her daughter. In a matter of spiritual moments, Elizabeth's heart machine showed zig zags and zig zags of lines.

The overbearing mother who killed her saved her. Elizabeth's mom turned to everyone.

"Who's the demon now? You dummies!"

Chapter 7

The abortion was a sad and bittersweet event. Elizabeth later found out the doctor had the wrong chart and that was why he called her Celina. As a result, she was given incorrect medication. The doctor blamed the mix up on the sonographer who he believed gave him the misinformation.

Ultimately, the doctor was sued by Elizabeth's dad but the side effects of the medications damaged her for life. There was a 50/50 chance Elizabeth could not have children.

The scars from the matted nine millimeter glock that invaded her leg, arm, and jaw healed virtually unnoticeably. The physical therapy and martial arts classes Elizabeth participated in nursed her back to health. The intact bullet was removed from her jaw, which allowed her to speak again. She also needed some extra work done to her mouth area, but nothing dental work and plastic surgery could not take care of.

But within, the scars were still noticeable.

She remembered right before getting shot, Casmir yelled at her from the car.

"You think I wouldn't find out about you killing our baby! Now I'm going to take your life!" He shot the whole magazine of bullets at Elizabeth, killing two innocent bystanders. He drove off before the police arrived.

Elizabeth knew it was important to never betray Casmir's trust as a betrayed Casmir would make it a goal to get even some day.

He said he would love me forever, and now, he has turned into my worst enemy, but thank God the bullets did not hit major organs. What a miracle!

Her only continual downfall was that she could not be under any stress due to the bullet that damaged her jaw. Consequently, she could suffer from migraines leading to panic attacks or, worse, seizures. *I almost joined my baby in heaven, but God kept me alive for some reason.*

Elizabeth, who seemed to have buried at least some of the details of the attack and the abortion in her subconscious, was grateful to know it did not burn her out. In fact she felt like she could conquer the world and for the first time in Elizabeth's life, she felt powerful. Elizabeth put her life back on the right track with God and practiced abstinence until she was to be married.

She also channeled all of her energy into volunteering at a center for abused women. Elizabeth was beautiful and smart, so if she could be brutally harmed by a violent and controlling man, she knew this could happen to other young ladies; her experiences could help many victims. But there was one overdue passion project she always dreamed of pursuing. That was to move to New York City to become a fashion model.

Elizabeth's sheer beauty, poise, height, and grace were unmistakable. Just before she dated her obnoxious boyfriend, a talent scout from a prominent modeling agency discovered her at age thirteen, while vacationing in Ocean City. The following week, the agency sent her and her family on an all-expense paid trip to the Big Apple.

Elizabeth and her family arrived by train and a car service picked them up to be transported to a hotel in Times Square. The next day, the agency set up an appointment for her at a famous hair salon catered to celebrities.

She had long dark brown hair with curls so stunning, perfect, and rare. But after they saw her ghetto Philly hairstyle,

A.K.A. "Hard Hair," they quickly made sure she had a twelve hundred dollar extra-long soft fierce weave straight down her back, paid by the agency as well.

This diamond in the rough potentially had a brand new life with an all new makeover.

At this point, mom and dad were understandably weary of the big city so Elizabeth was on tight reigns as she got her initial taste of high fashion and glamour. Her first casting was with Seventeen Magazine, and then Allure.

"WOW!" Elizabeth said to her mom. "The agency must really think I have a chance to be a great model."

The New York City lights, the pushing and shoving, the honking horns from the churlish cabs; everything was music to Elizabeth's ears. She remembered leaving a building with her parents and it seemed like all of New York was coming down the sidewalk at a rapid pace. Elizabeth and her family had to go in the opposite direction on the same sidewalk. They had to push their way through the crowd just to get up the street.

By the time they returned to the hotel at 5:00 pm, they were already exhausted. Her mom and dad had huge headaches and they were ready to return to Philly. Elizabeth on the other hand, loved the entire fascinating hustling and bustling experience. She had found her calling; modeling was what she wanted to do for the rest of her life.

The next day Elizabeth was scheduled to do a photo shoot for her portfolio. Each shot was as tight as a drum but her strict religious mother seemed to have a heart attack from the poses the photographer was telling her to do. Her dad did not seem fazed; he was more concerned about the location the photographer chose, in front of a bright colorful wall not too far from the Hudson River. Traffic was heavy on the street and some people stopped to watch.

He was on the lookout.

After the shoot, Elizabeth's agent invited them out for lunch. He explained that Elizabeth's first show was going to be with Naomi Campbell. She had never walked a runway a day in her life and now she had to do it with the biggest name in the industry. *This is amazing,* but her unafraid attitude took a backseat, she was scared out of her mind.

The next day her booker met them at the location to teach Elizabeth how to walk on the runway. Elizabeth saw Ms. Campbell walk across the floor to meet her stylist. Her hands trembled while her teeth grinded rapidly. Elizabeth felt like she was about to pass out and it didn't help when Elizabeth's agent pulled her to the side.

"Naomi Campbell was asking about you."

"About me?" Elizabeth replied, surprised. "I didn't think she saw me."

"Well she did," her agent smiled. "She asked me, what agency were you with and then said, 'She is beautiful. She almost looks like me.' Now that is classic."

"Wow, that's cool," Elizabeth laughed.

I look nothing like her, she said to herself.

About an hour before the show, Elizabeth's nerves got the best of her and she talked herself out of walking in the show. That was the biggest mistake of her life.

Elizabeth's parents took her back to Philly. They had enough of New York. On the way home, her mom stressed implications of modeling and instructed Elizabeth to finish school and forget about it. She thought modeling was sinful and a waste of time.

Later that week, Elizabeth's agent phoned her mom. He wanted her to return to New York with Elizabeth. He told Elizabeth's mom they needed her to be like Tyra Banks' mom. Tyra Banks and Elizabeth were with the same agency and they both started at the same time, but Tyra's mom was by her side and understood the business; Elizabeth's mom did not.

It was like talking to a wall: Elizabeth's mom was not giving in.

Elizabeth had no choice but to focus on local modeling jobs and hone her skills while finishing high school, longing for the chance to return to New York City when she was of age.

Unfortunately, during the time she modeled for a local agency in Philadelphia she also met Casmir. She thought about the time Casmir made things difficult for her at her Philly modeling agency. His bad temper always had him in fight mode.

The agency wanted to represent her but first she had to build a portfolio since she could not complete the one she initiated in New York, so the booker set up a free photo shoot for her. After leaving the photo shoot, she called her booker to find out what day she could pick up her photos. The booker said she had to pay hundred dollars first.

"You told me the shoot was free," Elizabeth reminded.

"I never said that and if you want the pictures we need a hundred dollars," the booker demanded.

Later that day, Casmir called her and Elizabeth casually explained the situation about her photos. Assuming he wouldn't make a big deal out of it. The next day, however,

Casmir went to the office and stole the photos. Elizabeth had no idea he was going to steal the pictures, but the agency called the police on her. But as usual, the clever Casmir was a step ahead of everyone.

Before Casmir arrived at the agency to steal the pictures, he was able to work his magic again. He made friends with Elizabeth's booker over the phone and tricked her booker into talking trash about another modeling agency in the Philly area. During the conversation, Elizabeth's agent had no clue, Casmir recorded the whole thing.

Casmir told her booker if he did not drop the charges against Elizabeth he was going to send a copy of the tape to the other agency. Needless to say, her booker dropped the charges.

Elizabeth heard the images were extraordinary. The only problem was that Casmir kept the pictures. As far as Elizabeth was concerned, Casmir was no better than her booker and this was just another way for Casmir to hurt Elizabeth.

But regardless, if I knew today, where Casmir stashed those pictures, Elizabeth said to herself. *I would return them to the agency.* The good thing was Elizabeth broke up with Casmir so there would be no more incidents. *What a relief.*

Well, except for when Elizabeth attended a casting auditioning over five hundred models who were standing in line waiting their turn. When Elizabeth and Casmir arrived he put her in the front of the line and looked at the models like, what? *That was gangsta!*

Elizabeth felt guilty for the unprofessional series of events Casmir caused her Philadelphia agency, and even though Elizabeth made an enemy in the modeling world, she gained a friend, a stylist named *The Sugar*. Sugar was a character in and of himself. Everyone always wondered if Sugar was gay or not, but Elizabeth did not care. He was hilarious and he loved Elizabeth like a sister, and since the situation did not work out with the agency, she vowed to book other modeling gigs to keep herself in the game, including a modeling contest in Virginia and Sugar was there for her.

Elizabeth was passionate in all that she did and she did it in grand fashion.

Sugar did Elizabeth's hair and prepared her for the runway. One of the judges from the contest was a lady from Elite Modeling agency in New York City. Elizabeth was so excited because this was her chance to be able to go to the Big Apple again and model for a huge agency.

The night before the show, all of the girls had to be interviewed by the judges. Sugar told Elizabeth to come across as the dreamy, new, fresh girl.

"Don't tell them you've already been to New York," Sugar advised. It made sense at the time.

She went into her interview with buckled knees, tension rushed through her body. Her confidence overpowered her anxiety as they introduced themselves. So far, Elizabeth's meeting was going great.

"Tell us a little bit about yourself," one of the judges said.

"I was born on a plane between London and Paris but I grew up in Hawaii," Elizabeth replied.

"Really?" another judge said.

"No," Elizabeth smiled. "But I thought it sounded more interesting than growing up in Philly with my mom, dad, and younger sister." The judges laughed. "I'm eager to become a top fashion model and I feel like I have what it takes to be successful," Elizabeth continued.

"Very nice," a judge from Milan said, pleasingly. "You are definitely a beauty."

"Thank you," she replied. Elizabeth wanted to be unforgettable so before leaving the room she looked everyone in the eye, shook their hands, and said goodbye to all eight judges by their first name.

As she strutted out the door, she could feel her sweaty palms and shaky legs.

The judge from Elite stopped her before she opened the door to leave and said, "One more question Elizabeth, have you been to New York City?"

Elizabeth did not want to lie but she remembered what Sugar said. She took a deep breath, slowly turned her head and looked at the judge, this time not in the eyes.

"No, I have not."

"Very well. See you tomorrow night," the judge replied.

After she completed her interview, her mind was on preparing for the show.

There is no room for disruptions, she thought. Sugar met her outside the door.

"How did it go?" Sugar asked.

"I nailed it!" Elizabeth smiled. "But I had to lie when they asked if I've been to New York City."

"Whatever, that's what Oprah had to do," Sugar reminded.

"I'm not Oprah," Elizabeth muttered. "But anyway I have to get ready for the show. Let's head back to the room."

"Yeah," Sugar said. "About the room, we have to stay with my designer friend."

"Why?" Elizabeth questioned.

"I ran out of money," Sugar laughed. He reached in his pockets to put fifty-three cents on the table. Sugar came all the way from Philly to Virginia with no money. Elizabeth spent all of her money on contest expenses and the two other people Sugar brought along with him were broke too.

This mother fuc...

They all moved their stuff to his friend's room. The beds were taken so Elizabeth took the floor. Her focus was on the contest and making it big time because although she knew how to adapt to any situation, this right here was ghetto.

"Do you have any blankets?" Sugar asked. He was on the phone with housekeeping.

Is he stupid? If they found out we were all in this one room they would throw us out.

"Get off the phone boy. We don't need any more blankets," Sugar's friend demanded.

"And where is your sister?" his other friend wondered.

"I don't know," Sugar replied.

Elizabeth bit her nails.

"Do we have any money to eat?"

"Nope," Sugar snickered. "We are going to help clean up backstage at the show to earn some money for food.

"I'm not here to clean up. I'm here to do a show," Elizabeth reminded.

"Then stop thinking about eating," Sugar said. "Look at you, you already a size two. You need to be a zero if you want to be a Super Model and stop biting your fingernails. You just got them done." There was a knock on the door.

"Hello, housekeeping," the lady announced.

Sugar marched himself right to the door and received the blankets from housekeeping. They could not believe this was happening as they all laughed. Five minutes later they were not laughing anymore.

Bang, bang, bang!

"Front desk!" the woman said with authority.

"Why is she knocking like the police," Sugar said, sarcastically.

"See," Elizabeth said. "I knew this was going to happen."

"I knew this was going to happen," Sugar's friend mocked as she laughed.

"It's not funny," Elizabeth retorted. Sugar answered the door.

"Sir, how many people are in this room?" the woman questioned, while peaking over Sugar's shoulder. Sugar raised both of his eyebrows and said something off the wall. *Great, now we all have to leave except for the designer who was paying for his room.*

They all gathered their things; still no sign of Sugar's sister until they arrived in the lobby. She was on the sofa hooking up with a hot French guy.

"Silly girl. We have been looking for you. We have to go," Sugar said. He hit her in the head with the lobby newspaper.

His sister was very cute and snazzy. Her name was Alexis.

"I'm not going anywhere. We can stay in my friend's room," Alexis suggested.

"We already tried that," Sugar informed.

"Well, let's try it again," she said. "What you think we are going to sleep in the car?"

"Oh, yeah we need gas money to get back home," Sugar laughed.

"This is not funny," Elizabeth said.

"Look," Sugar responded. "We are here for you, rain or shine you are going to be at the show tomorrow and everything is going to work out. Now let's go to my sister's friend's room." Sugar continued to laugh.

They all gathered their things once again and as quiet as a mouse they were almost able to sneak by the front desk. The only problem was tippy-toed Alexis was making too much noise. Sugar glanced down at the black marble flooring when he saw something hanging and dragging from Alexis' suitcase. A grimace crossed his face when he realized it was her metal buckle that was connected to her belt.

The sound was so irritating,

"Screereeeeeeeeeeeeeeeeeeeeeeeeeeeeeeeeeeeeeeeeee!!!"

"Pick up your belt, Alexis," Sugar whispered.

"What? My belt is not dragging," she replied.

"Screeeeeeeeeeeeeeeeeeeeeeeeeeeeeeeeeeeeeeeeeeeeee!!!

"Yes it is girl, pick it up!" Sugar shouted.

The lady at the front desk ran up to them.

"I'm calling security!" the lady threatened. "You have to leave unless you pay us for the night."

"We are leaving, miss," Sugar said. "Goodness. Is she on her period or something?"

"I heard that," the lady said as she walked away, grabbing the telephone.

"Thanks a lot Alexis," Sugar said. "I know you are not blaming me, you should have money," Alexis sassed.

"Shut up!" Sugar laughed.

They all slept in the car and the next morning it was a mess. Elizabeth felt like she was going to pass out from the beaming hot sun and her lack of nutrition. Not to mention, the restless night due to the small space and Sugar constantly talking in his sleep.

Elizabeth glanced over at Sugar and she could not believe her eyes. She tapped on Sugar's friend.

"What?" he asked.

"Look," she answered.

"Oh goodness." He smiled...Elizabeth giggled.

"Alexis," Elizabeth said, shaking her head slowly. "Look at your brother."

Sugar's circumcised flag pole was shooting straight in the air, flying around saluting all of Virginia.

She looked at her brother and looked away, and then quickly looked back. Alexis was shocked, grossed out, and embarrassed for her brother.

Alexis hit him in the head.

"Wake up pervert!" He did not move. His sister hit him again, and Sugar said hysterically in his sleep, "Who! When! What! Stop! Twinkie!"

"Twinkie? Who is Twinkie?" Alexis wondered.

"And whowhenwhat did Twinkie do?" Elizabeth laughed.

"I heard him calling out Twinkie in his sleep all night," his friend replied.

"Me too," Elizabeth said.

Sugar finally woke up, noticed his hard boner, and tried to hide it.

"You cannot hide that," Elizabeth laughed.

"Yes he can," Sugar's friend snickered. "I did not know you were carrying such a small package. What were you dreaming about?"

"None of your business," Sugar said.

"Obviously Twinkie," his sister responded.

"Come on Twink Twink," Elizabeth continued to laugh. "We got a show to do."

"Don't call me that!" Sugar said angrily.

"Don't be mad," Elizabeth smiled. "Everyone has wet dreams about Twinkies."

Elizabeth managed to get herself together but she was upset when Sugar spilled orange juice all over his white shirt almost missing her.

"Goodness Twink Twink," Elizabeth said, just to agitate him.

"You keep calling me Twinkie," Sugar warned.

"Oh, stop being that way," Elizabeth said as, believe it or not, snack truck pulled up in the parking lot with Twinkies. Everyone laughed hysterically.

"What on earth?" Sugar's friend said. "This is funny. I'm going to get some Twinkies since y'all did not bring any money for food."

Elizabeth walked towards the building as her things fell all over the street. When she picked up one thing, another fell. She finally managed to gather her belongings and walked and stumbled and walked and stumbled, then stopped. Elizabeth saw a lady asking for a dollar. She only had a dollar to her name but she could not resist.

After all of that, she dropped everything on the ground and gave the woman a dollar and some nail polish. The lady smiled. Elizabeth smiled back, grabbed her things, and entered the building that she believed might change her life forever.

Hours later, the evening show began, and Elizabeth looked ravishing in her pearly white gown. Aside from one of the models backstage trying to ruin her dress, she turned the show out. Every time she came out to walk the runway, the crowd clapped. Elizabeth was even better than the strikingly beautiful 13-year-old blue eyed, blonde girl.

With that said, Elizabeth won!

But that little white lie she told the agent during the interview later would bite her in the ass.

Elizabeth was relieved to be back in Philly. The contest did not take her as far as she would have liked it to, but she was able to go to Florida to do her first professional shoot for a known client. The shoot was awesome but she longed for bigger and better things. She was now old enough to move to New York City on her own.

Chapter 8

Elizabeth took a break from Philadelphia and moved to New York. A new life for sure, and a new world – what world? She was ecstatic about being away from Philly and returning to New York, but now what? Tyra Banks was already a supermodel, so Elizabeth felt like her time may have passed sometime in the six year hiatus. But she was determined to not let anything discourage her and to give it her all.

Her plan was not just fit in; she wanted to be an innovator.

Poised for success, she set up a number of appointments with some modeling agencies. So far, things were going well but nothing concrete, probably due to the glitter Veneers she allowed her dentist to test out. She literally had a sparkling smile. It's a cool look; Philly loved it, but New York City did not know how to market the sparkles and the ones that could market her did not want to take a chance.

Elizabeth came to the conclusion to only smile when need be.

One afternoon, Elizabeth was ordering food at a Manhattan corner deli when opportunity knocked. A short, broad-shouldered man with a huge nose, brown slicked back hair, and sucked in obscured brown eyes approached her. He was dressed in tight jeans and a t-shirt with a back pack.

"What is your name?" the man asked in a thick Italian accent.

"Elizabeth Tight," she answered.

"What is your middle name?" he asked.

She paused. "Lyla, why?" she wondered.

"Come with me Lyla," the agent replied.

"Who are you?" Elizabeth asked.

"I'm Antonello, a scout at Ford Models. You are just what we are looking for."

He could have been a maniac for all she knew but this was New York City and a person had to take chances. Ford was one of the biggest agencies in the world and she was fortunate to have caught the eye of a scout from that agency.

The agent introduced her to everyone at Ford as Lyla. *I hate my middle name,* Elizabeth thought. *I don't know why my mom named me that.*

One agent pointed at her teeth when Elizabeth smiled at the booker. *Oops, did not mean to do that.* After she was introduced, Elizabeth was uncertain if they wanted to sign her but something else caught her attention. She saw a good looking guy with beautiful gray eyes and milky brown skin answering the phone. She figured he was one of the bookers.

Elizabeth took note and left the office.

After a long day of seeing agencies, she felt positive but not happy with the results and for some reason she could not get the guy off her mind. She normally did not make the first move, but Elizabeth pulled out the business card for Ford and gathered enough courage to dial the number hoping he would answer the phone.

"Hello, Ford," a man on the other end said. By the sound of his voice she could tell it was Antonello.

She panicked.

"Hello, this is Lyla."

"Where are you?!" he said with excitement.

"Huh?" she replied, puzzled.

"I turned around and you were gone," Antonello said. "We want to sign you!"

The next day, Elizabeth immediately signed a three-year contract with Ford; from then on she went by her more alive middle name, Lyla, as suggested by her booker. Her name went along with her sparkling smile, that her booker nicknamed 'Peppermint' for its cool and refreshing look.

The agency asked her to get rid of her weave and to cut her hair short. She told them the name change was cool and she would remove the weave, but she was not cutting her curly hair.

It didn't take long for Lyla to get noticed. The agency sent her out to many of the same clients she first met when she was thirteen and they seemed to like her hair better long and curly then the straight long weave. *My career as a model had finally come full circle, thanks to my booker who took a chance on me, one that I almost missed out on.*

To this day, the gray eyed guy did not know that he was the reason Lyla signed with Ford.

Chapter 9

Lyla was well on her way. It turned out that the gray eyed guy at the agency was one of their models and he had six children. Not her thing, but she met new people, including new guys without kids. One of whom, a malicious head huntress sabotaged for her. Lyla referred to this girl as a huntress because of what she did to her.

Already, Lyla was running into haters and this mean huntress was a professional one.

She and Lyla were friends with the same person. The wicked huntress was out for his money and Lyla actually liked him as a person. The conniving huntress felt threatened, so her plan was to get rid of Lyla by telling their mutual friend, Sir Kristoph that Lyla was after his money which resulted in him slitting Lyla's car tires to her brand new silver four door Lexus LS 400, she purchased from booking modeling gigs non-stop for about a year now. He also took away her keys to his three million dollar home.

Lyla was not surprised this low-life huntress would pull this scandal but what she thought was selfish was when she found out the huntress already had another superstar plan in motion, so why mess up Lyla's relationship with Sir Kristoph?

Later Sir Kristoph found out, thanks to the cover of Ebony magazine, that the huntress married a celebrity NFL football player for the Cowboys. Sir Kristoph was upset that he was not invited to the wedding.

"See?" Lyla said. "I told you she did not care about you. *She* was after your money, not me."

The huntress' game to attract men was to tell them she was a virgin. Apparently the NFL player fell, the hardest, poor thing. *She should write a book called* <u>How I Married a NFL Player</u>, Lyla thought. No need to mention the huntress name; she knows who she is *Pillow.*

But this little bit of experience made Lyla grasp the reality that her new world was cut throat. She was not worried about the fluffy Pillow. Lyla actually dated a few celebrities herself.

She picked up her friend Allusion for a party where a famous artist was performing. The plan was to follow Lyla's boy uptown in her vehicle.

"Girl," Allusion said. "You may babysit lanes and go down one way streets the wrong way but you are an amazing driver."

"Yes," Lyla agreed. "I have to drive like this in New York City. They call me the girl cabby...007...the best driver in the world. I should've been a race car driver, boo-yah!"

"Okay I got it," Allusion said.

Honk, honk, honk!

"Get out the way!" Lyla called out to a driver, speeding by in a red Camaro.

"I'm just saying I get us from point A to point B in no time, and in more ways than one," Lyla continued, confidently.

"Ah Lyla," Allusion replied. "You better use your driving skills to get us out of here...turn the car around."

"What? Why?" Lyla asked.

"This is the Bronx, we don't want to be here," Allusion answered.

Lyla disagreed, "Yeah, but my favorite artist is performing. Besides, my friend would not invite us to anywhere dangerous."

Allusion's beautiful and eccentrically shaped snake eyes looked Lyla dead in hers.

"I don't care if your favorite artist is performing or what you think your friend won't do. These girls will cut you!"

It did not take too much to convince Lyla to turn around because she actually hated the Bronx. She remembered getting robbed at 4:00 in the afternoon at a corner store while visiting her aunt-in-law one summer.

Not paying attention, Lyla backed the vehicle up and BAM! She hit a car.

"Uh oh," Lyla said. She and her boy were backing up at the same time.

"There goes your best driver in the world record," Allusion laughed.

"Ha, ha," Lyla replied.

"Don't tell him why we are leaving," Allusion suggested.

"Why?" Lyla asked.

"Because," Allusion answered.

"Because what?" Lyla continued to question.

"Just don't tell him. He doesn't need to know why," Allusion responded.

"I don't understand," Lyla said as her friend approached the car.

"We backed up at the same time," her friend laughed from outside the car window.

Lyla stepped out of her car to check it and said to her friend, "I'm sorry."

"It's cool," he said. "There's no damage, it's just funny as all hell; so you looking for a parking space?"

"No we are leaving," Lyla responded. She returned back to her car.

"Leaving?" her friend said while peeping inside the window, checking out Allusion. "We just got here."

"I know but..." Allusion shakes her head no.

"Something came up so we gotta leave but thanks. I will talk to you later," Lyla said.

"Aight," her friend replied. It's a good thing she did turn the car around, because Allusion and Lyla saw a parked car burned to a crisp. The last thing she wanted was for someone to put fire to her Lexus. "I will show you where the party is," said Allusion. "Let's head back to the city."

Lyla could be assertive at times but Allusion was a social-climbing beast who was of somewhat respectable in the industry. Allusion always found out about the good networking parties and she redirected that night from a party in the Bronx to a celebrity filled, A-lister, ESPN after party in mid-Manhattan.

"Why didn't you tell me about this party before girl," Lyla wondered.

"There is one problem, we are not on the guest list," Allusion said, embarrassed. Would this stop her?

Lyla and Allusion searched for a parking space only to be stopped by a supped up muscle car with Illinois tags parked in the middle of a one way street.

"Isn't that the same car you honked at uptown?" Allusion questioned.

Lyla looked at the car and answered, "Oh yeah! I did not realize it. Everything happened so fast." Lyla waited and waited for the driver to move his car.

"I can't believe how ignorant this person is," Allusion said as Lyla and the other cars behind honked their car horns.

"Yeah, first he was in my way uptown and now he is in my way downtown!" Lyla screamed with an impatient voice. Everyone continued to wait and wait, the traffic behind Lyla growing stronger while Lyla became more irritated.

Without warning and unshakable confidence, Lyla jumped out the car and marched over to the custom tailored red Camaro. She tugged on the locked car door handle. Lyla turned around to walk away, so everyone thought. One of Lyla's long tanned legs, she recently paid for at the tanning salon, did a vicious kick through the window. She then stuck her hand in the door to unlock it.

After she put the car in neutral, with all her strength, she pushed it to the side, just enough space to let her car and the ones behind her through. Everyone cheered while Lyla bebopped back to her car, hair blowing in the wind as she gave them a gangsta nod like *yeah-what*?

Allusion looked aghast at Lyla at first and then laughed.

"That is how you keep the traffic moving in New York, boo-yah!"

Lyla was in gear to drive off until she spotted the driver dropping the boxes he was carrying out of the four-level Brownstone he was parked in front of. He ran and yelled, calling Lyla awful names, threatening to phone the police as he looked at her license plate number. She stepped on her brakes, shifted her gear to reverse, and backed up. Lyla then used her car like a monster truck and rammed the front end of his car with her back end to hide her license plate.

Allusion feeling a whiplash.

Lyla was not worried about her vehicle, that bitch had a flexible bumper guard attached to her shit.

She reached for her steel baseball bat from the backseat and stepped out of her car again, swinging her bat with one hand, like a professional baton twirler. The white scrawny male in his early thirties dressed in a pin stripped shirt, black blazer, a pair of A.P.C. jeans, and black Armani shoes saw her coming, ran a little, and then stopped and attempted to act badly, while he shook.

"You dummy!" Lyla said to herself.

She took his cell phone and threw it. Lyla then swung the bat at him. He ducked...she missed. She swung again. He ducked...she missed, but managed to smash his back window shield in.

"Tell the police that!" Lyla screamed. The guy tripped over the curb while running from her.

Lyla walked over to him and raised the bat over her head, ready to smash his in. The stain in her face was pure rage as she continued to shout, "And I dare you call me a bad name again!" A woman who seemed to be his wife came running out the building they were in. Allusion stepped out of the car ready for warfare.

"What is going on here?!" Please, stop! That's my boyfriend!" the woman ranted, as she grabbed a huge rock.

Lyla walked away from the guy, after she saw the weak man was no match for her. She refocused her attention on a new dummy.

Lyla stood in a baseball pro stance, with the bat held to the right of her head, ass poked out, back curved in, knees bent, like she was ready to go to bat. *Throw that rock bitch,* Lyla said to herself. *I'm hit a home fucking run.* The woman stopped coming towards Lyla after, she saw her stoned cold eyes. Allusion was watching the lady from out in left field, like she was a catcher with no protection.

The woman dropped the rock and Lyla lowered her bat as she walked towards the lady and said, "You act like we are on your time. You don't own these streets."

From a mixture of being concerned for her boyfriend, the disrespect from Lyla, and the shattered car window, the outraged woman shouted, "You bitch!" Lyla dropped her bat and punched the lady in the face as she slid easily across the car trunk. A broken piece of glass sliced the woman's right thigh, just above her knee.

Lyla hurried back to her Lexus, as the bloody lady hit the ground. Allusion stepped back in the car. Lyla did not need her help.

The guy, Lyla thought she got rid of, approached her car.

"I'm a lawyer! I will see you in court!"

"Look me in my eyes and ask me if I care. You are the lawbreaker, you pussy!" she hissed out her car window. Lyla sped off as he kicked the side of her bumper.

"I can't believe I had to turn into Mighty Model to get to a party," Lyla said. Allusion could not stop laughing.

"That was your alter ego, girl," Allusion informed.

Lyla and Allusion finally made it to the club. While standing outside, Lyla saw one of her ex-boyfriends. He was a stunning male model from Sweden. She reminisced about the time they spent the night outside on the rooftop of his apartment, star gazing. *It was beautiful.*

She wondered how could she let him go, but guys had a hard time accepting the fact she was celibate. The relationship lasted for three hot and steamy months of intense foreplay and role-play that lead to no sex.

Lyla would never forget what he said to her one night, at his Manhattan loft, when she wouldn't have sex with him.

"Don't ever disrespect my place again," he said graciously in his Sweden accent.

Lyla left; no hard feelings – they just weren't on the same page.

Funny how she broke it off.

"If he does not call me by midnight to apologize, I will be the Cinderella breaking up with him." He called at 12:01. She dumped him, but at least they were still cool.

He saw Lyla as a timid, quiet natured, sweet, virgin girl, which she was until Allusion smeared her good girl image. Allusion pushed Lyla in the club while she took off her coat.

"Keep walking; follow me downstairs."

"Where are we going?" Lyla asked, the music blaring around them. She turned her head and noticed the bodyguard was searching for something. Lyla pushed her way through the crowd of people and over the loud music she answered, "Oh, man what did you do, Allusion?"

"Just keep moving and take off your coat," Allusion commanded. Lyla took off her coat, showing off her long thin legs and slender body, fitted in a Givenchy plain but sexy black dress with high heels, but it couldn't compare to Allusion shiny, elaborate metallic mini. After a few moments, Lyla realized Allusion snuck in the club while the bodyguard had his back turned, and he was now searching for them. Allusion's skinny waist and Melissa Ford booty; in attracting men was as slick as an eel.

She motioned Lyla to stand at the bar and turn their backs to the crowd.

"We are going to jail," Lyla said.

"Girl, we are not going to jail," Allusion laughed. "You think this is funny because you were taking pictures and making friends the last time you were in jail," Lyla said.

"Yeah girl," Allusion continued to laugh. "When I got there one of the girls asked me what I'm in for, and by the time the night was over, when a new girl would come in, I was like 'what you in for'?"

"Yeah," Lyla said. "You couldn't tell them what you were in for because believe me, you would not have been taking pictures. They would have given you a hard time."

"Right," Allusion agreed. "Throwing a parking ticket on the ground that an officer was giving me doesn't make me sound dangerous, so I told them I killed my husband. But you know what is even funnier?"

"What?" Lyla asked.

"You just assaulted two people and destroyed a car but are worried about going to jail for sneaking in a club?" Allusion answered. "Come on girl, get over it."

Lyla giggled as she turned her head slightly around and saw the bodyguard walk right past the both of them. She felt like she was in a comedy movie. The funny part was Allusion's plan worked. It was embarrassing to say the least, but they were in the clear.

At first it was hard to pick out familiar faces, if there were any at all – the place was packed like a sardine. But eventually Lyla saw a few people she knew and she was the life of the party, socializing and having a good time. When her favorite song came on, she dropped it like it was hot.

"Yeah, this party is the bomb!" Lyla said to Allusion excitedly as she told her, "this is my first time at a club."

Allusion shook her booty to the beat of the music and replied, "Yeah right."

"I'm serious," Lyla said, observing the party people mingling in their small groups.

"Wow and just think your first night at a club would have been in the Bronx getting cut," Allusion laughed.

"I see Marshall, the photographer. I'll be right back," Lyla said. She danced her way over to Marshall like she was in a music video.

"What's up Marshall," Lyla said, moving to the rhythm of the music.

"Get out of here," Marshall responded. He was talking to some girl.

"Whatever, I'm like your little sister," Lyla said.

"Get out of here, you are messing me up," Marshall laughed.

"Who is this?" the girl asked.

"Oh, nobody," Marshall answered.

Lyla gave Marshall a kiss on his cheek.

"See you later Marshall." She walked away to find Allusion.

While Lyla looked for Allusion, she noticed an old drunk man on his knees.

"Come here baby. Daddy wants to marry you," the old man said instinctively licking his lips.

He looked like Chuck Brown with a bad suit. *He must have snuck in too,* she thought. Lyla swiftly walked away, but he slid on his knees in beat of the music swaying them side-to-side which allowed him to follow her everywhere she went.

She ran until she finally caught up with Allusion.

"How is Marshall? I'm about to...Who is that?" Allusion asked while observing a lecherous man on his knees.

"Let's get out of here," Lyla answered. They ran up to the first floor where they started.

"Oh, man that was scary," Allusion laughed.

"Who you telling," Lyla said.

Lyla looked at Allusion; she could tell her overconfident friend was not finished scheming for the night. She wanted to get in the VIP room which was right next to the front door where the bodyguard was posted.

Lyla expressed to Allusion that it wouldn't be in their best interest to push this any further, but Allusion was not listening. By this time, Lyla did not care too much either because she already had a couple of glasses of red wine. Lyla and Allusion approached the VIP rope. The attendant asked if they were on the list and of course Lyla and Allusion weren't.

They left the front of the line and stood to the side of the rope on the other end of the VIP section. Lyla was talking to her DJ friend who was working in the booth. Suddenly, Allusion stepped over the VIP rope and then Lyla followed.

Lyla and Allusion settled in, socializing, getting their party on. Moments later, someone caught Lyla's eye across the room, but he was talking to a famous television host so Lyla waited.

She remembered listening to a popular male pop star on the radio that morning: "I like it when a girl approaches me."

Lyla thought she would try it on the former heavy weight champion of the world. She was still warmed up from making her first move on the model at the agency as Lyla swirled her body in a seductive manner, allowing the music to take over her body.

This will be a piece of cake.

The champ ended his conversation with the host and started towards the exit.

"You giving all these girls your number, why not give it to me," Lyla said. The heavy weight brushed her off and kept walking. She felt like an idiot.

Lyla ordered another glass of wine as she noticed a huge man walking towards her, and she quickly realized it was the bodyguard from the front door. He escorted both of them out the VIP area, and directed them towards the front door to leave the club, but on their way out, the champ returned.

"Where are you going?" the fighter asked while Lyla looked at the bodyguard.

"We are not on the list," Lyla said truthfully.

"What she means is, they lost our names," Allusion sighed.

"Let's go!" the bodyguard shouted.

"They're on my list," the champ told the guard as he directed them back to the VIP section.

"Thank you," Lyla said to the fighter, rolling her eyes at the bodyguard.

"How old are you?" the champ asked Lyla.

"I'm legal," she answered. *So, he thinks I'm a kid.* He was not amused so Lyla told him her age. The fighter still did not seem convinced. He asked for her driver's license. Lyla pulled it out.

While the champ glanced at the license, Allusion came behind her and whispered, "Look at his ear." Of course, Lyla looked right at it the same time he handed Lyla her license back. She could tell he was insecure about it.

"Well would you like to do me a favor and bless me with your presence at a restaurant to grab something to eat, Elizabeth," he said.

"It's Lyla, my friends call me Lyla," she replied. "And yes I would and so would my friend." Allusion and Lyla left with the champ and his friend.

On the way out, Lyla chatted with a couple more of her friends, one of which was YCliff's old publicist. YCliff was a famous artist and Lyla's ex-lover, but they were still friends. She couldn't wait to tell him she ran into his old publicist.

Shortly after, Allusion and Lyla finally arrived to the location of Lyla's car, but when she got there, her car was missing. She realized her car was in a towing zone, and already owed three thousand dollars in tickets. Lyla and Allusion rode in the fighter's limo.

Not bad for Lyla's first night at a club.

Lyla's car was released the next day, thanks to YCliff. Meanwhile, Lyla and the champ became friends. He called her a *Supermodel*.

Allusion was the best, Lyla thought until the champ showed her his true nature. He wanted to have sex with Lyla one night, and when she refused him, he forced himself on her. Lyla pleaded with him to get off of her.

She was no match for this huge fighter, so she yelled, "Stop! Before I have to be rushed to the hospital to have my tampon surgically removed!" Thank goodness he impeded.

Needless to say, Lyla could be a little rough around the edges at times. She remembered what Allusion said to her.

"That was your alter ego, girl."

Allusion was right. At times, it was like Lyla's mind went somewhere else, and she became someone different. The scars from her past with Casmir made her angry, and she was no longer playing the victim. Needless to say, she was not that nice innocent teenage girl from the mall anymore. She also knew that she had a suppressed temper that had not been fully ignited.

But she did not know it was to a point where she would kick in a car window *like she was Beatrix Kiddo from Kill Bill. What else is my alter ego capable of?*

Lyla thought back to how she responded to the sonographer; though she was unkind to her, Lyla knew she was out of character.

"This is your fault! You left me here on purpose. I ought to slap the taste out of your mouth!"

She also knew she was out of character when she thought vulgar things:

"What have I done? Casmir's dick was good and all, but it's not worth all of this."

"This mother fuc..."

"Throw that rock bitch. I'm hit a home fucking run."

"You dummy!"

Well I probably got that one from my mom, Lyla thought.

"Who's the demon now? You dummies!"

It seemed as though Casmir had sucked out nearly all of Lyla's inner being. The bad part was Lyla was taking it out on everyone else, when she should be taking it out on Casmir. It had become her life's struggle to get her true self back before it was too late.

"God help me," she whispered.

The good part was no one saw her other side unless she showed it to them; and although her secrets from her past life were looking to surface, she kept them repressed. This was what everyone knew about Lyla Tight:

"Hailing from Philadelphia, this butterscotch complected, long-legged, young lady with dazzling almond shaped eyes exudes confidence and elegance and has a smile that is as bright as sunshine.

Growing up in Philly with her supportive mom, dad, and sister, Lyla enjoyed a quaint lifestyle but she always dreamt of challenges outside the City of Brotherly Love. Instilled with self-confidence and a sense that she could be whatever she wanted to be in life with persistence and determination, Lyla set the sky as her limit at a very early age.

Chapter 10

Years Later

As Lyla sat alone in her kitchen, waiting for her black bean noodle soup and rice to cook, she sipped on a glass of wine and bit her fingernails, questioning her modeling career.

"Life is easy when you know your purpose." Lyla posted on her blog about an hour ago. Based on the eighty eight posted comments, people could relate.

Lyla thought she knew her purpose.

During a modeling gig a make-up artist asked Lyla, "Why aren't you famous yet?" Good question. But Lyla's career had its ups and downs.

Though she hated her middle name, she was attached to it, so she kept using Lyla. Regardless, she never became truly successful, and Lyla's passionate and high-spirited personality unfortunately left her feeling exhausted and unfulfilled. She had lost both her Manhattan apartment and her car. Neither the champ nor any other known name could get her to where she wanted to be as a model.

By the smell of burned white rice hitting the air, Lyla's food was ready. *I was never much of a cook.* She grabbed some seaweed and some hot sauce to add to her dish from a nearby cabinet that hung over the kitchen sink. Lyla loved to drink a bit of wine before eating so she was a little tipsy.

She continued to look inward and outward of her career. *I had faith I could succeed*, Lyla thought. *But I missed out on opportunities. Some would say my good morals and values got in the way, but I was not going to compromise on those. No, I'm not perfect, but I did not count on practicing the wrong thing. I want to be known as the model that made a difference and did not sell my soul, maybe witness to a model or two about God.*

As she played opera music she had an affinity for about two years ago she asked herself, *Is this realistic?*

In contrast, there were a few things she thought held her back. For one, her time had passed like she thought years ago. For another, although she was a business minded person, appeared in plenty of magazines and commercials and walked in exclusive runway shows, Lyla did not recognize that modeling was a business until it was too late. Instead she took it for granted and did things half-ass.

Lyla's biggest mistake was her financial irresponsibility as she looked at the razor blade close by. She spent all of her money and had nothing to show for it. Even the money from the small hospital settlement was gone. That wasn't worth much because they could not prove the doctor had called her by a different name. Somehow, his paperwork was destroyed and the nurses in the room disappeared.

What made Lyla really upset was that she wanted to make life easier for her family. With that said, she believed there was more than one way to skin a cat so she used some of her 101 ideas she started and never finished to attempt to rise to the top and even went to college to receive her Master's degree in business. Nothing worked and she was at the end of her rope wondering where she had gone wrong in her life. Lyla stared harder at the razor blade while she poured another glass of wine.

Maybe I should have cut my hair short.

Before Lyla was scouted by a modeling agent, she had planned on becoming a physical therapist, getting married and having lots of children, the American way. But she couldn't turn back the hands of time and she was so far behind that all she wanted to do now was find an island with just her laptop for company. She would throw away her cell phone, work at a juice bar, and call it a life. But that was not realistic unless she had a million dollars saved up.

Ah, that would be so nice, Lyla thought. *If I had a million dollars in bank I would only spend the interest.*

Lyla did not like to be negative but she also felt like her dreams had been contaminated by people she had in her circle, mainly her "family."

It wasn't until after her grandmother passed away that Lyla found out that her grandmother was born in this world through an affair. Some say her mother was raped. In turn, Lyla's grandmother was shunned and abused by her own drug addicted, alcoholic mother. She raised Lyla's grandmother to sell herself from the age of six to support her drug habit.

Before Lyla's grandmother turned ten, her mother died of a drug overdose.

Later Lyla's grandmother became a prostitute and a street hustler. Undoubtedly, Lyla's grandmother followed in her mom's footsteps, which made her damaged goods. In the process of being sexually abused by her uncles, selling her body, and prostituting, she had seven children. One of the men in her grandmother's life stood by her, even though - everyone including himself - questioned whether or not they were his children.

Unfortunately, he was a mean and abusive man that used guns and threats to make Lyla's grandmother and her children obey.

Lyla did not believe in generational curses until now. She looked back again on her life and she now fully believed that everyone born through her grandmother was cursed, including Lyla and her mom. Now she could see why she was screwed up, started things and didn't finish, and made the wrong personal and business decisions. She was doomed from the beginning.

She continued to sit for hours pin pointing her evasive decisions and unsuccessful life, her heart towards God becoming dimmer. *Is God punishing me for having an abortion?*

Lyla eyes watered as they became red with anger. She threw her glass of wine against the wall, rubbing her eyes while mascara streaked her face.

"Why God? I have done everything you told me to do! I feel like you put me through so many unfair obstacles and test. You lead me to paths that only lead to a mountain I can't move, and you won't move! I obey your word and everything leads to a dead end!

"Why? Why am I here in this world?! My career...my love life...my family; it's all cramp. You don't care about me! I'm beginning to think you are not real!

"I'm tired!"

Lyla grabbed the razor blade and pushed it down on her wrist, causing blood to drip on the floor. She continued to whimper as she fell to the ground. Lyla was passed out.

After a few hours, she woke up with a bloody wrist. Lyla wondered where she was, as she looked around and touched her forehead. *My head is feeling heavy and the room is too bright.* She lifted herself off the bloody floor and picked up her wine bottle, tilted it to the left to get a good look inside. *Oh goodness, I drank the whole bottle.*

As she slowly remembered what happened before she fell out from the wine she said to herself, *I passed out fussing at God. He could have done anything to me, but yet I'm still here,* as she threw the bottle away, realizing she was in her kitchen.

Did I make God cry?

Lyla also realized she was acting like a spoiled ungrateful brat, and she wanted to give God a tissue to wipe his tears. She cleaned her wrist, prayed a grateful prayer, and instead of mentally beating herself up and listening to the devil's lies, Lyla unlocked her diary of secrets to write down all of her feelings and negative thoughts. She would do this from time-to-time to get things off her mind and to move on. But first, she read something she wrote a year ago. It said:

Dear God,

I had a revelation today. You showed me why I have a problem with starting things and not finishing them. As settle as this revelation is, it's real, and after all these years, I'm just realizing this...it all begun with my cousin Ryland. She is ten years younger than me. I never thought she would be the one who would attempt to indirectly take me down.

It's upsetting because she and I are the only female cousins with the same interests. Ryland was in pageants, she had way over hundred trophies from ballet, jazz, tap, and baton and everyone praised her, including me. I was so proud of my cousin, but when Ryland found out I was scouted by a modeling agent, everything went downhill between us. Ryland wanted the family to only talk about her and now she saw me as a threat; therefore, she is always in competition with me.

My little cousin is no ordinary girl; she was quite aggressive from a young age. Ryland would say and do whatever she wanted and no one ever corrected her, especially her mom, Liza.

I was at the beach with my cousin and her mom building a sand castle and Ryland marched over and knocked it over. Without getting upset, I moved to a different area and let her finish kicking it down while I built another one.

"You are going to be a wonderful mother one day," my Aunt Liza said.

At the time I felt good about being able to build a new castle without fighting my cousin, but now I realize in my adulthood that I should have fought for what was mine and not let my cousin knock it down. She had been kicking me down for a good part of my life until I put an end to it five years ago when I verbally knocked her down. But, unfortunately because I let her knock down what I started, in turn, I have let others do it to me as well. It's amazing what can be embedded in a person's mind at a young age through people you least expect.

Thank you for listening God. P.S. Where is that monster truck you promised me? Ha, ha.

Lyla now understood part of the reason why she never finished what she started: she learned as a teenager, and unknowingly brought it into her adult life as she thought about Casmir literally pushing her down at the park. Now she knew she could break this curse in her life. Lyla turned off her opera music and found a blank page in her diary and wrote:

Dear God,

This year is my revolution year, which means shaking and moving the world with every step, and not hanging on to fear and holding back. The only way to do this is to get rid of the unnecessary garbage.

I just read a previous letter I wrote to you about my cousin Ryland. I love her so much and loved being her cousin. She was so dear and special to me and a true gift. I absolutely adored her.

I remember the time we drove to New York City to audition to be in a singing group. We were asked to sing a song, and the only song we knew all the lyrics to was Twinkle Twinkle Little Star. Needless to say we did not get in the group, but we had so much fun.

A little over five years ago, I said some pretty harsh things to her about her arrogance and how she treats me. I have to admit I wanted her to feel how she had made me feel for so many years. I don't think she realized what she was doing when she was a kid, but now that she is older, I know she does. I apologized to my cousin, for how I said what I said, but she responded in a negative way.

I guess she is more fragile than I thought.

But the thought of us not speaking anymore brings tears to my eyes, on the other hand, I have learned something about people: if a person has not suffered through hard times, then they can't appreciate what it takes to get over them, and they miss out on the lessons learned in the process. It's better to be around friends and family who have been through challenges in life because those are the people who will be around forever no matter what.

Forget all of that, before we stopped speaking, this was the same girl who asked me when I was getting married, so she could plan my wedding. I thought that was so cute, and as difficult as this transition has been for me, I have grown accustomed to us not speaking; but, some things cannot be avoided. At our grandmother's funeral, we sat right next to each other and did not say a word.

I was crushed.

Almost the same thing happened at our grandfather's funeral. I miss my grandparents. I especially miss my grandfather asking me to get him a plate of pork chops and a high blood pressure pill.

Shortly after the funeral, Ryland told one of my family members that I need to be a woman and apologize; it is actually she who needs to be a woman, because if she was, Ryland would accept my first apology.

The ball is in her court.

But do I really expect an apology from a person who was served breakfast in bed from age two till now and has not washed a dish in her life because she does not want her hands to touch dish water. And if I really think about it, my cousin really can't help but be arrogant and mean. She is just like her mom, who took all of my grandmother's money while she was living and when she passed away to spend on plastic surgery.

I feel like telling my aunt Liza off, but that won't get us anywhere. She is who she is and so is Ryland. I'm just glad I can write what's on my mind and leave it be.

But I sent Ryland's mom a message and said that if she does not send my mom her part of the money, I would sue her. I know – legally - I could not collect my mom's money, but by the time I was done with her the money would be tied up in legal fees so no one can have it.

Of course, I said I was going to sue her to scare her. I would never sue my family.

Lyla took a break from writing, ate some food, drank some more wine, and then thought about her favorite great aunt. In the mist of everything, Lyla also found out after her grandmother's death that her great aunt, who lived in New York City, worked for the mob to make a living. She had so many husbands. The funny part is she never dropped her married names.

My great aunt could go down in the Guinness World Records as the woman with the longest last name.

Regardless, Lyla looked up to her growing up as a kid. If it weren't for her great aunt, she would have not been able to make it in New York. Lyla remembers her experiences when visiting her great aunt...

One day my great aunt and I were walking along Park Avenue South in NYC.

A guy was selling some tickets to a comedy show and I answered, "No, thank you." He followed us and would not take no for an answer. My aunt stopped walking and cussed him out. He quickly walked away.

That was when I learned not to talk to the salesman on NYC streets.

I was scheduled to go to an audition and I had to be there in twenty minutes - I ran to my aunt's room and told her I had to leave.

"Okay, but I'm not going with you," my aunt said. I would not go to the corner store of my aunt's building without her so I was horrified! But I had no choice. This would be the first time I had to ride the train in NYC alone.

Naturally, that day I learned the whole train system, and made it to my casting on time.

I also remembered when I booked my first magazine - I could not wait to show my aunt. I ran into her room.

"Look Aunty." She looked at it, rolled over, and fell asleep. That would be the day I learned how to be humble. The only time anybody hears about my work is through my agent.

It was always interesting at my great aunt's house. She was 71-years-old but she looked like she was in her forties. Her hallway in her Central Park apartment on the thirth floor, overlooking the Manhattan Bridge was filled with photos of celebrities. One of her husband's she was married to was famous. He passed away, but she still had a lot of famous connections.

She would take me to visit some of them.

My great aunt used to smoke marijuana all day; I guess that's how she stayed looking so young. One day, she asked me to open the door for her weed man. Boy, was I nervous. My great aunt would smoke her weed while we ate ice cream, drank champagne, and watched a movie.

On the other hand, when my aunt was tired of you, family or not, she got rid of you. One day I came home at 10:00 pm and she had all of my stuff packed in bags sitting next to the front door. Not because it was late, but because my two months was up. I didn't realize she had a time limit, but I found out that night. She told me I had to leave with no warning.

That would be the day I learned how to survive in NYC.

At the time, I was so upset with her, but years later I realized if she hadn't done that, I would not have been prepared to live in NYC on my own.

I heard she was dying from stomach cancer. I wanted to visit so I could thank her but it was too late, she passed away. I hope my cousin does not have to experience that. It was too late for me to say thank you to a person who was showing me hard love, like how I showed my cousin hard love.

Now that I think about it, just like my great aunt risked our relationship, I knew I was going to risk my relationship with my cousin when I punched and knocked her down with the words I said out of my mouth, but because I love her so much I took that chance. She is still my cousin and my intentions were not to be mean. With that said, I apologize to her again.

There was one particular child of my grandmother's that was treated the worst of all of the siblings: my mother. She would have to sit in the corner at 10-years-old, stand on her head, and read the Bible as punishment for hours if she did something wrong and when she became a teenager she had to give up her money from her part time job. The money had to go to her other six siblings. On top of that she had to make breakfast, lunch, and dinner for them while she was told by her dad to hula hoop while she watched them eat. She did not have time to eat because after hula hooping she had to clean up after them. Not to mention, that every Christmas she had to shop for Christmas toys in an elf suit for her siblings and received none for herself, just to name some of the abuse.

She was a modern day slave, so I expect my mom not to treat me right.

Growing up, my mom seemed like a nun to me. She was the total opposite of her own mother. My mom never saw the inside of a night club. She didn't prostitute herself, curse, steal, lie, or be envious; instead my mother lived a wholesome lifestyle and instilled good morals and values in me.

Although she seemed to go overboard when it came to her relationship with God, I loved the fact she introduced me to Christ. Then again, mothers hold a lot of power in mother-daughter relationships but some abuse and misuse that power. As I became an adult my mother dramatically changed on me in a negative way, especially as I grew as a person and when I started following my dreams. I know part of her would like to see me succeed, but the other part of her does not want me to do better than she did. As a child, my mom had the same dreams of becoming a model, but her mother and father would not let her pursue it.

When she looks at me, she sees her own failure.

For that reason, she has to be the center of attention and brag about her accomplishments. She continually seeks attention and overdoses of love and affection, which gets frustrating. No one can fill that void but God. She should know that.

To distract her from what does not make her happy in her life she works on her home, making sure everything is organized, even if it means throwing stuff away that does not belong to her.

I also understand that she is a blunt woman, but she does not realize it hurts. For instance, when she is mad she would attempt to kill my confidence with her murderous words.

Her favorite statement was, "God will not bless you. Nothing good is going to happen in your life." She would say the most hateful things. "You are ugly, the wife of Frankenstein with nothing to offer the world." or "You got a college degree and you're still dumb."

I admit I cussed my mom out that day, and that's the day I knew I had to get away, faraway. But that would be hard because she would reel me back in, because with that same mouth of curses, blessings followed in the next five minutes.

"I love you. God is going to bless you."

Some say she was a bipolar evil witch.

The way she treated me, you would think I was a stripper or drug addict like my grandma. None of my friends or her friends knew of her nasty ways because she only showed me.

Lyla stopped writing as tears cascaded down her face for a moment. She then walked over to the bloody razor, grabbed it, rinsed it clean in the sink, and tossed it away in the small trash bin under her kitchen sink. She continued to cry as she wiped up the drops of blood, poured another glass of wine, and proceeded to write.

Damn my mom! Oh sorry, God, but I'm a good daughter and regardless of how she treats me, I love her so much. I wrote her letters expressing how much I loved her and supported her in all of her dreams and she threw them out. When I was making lots of money from the modeling I would send her money all the time.

One special moment I remember was when I sent her flowers to her job for Mother's Day. Another great moment was when I made her and my dad Easter baskets. I wanted them to feel like kids again. They woke up and went downstairs to the kitchen and they had no idea I was going to have an Easter basket for them with all of their favorite things.

Nothing was ever good enough. I could not make her happy. I wish I had a t-shirt with her face on the back of it and it read, "Get Off My Back." That would be a funny t-shirt. Maybe it could make light of the situation, because her life goal for me is to feel the same pain her mother and father put her through.

That is the kind of sick success she wants for me.

She claims otherwise, but the only time she has something to say to me is when she's putting me down...pure death...pure sabotage, the same as my cousin. Normally, parents would adjust to what has happened in their past, and work on their future. My mom continued the curse of her mother and became my part time supporter when actually I needed her to be a full time one, but what goes around comes around.

Now I can see the generational curse.

I have much more to write to you, God, but I would rather not write with pen and ink. Instead I will meet life face-to-face. I still have faith and I'm never giving up.

But it wasn't until I met Nestle while I was working a night job that made me believe in life's possibilities again. I'm back on that love thing again.

Thank you for listening God.

Chapter 11

Now working the front desk in a new midtown hotel, priced for people with money and offering amenities to match, Lyla found herself staring at a tall, chocolate, brown-eyed, young stag with a bald head. She examined his features while performing her routine duties for the night, as the guy in Prada shoes walked towards her. Lyla could tell this chocolate stag was much younger than she, but he was absolutely fine as wine.

He came close to her, close enough that she felt his breath on her neck as he spoke.

"You make a man want to become a man."

That gentle statement sparked a light, illuminating her soul and building some confidence in her. Needless to say, Lyla got her groove back as she pounced back and forth taking care of business behind the desk, delegating orders to the rest of the staff as if she owned the hotel. The young guy took a couple of steps back to get a full view of this stunning beauty before his eyes, staring her up and down and down and up, making her feel almost naked. He was even more turned on by her take charge approach.

His desire for her was out of control.

Lyla continued to present herself in a professional manner, disregarding his stare.

Eventually, he took his hungry eyes off of Lyla as the guy and an older white male, who seemed to be with him looked around as if they were looking for something or someone.

"May I help you?" Lyla asked, wondering if this is his first time in New York.

"Yea, you can help me," the guy answered, gazing into her shining nut-brown eyes.

"Do you have a room booked for tonight?" Lyla asked.

"No. We don't have a room for the night but aren't you the least bit curious to know my name?" Lyla's face paled as she raised one eyebrow and did not reply.

"It's Nestle," he continued, attempting to break her silence.

Her eyes glowed.

"Like the chocolate."

"Like the dark and sexy chocolate, babes," he replied smoothly.

"Yum," Lyla's coworker interrupted. They all laughed.

"We are here to chill at the bar," Nestle nodded toward the left.

"Okay," Lyla said. "Please enjoy yourself, Nestle."

"I will Lyla," he said.

"How do you know my name?" Lyla instantly blushed.

"It's right there on your chest," Nestle pointed out.

"Oh!" Lyla laughed, feeling a warm stir in her stomach.

He noticed her unique smile.

"You are beautiful, sparkles."

She blushed again.

"Thank you." Nestle was really cute and she wanted to get to know him a little bit better - taking her time of course.

There was only one problem: she thought this suave good-looking GQ guy was gay. *That is so weird because I'm sure he was coming on to me,* she said to herself. Lyla went to her colleague.

"The gay guy just said I'm beautiful," Lyla said, puzzled.

"What's wrong with that? Gay guys have secret crushes on females. They still got a dick," the colleague responded. "This seemed more than a crush. Do you think he is gay?" Lyla asked.

Her colleague glanced at the potential gay guy and he could not figure it out. Lyla's manager walked by so she asked him and he was also puzzled.

"Don't get any ideas," her manager warned.

"Why?" Lyla wondered.

"Because whether that guy is gay or not," her manager answered, "you are not his last stop. He is definitely a player."

Lyla's manager wanted to be with her so she couldn't listen to him.

"If he is a player, I'm going to change him from the inside out," Lyla said, confidently.

"Yeah. Good luck with that," her manager chuckled. Lyla thought back to what her Aunt Iris told her.

"What you see is what you get. You cannot change anyone especially not a man. He has to want to change."

If he is a player he will adjust for me, Lyla said to herself. *I can feel it.* Lyla's last attempt was to ask her gay colleague. He would surely know.

"Is that guy gay? Over there on your right hand side?" Lyla pointed out.

"No, definitely not," her coworker laughed.

Lyla was pleased to know that.

She giggled and said to the girl at work, "I'm in love."

Lyla's shift was over. On her way to the area to punch out for the night, she saw the young guy, along with the older man sitting at the bar. Nestle stopped her and she smiled. The older man was doing most of the talking, but then Nestle told her he was Dominican and African-American, and she noticed he had one tooth missing.

Another guy with a missing tooth? Lyla hoped this was not a sign to run. Needless to say, that missing tooth brought back some disturbing memories. Lyla considered what happened to Casmir after he shot her.

The Philadelphia District Attorney convicted him for attempting to murder her, but when special agents George Miller and Garrett Collins crashed their patrol car during a secretive prison transfer, they unleashed Casmir. His rough-edged partner died in the crash, but Special Agent Collins survived, limping from the wreckage to track Casmir through a downpour in the remote Philadelphia backcountry. Casmir lead him to an empty road, but the special agent arrived too late. He had already emptied his gun into the driver of his getaway vehicle.

Casmir became a fugitive gone mad.

The police work of recapturing Casmir was incompetent and messy until Lyla found out some traumatizing news: four years ago, her first love was murdered by a gang member in Philly.

Casmir was gone forever.

Although Lyla missed the funeral she mourned Casmir's death and after everything Lyla went through with him, he still had shared a special place in her heart. She felt like she lost half of her soul and now and then, the pain felt so deep. For some reason, though, she could not visit his grave, so she never had closure.

Nestle was the next best thing.

They exchanged numbers after Nestle invited Lyla to his upcoming birthday party. Playing a little hard-to-get, she did not make it to his event. But Lyla finally gave in, after several attempts on his behalf to take her out. She saw nothing wrong with a little casual evening with him.

While getting dressed at her apartment in Jersey City Lyla noticed the time. *Nestle will be here any minute,* Lyla thought. She finished up the final touches to her make-up.

"He should be arriving any moment," Lyla murmured. But there was no Nestle, so she figured she would eat a little snack especially since Nestle did not tell her where they were going on their first date. She sat and ate and, suddenly, she heard loud Vroom! noises outside of her building.

Lyla lifted the heavy unscreened window, poked her head out, and looked up the street. She saw some crazy person popping wheelies on a motorcycle. *That is so dangerous,* Lyla thought as the black and blue glow-in-the-dark motorcycle stopped, and parked right in the front of her door. The rider dismounted in a pair of dark jeans, white V neck t-shirt, and Supa sneakers. He took off his helmet, and it was none other than her date for the night.

Such a change in appearance, Lyla thought. *The first night he looked all GQ and now he looks like a troublemaker who did not play by the rules.* It fascinated Lyla and she needed some drama back in her life as she looked down at her watch. *Fifteen minutes late and loud,* Lyla thought. *He better be glad I always wanted to ride on a motorcycle and I'm dressed for the occasion.*

"Up here," Lyla hollered. Nestle looked up and fixed his eyes on hers like he did on the first night they met. *He looks so sexy.* Her landlord came out of his office from the first floor to see who was making all of the noise.

"Its okay, Mr. Cohen!" she yelled out the window. He shrugged, and went back inside.

Lyla could hardly wait to meet Nestle downstairs. But first she simmered down and made him wait thirty minutes for her.

Lyla finally sashayed downstairs. She just knew Nestle was waiting for her to jump in his arms, but instead she overheard Nestle say to someone on his phone, "Alright talk to you later babes."

"That sounded interesting," Lyla said.

"Just some nagging bitch," he replied.

He handed Lyla a helmet and they drove off swirling and dodging every bump and vehicle in New York City, each turn feeling like she was going to fall off. *What a rush,* she thought. Nestle pulled up in front of a hookah bar. She had never been and was regretting it the deeper she walked inside as the stark smoke hit her nose. But she remembered watching her ex-boyfriend from Sweden smoking hookah at his house, so she wasn't a stranger to it.

Minus his phone constantly ringing during the date, she and Nestle were having a stimulating conversation. He frequently offered kind words and useful advice about different situations with her professional career. Nestle seemed to be very confident and had strong morals and ethics, a true alpha male. He made Lyla feel so good inside and he wanted to become deeply involved in her life.

As they continued their conversation Nestle asked her to smoke the hookah. Lyla never cared for it, but Nestle insisted. She put the pipe in the corner of her mouth, took a couple of puffs, and faked it like an orgasm. Lyla blew it out and Nestle had no idea that she did not actually inhale the smoke. He stared at her and from the look in his eyes he thought that he could get Lyla to do anything he wanted her to do.

As mentioned before, and little did he know, Lyla had a suppressed temper that still had not been fully ignited but she knew it could quickly flare up out of nowhere; she didn't even know what would happen. Lyla was not to be played with.

Nestle and Lyla danced the night away to house music, gently pulling her close at moments slow dancing to the melody in their heads, and his ring tone from the non-stop telephone calls. *Goodness, how many people call him in one night,* Lyla thought. He held Lyla tighter in his arms, feeling the beat of his heart beating with hers as they continued to dance.

Suddenly, Nestle quickly pulled away from Lyla.

"I thought I would be fighting guys off of you by now." *Surely this was a bad joke,* Lyla thought, as Nestle laughed. He held her close again and said, "You are hot! I dare a nigga approach you."

Despite Nestle's macho man appearance and bad jokes, he was sensitive and very nice. Lyla normally went for white guys but in the months that followed, a romance blossomed. They became an exclusive couple and the phone calls stopped coming in.

She loved the quality time he was spending with her. It was all about them. He went to her modeling auditions with her, he took her to work and picked her up, and he met her at her apartment almost everyday just to hang out.

He introduced her to his family members, friends, and business associates. They all loved Lyla and thought she was perfect for Nestle, maybe even calm his life down. *Whatever that means*, Lyla thought.

Eventually, Nestle told Lyla he was in love with her and Lyla told Nestle she had the same feelings for him. He asked Lyla to move into his apartment. She was so happy that he invited her to stay. This would be good, but she still kept her apartment in Jersey.

Lyla moved in and the first thing he asked her to do was to decorate. She did notice he needed a woman's touch. A candle there, a plant here, and a few furniture purchases to complete his pad. They made a home together. Nestle valued her, and life and love was finally good to Lyla and after all of these years she let her guard down.

Sadly, a few months later, the couple's cozy life together, frizzled out and was disrupted by Nestle's new attitude. Still, Nestle was very nice and entertaining, but he was not adding up to be her ideal boyfriend anymore. He was what you call a good and bad guy; to Lyla that was the worst kind and it caused their relationship to become complex.

But instead of giving up on their relationship, she thought she could take this bad boy, and, like a piece of clay, mold him into what she wanted – but it was actually him molding her into what he wanted.

He praised Lyla at the beginning, and then broke her down so she would come running to him no matter what. It was the old school pimp move and she fell right into it.

How did this little boy turn me out? she asked herself.

Not only that, she could tell this once-caring and sensitive man was drifting away and not only into her anymore, mainly from the phone calls pouring in again. Nestle was withdrawn and the relationship was coming apart at the seams, headed toward reckless disaster and because she did not want to let him go, she went down a dangerous, unpredictable, and wild road with him.

After all of these years I'm stuck in yet another complicated relationship. I did not think anyone could take over my mind again, Lyla thought. *But it was like* déjà vu *and I complied with what Nestle wanted. I kept his place clean and his food ready. I became his "bottom b."*

The maltreatment was vile, but what Lyla did like was his enthusiasm and ambition for fighting. Nestle was a ripped, well-built, professional fighter — Lil Nestle Crunch was what they called him. He was determined to be famous one day. It sort of brought out that aspiration she once had for being a fashion model.

Lyla wasn't totally out of the modeling game, but after the rice diets, hard-core physical training, and fasting for days on only black coffee, she eventually had to think about her health instead of remaining a size two.

She was so obsessed with losing weight Lyla went to a weight loss meeting and sat in the first row at 110 pounds, asking questions as the overweight people behind her looked at her in disgust. Lyla did not care; she wanted to know how she could get down to 100 pounds and still eat her favorite red-coated popcorn.

Worse than that, one of Lyla's weight loss diets caused her to be rushed to the hospital. Although her health was still not to where it used to be, she did eventually gain some weight, and at a size six, her agency put her on the plus size board. *Crazy, eh?*

What Lyla really wanted to do was to lose the weight, model full time again, and in a perfect world, marry Nestle. But that was impossible, because what Lyla did not like about Nestle was his loud boastful attitude, his entitlement, his self-centeredness, and his pride. He knew he was going to be the world champ and he had to let the whole world know even though he had nothing significant to back it up, signs of narcissism.

"I'm going to carry the Olympic torch because I am the best in the world, yeah," Nestle bragged.

Also Nestle would sometimes forget to leave what he did in the ring and bring it into the relationship. No, he never hit Lyla physically, although it almost came to that once or twice; if he had hit Lyla, she would have knocked out his other teeth before she let a man or anyone beat on her again. However, he was mentally and emotionally abusive.

What caused a lot of emotional abuse was his constant cheating and lying. Lyla had been with jerks that mistreated her in different kinds of ways, but she had never experienced a cheater before let alone a blatant one. He had to be the center of attention, especially with women. By the time she found out he was cheating, it was too late. Her heart was already entirely wrapped up into this man, and she was dumb struck in love, over the moon for him.

Whenever he wanted to take her heart from out of his pocket and stomp on it, he did so. Whenever he wanted to put her heart back in his pocket like a hostage, he did so. They fussed about his cheating all the time, but it did no good.

When Lyla asked him about wooing women, his recurring line would be, "Did you catch my dick in a pussy?"

"I know you are seeing other women Nestle," Lyla said. "Whether I see you actually doing it or not, I know you are."

"For real," Nestle responded. "I went shopping."

"Oh really? What happened?" Lyla asked.

"I didn't find nothing. But if I did, you still my lady," Nestle answered.

"Whatever," Lyla said. "And what if you get one of these girls pregnant...then what?"

"You are going to be the stepmom and take care of it," Nestle said. "But like I said, I'm not cheating, bitch."

Ever since Nestle found out his best friend, Da Mac calls his sister a bitch for fun, and she doesn't mind, Nestle thinks he can call me one now, Lyla said to herself.

"I told you to stop calling me that," Lyla reminded.

"Da Mac calls his sister a bitch and she don't care," Nestle replied, "so, I can call you one."

"Da Mac and his sister are close," Lyla said. "You and me are not, at the moment, to me it sounds disrespectful, so stop it!"

126

"I think it's funny," Nestle laughed.

"Well, I don't!" Lyla exclaimed.

"That's because you don't got no swag, bitch!"

Pure arrogance - pure ego; and that huge ego made Nestle continue to call her a bitch when he felt like it, but her main concern was the women. She knew he was lying through his teeth about the cheating. But to make him happy, Nestle was allowed to call her a bitch and see other women. She told him she did not want to know about the other girls. By telling Nestle that, it was like giving him a key to do the opposite of what she asked.

Nestle threw it in her face even more so and made sure she saw every text and phone call of all of his women. He stayed out all night and women approached her. But what pissed her off the most was when she noticed a reservation for two at the hotel she worked for.

The room was on the eighteenth floor under Jell-O. Lyla knew that name. After work, she took the beautiful glass-elevator upstairs to see if it was who she thought it was. Lyla loved riding that elevator. She felt like Michelle Pfeiffer in Scarface.

Lyla knocked on the door and the person standing in the doorway was who she expected: Jell-O, the stripper from LA, Nestle's ex-girlfriend.

Lyla's eyes burnt ferociously with emotion.

"Where is Nestle?!"

"He ain't' here," Jell-O answered as another girl approached the doorway looking like a broken down Lil' Kim.

"Who is this?" the girl asked Jell-O.

"This is Lil Nestle Crunch girl," Jell-O answered. "Puddin' Pop...Lyla...Lyla...Puddin' Pop."

Lyla rolled her eyes.

"So what is she doing here?" Puddin' Pop said curiously.

"She! Works here," Lyla said abruptly.

"Well I need some KY Jelly, housekeeper," Puddin' Pop laughed.

"Funny," Lyla said disgustedly. "You Lil' Kim wanna be."

"Who you think you talking to," Puddin' Pop said.

"Puffy hold me down baby," Lyla snickered.

The girl was getting ready to respond back, but hesitated. She saw Nestle and his entourage stepping out of the elevator.

Jell-O and Puddin' Pop chanted their slogan for Nestle, "Knockem Out Lil Nestle...Knockem Out...Knockem Out Lil Nestle," and in unison, the two girls said, "Crunch!"

Lyla and both girls ran up to him while the elevator doors were closing.

"Hold the elevator Nestle, we are leaving!" Lyla shouted.

"No he ain't," Jell-O said to Lyla with mean energy. "This room is paid for and ready for use. Where is my 'Please Don't Disturb' sign? It's time for YOU to leave."

"Whatever," Lyla snapped. "I thought you were off tonight for your birthday," Nestle said to Lyla.

"You kidding me right," Lyla said. "Why are you here at the hotel where I work with this hoe, on my birthday?"

"Hoe?" Jell-O repeated.

"Yes hoe," Lyla affirmed. "Do you need me to spell it out for you? H-O-E...hoe!"

"Look ah here, I'm the one he is always going to come back to no matter who he is with. I hold it down. They don't call me Jell-O for nothing," she said, shaking her booty like no other.

"So, you think," Lyla sneered.

"He is only with you because I had a miscarriage," Jell-O assumed.

"You think he is with me because you lost the baby?" Lyla chortled. "In other words, you lost the baby so you cannot trap him anymore so he left you."

"Believe what you want," Jell-O responded.

"He's not at this hotel with you because he loves you. Nestle is using you for sex and money, foolish girl!" Lyla said. "And you may have a lot of booty, but he told me he did not like girls with big booties."

"He lied," Jell-O said.

"It doesn't matter. Like I said he does not love you!" Lyla shouted.

"Like he loves you," Jell-O said. "If he did, he would not be here with me, and he definitely would have told me to book a hotel you don't work for, especially on your birthday. It's obvious his heart may belong to you but his dick belongs to me!" Lyla gasped. "And he wanted to throw that in your face," Jell-O continued.

"Nah, nah, Jell-O," Nestle replied, "you said you love this hotel and Lyla was supposed to be off tonight."

Nestle could tell Lyla did not like his response by the rock hard glare Lyla gave him which made Jell-O speechless with fear.

"This is not cool, Nestle!" Lyla hissed as Nestle looked away from her glare. Lyla directed her attention back to Jell-O. "You don't seem to get that he is in a relationship. You are just mad because the guy that every girl wants wants me, now back off." Lyla swung a vicious punch missing Jell-O, but leaving a serious dent in the wall.

"Oh no she didn't!" Puddin' Pop said as she threw Lyla a dirty look.

"You are crazy!" Jell-O shouted.

"Next time that is going to be your face," Lyla said to Jell-O. She hit the down button on the elevator. This was the side of Lyla she wanted to keep concealed but it was too late. Her alter ego had been released once again and she had more to say.

"Bitch!" Lyla said shrilly. "You have FUCKED," she paused, "with the wrong one. Fuck you and the mother you came from." Nestle had never heard Lyla curse nor seen her fight before. "Come on Nestle," Lyla commanded.

"I don't think so!" Puddin' Pop screamed. She stormed after Lyla as the elevator doors opened, followed by Jell-O. Lyla took the both of their heads, bashed them together, and kicked them in the elevator. Lyla stepped in and the elevator became her battleground. She wasted no time fighting for her man.

Jell-O and her girlfriend landed a few lucky punches, busting Lyla's lip, but she overpowered them as the onlookers watched from the ground level. Lyla kicked and punched Jell-

O and Puddin' Pop repeatedly, both hitting the floor. The elevator dinged and the doors opened on the thirteenth floor. An older couple stepped in and hastily stepped out, after they witnessed the brutal caged cat fight.

The unhinged Jell-O crawled like a hermit crab to the opened elevator door to escape while Puddin' Pop stood painfully in the middle of the elevator. Lyla yanked Jell-O back in the elevator and punched her while on the ground, pushing her girlfriend into the elevator glass wall.

Puddin' Pop fell to the ground jumping right up and getting the best of Lyla with harsh and aggressive kicks to her stomach.

"Here are your birthday licks, bitch!"

The disoriented Jell-O managed to sound the alarm. The doors opened on the ground level, Lyla holding her stomach and coughing blood in pain.

The insensible Nestle stood there, watching. He left with that freak Jell-O, leaving Lyla in a state of shock. Lyla's manager had warned her about this dude. She was heartbroken.

The next day, she and Nestle had to do an interview with a popular sporting network about his fighting career. After a long cry and a glass of wine, she had to put on a smile after everything that had happened the night before.

Nestle talked about how great his career was going when the interviewer mentioned how he loved when Nestle threw chocolate cupcakes at the girls after a fight for the girls to catch. *Please.* Lyla just wished that he would put his fake tooth in for his interviews. *He says his missing tooth shows* character. *I say it shows he got beat up in the ring. Not a good look for a professional fighter.*

Nestle then spoke about how great of a girlfriend Lyla was. All she could hear in her head was Jell-O and Puddin' Pop's chant for Nestle.

"Knockem Out Lil Nestle...Knockem Out...Knockem Out Lil Nestle...Crunch!"

The interviewer asked how Lyla and Nestle met and Nestle answered, "Well, this is how it all went down." First, Nestle said he asked Lyla for the time. He then put his cock up on the counter.

"What are you doing?" Lyla asked.

"I thought you said you wanted to see my cock," Nestle answered.

"No, I said its five o'clock but I like what I see," she replied as she became speechless from his good looks and big cock.

Nestle walked towards a sofa.

"You can have some right here, baby."

He continued the story by saying he snapped his fingers and Lyla came gliding across the floor, batting her eyes.

Then in a slick pimp-like voice.

"So what's up? I saw you watching me watching you me watching you you watching me. What is your name?"

"My name is Lyla Tight."

"Don't get too heavy on me baby…I am a bad boy," he said, and then he hard kissed her neck as she pleaded with him to be hers. *"Keep it tight, aight,"* Nestle continued.

"Wow," the interviewer said.

"Yeah!" Nestle laughed. "And then she passed out from all my swag.

Nestle thought he was so neat, so swell, and splendid. Lyla sip on some wine in a Styrofoam cup posing as water while she told the interviewer that story was not true, trying hard to keep her voice from trembling.

She then said to Nestle, "Keep me out of your sick perverted dreams and stop telling lies." Nestle's manager was present during Nestle's and Lyla's first engagement and he knew Nestle was not that fly.

Clearly, Lyla stayed with Nestle, even after losing her job over the loser. Lyla was an emotional mess, and he continued cheating and being arrogant.

Nestle didn't know that before she dated him, she went out with two celebrities he admired. His arrogance made him miss out on so much and Lyla could have crushed both of his balls at the same time if she wanted to. One of the celebrities was already a famous fighter – exactly what Nestle wanted to become - and the other was one of his favorite R&B singers.

Lyla would never forget the day Nestle was playing one of his songs at the apartment. He danced and sang while she laughed. If he was a good boy, she could have introduced him to *Fiesta*.

Chapter 12

It was a lazy day. Lyla passed fruitless trees as autumn's warm eyes stared at her on an early day in New York; waterless clouds, swept along by winds. The sky was blue and the air was crisp, another Sunday she would have much rather spent in bed, but instead, Lyla was getting her praise on at church. No matter how many mistakes she'd made or how many times she was upset with God, she made it a point to go to church every Sunday, eventually working her way to attending prayer meetings on Tuesdays.

Looking at her past, she can admit she had made questionable choices which resulted in plenty of mistakes, but who didn't? *Sometimes I feel my life is like a game with no referee,* Lyla thought. But she knew she needed forgiveness especially because her biggest downfall seemed to be men.

Guys were like dogs with no bone. Just lost little puppies with nothing to play with until they see the first sign of a pussycat to chase after.

Lyla came across all different types of dogs; poodles, sheepdogs, bull terriers, pugs, and especially pit bulls. Lyla knew the dog she had to get rid of was Nestle.

As the offering pan was passed around, Lyla noticed a guy checking her out two rows away from her. *He looks like a lamb until I tell him I'm not having sex until I get married then all of a sudden they forget who God is. I call those types the 'Hoellaujahs'* Lyla thought as she put her tithes and offerings in the pan.

The worst part is I find myself slowly giving into the pressure just for a moment of dishonorable passion with some of these dudes. I become what every man wants: a bad girl who loved God. But just like girls who want a bad boy on the outside, but a softy in the inside; most likely it's not going to happen.

She enjoyed church. For the most part, there were nice people singing and worshiping God from different ethnic and social backgrounds and Lyla's pastor always brought a good message. But, this Sunday, something out of the ordinary happened.

After the sermon, her pastor said openly to the congregation, "There is a young lady here today and God is telling me to speak to her. I don't know who she is but I see a dark cloud over her current relationship. You need to get out now before something terrible happens to you. God will send you a man that loves you. There is no need to stay in this horrific situation."

Later that week, Lyla called her pastor. She wanted to know if he was speaking to her, but she came to the conclusion that the pastor was not as available as her principal was back in high school. After several failed attempts to reach him, deep down inside she knew he was talking directly to her. She admittedly was searching for an excuse so she would not have to break up with Nestle.

It was up to Lyla to listen or be destroyed once again by a man.

The next day Lyla sat alone at her favorite café, no bigger than a small studio apartment in the city, enjoying another nice day.

"Milk and honey for your tea?" the waitress asked. Lyla smiled and politely answered, "Neither, just a Sweet n' Low please." Lyla woke up this morning thinking to herself, *Today is going to be a great day.* Every time she spoke that, she thought she messed up the whole day because it always turned out to be the craziest, as she watched happy couples holding hands and laughing. The sight of that made her sick to the stomach but no matter what, she planned to have a good day.

Lyla continued to sit and sip her tea, contemplating on the pros and cons of her relationship with Nestle. She reached in her purse to pull out her phone and viewed the video posted by one of the bystanders at the hotel labeled, "The Elevator Cat Fight." The epic fight had over 75,000 views and counting.

"Good thing my face is not showing," Lyla mumbled. She shoved her phone back into her purse and made up her mind that she was tired of always helping people that did not want to be helped. Lyla claimed to be helping Nestle become a better man, but Nestle was too much drama, more drama than what she thought she needed.

Needless to say, Nestle gave Lyla no choice but to eliminate him from her heart for good and focus on her modeling career. Lyla's biggest dilemma was making sure she did not go running back to him like she used to do with Casmir.

Once I'm gone, that is it.

Lyla progressively released herself from Nestle. She moved her things back into her apartment a little at a time. He would ask what she was doing every so often but Lyla told him she had to switch out her fall clothes for her winter clothes.

"That's funny, because you are taking your fall stuff but I see no winter clothes," Nestle observed.

"Okay smarty pants," Lyla said. She went to his iPod and played one of his old school songs he loved by the Manhattans, "Kiss and Say Goodbye."

Nestle was laughing until she sung and acted out the words to him, karaoke style. He got down on his knees, cried and pleaded for her to stay. Lyla kept singing the words, ignoring Nestle.

After a few more lines Nestle stood up.

"Walk out then, bitch!"

"Who are you talking to," she replied. Lyla poured lighter fluid on his package and set it on fire like an Olympic flame, his body temperature rising right in front of her.

"I'm going to carry the Olympic torch because I'm the best in the world, yeah."

"Nice, you are now carrying the torch," Lyla jeered. "You clingy nagging bitch," Nestle said.

"How could I have loved such a vain, pretentious, and pompous little boy?"

She watched him shake and quake and wiggle like a little worm in his He-Man pajamas.

"You are pathetic and your swag is ineffective now," Lyla continued. "You look like a whining little girl, maybe you are gay. Call me when you are ready to be a real man, weirdo."

Lyla snapped out of her deep thought and realized the karaoke disaster was just a dream but a few days later she finally let him go completely especially after she realized Nestle was just another Casmir – and maybe even worse.

Lyla's phone rang. She did not recognize the number, so she let it ring a few more times as she mused over who it could be.

"Hello?" she said, hesitantly.

"Hello," the man on the other end replied. "I'm returning a call left by Lyla Tight."

Still puzzled.

"I apologize, but I leave a lot of messages. Who is this, please?"

"This is Pastor Bill."

"Oh," Lyla responded, happily. "Yes, I was not sure if you received my message."

"Yes, I did. My days are busy but I do take the time to answer my messages. What can I do for you ma'am?"

"Well, I feel a little stupid talking to you now about it," Lyla said.

"Don't be. Nothing is stupid in the eyes of God. He loves all of us and he loves you. Tell me, what is on your mind, Lyla?"

"I attended your service on Sunday," Lyla recalled, "and you mentioned that there was a girl in the congregation in a bad relationship, and she needs to get out."

"That was you?" the pastor asked, gently.

"Yes, I believe so," Lyla answered.

"God tells me what to say, but I never know who it is for," the pastor said. "What happened?"

"At first I was in denial," Lyla admitted. "That is why I called you for further confirmation, but ultimately I knew you were talking to me. I broke up with the guy."

"How did that go?" the pastor wondered.

"Well, leaving him alone wasn't hard because his narcissistic behavior allowed me to easily walk out of his life."

"Wow," the pastor said. "A narcissist, huh? One thing you can count on with a narcissist is when their self-image or self-worth was tampered with they will go into a mental rage. He would do anything to make himself look good again in front of his friends, family, colleagues, strangers, dogs, cats, whatever."

"You're right," Lyla chuckled. "He had the nerve to say to me he'll find someone to love and I will not."

"Don't believe that, God has someone for everyone," Pastor Bill reassured.

"Thank you for calling me back," Lyla smiled.

"Not a problem," the pastor said. "You can call me anytime, or you can actually come in if you like to talk more in detail about the break up or anything that is heavy on your mind."

"No," Lyla said. "I don't do to well with counseling."

"It's not counseling, it's more like a friendly conversation," Pastor Bill said.

"Thanks," Lyla responded. "It's just not for me. Have a good a day and thanks again for calling me back."

"If you change your mind, I'm here," the pastor said. "God bless."

Lyla actually did need someone to talk too because she was a wreck. Casmir and Nestle did a number on her mind and she did not know which was worse: being physically and verbally abused by Casmir or being emotionally abused by Nestle.

What she did know is that Nestle was like an addictive drug and he truly captured Lyla's heart, which he hurt to the core. *Now, I'm left with a big hole in my heart,* she said to herself, *wondering if I will ever be emotionally the same.*

But like with most drugs a person has to go through rehab. Lyla's rehab center was in Philadelphia with her family, secluded from everyone. She returned home to stay for a short period to go through her withdrawals.

Lyla cried all day and before she went to bed. If she did not have the support of her family and friends and Nestle's family and friends, she would have died from a broken heart.

You know it's bad when Nestle's family and friends were on my side.

On the other hand, although she fully appreciated their support she had to let his family and friends go so she could fully heal. But there was one person she did not want to let go, and that was Nestle's mom. Lyla felt bad because she told Nestle's mom she would stay in contact with her even if she and Nestle broke up, but getting Nestle out of her system was harder than what Lyla ever imagined, and his mother was a part of him.

I hope she forgives me, Lyla thought. *I wonder if she still has my picture up on her living room wall. I hope she knows I love her and I think about her all the time.*

Before Lyla broke up with Nestle, she and Nestle had an interview scheduled on a popular entertainment channel, *Why Do Good Girls Love Wild Guys.*

How can you have a show like that? Lyla thought. *Most likely the couple will break up sooner or later, and that is what happened.*

Lyla called and cancelled their appearance.

The lady asked a silly question, "Why?"

"Well let's just say I do not want to be in anymore crossfire because of Nestle. I was in a fight with a stripper from LA, and not too long ago had to throw away a suicidal poem from another girl he was sleeping with."

Lyla phoned Nestle and told him she cancelled their appearance on the show and he said in a nasty tone, "How dumb can you be?! You better call them right now and get us back on the show!" Lyla remembered Casmir saying almost those same words to her.

"How dumb can you be?! You better call them right now and tell them that is not my business card!"

Right there, Lyla knew it was time for her to leave. The only difference was it took her a little over four years to get rid of Casmir it only took her less than a year to get rid of Nestle.

On a brighter side, she was grateful to God she was not a basket case from going through bad relationship after bad relationship.

Don't misunderstand, some of the relationships she had been in were with great men, but of course those were the nice guys. Lyla had this thing about keeping drama in her life, whether she wanted it or not.

Undeniably, Lyla took a few hits, but she was always able to get back up and fight! She took a minute to do another maintenance check about her life without a razor blade this time. Lyla thought about two of her main relationships, her family, her 101 ideas, and although she went in and out of her modeling career that was one thing she was determined to be successful in. Lyla believed she had one more, good try before totally giving up. Sugar the stylist felt the same way too.

Yes, a blast from her past.

Although Sugar gave Lyla some wrong advice when he told her to tell that little white lie, he was still her number one fan. But that little white lie caught up with Lyla when the woman from Elite found out she did go to New York prior to the interview. She had not forgiven Lyla yet and never signed her to Elite. Lyla was only 17-years-old and she listened to wrong advice. She felt like the lady should not hold that against her but the lady did.

It was funny because in the modeling industry, they tell lies all the time but the number one rule was to never get caught.

As expected, Sugar had some making up to do. Lyla contacted Sugar and he said he was at the point where he wanted to give it one last shot at becoming a successful stylist. He knew this could happen through Lyla. Letting Sugar back into her life was probably not the wisest choice but she was desperate.

Against all odds, she pursued her career and aspirations. Sugar became Lyla's manager. Little did she know, this bought on more of a headache then she bargained for, but it did take Lyla into the next chapter of her life. Sugar moved Lyla back to the city through a superintendant he knew.

As far as relationships were concerned, Lyla was not sure when she would actually take that monumental walk down the aisle, but she figured the right man would come when he came.

I'm not looking for a man right now, Lyla said to herself.

But of course, when a woman is not looking that's when the man appears and believe it or not this is where the story begins!

Chapter 13

Living in New York City again and back on the regular size modeling board, Lyla booked a huge exclusive promotional job for Disney at Madison Square Garden. *It was lovely to be reintroduced to the modeling world at a respectable size.* During her lunch break, there was a winsome man that caught her eye, sort of how Casmir caught Lyla's eye when she first met him at the mall. She thought no one would be able to grab her attention like that again and years later, it happened. *This man had the same body structure and walk as Casmir*, she said to herself.

Lyla wondered if the gentleman was related to Casmir. Of course not, but this was definitely an older more dignified and sophisticated version of Casmir and Lyla had to know who this attractive man was.

After three days of promotional work, the client had an after party at an upscale lounge in downtown Manhattan. Lyla and the rest of the models had to host the event and while working, she saw the gentleman there. *What a blissful moment.*

Lyla simply asked, "Where are you from?" The simple question was enough to warrant a conversation. He told her Cuba. His mom was white and his dad Cuban, as he handed her his business card.

The handsome man then told Lyla he was an accountant for Elite clients but also had a music company. He was organizing an event coming up. He invited Lyla and her family and friends.

This well-dressed man in a tailored suit with a fancy watch and shoes sounded like a really genuine, sweet person. Lyla looked at his business card and it said he was the

President of the accounting firm. She was now doubly intrigued. Lyla also noticed his name is Ritchie Perez; bizarrely, the same name as Casmir's street name, though spelled his with a "T."

"Well, nice to meet you Ritchie, my name is Lyla Tight," she said.

"Nice meeting you too. May we meet again at the event," Ritchie replied, charmly as he walked away.

The last day of her promotional work at Madison Square Garden, Lyla did not have to wait for the music event – the well-groomed Cuban guy showed up. Of course, the other models already knew about chiseled chin Ritchie. They saw Lyla talking to him at the party.

Lyla blushed as he walked over to her. She looked down, searching for her purse to grab one of her delightful fruity lifesavers and when she looked up, he was gone. Lyla thought nothing of it and then, just as suddenly, he reappeared. *What a whimsical man.*

"It's lovely to see you again. What time are you going to be off, Mademoiselle?"

Flashing her most dazzling smile she replied, "I'm off now."

She noticed he had a lower missing tooth, much like Nestle and her ex-boyfriend Casmir, except their respective teeth were missing at the top. Funny that she had not seen that at the lounge. The question was, was this yet another sign to run the other way?

The models working with Lyla wanted to hang out after the job, but they could see she was busy. Ritchie took Lyla over to the computers set up at the Garden to show her the website for his entertainment business. He was also the CEO of several other companies, and newly working alone at the top, as his business partner was recently found dead after falling off an unstable cliff. The site was filled with interesting visual effects; absolutely superb.

One of the companies that caught her eye the most was a cosmetics line called *Heavenly Secrets*.

While they were still in front of the computers, he logged in to the Heavenly Secrets website to view the products and just like the entertainment business site, it was epic. The website was chic with lots of information as well but it was missing one thing: Lyla! Lyla always wanted to help others but rarely would she ask for help. At this particular moment, she saw the opportunity and asked if they needed a model for their ads.

He told her the company was actually looking for a new face. Ritchie then invited her to go with him right that second to meet the people in charge.

"Spontaneous. I love that in a man," Lyla smiled.

"I like to get things done, no time to waste," Ritchie said.

As Ritchie and Lyla headed out for some reason, she imagined him walking her to a flashy red sports car, matching his fancy watch and shoes but instead, he hailed a city cab. They were on their way to the make-up counter at Saks Fifth Avenue. *Good enough.*

"I have twelve cars but I haven't had time to renew my insurance," Ritchie said out of nowhere. Lyla did not respond; she just wanted to meet the people at Saks.

When they arrived, Ritchie introduced Lyla to an older and average looking Russian lady. She and her mother were the co-founders of Heavenly Secrets. They were billionaires and Ritchie, with his scientific background, helped formulate the products. They all seemed to have great respect for him.

"What an interesting smile you have," the Russian lady said to Lyla.

"Thank you," Lyla replied. The Russian lady seemed to like Lyla's look a lot, and Lyla knew this marvelous cosmetics line would be a nice launch for her modeling career. But also Lyla thought the Russian woman was more concerned about her and Ritchie hanging out. Either, both she and Ritchie had been previously involved and now she was old news, or she had the hots for him and now saw Lyla as a threat. All Lyla had to say was, "May the best woman win."

Ritchie asked Lyla out to dinner the next day. As she walked in, the atmosphere of the restaurant was quiet and romantic. He pulled out Lyla's chair and she sat down with a grateful smile and a "thank you."

The waiter came over and asked if Lyla and Ritchie would like to begin with a drink. He ordered a bottle of red wine; already, they had something in common. Ritchie then ordered a side dish of Black Caviar to begin the evening dinner.

"When the lady makes her choice of meal, I will be ready," the waiter said as he walked off.

Ritchie was very alluring. He spoke with an endearing accent. It would be hard to pinpoint where it was from since he spoke over six different languages.

"Where did you learn how to speak so many languages?" Lyla wondered.

"I taught myself," Ritchie said, humbly. "I can pick up a language as soon as I hear it. I don't know how I do it."

"Wow, I thought you learned it in school," Lyla said.

"No," Ritchie corrected. "I focused on science in school. I received my PhD in Chemical Engineering from Yale."

"What about accounting?" Lyla questioned, a bit confused.

"I don't need school for that," Ritchie answered. "I taught myself that as well."

"You are a self-taught kind of guy, huh?" Lyla smiled as they ordered their food.

Shortly after, the waiter brought their food to the table. The small portion of food was so elegant and fancy.

Before eating she bowed her head to say her grace but something unusual happened. Ritchie held her hands and said the grace. *Wow*, she thought. He then told her that he was a Christian, which was right up Lyla's alley.

While she ate grilled salmon with steamed green beans and creamy garlic mashed potatoes sprinkled with chives and he, a seafood pasta dish dipped in lobster sauce, Ritchie began to tell her a little about his life as he offered and fed Lyla some of his pasta. Lyla felt like she was in a storybook with Prince Charming. *There is something really special about him*, Lyla said to herself. *He has all of the right elements and is easy to be around. I find myself slowly but surely falling for him.*

Ritchie gazed at Lyla.

"You are good natured, well grounded, and easy going. On the other hand, you are inspiring, very perceptive, business savvy, determined, and eager to learn new things and reach new heights. You thrive off of knowledge. You have the gift of faith; that keeps you going even after everything you have been through."

Somehow, Ritchie knew me like a book.

"Don't forget adventurous," she said.

"Yes," Ritchie laughed.

"And how do you know I have been through something?" Lyla asked.

"Trust me I know." He could look at anyone and tell who they were. Ritchie would later tell Lyla he learned how to read people through the CIA work he did. This was truly a man of many talents.

"One more thing," Ritchie said.

"What's that?"

"God is first in your life."

"Yes, he is. How can you tell?"

"Your first app on your phone is the Bible."

"Very observant, Ritchie," Lyla said.

"That's my job," Ritchie smirked.

The check came and Lyla reached for it. Ritchie gently grabbed her hand.

"A woman should never touch a bill." He paid the $219.30 tab. Lyla smiled and thought, *My kind of man.*

They left the restaurant to rain rumbling down over New York like cats and dogs. The city was soaked. Ritchie told her to wait under the canopy. She half-expected that he would return with a white horse, both he and the horse wholly unaffected by the rain.

He seemed untouchable, like Iron Man, Lyla thought.

As he motioned a cab to follow him to where Lyla was standing, she searched for one of her lifesavers. She was sure the garlic in the mashed potatoes was kicking. Ritchie made his way back to her with the cab, wearing a pair of dark shades.

"You know its dark out," Lyla smiled...Ritchie grinned. "But you pull it off well." His caring heart safely kept her out of the rain and in the cab, as he gave her a handful of cash to get home. Ritchie closed the door and Lyla waved goodbye.

On her way home, Lyla daydreamed about Ritchie. He was the opposite of Casmir and Nestle. Lyla longed for a gorgeous and smart man like Ritchie, but out of nowhere, became very emotional and began to cry for her ex-boyfriend Casmir. She missed him and she didn't understand why.

Lyla quickly got her head straight.

I give into love too quickly, she thought. *I have to guard my heart this time. No matter how good it looks, how smitten, or how warm and fuzzy I feel inside, I cannot give myself totally to a man again unless he truthfully earns it.*

Lyla arrived home. Before leaving the cab she gave the knot of money, Ritchie gave her, to the driver. It had to be at least five hundred dollars. She could not help it. Her heart was as big as a whale.

Chapter 14

For the past few days, Ritchie and Lyla had been hanging out and getting to know each other even more. Each time he would make an effort to come home with her, but she would not let that happen. He didn't overtly show his frustration but she could tell he was. Ritchie attempted to penetrate her determination by sending a dozen, long-stemmed red, white, and cream-white roses to her building.

Lyla's superintendent knocked on the door and handed them to her.

"Who are these from?" he asked. Her super sometimes acted like her father.

She viewed the tag, sighed in contentment and said, "It's from a secret admirer. I have to go now. I'm in love." Naturally, his curiosity went through the roof.

Of course the tag actually said from Ritchie. Lyla took one last look at the vibrant roses and then tossed them in the trashcan, with a satisfying plop. She thought about her parents.

"My parents were married on Valentine's Day, and still together, but sometimes it was war of the roses between those two."

Lyla favored exotic flowers, not roses. She forgave Ritchie because they were still getting to know each other. Lyla's main concern was how Ritchie knew where she lived.

After a few more casual outings it turned into intimate dating. On one of those dates Lyla gave him permission to enter her apartment. He was shocked to see how small it was but after Lyla dropped Sugar again as her manager her superintendent and his friendly wife took Lyla under their wing. They moved her in one of their many apartments until she earned enough money to afford it.

The superintendent even offered to manage her modeling career. Lyla assumed that was the real reason he interfered in her life at times, and although his offer sounded great, she learned to divine if people were just talking or making a commitment.

Ritchie brought his high tech camera with him. He wanted to help Lyla perfect her poses before shooting for Heavenly Secrets. She loved it when he showed he cared and supported her.

"You know I picked you out of 2,500 women," he said so eloquently as Lyla laughed. She thought that was hilarious, especially since it was she who approached him at the lounge. Lyla let him broadcast that fantasy in his head like he was Daddy-O, but she was the one in control of this rodeo.

"I am glad you found me. My life is complete," Lyla giggled.

"I really did pick you. But who was the model working with you at the party?" Ritchie asked, curiously.

"Why? You like her, babe?" Lyla wondered.

"No, just wondering what her name is. She had a lot of character - good character."

"So, are you saying I have bad character?" Lyla said.

"It's important to have good character, but you my love, have excellent character," Ritchie replied. Lyla smiled as she said, "I'm not sure, but her sister was one of the models I worked with at the Garden." For now they skimmed that conversation, but she had to wonder, *Is he really more into the model chick I was working with and using me to get her information?*

Moving on, Lyla let Ritchie take pictures of her. She trusted him because Ritchie was very skillful and smart like Casmir had been. But Ritchie seemed to use it to help people, unlike Casmir. On the other hand, they both have that talent called, "the gift of gab." This meant she had to ascertain whether the things he told her were credible or total nonsense.

For instance, "How did you know where to send the roses?" Lyla asked.

"Oh, I invented the technology for the satellite, of course," Ritchie answered. "I can see everything and take pictures or video, so don't be surprised if I send you material of you and the guy you cheat on me with." They both laughed but she looked at him and thought, *Was this legit or nonsense? I'm going to go with nonsense, but something tells me he is not playing or in a weird kind of way he believes his own nonsense.*

"Wow that is amazing! And don't worry, babe, I don't cheat," Lyla said.

"If you do, I will send black roses instead of red," Ritchie smirked.

"How about not sending me any roses," Lyla suggested. "I hate them but I love exotic flowers." He moved in on Lyla slowly and softly said, "Close your eyes." Lyla closed her eyes, allowing herself to enjoy a moment of stillness. She felt his fingers on her skin, the warmth of his lips on her cheek, as Ritchie murmured, "Ahhh, but all the love that's rich in history is said to be in a rose.

She smiled and spoke softly, "How so?"

"A red rose whispers, of sincere love, the intensely white rose breathes of purity, and the cream-white rose is for the love that is innocent and sweet with a kiss of desire on the lips," he said.

He slowly moved back and she found herself drifting away in a magical moment, not realizing he had stepped away.

"I have learned something about you today, my love," Ritchie continued observably. She opened her eyes and Ritchie held a blue rose in his hand. He gave her the rose and proceeded to say, "The blue rose represents mystery and attaining the impossible."

Lyla let Ritchie stay the night, but before he went to sleep, he showed her the most exquisite diamond ring. She gasped in delight as she stared at the beautiful ring.

"You and your family are going to be okay," Ritchie said. Lyla discussed her family situation with him not too long ago, so he knew her goal was to make enough money to purchase a house for her family and to live a comfortable life again herself. Ritchie claimed to be a multimillionaire, and told Lyla that if she wanted to be equally successful, she should listen to every piece of advice he offered or she would fail personally and professionally.

Overwhelmed with excitement, Lyla allowed him to give her the fine piece of jewelry. He placed the ring teasingly on her ring finger. She smiled...he grinned as he placed the ring on her middle finger instead. Perhaps accepting the ring wasn't the wisest choice, but in her past relationships, they took everything from her and she was left with nothing.

This time, I'm taking it all.

Lyla put Ritchie to sleep by performing one of her hypnotizing finger moving rituals that would relax anyone. She slowly and very softly went up and down and side to side on Ritchie's back, purposely keeping her randomly selected fingertips from touching his skin.

"Your fingertips are like magic," Ritchie said. She did this continuously all over his back, eventually putting him to sleep. After a few moments, Ritchie was on his side, and Lyla fell asleep in his arms. Moments later, Ritchie was on his back snoring loudly.

Lyla gently pushed him back on his side to see if that would help quiet the snore, and succeeded.

But she actually wanted to wake him because her body screamed, "Take me!" It would be so incredibly nice to have sex with Ritchie all night long, but even after his several attempts of seducing her she did not give in. A few times he managed to go down her pants, fumbling around her asshole. *Was this another sign?* Lyla said to herself. *I was going to stop him because it may bring back bad memories, but it actually felt really good, unlike when Casmir did it.*

The next morning Ritchie had to leave to go to work. Lyla was upset with herself because she overslept, and instead of waking her so that she could wake him, the sounds of birds chirping and waterfalls that made up her alarm sent her into dreams of being on a Caribbean island.

She gently cupped both sides of Ritchie's face in her hands, lightly kissing his bottom lip, his upper lip, back down to his lower lip and warmly said, "Good morning." She could tell Ritchie was upset with himself for not setting his alarm, but he turned to Lyla and softly said, "There's no better alarm clock than your personalized ring of kisses to begin my day."

Lyla kissed Ritchie deeply, and then thanked him again for the lovely ring.

"Be careful where you wear the ring. I don't want anyone to hurt you," Ritchie said.

"I will be," she replied, as he looked down at his watch on the bed.

"Your watches always look awesome," Lyla acknowledged.

"I take great pride in my watches. They are very expensive and some are one-of-a-kind sent to me from different designers," Ritchie bragged, as he quickly put on his pair of pants and shirt from the night before.

Lyla walked him to the front door and laid a gentle and delicate goodbye kiss on him, wishing he did not have to leave. She waved goodbye as he cast one last lingering gaze at her before walking down her hallway.

Lyla headed back to her room feeling like a young teenage girl in love again, minus the abuse. She plopped down on her bed enjoying the leftover scent of his sexy and manly cologne, turning her on. *I need to let out some steam.*

She shifted her body to feel more comfortable, but that was impossible because she felt something poking her back. Ritchie forgot his fancy watch.

"I must put it away in a safe place," she murmured.

This would become one of Ritchie's quirks that he had no idea wrapped itself around Lyla's heart.

Chapter 15

Ritchie and Lyla continued to hang out almost every day. He always spoke to her in sweet gentle honesty, always pleasant, and their quality time made her happy.

We flew to Martha's Vineyard just for lunch and came back the same day. How romantic.

Over the Christmas holiday, Lyla would have preferred to stay in the city to be Ritchie's "Santa Baby," but instead she went home to Philly for two weeks. During this time they spoke on the phone, and she quickly realized that this man was not only very skillful, but he was also a genius.

The information he spoke about was not normal knowledge; it was specialty knowledge and she could learn a lot from him. This was why Lyla could almost believe him when he said he invented the satellite, but that was still a long shot. Lyla also acknowledged the things he spoke about could probably be found in books but the way he delivered the message was enchanting. It made Lyla want to apply it in her life.

She could talk to Ritchie about anything and he always had an intelligent response or something enlightening to say. One thing he told her was that it was important to be wealthy; not just financially but also spiritually, mentally, and physically too.

"When someone asks me, 'how are you doing?' I don't say 'well,' 'good,' or 'fine.' I say, 'wealthy,'" Ritchie explained. "You will be there one day, Mademoiselle." She could tell he was wealthy. He told her his money was old money straight from the oil company his family owned.

Ritchie constantly turned Lyla on and she was not sure where this was going but she liked where they were. He became Lyla's mentor and her part-time lover. She says part-time lover because when she returned to New York, Ritchie and Lyla had coffee at their favorite diner in the city. During her chat with Ritchie he revealed some disturbing news.

"So! Tell me your deepest darkest secrets," Lyla said, feeling a little uneasy asking.

Ritchie sat at the table with one leg crossed over the other.

"I think your secrets would be more interesting. I know you have a dark side."

Lyla felt like her relationship with Ritchie could finally be true love and she did not want this feeling to go away over something she stuck her nose in. Conversely, she wondered why he mostly spoke about his professional life, but very little about his personal life. Lyla was sure she could handle a mature conversation without getting upset over something she did not want to hear. She continued to pry.

"Oh, come on. What are you, a wanted man?" Lyla asked jokingly.

"Yes, I'm a straight lunatic on the run," Ritchie said sarcastically.

"Ha, ha, ha. I'll show you mine if you show me yours," Lyla smiled.

"What is it you want to know, Mademoiselle?" Lyla loved it when Ritchie called her Mademoiselle with his sultry accent.

She took a deep breath and asked with all jokes aside, "Are you married?"

"Yes, I am," he said without hesitation. "I have been married for 23 years and I have two girls, 7 and 13 and a boy, 6." Lyla played it off like it did not bother her so she could get more information from him as he showed Lyla pictures of his children. Ritchie looked nothing like his kids except for his teenage daughter.

He then told Lyla he coaches his teenage daughter's swim team and plays tennis with his younger daughter on Saturday mornings while his son sticks to the sidelines until he's old enough to pick a hobby. Lyla continued to play it cool while he spoke highly about his wife. Him and his wife attended weekend ballets when she was not at one of her monthly charity events. His wife supported him in whatever Ritchie wanted to do.

From the sounds of it, his world was wrapped around his family, not to mention his mother who lives with them too. Lyla could no longer keep her composure. She almost fell out of her chair as she put her hand over her chest and gasped for air like she had asthma. Ritchie handed her some coffee and she slapped it out of his hand.

"Bastard!" Lyla hissed while Ritchie stared at her like she was the one married with kids.

"I had no idea until now that I was just something on the side. Why didn't you tell me this the first night you took me out to dinner or when you spent the night at my apartment or flew me to Martha's Vineyard?!" she screamed. The couple at the next table looked at Ritchie and Lyla until they realized they were impolitely staring.

The multimillionaire did not flinch.

"I did tell you the first night, during dinner, you must have forgotten."

"No you didn't," Lyla replied, sharply.

"Yes I did," Ritchie said, and with a vain effort, he continued to claim he told Lyla on the first date. Lyla was angry and he could clearly see that. She was trying so hard not to show him her alter ego, but she was two seconds away from strangling him.

Instead she glared him straight in the eye.

"Tell me this, Ritchie," Lyla said. "What woman would forget about something like that? I am a Christian woman, not a home wrecker, and you are supposed to be a Christian man."

"I am," Ritchie replied.

"Okay, Christian man," Lyla doubted. "It would have been a dead giveaway if you were wearing your wedding band, Ritchie."

He was not backing down.

"The love I have for my wife I do not need a ring. My love for you, you should never have to doubt," Ritchie said.

Lyla calmed down visibly while mocking.

"You love me?"

"Yes. I love you," he replied. Lyla sighed. *Another declaration of love.*

"Saying I do after your wife walked down the aisle to meet you is more than saying I love you; that was a promise you made to your wife, family, friends, and God until death," Lyla reminded, her heart silently wishing that she was in his wife's place.

"You and I are together and that means the world to me. God does not have to know," Ritchie laughed.

"Ha," Lyla said.

Regardless of how hard she tried to get him to admit that he did not tell her about his marriage, he was sticking with the "fact" that on their first date, he was crystal clear about his wife and kids.

In turn, Lyla felt like he was insulting her intelligence, by making her believe something that wasn't true - *the Jedi mind trick*. She wanted to throw her hot coffee on this man's married dingaling, get up, and walk away for taking advantage of her. He stole the right for Lyla to make a decision whether or not she would want to pursue a married man.

Now Lyla understood why she never saw him on the weekends. *I'm a full-fledged grown woman*, Lyla said to herself. *The nerve of him to play mind games with me!*

She took another deep breath and then it dawned on her: *My heart is not entangled in all of this anyway*. She had developed some feelings for Ritchie but she was not in love. For now, she figured they could do business together, although she wondered, *What else is Iron Man lying about*?

A middle-aged woman walked over to the condiment stand next to Ritchie and Lyla's table. While she stood, taking some napkins, Lyla realized she was high.

The woman looked at Lyla and prayed, "May the Lord Bless you." She did the Catholic cross by her chest, and then walked away.

"That was weird," Lyla said. Later she found out why the woman was sending that message to her. It was from God. He sometimes uses a person you least expect to deliver an important message.

Ritchie drank the last drop of his coffee.

"I have to leave."

"Wait a minute," Lyla said with frustration. "I'm not done with your examination, Ritchie."

"Examination? This is more like interrogation," Ritchie laughed.

"Examination, interrogation, whateveration, it's all the same and I'm sure there is a lot more for me to know, like your age," Lyla said.

"We are finished here. Now are you coming with me?" Ritchie responded.

"You are *such* an afternoon delight," Lyla said mordantly.

"Yeah," Ritchie replied. "And you cannot get enough of me."

"So you think," Lyla said.

"My love you cannot live without and I'll share it with you always. Now apologize to me."

"For?" Lyla wondered.

"For calling me a bastard," Ritchie reminded.

Fuck you! Lyla laughed to herself as she rolled her eyes at him and yelled, "That's what you get for being married, you bastard!"

Ritchie laughed.

"Feisty, I like that."

"You haven't seen anything yet," Lyla murmured.

Keep fucking with me.

Chapter 16

Despite the consequences of what Lyla learned about Ritchie, he was right; she couldn't get enough of him. He had a type of charm that snuck up on a person and a contagious personality that had no equal, even in Casmir. Ritchie was perfect and so was the love they shared.

I know I told myself I'm not in love with this man, she thought. *But as time goes on and the spring months roll in, I grew to genuinely love him more than I ever thought I could, and now I'm hooked. A stranger Ritchie was once, but now he would become my full-time lover, his official girlfriend.*

I will never label myself a mistress.

He would stay the night, sometimes leaving his lavish watch behind.

And whenever she had doubts about the two of them, or wanted to break it off because of guilt, his choice of words would be, "I see our past, present, and future."

"How do you know?" Lyla asked.

"By the way you stare at me," Ritchie answered. "I know we will last for eternity."

"Okay, but your life is complicated," Lyla reminded.

"You don't understand my situation," Ritchie said.

"You're right. I don't understand your situation," Lyla agreed.

"I hope that one day you'll realize how important you are when seen through my eyes," Ritchie said. "But again, you don't understand my situation." This became his famous line, turning him into a mystery man, turning Lyla on even more.

The next day, Ritchie met Lyla at her place. She had her feet up on the wall while playing her favorite childhood game UNO on her phone as her upper body lied next to Ritchie's. He sat and admired her.

He noticed her nails and asked if she bit them. Lyla hated that question with a passion. She understood she was a model and people expected her to not bite her nails down to the skin, but it was a habit Lyla would stop when she was ready.

"Yeah, it's a skill," she passive-aggressively replied.

"Well you have pretty feet," Ritchie chuckled.

"Funny," Lyla said. "Man!"

"What's wrong?" Ritchie asked.

"You're not hot? My hair is frizzing up," Lyla answered. She walked over to the window.

"It is hot," Ritchie agreed. He grabbed his bottle of water sitting next to the bed and quaffed it down.

"My body likes to be hot but this is too hot," Lyla said. "I wish my super would put an air conditioner in here like he promised."

"Turn on the fan too," Ritchie suggested. Lyla opened the window and then quickly slammed it shut. Construction workers were outside her building fixing the sidewalk. The sound of the machine was like a screeching dentist drill.

"I will turn on the fan," Lyla said as she turned it on high. "That's a little better. Now I can finish my game."

Ritchie welcomed the light breeze as he took Lyla's hand.

"So your body likes it hot, eh?"

"Yes," Lyla giggled while grabbing Ritchie's bottled water to drink. "It came out the wrong way. My body does better in hot weather. One day, I'm going to move to Florida to live. And if I don't get married soon, I will be moving there with my friends like the show Golden Girls. So set me up with someone Ritchie."

"You have someone," Ritchie reminded. He slowly ran his hands up her arm, neck, down to her smooth back, sending shivers up and down her spine. Ritchie stared into her eyes and whispered in her ear, "I love your hot body; because of you my world is now whole."

"I love you, sweetness, with all of my heart," Lyla said. She flipped him over to his stomach and straddled him while she popped the top of her lavender body lotion to massage his shoulders. She soothed his tight muscles as she continued to say in a sensual tone, "They say two minutes of massaging can take away two hours of stress."

After a few moments, they kissed hard, pressing their lips against one another with a new kind of passion. This was perhaps unacceptable behavior for a Christian woman's but she cared nothing about her spiritual beliefs right now. Ritchie made her feel so good inside and he truly understood her.

She laid on the bed as he climbed on top of her steadily stripping all his clothes. He gazed into her eyes with his eyes as they continued to kiss. She moaned. He moaned and it was obvious they were both in the mood to have sex for the first time.

After her clothes were almost off they stopped for a second and blurted simultaneously, "I want to tell you something."

Both looked at each other, smiled and said in unison, "Never mind." They continued to kiss as Ritchie moved his hand up her blouse touching her sexy breast that needed no bra. Lyla kissed him harder and harder and then she suddenly grabbed Ritchie's wrist and stopped him from feeling on her boobs.

"What?" Ritchie said.

"What di-"

She heard a knock on the door as Ritchie covered his naked body with her blanket.

Lyla quietly and quickly sat up, turned her back to Ritchie, yanked off the remainder of her clothes and selected a pink shoulder less lightweight spring dress to wear. The top part of the dress was fitted while the bottom half was loose with well-thought out bunches of perfectly placed ruffles, one side longer than the other. The style and color were just right for Lyla's skin tone, shape, and rouge cheeks, as she shook out her easy breezy curls.

Ritchie admired her confident stride and beautiful attire as she gracefully swept out of the room and walked towards the front door.

Lyla answered the door and found that it was the superintendent's assistant. He stood six inches eleven feet tall with a size sixteen shoe and creepy lower lip. The assistant startled her because she always had to keep an extra eye on him. He was a gentle giant but he had some emotional challenges. She could never tell if he was on his medicine or not.

The assistant told Lyla she needed to take care of a cleaning job for her super.

She had a deal with the superintendent to help him with his cleaning business in exchange for letting her stay at his apartment for free. He always needed her at the wrong time. Lyla told the assistant she would be right down, went back to her room, and told Ritchie; she would be back as she slipped on a pair of jeweled sandals to match her cute and trendy dress. The door closed behind her, barely catching the flowing fabric as if air was blowing in from off the ocean.

The superintendent was downstairs waiting for her, but before he noticed she was there, he was fussing with a young man who was flirting with his daughter. They used vulgar words but the superintendent quickly shut the guy down when he lifted his shirt and showed him a 357 magnum that never left his waist side. The guy was not prepared for that, so he ran.

"Punk!" the super hollered.

When Lyla stepped into the car she asked, "Is that gun registered?"

"Look, at the end of the day, it really doesn't matter," he answered.

Lyla's superintendent was crazy like that.

Chapter 17

An hour later, Lyla was back in Ritchie's still-naked arms. He dripped charisma and flare. With her heart pounding, anticipating his next physical touch, she could tell Ritchie was very experienced, and Lyla's body was ready for him to be inside of her.

As he continued to touch her body Lyla asked softly, "What did you have to tell me?"

"I said never mind," Ritchie reminded.

"I know, but I'm curious now," Lyla said.

He kissed her lips tenderly.

"You exude sex appeal. I have never felt this way for someone before outside of my..."

"Shhhh...Neither have I," Lyla interrupted. They held each other intensely.

"If I could have just one wish, that wish would be to wake up every day to the sound of your breath on my neck."

"That could happen," Lyla said in a teasing voice.

"Say it again," Ritchie responded.

"That could happen," Lyla repeated making herself believe this could happen if she said it enough times. "That could happen. That could happen. That could happen."

Each sound went deeper and deeper and Lyla and Ritchie were kissing again as he said, "I love the way you kiss me, your mouth is so soft and smooth. The way you look at me with your bright almond eyes. I'm so happy when I'm with you."

Cuban guys are so romantic, Lyla thought, as she whispered to Ritchie, "I love you."

"I love the way you say I love you. You are the first person I think about when I get up in the morning and last before I go to sleep," Ritchie replied.

She felt like a "but" was coming on, "But?" Lyla said.

"But I do love my wife," Ritchie said. "Since we no longer have sex, though, I have to pursue other alternatives and that means being selfish and looking outside my marriage for it."

"Well I notice we share a lot of things in common, but there is one that just stood out the most," Lyla said.

"What's that?" Ritchie wondered.

"We both want to be loved," Lyla acknowledged, though she could clearly see in his eyes, his heart was with his wife. "But there is one thing we don't have in common. I'm not willing to do anything for it like you are!" Lyla jerked away from him. *Cuban men are not so romantic.*

He gently grabbed her, holding her tightly in his arms.

"Let go of me!" She pulled away from him again. "Just think I almost gave in and was about to have sex with you!" Lyla shouted.

"I thought we could talk about anything," Ritchie said.

"We can. But I have slipped in the past and you know what my selfish alternative is, Ritchie."

"What's that?" he asked. "To wait until I'm married to have sex!" Lyla answered.

"Mademoiselle," Ritchie said.

Now he is aware of my good morals and values and hated them, Lyla said to herself. *But he wouldn't leave though,* as she said, "But for some reason when I'm with you I want to give you all of me."

He smoothly pulled her back into his arms and held her lightly.

"With a body like yours, why let it go to waste?" And in the next moment, they fell to the floor of her bedroom crushing each other's soft mouths and necks, hard and sloppy, Lyla snatching off her dress, but suddenly slapping him in the face and pushing him away.

"I have always struggled with men not accepting what I believe about sex," she said boldly as she put on a pair of jean shorts and a wife beater. "I have to be strong and stop this nonsense. I know right from wrong, and this is wrong. I'm not having sex, especially not with a married man. What kind of Christian are you?"

Ritchie put his shirt and boxers on and left the room with a childish temper tantrum. He was pissed off but that was his problem, not hers.

Lyla waited and waited for Ritchie to return to the room but he was taking a long time so, like a mother who gives in to a child, Lyla went searching for him. She heard Ritchie in the bathroom with the door almost shut. Before he could stop her from entering, the door flung open, hitting the cement wall. She looked at him and thought, *This is like a ship with no sail.*

Ritchie was sniffing cocaine.

Remarkably, Lyla had not let the lures of the industry and its potential ills spoil her. Many commented that she was not the "typical model babe." Smoke-free and drug free.

Lyla quivered and sighed.

"What on God's green earth are you doing?" Not sharing with me," just rolled off her tongue. She wanted to try whatever Ritchie did. "Let me have some," she continued.

Ritchie ignored her and flipped off the lights, the sunlight only hitting the bare walls, as he promptly ran warm bath water and said, "Get in."

"Why?" Lyla said. "I'm not taking off…"

"Shhhh," Ritchie interrupted. "And get in. Trust me." Lyla dipped her toe in the water then fully stepped in as Ritchie followed. She heard a thump. Her peppermint soap fell from the arm of the tub. Lyla picked it up while Ritchie sat down to get comfortable.

She replaced her soap on the shelf, feeling self-conscious.

Finally Lyla sat down as she eased her body into the warm water, to her surprise, it felt so romantic and beautiful in a weird kind of way, snuggled in between Ritchie's legs while wet and clothed.

As Lyla sat in the large tub, listening to the sounds of water filling the tub and falling off her body she turned to him and said, "Who would have thought?" He held her with an affectionate embrace.

"Imagine just you and me in this world all alone," Ritchie said as she painted a mental picture.

"Never have I fallen but I am quickly lost in your magic," Lyla replied, thinking of that wonderful mental picture.

After a few minutes of caressing her body, he held the cocaine by her nose and she snorted a small amount. It did not take long before Lyla felt the effects of the drug.

"Look," she slurred, leaning sluggishly against Ritchie's chest. "Sugar-cane dust and purple skies." Her fingers were raised high. "I'm writing your name in the cloud as I tickle the sky," Lyla continued.

She was definitely in another world and feeling extremely nice.

"Yes, I see it too," he responded, dismissing her words that don't mean anything.

"Can I ask you something?" Lyla said.

"Ask me what," Ritchie said while he flipped off the water.

"Is there a yellow brick road?"

"What?" he said.

"You know the yellow brick road from the Wizard of Oz?" Lyla explained.

"I know what it is," Ritchie laughed. He did not know what to say. Telling Lyla there was no yellow brick road would be like telling his little boy there was no Santa Claus.

He did not want to spoil it for her, so he told her, "You know I could do a one man show of just you."

"Ha, ha, ha," Lyla said.

"Seriously," Ritchie chuckled. "At moments the things you do and say are original especially when you're high."

"I just want to know if there is a yellow brick road?"

"Sure, Lyla."

"Really?!" Lyla smiled. "Where?"

"Right next to Lover's Lane," Ritchie joked, shaking his head.

"Where's that?

Ritchie responded to Lyla by dick punching her lower back. She was not sure if she was hallucinating. Lyla stood up, water splashing in his face as she slowly stepped out of the tub regaining her balance after a few stumbles, making the tile slick. She turned around and realized she was not hallucinating. Ritchie was rock hard making her horney.

Lyla strip-teased until she was fully naked. Ritchie then stood up and stepped out of the tub and saw the wounds on her body from what occurred when she was a teenager. Lyla felt vulnerable, covering the scars with her favorite soft pink towel, pressing the cool material to her body.

"You don't have to hide them," he said. "I know that when the time is right, you will be able to talk to me." He gently slid his hand up her towel to softly touch the abrasions. "These wounds show how strong you are and how much valor you have," Ritchie continued.

Lyla received his kind words with open arms, or at least the drugs did.

"Your lips speak of kindness and soft sweetness," Lyla said. He dropped his boxers. She dropped her towel.

"Your skin is as smooth as silk," he added, rubbing his dick against her thigh, holding her, and feeling her secret pulses. *Ritchie was so hard he can hardly stand.* He aggressively spun Lyla around and stretched out his hand, past her ass, to touch between her legs. Ritchie kissed and licked her neck while pulling Lyla's hair, causing her head to fall back on his.

She hastily stopped to run to the toilet; Lyla could barely keep her head up. The drug made her sick but it also made her need more. Ritchie lifted her head as she sniffed more of the cocaine. She then wrapped her arms around his neck and pulled his face to her and asked, "Have you done 69 before, babe?"

"Is that a trick question?" Ritchie answered. Lyla giggled as they both got into scoring position. She craved the heat of Ritchie's tongue against her pussycat and dreamed of feasting on every delectable part of his nuts, as Lyla did things her tongue was never intended to do.

She twirled her tongue around in a circle at the head of his hard throbbing cock until he could not take the sensation anymore. Ritchie came out from between her legs and gently pulled her down until the head of his dick hit the back of her throat. Lyla pulled up, slapped him on the thigh, and went back to the 69 position to take control of the situation. She circled his dick with her tongue again.

Lyla then went up and down and down and up, letting his dick throb against the back of her throat over and over again while Ritchie took his time and sucked on her like a succulent, juicy, piece of fruit.

"AHHH!" she screamed. She could feel the steam coming off his body, making Lyla moan louder.

Ritchie then picked her up and gently laid her on her back.

"There is more?" Lyla whispered with anticipation. "Was that just the appetizer?"

"Yes," he nodded. "This is the full meal."

He slowly kissed and toyed with her, from tits down to her belly button, touching the lip of her divine wetness of her cunt again, softly working on her clitoris, arousing her carefully. Her hands were everywhere — caressing, stroking holding Ritchie closer as she rubbed her feet up and down his leg.

"Every inch of you is as delicious as honey," he said softly.

It felt so good to enter her. He loved the way she held her hips beneath him as he kept up with the waves of her body. Ritchie could not help but cry out in pleasure. He covered her mouth with more kisses as he grew harder. She wanted it faster and harder as her moans billowed like sheets in the wind.

She stopped him.

"So what is for dessert?"

"Would you like second helpings?" he answered with a question.

Lyla closed her eyes, opening her mouth to feel the might of his crotch again, but this time it tingled and sent ripples of ecstasy through her taste buds. So sweet, so wonderful, so special. She kissed, she touched, she teased, and she swallowed her dessert like she was drowning in a sea of love, cum running down her chin.

After the erotic courtship on the bathroom floor was over, Ritchie kissed her closed eyes, praying she wouldn't leave him.

Meanwhile, Lyla laid on the floor as she felt the drug take over her body. A few moments later, Lyla pushed Ritchie out of the bathroom into the uncomfortably cold hallway and shut the door. Ritchie scuttled to Lyla's bedroom shivering while searching for his clothes.

Ritchie eventually opened the door to the bathroom fully clothed. He told her to get off the floor as he gently pulled her up by the arm. She managed to get herself together to listen to Ritchie tell her he was on his way to his office in midtown and to meet him there later on.

She snorted more cocaine.

"Okay."

"Be careful with that," he urged. "And make sure you meet me; I have some things to show you."

"Okay babe," Lyla replied. He placed the rest of the cocaine in his pocket as Lyla walked him towards the front door to leave, and out of nowhere he said, "I am an insanely crazy scientist. I don't know why. I can cut a person open and drain their blood without making a mess."

If that is what he wants to show me than I will stay home, Lyla said to herself.

"I like to eat the people I kill. You taste like tuna," Ritchie continued.

Lyla was too high to take what Ritchie said seriously. She assumed it was more nonsense as she laughed hysterically and said, "Yeah, well, I like to fight until I see blood, so now we're crazy together." *Don't play with me,* Lyla thought.

Instead of walking Ritchie to her front door, Lyla walked him downstairs to the lobby of her building. She was still as high as a kite so she held on to Ritchie while singing, "I believe I can fly." Ritchie guffawed and Lyla kissed him good-bye.

On her way back upstairs, the superintendent asked her if she was okay.

"I'm fine," Lyla muttered. She slowly used her knees and hands to seize the steps in front of her but in a matter of seconds she lost her grip and tumbled down a couple of stairs. Lyla repeated this a few times before saying again in a slow low tone, "I'm fine."

When she woke up the next morning, she was in her bed, but had no idea how she got there. Lyla looked to her left and grabbed her cell phone. She noticed several text messages from friends and family and eleven missed calls from Ritchie, eek! Lyla had finally come down from cloud nine.

She only responded to Ritchie's call.

He was not very happy about her passing out until the next day. *What did he expect?* Lyla thought. *My body is not use to hard drugs,* as she turned off the fan, now blowing warm air. Ritchie asked her to meet him at the office. Her body felt like she worked a double shift, but she proceeded to make her way to the office.

On the train, the sin-filled afternoon with Ritchie replayed in her head as she held back tears while dealing with the harsh blow of reality that she gave in to temptation and slept with a married man. Her mind switched over to his wife and her tears could not help but fall. She wiped them away only to endure more drops of sorrow, hiding her face from the other passengers in eternal rains of shame.

I can't believe I had sex with a married man and did drugs, Lyla thought. *I'm a hypocrite and God hates me. I do not deserve his mercy or love.*

Lyla did something she thought she would never do. She called the pastor's office and made an appointment. Lyla needed to talk to someone, mainly because she was beating herself up about what she did with Ritchie and how it might affect his wife. She could only imagine what he was telling her, especially since he was at Lyla's place almost every day of the week. He said it was more convenient for him to stay in the city then to go to his home in Connecticut. The bizarre part was his wife seemed to believe everything Ritchie said.

What disturbed Lyla the most was that Ritchie would lie to his children, made even worse by the fact that his kids thought he was a god. Ritchie had so much self-control and always so mild tempered no matter what the situation was; it was easy for his kids and wife to believe his lies. He would lay right next to Lyla in bed or sit next to her at his office while he talked to his kids on the phone. She would look at him, amazed, as he told lie after lie of his whereabouts.

He speaks as if there was nothing going on between us, Lyla thought. *So, since he lied to his wife and kids with ease, he could lie to me.*

Lyla reminisced, remembering one morning that while at her place, he was on the phone with his wife. Without warning, Lyla made a loud noise that sounded like a fart. She was just as surprised as he was. *That's never happened before,* Lyla thought.

Ritchie put his wife on mute and looked at Lyla. He was speechless for a second.

"Did you just fart?" he asked. She was mortified and wanted to end her life right there. "Girls don't fart. Well, not in the way you think. It was pussy fart," Lyla cackled. *He did not understand, but that became one of our running jokes,* she said to herself.

Lyla had a whoopee cushion app on her phone. After his phone call, they were preparing to fall back to sleep, but first she had some fun with the pussy fart situation. She pressed the button on the whoopee cushion app. No response, so she did it again. He still didn't say anything.

Lyla did it again and he finally gathered up enough nerve to ask, "Are you farting?" They both expressed uncontrollable amusement.

After a few more times she told him it was her phone app.

"Was the fart you did while I was talking to my wife also the app," he said as Lyla's phone rang. It was her super.

"Saved by the bell; I have to run," she replied. Her superintendent normally called her at the worst times, but this time it was perfect. Oddly enough, she thought the pussy fart made her and Ritchie closer, which of course compounded her feelings of guilt that stemmed from messing around with a married man.

On the other hand, despite her feelings of love for Ritchie Lyla felt dirty. She asked God for forgiveness and to spare her the consequences.

Ultimately, his wife had the upper hand. She was the one with the kids, the big house, and money. But sometimes Lyla wondered if Ritchie really had money. Some of their past dinners, 'a woman should never touch a bill' flew out the window; Lyla had to dig into her pockets. She didn't mind if she had it to spare, though, and she knew he would always be there for her.

Ritchie was where she found her rest.

Chapter 18

Ritchie and Lyla often did things that didn't make any sense, and he talked her into things she normally would not do. Aside from their sex life — with an occasional temper tantrum if she rejected him — her diet consisted of cigarettes and hard liquor from the corner store instead of her usual red wine. She stopped snorting cocaine after the second time, because it was already killing her cute button nose and she was absolutely not going to smoke it or shoot it up.

In any case, they were having fun and she loved him deeply. He brought joy to her life every day. She still often wondered, though, why they spent so much time at her place. It was convenient, but not half as nice as his house on the hill.

Roger, the accountant who worked with Ritchie, said that he once visited Ritchie at his house. He saw one bright red Lamborghini only a blind person would miss, but assumed it didn't belong to Ritchie because he did not know how to drive it. Roger also said his house was nothing special. Lyla begged to differ; Ritchie claimed to have at least twelve very expensive exotic cars including the Lamborghini, and an awesome house on the hill with horses, maids, a butler, and a huge island-like pool. Lyla thought that Roger was a jealous 68-year-old who had never and would never achieve as much as Ritchie.

However, Ritchie's money was always tied up in something. Either it was the IRS or the bank holding his money; the excuses always sounded reasonable, so it was hard to question him. Sometimes Lyla attempted to take a peek at his bank statement but he moved away before she could see it.

Also, Lyla wondered why Ritchie bought lottery tickets. Originally, she thought it was for amusement, but, like she wondered before, maybe he was not the millionaire he claimed to be. On top of that, there were times when he asked Lyla for money other than for some of the dinners.

Collecting on the loan meant fussing with him to get it and sometimes she couldn't even get the full amount.

"You owe me for some of the cocaine purchases!" She simply laughed at him. Lyla used it twice. If anything, he owed her for buying it for him. *He loved to turn things around on me.*

He also attempted to con ten thousand dollars out of her aunt and her superintendant. Both dishonest incidents displeased Lyla, so from then on, when it came to Ritchie borrowing money from Lyla or anyone she knew, the bank was closed.

Nonetheless, one night she blurted out, "I'm not into your money. I'm into you because you are kind to me and supportive. But if you need money let's talk about it and maybe I can help you even if I do not have cash to give you." *Why did I say that?* as she lit a cigarette, and offered him one.

"Let me have some of yours," Ritchie grinned.

Chapter 19

That afternoon, a deluge of pigeons assembled on the tall building in front of the office. Over the next few days, Ritchie and Lyla came and went like clockwork, until Ritchie discussed an important job to Lyla during their smoke break. Lyla thought it had something to do with Heavenly Secrets.

"What kind of job?" she asked while inhaling smoke through her glossy lips, forgetting to ash.

"First you need to learn Spanish," Ritchie suggested.

Lyla simply replied, "Yo hablo Espanol y Francais."

Ritchie was surprised but relieved. He knew this was meant to be. They continued to smoke their cigarettes outside as he explained the job. Ritchie's accent was stronger than normal. He did this when he was nervous or when being sneaky and Lyla had to read his lips in order to understand him.

The next month — on the day she was supposed to meet with Pastor Bill for the first time, no less — Lyla was on her way to the airport with a luggage full of cash. She had to deliver money to a drug dealer in Monterrey, Mexico to collect heroin and some cash for her man.

On her flight to Mexico, Lyla reflected on the situation and could not believe she had cancelled her appointment with the pastor to meet a drug lord. Her priorities were out of order. She knew this trip was dangerous and as she thought about it, an excruciating headache developed, a side effect of the jaw operation she endured when she was a teenager; her doctor had warned her to stay out of stressful situations.

How did I get myself into this? Lyla asked herself. *Anything could go wrong in Mexico.*

Ritchie told her she had what it took to pull it off because no one would suspect her. Lyla walked, talked, dressed, and acted like she was a million dollar woman but was still considered the pretty girl next door.

Lyla was under too much pressure and the headache was getting worse, so she asked the flight attendant for some aspirin but she had none. The only option she could think of was to do a little bit of cocaine she stashed away in her suede and leather handbag, in a container otherwise filled with moisturizer.

I know I said I would never use it again but I had a feeling I may need it for this trip, Lyla thought. *It wouldn't be so bad if I rub it on my teeth to numb my body, a trick I learned from Ritchie,* as she thought about what Ritchie said to her.

"Be careful with that."

After using the drug in the bathroom, Lyla fell asleep and when she woke up, she was free of her headache, but arrived in Monterrey, jet lagged. *That was unavoidable.*

After navigating customs successfully, she saw her driver right away. It was burning hot and humid as the brightness of the sun hit her so hard that she had to at least cover up her eyes with sunglasses. But what she really wanted to do was to get to her hotel to take a cool shower and climb into bed, as she stared at the driver. *I can't be too careful these days,* while he took her bags.

His long graying hair was well kept and his wimpy looking body seemed harmless enough as she stepped into the car.

She spoke to soon.

While searching for her hotel information, she caught the driver giving her an evil eye, and immediately felt goose bumps up her arm. He gripped onto the steering wheel and sped off.

Before she left New York, Ritchie quoted Matthew 10:16, "I am sending you as a sheep in the midst of wolves, so be wise as a serpent and innocent as a dove."

In less than two minutes, Lyla found her information, but before she could hand it to him the driver said, "That's okay. I have the information." Lyla looked at him strangely and after twenty minutes the man pulled over to the side of the road. Lyla's heart was racing from fear but she did not show it. Her door opened and a bag was roughly put over her head, while guys chattered in the background.

Lyla screamed and kicked like a wild fire, knocking some of the guys to the ground.

"I thought this was going to be easy! This bitch is out of control!" one of the guys shouted.

"Hold her down. Can you manage that? She's just a girl," another guy said. In a matter of seconds, Lyla had been drugged and was out cold.

She woke up and did not know what time or day it was. Moreover, she was feeling sluggish from whatever they stuck her with, and the cocaine in her system was not helping. Lyla attempted to get up, but she wobbled and fell to the ground.

She lifted up again with the same result while touching her weak legs. They were a bit numb, part of the reason why she couldn't stand. She put both of them in front of her. Frustrated from not being able to walk, she forced out a thunderous, Banshee-like scream while shaking her bed-mussed hair.

"Calm down," came a woman's voice from nearby. Lyla saw rows of young and old female and male bodies with dry blood under their fingernails and in between their toes. They were committed to chains of gloomy chairs with eyes full of fear and concern in their voices.

Lyla looked at them with grave interest.

"Don't tell me to calm down."

"We're not the enemy. They think you're dead. You are supposed to be our food," a young scared girl in a dirty pink dress whimpered.

"Over my dead body," Lyla said. She shouted for help.

"No one is coming until they decide," a man said.

"Where are we?" Lyla wondered.

"We have no idea," he replied.

Lyla saw padlocks on the blacked out windows. She could tell someone tried to escape by the picking, scratching, and biting at the windows and doorknob.

A few minutes passed, and Lyla heard footsteps coming to the dark, musty room. She looked toward the door and then looked back at the people. Lyla was now in survival mode. She laid back down on the hard cold ground and closed her eyes, to seem dead until the man left.

The armed man came inside the room with cruel intentions.

He stood over Lyla, prepared to brutally carve her into little pieces for the people to eat. But first, he saw how beautiful she was and, like a creature of instinct, he wanted a little bit to eat for himself.

He leaned over Lyla and forcefully stuck his tongue in her mouth, digging his filthy nails into her numb leg. He dragged his nails up her thigh causing streaks of blood to follow while he fondled her breast. Lyla held in her scream as he licked her cheek and then back to her mouth. He was prepared to rape Lyla's corpse body.

She opened her grizzled eyes wide. At first it startled him, but he quickly recovered, slapped her with his massive hand, and held her down tightly by the front of her neck. He sat his beefcake on her stomach. That thing was huge enough to do some serious damage to her secret garden. He rammed his huge horrible dick inside her; Lyla screamed for mercy.

He continued to rape her until he used Lyla as his cum dumpster.

The gruesome man released her arms from the ground, and reached for his knife to kill her, but Lyla yelled, "Wait! Can I have one last kiss, my mighty king?"

He groped and then laughed, "Sure I know you cannot resist me."

You dummy!

He kissed her, and Lyla bit down hard on the intruder's tongue like she was out to destroy. She grabbed his hair and pulled it. He struggled and leaned back with all his strength to come undone from her tenacious grip. Lyla pulled back from his mouth and spit out the piece of his tongue as she looked at the chuck of hair from his scalp in her hand.

She tossed it aside, blood dripping from her mouth as she watched him gnaw his tongue in anguish.

Lyla seized the knife from his pants pocket and sliced his throat, puncturing his windpipe and spurting blood. Her fellow prisoners gawked as the blood fell from the ceiling and dribbled down the walls onto the ground.

"She is a rebel in disguise," a man said. "Can she save us?"

Lyla's legs were still numb, so she wiped her slippery hands off and crawled over to the dirty man, disarming his corpse of his machete. Lyla placed the knife in the pocket of a flimsy black satin negligee she was not wearing when she arrived in Mexico. She did recognize the heels and the blonde wig. Lyla also felt her irritating gray contact lenses.

She strapped the machete across her shoulder and waist like a ninja. Lyla was ready for combat, as she heard soft babble approaching the opening of the foul-smelly room.

She slid to the opening using her arms, pushing off of bumps or any other surface to arrive to her destination. The chatters were closer now, as she sat against the wall waiting to demolish her enemies, her heart pounding rapidly.

Shortly after, Lyla heard them walk away except for one. The loud door squeaked open to a shadow figure with razor-sharp claws. The creature-like villain walked in without seeing Lyla lying on the floor behind him. As he took in the familiar body on the blood stained ground, he pulled out his gun.

Lyla took a deep breath and slit the backs of his ankles with her knife quicker than a shooting star, immobilizing the prowler. The guy dropped forward, face first, screaming with rage and agony to the dusty ground.

She felt some movement in her legs as she got on all fours like a cat; ready to pounce on anyone in her way. Lyla turned the guy around and dragged his body to the huge door, head first in the doorway.

"Where are we?" she asked. The injured man ignored Lyla, so she closed the heavy door on his head. He yelped.

"Where are we?" she repeated.

"I don't know," he lied as she shut the door on his head again.

"Where are we?"

"You are in a place called 'The Monster,' deep within the Monterrey Mountains," the man growled. "You and the rest of the captives will never get out of here." Lyla slammed the door on the guy's head one last time, killing him. She seized his weapons, sat up against the wall and did leg stretches, push-ups, and sit-ups for hours to rebuild her strength.

Lyla was ready to finally walk again.

The doors opened and what already seemed like a bad dream turned into a nightmare. There were at least fifteen gun barrels staring her in the face.

"When they deliver you over, do not be anxious to speak," Ritchie said, as she daydreamed for a second. "You will be given what to say in that hour."

"Estoy aqui en nombre de Ritchie Perez," Lyla said.

"No need to speak Spanish. Who are you?" a guy who seemed to be the kingpin she was supposed to meet asked. But to her surprise, two men, who looked like pimps were approaching her as if they were one.

"I'm supposed to meet one person: D'Italian," Lyla answered.

"We are one," the kingpin corrected. "Can't you see that? I'm D."

"Yea," the other kingpin said. "I'm Italian."

"Oh, I see," Lyla replied.

Still confused, Lyla repeated herself.

"I'm here on the behalf of Ritchie Perez." One of the kingpins placed his gun in her face.

"I know that! But how in the hell did you take the life of my trained killers?" he questioned as he surveyed the enormous amount of bloodshed surrounding him and his men.

"Who do you think I am?" she asked.

"Ritchie's girlfriend," he answered. "Think again," Lyla said.

She quickly kicked his hand and the gun fell right into the palm of her hand as planned; she pressed the gun against his forehead and said, "Now, tell your friends to get their guns out of my face and then you give me what I came here for and let me out of here." He then snatched the gun back while the other kingpin and his friends guarded him.

I had a bad feeling about this whole Mexico trip, Lyla thought.

He told the gunmen to lower their guns as he lowered his. D then gave her the drugs in exchange for the money he obviously already had. The kingpin was counting some of the folded money in his hand one by one. He lifted the top half of one bill, tugged on it a little and then plucked the money. *I guess that's what passes for style*, she thought.

Idiot.

Lyla checked out the heroin and it was definitely that China pure white that's not stepped on.

She put her shoulders back, raised her chin more than normal, and changed her attitude. Lyla politely asked if she could leave. She did not want any more trouble.

"Yeah. I will get the driver," D said with deceit on his lips.

One of the young girls screamed, "Please, let us go!"

The kingpins looked cooly at the girl and D said, "What you say?" The young girl did not say anything. "That's what I thought," D continued.

"She said to let us go!" another young girl shouted, unafraid. D did not ask any questions this time. He walked over and slapped the girl so hard that she and the wooden chair she was tied to fell over.

"Leave her out of this," the girl who originally cried for freedom said. "I'm the one who said to 'let us go!'"

D ignored her as he kicked and punched the girl repeatedly, breaking her nose as she laid on the ground. Lyla could do nothing. The guys held her captive again with guns cocked right at her head.

The young girl threw up from the unbearable beating. Lyla was sweating bullets thinking of a way to help this girl.

"Man, don't bruise up the merchandise. She makes good money for us," Italian reminded.

What? Is this sex trafficking? Lyla asked herself.

D stopped and said to the girl on the ground, "You know what? My brother is right, but for opening up your mouth? I'm going to find your sister and hold her here to replace you." He showed her a picture of her sister.

"How did you get that?" the girl said weakly.

"That's a silly question," the kingpin said with an evil heart. "But here is a little gift from me." And with an irresistible impulse he overdosed the severely beaten girl with heroin, urinating on her open grave.

"I don't need her. I can find another hot commodity," he continued as he looked at Lyla, his heart trained with greed. "There are at least ten guys I can call right now who would love to have sex with you today."

"So you are a pimp, too," Lyla said.

"No. A slave master," D corrected.

"Impossible, slavery was abolished in Mexico in 1829," Lyla informed.

"My empire un-abolished it," the kingpin responded as he directed the gunmen to lower their guns and to step away. "I can at least sell you for about twelve hundred dollars."

"Such a disturbingly low figure, how insulting," Lyla said. "I thought a sex slave was worth more than that."

D and Italian laughed.

"I'm sure these girls do shameful and appalling acts just to please you...sell their souls to please you...to survive, but don't push your luck," Lyla continued.

"Don't worry, I will make sure you are handled correctly. Take her measurements, Italian. Let's see what we are working with," D said with flattering words of ruin.

"I don't think Ritchie would approve," Lyla responded.

"I answer to no one, especially not to your absent boyfriend. But just like I didn't need that slut I just killed, I don't need you. Get your shit and get out of here," the kingpin said.

Lyla wondered why D let her go so easily, but in a matter of seconds she found out why.

As D and Italian walked away, the other guys standing there looked suspicious. They walked towards her and one of the bloodthirsty guys pointed his gun at her head, and she knew he was born to be caught and destroyed.

"You have pointed your gun at my head one too many times today," Lyla said. "I advise you to put your weapon away."

"You are about to meet your maker," the guy replied.

"Someone before used my heart as a chessboard and they knew when to strike. Now life is a chessboard and I know when to attack. I warn you one last time. Put your gun away," she said.

He cocked his gun, while Lyla rapidly somersaulted, using her legs to grab the gun from the grizzly man. She was in autopilot as she shot him, followed by a firestorm of bullets ricocheting. Pow! Pow! Pow! Pow!

The rest of the men threatening her life each caught a bullet like a deadly kiss. In a split second, she watched them all tumble to their death, blood splattering everywhere, hitting her face, gun smoke stinging her eyes. The black smoke cleared, and one man remained standing with rotten rusty eyes beating his chest. She shot him in the head as he landed in the blood bath alongside his semi-automatic.

Everything happened so fast that not even Lyla knew what had just occurred. *Checkmate.*

She heard someone else coming. Lyla took two Shuriken from one of the guys' pocket and slung the steel across the room. They hit the wall and stuck there and, with no time to waste, she did a front flip, cartwheel, and then a back flip, landing right on top of the blades. With bent knees, unbelievably focused strength, and balance, she quickly took out two knives to hold in her hands. Lyla waited patiently for the perfect time to make her move.

The attacker entered the room. Lyla was seemingly no match for this guy. She stood against the wall with only her toes holding her steady.

"Pssssst," Lyla said.

The ugly, strange man turned around and as bold as a tiger, she raised her arms and plunged her knives into either side of his neck, right at the spot most likely to knock him out instantly. Lyla fell to the ground and as she arose, another guy threw a knife at the center of her lower back. She pulled the weapon of opportunity out of her single stab wound and hurled it back at the guy's forehead as she fell to her knees. The knife held the bloody man against the wall, eyes as big as saucers shedding bloody tears.

She lied down in pain until she saw a cigarette lighter. Lyla grabbed the lighter and made a fire stick with the materials around her. She used the fierce heat from the stick to scorch her wound to stop the bleeding, she shouted for Jesus to help her. Then she took a shirt off of one of the guys and tied her back up.

Lyla knew she could not stop trying to escape the deadly room as she felt a second win. She stood up limping with her persistent back pain growing stronger only to be introduced to an abnormally tall individual walking in with an all-black Bruce Lee cat suit, long fat thighs, and a mask with dark menacing eyes. Lyla sized this triumphant low-life up with fingernails like swords as she made her move, adrenaline keeping her keen. She attempted to lift the malleable flesh over her head, but failed.

The heathen choked her. Lyla kicked and squealed as the attacker continued to squeeze. The blood rushed to Lyla's head, leaving her gasping for air. Lyla thought her eyes were going to pop out.

She struggled to release the strong hold with her hands but did not succeed. In a moment of clarity, Lyla grabbed a sharp object from her pocket, and hit the monster. Lyla fell to the ground, clasping her throat, searching for air. She finally caught her breath as the madman charged after her.

Lyla stood up only to be pushed through the opened door and out into a dimly lit hallway, smashing into a glass shelf. She lost her balance and fell to the ground as the masked maniac stomped on her fresh back wound. Lyla screamed in pain as she was picked up by the neck and thrown against the wall.

"Fuck this!" Lyla screamed.

Lyla threw an aggressive punch and made the slugger lose balance. She then threw several additional punches and then lifted the behemoth over her head. With anger on Lyla's face and a furious yell, she lifted one knee high and threw the screeching rogue down on it, breaking the good-for-nothing creep's back in half. Lyla tore off the mask; before her was a dead Spanish woman as beautiful as a shining sun, eyes still screaming.

Lyla stalled. She heard sounds, and followed the echo deeper into what she thought was a building but actually was a dungeon. Lyla saw a closed door. She peeked through its feeding slot only to witness more people being held captive in a dark room with only one light glowing, albeit brightly.

"Please!" a woman called out. "Help me! My skin is burning! I need some heroin!"

Lyla was devastated by what was before her, as she turned around. There was a short, skinny, hairy man with dark shades standing behind her. He looked like a wild man. She quickly lifted him over her head.

"Wait!" the guy said. He knew he was no match for Lyla, who could fight to the death. "I'm on your side."

"Sure you are," Lyla said sarcastically.

"Look! I have the keys to let you and everyone go, and I have Ritchie's money," the guy replied as he shook the keys. For some reason, Lyla believed him, but if he tried anything, she was ready. She dropped the guy down on the ground like a bag of trash.

He got up off the ground and wiped his knees.

"Was that called for?"

She pulled out her gun.

"No, but the bullet that is about to be between your eyes will be."

"Hold up, hold up, I'm on your side remember," the guy reminded.

"Then what are we waiting for," Lyla said.

He quickly began to unleash the innocent prisoners, one of them picking up the abandoned semi-automatic assault weapon for protection.

Lyla grabbed the bag of drugs and asked, "Are they safe to run out of here?"

"Hurry," the man commanded. He grabbed Lyla's hand like they were partners to the end. They both ran out the door and the others followed.

Once outside, a car was at the base of the mountain with no driver. The guy threw her in the backseat of the vehicle and he jumped in the driver's seat, pressing his foot on the gas as the rescued prisoners ran off. Both were quiet.

It was today that Lyla realized pain ignited her alter ego, and fully released her temper. But she was happy to be able to use the secret weapons she learned through taking martial arts training as a young adult and after Nestle saw that Lyla had some potential fight in her; he took it to the next level and trained her at his gym in the city and on the side she learned how to use weapons through her Kung Fu lessons.

An effective warrior I have become and now I have shown it to the world. The moves I learned came in handy today. At least Nestle had been good for something, Lyla thought.

She eyed the driver in his rearview mirror. He looked familiar. In fact, like one of the goons her ex-boyfriend brought with him to her high school.

Lyla could not tell because, of course, he was much older now with a bushy beard and sunglasses that just barely covered the teardrop tattoo under his eyelid. He detected she was checking him out, so he moved the mirror over.

"Where are you taking me?" Lyla asked. He never replied, but after what seemed like eternity, she was at the hospital to get her wound patched up.

Lyla opened the car door.

"Wait," the bearded guy ordered.

"Yeah," Lyla said with one hand on the trigger.

"Take this."

Lyla reached for a fairly large envelope.

"What is this?"

"Don't open it right now," the guy said.

"When do I open it?" she questioned.

"You will know when," he answered.

"Okay," Lyla said.

"Watch your back, keep it cool, and get rid of the weapons Lyla," he said and the mystery savior sped off.

Lyla did not look back. All anyone could see was Lyla's smoke. She wanted to get her stab wound to the back cleaned, pack the drugs, and get out of Mexico.

After the doctors treated her wound, Lyla went to the bathroom to do what would have been unthinkable just a few short months ago: she had to stuff the heroin in her ass and her pussy. Now she knew why Ritchie loved assplay so much; he was grooming her to be an international mule to hold bags upon bags of heroin. He loved her over and over again to make her butt hole large enough to stuff a lamp in.

Instead of using bags, she used condoms. Lyla filled one condom. Then she took that filled condom and put it inside of another condom to prevent it from breaking inside her. Lyla tied a tight knot and, for the first time in her life, she put the drugs inside of her bruised pussy still in pain from the brutal rape.

She shoveled more heroin in her coochie and then put dozens more of the drug pellets in her ass, using oil to help break her open even more.

The plan was to meet the security guard Ritchie paid off to get her through customs with flying colors. When she arrived, everything seemed to be going as planned, until the security guard she had to meet at customs was not there. No worries, Lyla was next to last in the long line, but the line was moving quickly, and she did not know what to do.

Lyla was sweating bullets again. Out of nowhere, one of the bags fell out of her coochie while standing in line.

Man, I should have on jeans. The only garment she could grab from the dungeon was a halfway decent knee length dress from the dead girl's body.

"You dropped something," an elderly man behind her said as he cleaned his bifocals. Lyla quickly picked up the drugs, hoping he did not know what it was. Thankfully, no one else was paying attention, but the real back breaker was the security camera staring at her from the ceiling. Lyla put the drugs in her bag and got herself together, but her heart was still pounding like when she and Ritchie first made love.

The next person in line was Lyla. As she was called, a man came running down the hallway.

"I got this! I'm finished eating!" the security guard Lyla was looking for hollered.

"It's about time," the guard standing post snapped.

Lyla was jovial to be out of danger, but she could have smacked him for scaring her like that.

She whispered to the guard, "Get rid of the security footage."

Chapter 20

After the Mexico fiasco, Lyla could not wait to confront Ritchie. She felt like she was in a Lifetime movie and she had war stories to tell. *Goodness, I'm just a model.*

Lyla assumed Ritchie would be proud to know that she was a down chick for him as she removed the heroin from her body. A bit of the heroin leaked through the condom. It was stinging, but it was just enough to numb her coochie to stop her pain from the rape.

The doctor in Mexico did an examination on Lyla for the sexual assault. She was blessed to be alive and grateful the doctor said there was no permanent physical damage. Lyla took off her wig and took out her contact lenses. *I'm so relieved to get these...*

"Did you see the letter?" the superintendant's assistant said in a husky voice, interrupting her train of thoughts.

Lyla promptly covered the drugs.

"What?" Lyla wondered.

The assistant directed her attention to her dresser near the doorway.

"Look. Your boyfriend Ritchie asked me to sit it in your room."

"First of all, he is not my boyfriend," Lyla corrected. "He is a friend."

"Yeah, okay," the assistant snorted.

Although Lyla hid the fact she was Ritchie's girlfriend, people assumed they were a couple. Lyla saw the letter with a rare loose diamond lying next to it and continued to say, "Second of all, thank you for letting me know, but please knock before you come in the front door, not to mention my bedroom."

"I thought you were still away on your trip, sorry." *Liar.*

There was an enduring love letter enclosed in a glossy gold envelope. Lyla traced her finger over the fancy envelope, eventually reaching inside to read the sweet and pleasant words Ritchie chose to flatter her with. She then held the beautiful diamond high, watching it sparkle as she directed it towards the light.

Lyla put the diamond in a safe place still thinking about the touching words in Ritchie's letter. She appreciated him so much as she showered and washed her hair.

After showering she shook out the tiny water droplets from her hair as she walked back to her room in hopes to take a quick nap, but instead she found herself staring at the bedroom wall in front of her as she moved back towards the wall behind, sliding down it slowly. She just took a shower, but did not feel clean and she should be feeling good right now, as she just received a lovely new diamond and a beautiful love letter from Ritchie, but the excitement from it all only lasted for a few minutes. Lyla pressed her knees to her chest and wrapped her arms around her lower legs tightly, her watery eyes were exposed, nose and mouth tucked down in her black-and-blue knees.

She sat in her quiet room like a breathless mannequin until she gushed out a frightful cry and shouted, "Sex, money, and drugs! A rock star life I'm not happy about. I have betrayed my principals once again!" But the life drew her closer to Ritchie, and though her spiritual beliefs attempted to tear them apart the lifestyle was getting the best of her.

On top of that, visions of the rape in Mexico, the group rape, her abortion, and being shot appeared in her mind.

She turned on her side and slid down to the floor into a fetal position and continued to weep, bitterly asking God to help her.

At the hospital in Mexico, Lyla was told to seek counseling when she returned to the States. Since she missed her session with the pastor she called him, continuously crying and shaking while she dialed the number.

"Hello," the pastor said.

"Help me," she cried.

"Lyla?" the pastor said.

"Yes," Lyla confirmed.

"What's wrong?" Pastor Bill asked.

"I have a rage in me I cannot hide any longer," Lyla admitted. "It hurts, it hurts!"

"Lyla come to my office today," the pastor insisted.

"The pain!" Lyla screamed. "I have dark urges and this pain may never go away!"

"Lyla!"

"I wish he was still alive so I could kill him! Like he tried to kill me!" Lyla cried.

"An eye for an eye. There has got to be another way," the pastor said.

Lyla stood up, grabbed a lamp, and flung it against the wall.

"This is not going to hold me back."

"Lyla! Stop trying to handle this by yourself! Let God help you. Come in today!" the pastor said without backing down.

"I have to go, Pastor Bill," she said.

"Lyla!" the pastor shouted. She hung up.

Lyla looked up and notice she smashed her long mirror instead of the wall. *What's seven years of bad luck? I can't seem to get away from it anyways,* as she stood in front of the cracked mirror, affecting a confident pose, air drying hair growing so full and curly. She then dried her tears, buried her tragedies, and slipped on a fitted black cotton spandex bodysuit. Lastly, she put on her game face and kept it moving. Perhaps this was foolish, but she was not going to die mentally or physically.

Lyla contacted Ritchie to let him know she was back in town. He sounded upset to hear from her.

She asked him, "What is the matter with you?"

"I have some bad news. Unfortunately, you did not get the make-up ad," Ritchie answered.

"Okay, life goes on," Lyla said.

"Because you got the make-up campaign! You're going to be everywhere, Mademoiselle!"

She screamed and thanked God. Lyla could not believe it. *See I don't need counseling, everything is fine,* Lyla thought.

"This is magnificent. I thought you were going to tell me something else," Lyla replied.

"Like what? You think I set a trap to get you killed in Mexico?" Ritchie said.

"Well," she said.

"Or leave your DNA somewhere so you would be thrown in jail for a very long time for something you did not do?" Ritchie continued.

Lyla hesitated.

"Not quite. But that's psycho, why are you thinking that way?"

"I'm joking!" Ritchie laughed.

Lyla gave Ritchie her new address and told him to come to her place. She may have been staying for free at her super's apartment buildings, but he certainly did not make it simple for her. Each day she did not know where she would dwell. *I know where I'm from but I don't know where I live,* Lyla said to herself.

Her super constantly changed her room. The bad part was he would either call her at the last minute to move and if he couldn't find Lyla, he would move her personal things for her, sometimes losing her things. She could have sworn she put her super large gummy bear she received as a gift in her room, but it was missing. Her Gucci belt was also gone, along with some money.

He also knew information he shouldn't. For this reason, she had to keep her personal documents and valuables on her person, especially the mysterious envelope.

Lyla appreciated her super but she also felt like she indirectly made him plenty of money, and should be able to stay put in one place.

For instance, Lyla was very creative and her super acknowledged that. One day, she turned one of his train apartments into a five bedroom and rented out the sections.

He saw that he could make some good money, so less than a week later, her superintendent made the sections into actual rooms. It was great, but inconvenient for the tenants who wanted to move in. Lyla had to tell them that the rooms were on hold, and she had to stay in asbestos and anything else that was lingering in the apartment alone while it was under construction.

One of the girls who wanted to move in was from Lyla's modeling agency. The girl had already paid a two thousand dollar deposit. Lyla's super gave the girl an option to stay at another building of his, but she declined and demanded her money back. Lyla's mistake in the matter was giving her shady super the cash, because he immediately alleged that Lyla had never given him the money.

The girl threatened to sue Lyla, and when she told her super, he responded, "things will smell for a few days, but everything will quiet down." Lyla's super had a way of saying things. If it wasn't her crazy lover, it was her crazy super.

Still, she remembered the time her super found out, at the last minute that it was her birthday. Lyla never made a big deal about her birthday, but he was knocking on Lyla's door at 11:59 pm with a cake and candles. That was a special and sweet moment, and reminded her that in the mist of all of his riff raff, her super had her best interest at heart in his own little way.

Ritchie arrived at Lyla's place with a bottle of wine. She stood in the door like a mystified shadow. Lyla smacked Ritchie's face before he could say a word.

He asked, without a flinch as usual, "What was that for?"

"You have no idea." She jumped into his arms and they kissed. Lyla thanked him for the diamond and the sweet letter. "Everything went well in Mexico, baby."

She hadn't forgotten that the guy in Mexico told her to watch her back and to keep it cool. If Ritchie did plan to get her killed, she wanted him to be confused.

"So you put that H up your rat hole?" Ritchie grinned.

"Excuse me," Lyla said.

"It's just an expression," Ritchie shrugged.

"I got your stuff," Lyla said. She handed him the bag.

"Let's celebrate!" Ritchie persuasively announced.

Celebration was Ritchie's MO when they accomplished something. In this case, they both had a lot to be grateful for.

"Congratulations on your modeling gig and your safe return from Mexico. *Salut!*" Ritchie said. Lyla and Ritchie lifted their large tulip-shaped wine glasses by the stem, pinky finger held high to toast. "I'm glad you made it back to me. I can't believe you pulled it off, my love." "For you I would climb the highest mountain peak. Swim the deepest ocean, even kill for you," Lyla said.

Ritchie gave her an odd stare.

"Did you get hurt in Mexico?" Ritchie asked, though the answer was visibly clear.

"Yeah, I was shot at and stabbed," Lyla replied. "See." She showed him her wound.

"How did you escape?"

"I did what I had to do. And I followed your instructions," Lyla said.

"Did you kill someone?" Ritchie wondered.

"Maybe, in self-defense," Lyla said.

"How many did you kill?" he asked.

"Enough," Lyla answered.

"I'm scared of you now, but it is turning me on," Ritchie smiled. He cuffed her hand in his and kissed it.

"Whatever," she said, yanking her hand away. "What're the twenty questions for?"

"I'm concerned. My love for you is real and forever," Ritchie responded. He reached in his pocket to pull out cocaine. "I will take care of you and be beside you in any situation. I definitely will keep you safe from crazy people."

"You deal heroin, but you use cocaine?" Lyla said as he sniffed a little.

"Don't use your own supply," Ritchie replied. "I don't have to worry about that, now do I? Were you on drugs in Mexico?"

"Don't go there with me Ritchie," Lyla warned as she held him. She was sure he did not want to know about the needle she was stuck with.

"Just stick with the plan for now on," Ritchie said as he shoved her away, heroin falling on the ground.

"Our first argument. How cute is that? Can we make up?" Lyla said seductively.

"Where is my money?" Ritchie questioned as they continued to bicker back and forth.

She sipped some wine and replied, "Oh yeah...that. Well, Ritchie while I was getting shot at and stabbed I ran out so fast I forgot the money. If it hadn't been for some guy saving me, we would not be talking right now."

What could Ritchie say? He surely did not want to ruffle her feathers. The last thing he needed was Lyla asking too many questions, especially if he wanted her killed out there.

"It doesn't matter to me. That money was for you, I'm already well-to-do...*Salut*," Ritchie said. They finished their glasses of wine, and made up all through the night.

Chapter 21

Lyla was happy to be back in normalcy and not being used as a body packer. Although she and Ritchie had been seeing each other for almost a year, at times she would rather be friends and business partners exclusively, and not his girlfriend. But he would beg her to stay with him and of course he would say his famous line.

"You don't understand my situation."

Sometimes Ritchie told Lyla his marriage was not working out and he was going to leave his wife, but he couldn't because they had to keep a specific image to look good for his companies. *To look good for his companies,* Lyla thought. *So she's a trophy wife?*

While that sounded great, Lyla was not getting her hopes up, not to mention, she never asked him to leave his wife. On the other hand, his words bounced around her head. She couldn't help wondering what it would be like if it was only her, minus Ritchie's wife and kids.

She talked to Ritchie about it, but for some reason, when Lyla said the word relationship, reality hit and he was frantic. His response would be somewhere out of left field.

"What relationship? We don't have a relationship." But five minutes later, she was his girlfriend again.

Though she knew he didn't mean it when he said hurtful things, it made Lyla want to only focus on gathering enough valuable information for her career and moving on. But at the moment, they were comfortable with one another, addicted to the secrecy, lust, excitement, and she found that she was not just Ritchie's conquest. The relationship became her antidote to all of the things going wrong in her life and to his dissatisfaction with his marriage. *A perfect storm some may say.*

In any case, Lyla and Ritchie met at an Italian restaurant to talk about their careers and where they wanted to be in the future. She noticed he did not have on his fancy watch, and recalled that this was happening more frequently. Anyway, he convinced Lyla that he could get her where she wanted to be in three years. She believed him because, so far, based on the meetings she sat in on, he seemed well liked and professional.

Now, Lyla was able to tell him about some of her dreams, but the ones she was working on the most, other than modeling, were her clothing line called *Steam* and her cartoon about fashion models called *Air Heads.*

Ritchie saw more of a future with the clothing design than the cartoon, so they focused on that, as they designed the logo and brainstormed ways to move forward. He said he would teach Lyla the secrets of business. *Electric!* This was what she was looking forward to.

In the next meeting, Lyla was sure he was going to continue to help move her goals along, but that wasn't so. He used his gift for gab and somehow turned everything around. Unexpectedly, Lyla was working only on his projects while her ideas took a backseat.

She remembered him telling her, "People always wonder how I walk out of meetings, having accomplished everything I set out to." Now he was doing the same to her. Lyla was dealing with a pro.

She found herself learning about his business and slowly forgetting about her modeling career and not pursuing Steam, or anything else. Now Lyla was working at his accounting office and for his entertainment business full time. Lyla abandoned her blog. She was abandoning her life. Lyla felt like Daniel in *Karate Kid*, and Ritchie was her Mr. Miyagi. Wax on, wax off.

Furthermore, she was attending meetings for the cosmetics line, not as a model as planned, but as Ritchie's assistant. Apparently, the Russian lady had another girl in mind to model for the ads. Lyla was hardly surprised; she assumed his watch had been there lately. Now, she believed the make-up contract was actually a smoke screen to take her mind off him possibly killing her in Mexico.

What happens in the dark will come out into the light? I will get to the bottom of this.

From time to time, she would bring up her ideas, but it never mattered. One day, Ritchie came to her house after an anniversary dinner with his wife, and they had sex. Afterwards she brought up her ideas again and he fell asleep. Well, Lyla had worn him out, after all.

She just saw *Sex and the City 2* with some girlfriends. Lyla normally identified with Carrie because of her style and sophistication, but she wanted to be Samantha in bed for once.

In the movie, the actress spread her legs open and screamed, "Yes! Yes! Yes!" while having sex with one of her younger boy toys.

Lyla wanted to do the same thing.

Ritchie worked on her buttoned down cotton shirt, fitted blue jeans, sexy crimson red heels hitting the floor. Her silky pretty white thong was shortly pulled off with his teeth. The flames of passion, love, and desire controlled them while

Ritchie and Lyla were fucking, and Lyla did just what she said she was going to do.

He pounded her insides while she laid on her back, legs wrapped around his waist and she screamed, "Yes! Yes! Yes!" Lyla then used her strength to flip Ritchie into a sitting position on the edge of the bed, showing off her flexibility, catering to every indulgence.

He touched his side and shouted, "Mademoiselle!"

Lyla slowed down.

"I'm in pain!" he said.

"Shut up and be a man!" Lyla said. She straddled him like a jockey and rode him like he was her horse, facing the wall in front of her. "Move the covers, they're in the way!" Lyla screamed, throwing the blanket away from her bare legs. "Is it all in? Faster! Faster! Faster!" she continued as she swung her legs to the center. Lyla then stopped and jumped to her feet!

"What the hell is wrong?" Ritchie asked.

"Shhh," she responded, placing her finger gently over her lips.

From behind the closed door of Lyla's room, she heard a faint movement and then low voices.

"Somebody is in the apartment," Lyla said, standing by her bedroom door butt balled naked. She opened it and listened.

He stared at her ass and muttered, "Nobody is in here."

Lyla's super finally moved her into a permanent duplex four bedroom apartment that she decorated in style. When guests walked in, a beautifully aging wooden round table with smells of delicious candles from Barney's, a relaxing water fountain and an antique chandelier hanging from the high ceiling — on a dimmer for just the right lighting — greeted them at the front door.

A custom beaded curtain separated the foyer from the living and dining room spaces, which she had decorated in Japanese style to give her peace of mind. Along the huge windows sat a long brightly painted bench with plants, and an indoor garden of vegetables and fruits that smiled back at her.

Lyla's friend helped her paint the rooms using a sponge to bring the texture out in her inviting personalized kitchen.

Her friend always told her, "If you just paint the place, it will look finished." Lyla's most distinct room was her canary yellow bedroom with a big brass bed with just enough pillows to position herself, a soft delicate bone-white duvet and flannel sheets, bamboo blinds, a huge wooden chest to sit Lyla's television and up-to-date music system on, a shabby chic tent she designed herself for a camping and reading excursion when need be, and a butterfly painting, made by her grandfather.

Her grandfather passed away a few years ago, but she always kept in mind when he used to say, "You are a Supermodel."

Across the hall of the bedroom was her New York City bathroom with black walls, a transparent subway map shower curtain, and matching bathroom accessories. Her guests were able to write on the walls in chalk, graffiti style. The room was always a conversation piece. The only thing she had to replace was the slow winding ceiling fan in her living room that had an annoying screeching sound. Ritchie offered to buy her a new one.

Lyla's super recently moved a couple into the room above hers, but she thought they were alone. If word got out that Lyla was dabbling with a married man her squeaky clean reputation would be ruined.

This is my life, Lyla thought. *I'm not proud of being with a married man, but I have to deal with it, not anyone else, including my super, and I want to keep it that way.*

Lyla did not hear anymore noises as she scrambled to the DVD player, kicking Ritchie's shirt out of the way. She hurriedly popped in a porno called *Hit it from the Back Door* and Lyla turned it up loud. It showed a girl squirting causing Lyla to jump back and grunt. *Damn cheap girl.*

Lyla rewind the movie to the beginning and they watched the provocative porn, it made their blood boil sending electrifying emotions through their bodies without even having to touch each other. The porn stars were stimulating pure intoxication as Ritchie's cock rose. Lyla looked over her shoulder peeking at him. She did not need to say a word. Lyla knew what to do as she backed her naked ass up, the head of his dick touching her ass crevice.

She lifted her ass allowing him to have a better angle as the sounds of penetration drove her crazy. Lyla was not wasting any more time. She began to moan as his hard dick penetrated her anal cavity, the freaky, sweaty sensation, making her climb up on her knees as she caressed her clitoris.

"AH! Ritchie! Fuck me!"

He did it so well as usual, no lubrication needed. Clap, clap, clap were the sounds of Lyla's butt cheeks as he thrust and plunged in and out; her bodily fluids splattered down the side of her leg.

"Fuck me daddy, Fuck me!" He pulled her hair as he climbed off of one sore knee; clap, clap, clap, clap.

She stopped right when he was getting ready to climax and then she went back and forth, back and forth, stopping at the top part of his head and then went back and forth again and stopped; driving Ritchie crazy as he said, "La La La La La, Lyla." She repeated this game until finally she let him let it loose as he pulled out and nutted on her face. A glob of it stuck to her forehead as he said, "AHHHHHHHH!"

After that everlasting moment of sex, they were both worn out as Lyla's breath came out in short pants while she wiped away cum with her hand and looked wildly for a towel to wipe the rest.

Lyla had never seen so much cum in her life. It was enough to flood a large bottle. She couldn't talk after cumming nine times; the rapes were definitely buried.

Lyla smoked her last cigarette and drank some Saint Ives. *The only thing missing from this raunchy R-rated event was an old school 2 Live Crew song in the background.*

Ritchie was astounded.

"You have demonstrated technique that is far from an innocent Christian woman's, Mademoiselle," he said as she used her one hand to yank off the sheets drenched in sweat and semen to throw in the washing machine.

"I never said I was innocent. I just want to do it with my husband, but you'll do for now, my love," Lyla said, forgetting to ash as usual. *The ash hanging off my cigarette was as long as Ritchie's dick*, she giggled to herself, *so short and skinny perfect for my ass.*

Lyla searched for her new pack of cigarettes, and then she happened to look in her mirror. *One thing I love about having sex with Ritchie is that when the sex is over, my skin looks like a baby's bottom, like I just drank eight glasses of water.*

She found her pack of cigarettes as Ritchie said, "Ash!" Too late! Lyla watched the ashes hit her floor while she put her cigarette in a cup with water and out of nowhere screamed, "Oh my gosh, oh my gosh!" Lyla dropped to the floor. "Ah! Oh yes, oh yeah!

"What the fuck," Ritchie said. Lyla laid on the floor, her body feeling numb.

"Did you just cum again?" Ritchie assumed.

"Yes," Lyla confirmed.

"You need to ash more often," Ritchie grinned.

"Ha, ha," Lyla replied, returning to the bed, offering a cigarette to Ritchie. He took one. "Thank you."

"Don't ever say 'thank you' when someone gives you a cigarette," Lyla said.

"Why?" Ritchie asked.

"Because I'm offering you cancer," Lyla answered. "Just take it, no need to say thank you."

"So tell me about your pain," Lyla said. "Was the pain from all of the sensational sex we just had." She stood up on the bed and demonstrated some of her moves. "I worked it and I can't wait to show you what I'm going to do to you next."

"Seriously, my love, you have to be careful with me," Ritchie replied.

"Why?" Lyla asked.

"I was in my Porsche going over a hundred miles and..."

"Were you sightseeing," Lyla interrupted.

"You are so funny," Ritchie said sarcastically. "I got into a car accident. I damaged my liver and it gives me great pain. I can hardly walk sometimes."

"Okay I got you, boo boo," Lyla joked as Ritchie farted. They both paused, and a few seconds later, filled the room with laughter as Lyla proceeded to sing, "Ritchie is a jolly good farter; Ritchie is a jolly good farter, which no one can deny. Now, that was no pussy fart unless you have a pussy."

"Fuck you!" Ritchie laughed.

His fart smelled like a filet of fish.

She did not tell him that but she did say, "Don't worry it smells like flowers."

"Funny girl."

So, yes, I do understand why suddenly sleeping Ritchie fell asleep easily and did not listen to me when I talked about my business ventures, Lyla thought. *But honestly, wild sex or not, it seemed like he was always awake when it pertained to his cause, but fell asleep on what I wanted.*

Instead of gently putting him on his side to stop his loud snoring, she ignored what he just said about his pain and shoved him.

"What are you doing?" Ritchie asked.

"Oh, nothing," she answered. Ritchie shrugged and he fell back to sleep.

Additionally, he seemed to be a lot of talk but no action. She had not seen any significant business deals go through, either from the meetings she attended or the ones she didn't.

Lyla did not want to think Ritchie was a loser but this Prince Charming was not so charming anymore. It was becoming more like a suffering fairy tale. She noticed he was wearing his fancy watch today.

Chapter 22

Lyla did not like to celebrate her own birthday but Ritchie's was fast approaching and she wanted to do something special for him, especially since the relationship seems to be going down a slippery slope. She thought it would be nice to have an intimate dinner at her place. Ritchie was okay with it and he offered to cook a dish. Thoughtful, and though she told him not to worry about it, Ritchie would not take no for an answer.

Lyla wanted to get her hair done, a new outfit, and tan. The whole shebang. She made an appointment for her tanning session. No one knew she tanned at the tanning salon, not even Ritchie.

She was getting ready to send a text to her girlfriend to see if she wanted to go for a day of pampering, but her girlfriend had sent her a text earlier. Lyla hadn't seen it until just then. Her girlfriend said she had something to tell Lyla.

She also saw a text from Ritchie asking Lyla to send him a naked picture.

Lyla wrote: "Sexting? That's teenage stuff or r u going to keep it in ur wallet, cuz u luv me so much."

Instead of texting her girlfriend back, Lyla called.

"Hello," her friend said in her peppy voice.

"Hello Isabella," Lyla replied.

"I'm sorry but I just received your text. It's been a little crazy."

"That's alright," her girlfriend said.

"What did you have to tell me?" Lyla asked.

"Can you meet me for lunch?"

"Yes," Lyla said. "Where?"

"Let's get some jerk chicken on Twenty Third and Sixth Avenue," Isabella recommended.

"Jerk chicken, ummm," Lyla said, discontentedly. "I want some Kentucky Fried Chicken."

Her friend laughed.

"That's why I love you Lyla."

"Better yet, I'm going to get my hair done at the Dominican hair salon, do you need to get yours done?" Lyla asked.

"Yes," her friend answered. "Sounds like a plan. We can talk there and figure out where we are going for lunch."

"Awesome," Lyla smiled.

"I wonder how much it cost to get my hair washed, blow dried, and cut up," Lyla continued.

"Cut up? Don't you mean cut. You make it sound like a school project," Isabella laughed.

"You know what I mean," Lyla cackled.

"I don't know how much it cost, but seriously when I find another type of hair salon I'm thinking about not going to them anymore."

Lyla was baffled because her friend was the one who introduced her to the Dominicans.

"Why not?" Lyla questioned.

"The blow dryer is too hot for my hair," she answered.

"How is it too hot for your hair when people use a hot comb," Lyla replied. "It's the same amount of heat. Y'all need to get with it and stop hating. The Dominicans are doing wonders for the hair especially mine. I have not seen my hair look so good since I was a little girl."

"Yah," her girlfriend said.

"Yes," Lyla said. "And you should know; you have been there since the beginning."

"Well. I don't use a hot comb so I wouldn't know. I got white girl hair," her friend reminded.

"That's because you are white," Lyla said.

"And what you know about hot combs," her friend said. "Your hair cannot take a hot comb? You are so silly Lyla."

"I was just using an analogy," Lyla said.

"Use another one," Isabella laughed. "But seriously, I understand what you are saying. Alright, I will see you Saturday, at our normal time, right?

"I will be there!" Lyla said excitedly.

Lyla was happy to know the specialty knowledge was rubbing off on her girlfriend as she laughed out loud.

Chapter 23

Meanwhile in Connecticut, it was a cold and dark night. While Ritchie was unloading the groceries he gathered at the store, his family was fast asleep. Although it was the middle of March, there was still snow on the ground. The snow created harshness that made winter even more dreadful, but being inside felt warmer and nicer for it. Ritchie was brewing up his infamous meat and vegetable recipe.

3 cups of chicken broth

1 cup of green pepper

1 cup of yellow pepper

1 cup of red pepper

½ cup of carrots

1 cup of mushroom

1 cup of onion

½ can of tomato plums

1 pound of your choice of meat

Simmer until tender and season to taste.

The fresh vegetables, authentic spices, and herbs boiled like lava in a slow cooker for thirty minutes. He then cut up pieces of meat to roast over the flaming fire like marshmallows.

When the tender meat was ready, he added the tasty vegetables. His wife still had some left over sauce from the day before. He poured it over the drained meat and vegetables. The dish was ready for him and Lyla.

His son Danny came into the kitchen and asked, "When are we going to eat, daddy?"

"Not tonight," Ritchie answered.

"Daddy will fix you breakfast, but here...taste a little piece of meat Danny boy."

"Tastes good!" Danny said with excitement.

"Shhhh, don't tell mommy. Now go to bed," Ritchie said, shoveling a line up his nose and preparing a killer Bloody Mary to end the night.

Chapter 24

Ritchie's birthday was here and Lyla looked like a lobster! Her tan did not turn out so well this time, and now her secret was out.

Despite Lyla burning rice, water, or whatever else, she took a big risk by making the dinner all herself, but it seemed to be worth it because between the aromas of her Dolce & Gabbana perfume and the food she prepared with love, it was as if the smell locked him in his chair when he arrived, and Lyla felt like she succeeded in preparing a scrumptious feast fit for a king. As Ritchie gave Lyla the dish he made, he saw something so amazing, so well thought out, it was unforgettable.

"Mmmm, it smells delicious," Lyla said pleasantly. "You are the most perfect precious jewel in my crown," Ritchie replied charmingly. Lyla blushed as she walked to the kitchen to add his dish to the food she already had arranged on the plates for them.

"Everything is ready, except for the dessert. I'm waiting for that to finish baking," Lyla said.

"Okay, my love," Ritchie replied.

"You know I feel bad about you cooking on your birthday," Lyla said.

"Oh, I don't mind. I love to cook, even on my birthday, Mademoiselle," Ritchie responded.

"Well I'm glad you did because it smells nice. I'm so hungry! I can't wait to taste it," Lyla smiled, feeling okay about sounding selfish on his birthday.

A few moments later, she says in her sexy voice, "Considered for two, our table is ready." Ritchie smiled and Lyla gave him a long, slow French kiss as the candles flickered softly. "There is no one on this earth tonight except for me, you and candlelight," Lyla continued.

"I am here, spellbound by your beauty, your soft peaceful face sent from God above," Ritchie said. "You were sent by an angel for me to love." Her heart skipped a beat. She was so happy to see him and everything was perfect.

Lyla drank her glass of wine before eating, as usual, while Ritchie ate his dinner.

"The food is bursting with flavor; you smell divine and your flawless, lean body looks awesome in your dress," Ritchie continued.

She softly kissed him on his bottom lip, pleased to know he likes her cooking.

"Thank you and HAPPY BIRTHDAY!" Lyla then tasted some of Ritchie's vegetable and meat dish. "Oh so lovely," Lyla continued. "This is so tasty. What is in the sauce?"

"It's a family secret," Ritchie said cryptically. "My mom used to make it for us all the time growing up. I'm happy you like it."

"How sweet of you to bring this," she said, putting a bright smile on her face.

Lyla couldn't stop sucking the juice from the meat, as she savored every bite of the mouthwatering vegetables, flavors changing with the color and temperature.

"Yum. That hit the spot, babe. My hunger is satisfied," Lyla continued.

"It does not compare to what you did tonight for me," Ritchie said, observing the extraordinary display he saw when he first walked in the door. "You really went all out, and it's all for me. What a special night."

Lyla prepared a dish from different parts of the world. The smells of food from Brazil, Spain, Italy, India, and France filled the air as the flags, hung in the background and the music played from those places.

"We are celebrating your birthday all around the world," she said. "It goes with your tan," Ritchie joked. "So you noticed," Lyla giggled. "Of course," Ritchie smiled. "I always knew you tanned."

Ritchie kissed Lyla, ready to undress her. He felt the fire kindling in his heart.

"Wait!" Lyla ordered.

As it turned out, the sounds Lyla thought she heard while Ritchie and Lyla were having sex were real. Her roommate was listening to them. This was what Isabella had to tell Lyla. Isabella was friends with Lyla's new roommate but her and Lyla were closer, so Isabella kept Lyla informed.

Lyla's girlfriend told her the roommate told everyone including her super. The roommate also put her two cents in and told everyone that Ritchie seemed like the married type. Isabella asked Lyla if Ritchie was married, but Lyla did not answer her.

"Let's go downstairs," Lyla said to Ritchie, checking on the dessert in the oven.

"What's wrong?" Ritchie wondered.

"Nothing, I just need some air," Lyla said, shutting the oven door. "The dessert will be done any day now."

"That's alright," Ritchie said. "I will stop by after work tomorrow to eat some."

"Ha, ha," Lyla replied as they headed downstairs.

They stood by the front door having an after dinner cigarette. *Those were the best.* She told him what happened and why she felt uncomfortable being intimate. He did not seem fazed, as usual, but it was tragic for Lyla.

Ritchie did send the nosy perverted roommate a text from Lyla's phone that made her feel so stupid for listening in on two consenting adults having spectacular sex, that the girl ended up moving out the following week from embarrassment.

Even so, Lyla's saw her reputation going down, right along with their relationship, if things did not change. The superintendant approached the front gate with his three daughters and his wife. They saw Lyla smoking for the first time.

"That's just want I needed," Lyla said with frustration. "Now he knows I smoke and I have sex." By the look on her super's face, he was not very fond of Ritchie.

Lyla and Ritchie returned upstairs to finally try her sprinkle surprise birthday cake for dessert and have another glass of wine.

He blew out the candles and Lyla asked, "So, how many birthdays have you had so far?"

"Ha, ha, ha. I told you forty-four already, but as of today, forty-five," Ritchie said, knowing he did not.

"You never told me your age," Lyla said. "Not that it matters. So a young forty-five, huh?"

He quickly changed the subject and told Lyla how grateful he was for the amazing evening.

"I'm glad you're happy. I wish I could do something nice for my own birthday," she replied.

"Why don't you?" Ritchie asked. Lyla thought back to her less enjoyable birthday moments.

"I can't believe he killed Freckles. My birthday gift. Birthdays don't matter anyways. They just remind me of the day I was born into this tragic situation."

"You kidding me right. Why are you here at the hotel I work for with this hoe, on my birthday?"

"I don't want to talk about it right now, but one of my birthdays I'm going to go all out and make up for all of the ones I missed. Maybe go to Paris with a group of my friends and have a slumber party and talk about my exciting modeling career," Lyla laughed.

"Do it," Ritchie insisted.

"I just need some money to do it," Lyla replied. "When can I get paid?"

"You are not ready," Ritchie said.

"What do you mean I'm not ready?" Lyla snapped.

"Why should I pay you?" Ritchie asked. "What have you learned?"

Lyla wanted tonight to remain perfect, but the one person she thought she could count on, just insulted her, and this beautiful night turned into an explosive argument with her only screaming about never having any money. She would like her bills paid, especially since she was working for free for all hours of the night. It's a shame Lyla cannot get a simple phone bill paid and then thought, *Why should he pay me?*

Lyla had a unique gift to give him after dinner, a gift made just for him. She bought twenty-seven gift bags, and each had a letter on the front of the bag with his desired item beginning with the letter. For instance, he loved apples so Lyla put an apple inside the letter "A" bag and that was the first bag she threw at him followed by all twenty-seven bags flying across the room, Lyla hoping one of them would hit his head. He swayed back and forth like they were playing dodge ball.

A key dropped out of the "K" bag.

She stopped to pick it up.

"This was supposed to represent the key to my heart; now I'm locking the door." Lyla tossed the key as hard, and as far as she could. Ritchie walked towards the front door to leave but first with a cold demeanor he said, "You threw your baggage at me. Stay away!" He opened the door and Lyla ran after him and clutched the bottom of his ankles, begging him to stay, thinking back to the incident with Casmir.

"I grabbed his ankles and begged for him to stay and he still walked out the door."

Lyla caught herself and let him go.

"No! Don't walk out. You are in pain, and that's why you're speaking this way."

"You have to control yourself," Ritchie replied.

"How can I when you insulted me," Lyla said. "I'm ready. I have learned so much from you Ritchie."

"Prove it! And you need to tell me what happened in your past; if not, there is no us," Ritchie warned. He slammed the door and left. Lyla paused at the door wishing it was transparent so she could get one last look at him while he walked away. He loved to change things around on her, and like a lost sock in a dryer, Ritchie disappeared for the rest of the night.

Lyla assumed he ran off to go home to receive more gifts from his wife and kids. She had mixed feelings about everything as she did one of her home remedies to get rid of her bad tan, but Lyla did not mean to say the door to her heart was locked. *Ritchie has my heart.*

The flashback Lyla had a few minutes ago had filled her with ire. She fell asleep thinking about the flashback.

In the middle of the night, Lyla woke up full of sweat and tears screaming, "No! No! No!" She sat up, pushed her damp covers away, and threw her trembling hands over her face, letting out a deep, long breath to cool down. She dreamt her ex-boyfriend Casmir was still alive.

It was almost like he was in her room, laying close, giving her a kiss. The pressure - the strong energy felt like he was pulling her to wherever he was. She was reassured to know it was only a dream as she regained consciousness, but it seemed so real.

What didn't seem real was Ritchie.

She thought about him, since she knew there was no way she would be able to fall back to sleep. *There is something about him that is not right. Things weren't adding up. He talked about driving to New York in one of his cars, but he always had an excuse. He claimed to have money, but he calculated every penny spent. Yelling at cab drivers for taking him the long way, which was not true at all. People with money looked for deals too, but goodness.*

Regardless, Lyla went on with their relationship as is. Despite everything, she couldn't overstate how great this man became in her life.

Ritchie loved when the office was clean, so as a peace offering, she went to the office and tidied it up. When she finally caught up with Ritchie, he thanked her. Lyla apologized for being a jerk, and they had a civilized conversation, although he did admit to her that he thought she was with him for what he could do for her.

How can he say that when I don't even know who this man is; he is such a mystery; he hardly tells me anything. And it would have been nice if he had told me he had decided not to pay me until I "prove" myself.

Ritchie reminded Lyla of the guy in the movie "True Lies" and it was not Arnold Schwarzenegger. More like the phony guy trying to con Schwarzenegger's wife by acting like he was bigger than what he was.

"That is how Ritchie acts," she said in an accusing voice.

Lyla reminisced about the time she was in his office and he was speaking to his wife on the phone in the hallway.

He came back in the room just so she heard him say, "Make sure the helicopter is ready." Lyla supposed Ritchie and his wife had a private helicopter waiting for them and he specifically wanted Lyla to hear that part to impress her. Little did he know, none of this impressed Lyla. She loved him, but not for his worldly possessions. *Maybe one day he would really get to know me,* Lyla thought.

Moreover, although she loved Ritchie and for the most part enjoyed being his girlfriend, he irritated Lyla at times. Especially when he changed on her or questioned her

Christianity. Guys loved to do that to her. Lyla told them she wanted to do things the right way and as soon as she gave in, they made her feel guilty and then claimed she was not a Christian.

She did not appreciate that shit.

Anyway, Lyla opened up to Ritchie. *Women hold secrets close to their hearts, but when they talk, be ready,* Lyla thought.

Ritchie and Lyla were walking along Third Avenue holding hands and teasing each other, eventually telling him candidly about her ex-boyfriend from when she was a teenager. He was surprised to know Casmir's 'street' name was the same as his name, especially after she told him the horror she went through with Casmir and revulsion she still felt. But he was happy to know the story behind her brilliant teeth. Lyla also told him about her family, and how dysfunctional they were.

After the conversation she felt so much better. Lyla was no longer a woman of mystery, but an open book for once in her life. Ritchie was still a mystery, but hopefully not impossible to reach.

They stopped at the corner of Third Avenue and Lexington to give each other a comforting hug.

"I love the smell of your hair," Ritchie whispered. Lyla and Ritchie walked to Seventh Street and crossed over to Sixth ending up on Second Avenue when suddenly Lyla saw a very fine looking guy on her path eating a hot dog. He favored Shemar Moore. The sexy man struggled with the messy hot dog, ketchup dripping down his fingers.

As his luscious tongue attempted to clean the ketchup from his fingers, he met the crossroads of hope and loss when he saw Lyla walk right pass him. He clearly forgot about the hot dog as his eyes traveled silently, followed by his head, slowly venturing into her arresting form and shifting curves. Not realizing the ketchup was still dripping, one glob of ketchup sat on top of his shirt. Ritchie and Lyla stopped at the corner waiting for the street light to change as she took one last glimpse at the guy for fun.

"Do you see how everyone looks at you?" Ritchie asked.

She blinked her eye at the Shemar Moore look-a-like.

"No. I don't notice those kinds of things."

"That is what I love about you," Ritchie said.

"What?" Lyla questioned.

"You are so beautiful and you don't even know it," Ritchie answered. "Your sense of style is timeless. Your smile is kind, that strength in your stare is amazing. Your personality is so inviting. I love everything about you. You have captured my heart." Lyla's face, redden. He always knew just what to say to seduce her.

Ritchie stopped talking when his phone rang as he motioned Lyla to wait while he walked a little bit away from her to answer his call.

While Lyla waited patiently looking around at the people on the street, and admiring some of the clothing shops, she saw a young guy dressed in faded old raggedy jeans and sneakers. Ritchie finished his call and walked over to where she was standing. He noticed she was staring at the young guy.

"I bet he owns an iPhone," Ritchie said.

"Yeah right," Lyla said. "Look at the way he's dressed! No offense, but he looks like a bum."

"He is the type that would save for one no matter what kind of financial situation he is in," Ritchie replied.

Lyla was in such disbelief and she wanted to prove him wrong for once as she walked over to the guy.

"Do you have a cell phone?" she asked. The guy's jaw dropped as he looked at her in admiration. He was pleasantly surprised that a beautiful woman was talking to him. The young guy pulled out his Blackberry.

"Yeah," the guy smiled, "and I got an iPod, too. You want it?"

"Thank you, no," Lyla giggled. "Nice stuff, though."

Wow! Close enough. Ritchie definitely had skills, Lyla thought.

Ritchie held Lyla again, kissed her on the cheek and then he did something strange. *Why is he hiding behind me?* she asked herself.

"Wait; do not move," Ritchie said, quietly. He was staring at something in front of him. Lyla followed Ritchie's eyes to see what he was hiding from. There were two white males in black suits getting into a black truck with tinted windows.

They looked like the mob.

The guys drove off and Ritchie smoothly came out from behind Lyla's shadow.

"Who were they?" Lyla questioned.

"Nobody," Ritchie answered. He quickly made a phone call speaking in a language Lyla did not understand but someone else did.

Ritchie hung up from his conversation and a homeless lady with a shopping cart filled with bags appeared out of nowhere.

"This is a very nice girl," she said to Ritchie. "You have a really nice girl." She kept repeating that and then walked away. Lyla did not know what to make of the two suspicious dudes and the homeless lady so she made light of the situation.

"Does the homeless lady have an iPhone?" Lyla joked. Ritchie did not hear what Lyla just said. Obviously his mind was elsewhere.

He told Lyla he had something to do tonight. It was top secret. She asked if he could tell her something about the two men he was hiding from. He explained to her it was best if she did not know anything. The only thing she did know was that he was talking to his wife on the phone both times. Lyla could see her name on the caller id.

This relationship is not supposed to be about being with a married man. It is supposed to be about being friends with a possible business person. But like Lyla said before, she had to wonder about his credibility in business. Was he as smart and business savvy as she thought? Still nothing tangible was happening like Ritchie promised, but now she was in way too deep.

To get her mind off the two guys, Ritchie pulled Lyla into a nearby alley behind a pile of empty boxes, and for a few minutes kissed her in the mouth. His tongue reached deep in her throat, hands reaching down her pants, while she held both sides of his jaw comfortably in the center of her hands.

Ritchie eventually moved towards her cozy hole, Lyla screaming his name.

After a few moments, she screamed louder, and Ritchie yelled, "Shit!" But not because they were enjoying each other, as an old lady on the fourth floor shouted, "Get a hotel!"

They looked up to see who was shouting. The lady slammed her apartment window. Lyla and Ritchie looked at each other in stunned belief. They were soaking wet from a bucket of cold water the woman dumped on them. But she was right, as they both laughed and shivered from the wet clothes and the fifty degree below weather.

Lyla and Ritchie checked in a rundown hotel on Saint Mark's Street. The bed was as hard as a brick and the door was hanging on for dear life, but it was all in good fun.

After they finished their afternoon fuck, they headed to Soho to shop, laugh, and play. While they stop to purchase some hot candy cashew nuts from the street vendor, Ritchie asked her to meet him at Central Park the next day to hang out with him and his children for the day. Lyla was not prepared for this outing, but she was going to make the best out of it. Lyla was so happy that Ritchie was finally letting her meet his kids, but she did have to internally marvel, *Why would his wife be okay with me meeting her children?*

Chapter 25

Lyla was excited about spending the day in Central Park with Ritchie and his kids, but also felt awkward. She didn't know why; the children knew her as the person who worked with their dad. Lyla was the first one to arrive at the park. She thought it would be a little chilly today for a picnic but it was not that bad out as she sneezed ineptly.

Lyla felt a little under the weather after walking around the city in wet clothes.

Thank goodness it is nice out. This had been the warmest spook winter I can remember, Lyla thought. *It's only been a few dreadful cold days. Weird weather, but I like it.*

Lyla laid out the blanket on short grass. She then neatly displayed the food from her traditional picnic basket. Lyla was sure the children were going to report back to their mom, so she wanted everything to be grand.

Shortly after, she saw children, a boy and a girl, running down the hill towards Lyla's wonderful arrangement. She thought they were about to hit everything, but they suddenly stopped right in front of her. Lyla then saw Ritchie walking slowly behind, confirming that they were his lovely kids.

"Hello," the boy said. "Are you Lyla?" the girl asked.

"Yes," Lyla answered, and gave them both a hug.

"You must be the handsome Danny and the gorgeous Celina."

"Yelp that's us," Danny confirmed.

Ritchie finally caught up with them and said he loved the whole set up, especially the square-shaped watermelon pieces topped with whipped cream presented in beautiful glasses.

"So, what's for lunch?" Celina asked.

"Oh we have lots of good stuff, sandwiches, potato chips, lavender lollipops, sodas..."

"I don't drink soda," Celina interrupted. Lyla was momentarily taken aback.

"Yeah me either," Lyla said. "It's bad for you. We have juice too, would you like a turkey or chicken sandwich?"

"Turkey with cheese and an apple juice," Celina said.

"Oh," Lyla replied. "I don't have apple juice but taste this." Danny already found what he wanted. Lyla set a separate special spot for her and Ritchie. A low table set for two with the traditional red and white checkered cover; a large bowl filled with spaghetti and meatballs and two forks to make it seem less intimate.

There was a short silence as they all ate. Danny broke the silence by talking about his new pony. His dad and sister expressed amusement because Danny slept in the barn with the mare the first night he received it. No one could find him!

"So Celina," Lyla said. "I heard you skipped a grade."

"Yes!" Celina replied proudly as she asked for more juice. "My dad has a way of making sure we stay on the honor roll and my teacher suggested to the board that I should be skipped a grade, maybe even attend a prestigious school in Paris to finish my high school education."

"That is amazing," Lyla said.

"Yeah, but I much rather be a model," Celina said.

"Really?" Lyla said surprised. "Maybe I can help you out with that one day."

"That would be awesome, Lyla." Celina smiled.

"So!" Lyla said. "How does your dad make sure you stay on the honor roll?"

"My dad pays us for good grades," she responded.

"Well, yeah, I would keep my grades up too," Lyla smiled as Ritchie, explained his philosophy on why he pays his kids for grades.

"I pay my kids so they will stay on the honor roll, in turn they receive scholarships for college," Ritchie said. "It saves me a ton of money."

Lyla agreed, "That makes sense. I mean if you think about it, when you grow up and you get a job, they pay you, so why not pay your children when they do a great job in school? It's the same concept."

Now Ritchie agreed with Lyla.

"Believe me, in today's society, the best way to go to college is with a scholarship because school loans are a beast," Lyla continued, drinking some hot tea.

"You know my dad is not..." Danny was about to say something, but she saw Ritchie kick him hard on his leg. *Are these kids being abused?* Danny rubbed his leg and walked off with a temper tantrum.

"Come back, Danny," his dad ordered, kicking grass.

Wow, Lyla said to herself. *It was simply unbearing to witness Ritchie acting like a child once again; mirroring his 6-year-old son...scary.*

Lyla did not know if she should say something, so she thought it would be a great time to bring out the gifts she brought for them. Hopefully Danny would feel better and Ritchie would stop kicking grass.

Lyla gave Celina a perfect pair of dainty earrings she made for her and some building blocks for Danny. He loved to build things, Ritchie told her. She had a beaded bracelet for his other daughter who did not show.

"My sister Sarah is sick," Celina said. "Our mom is home with her."

"Sorry to hear that," Lyla croaked, blowing her ruby red nose. "Please give the bracelet to Sarah and the necklace to your mom." She handed her the jewelry packaged so pretty in jewelry bags.

Celina looked inside the bag and asked, "You made all of this?"

"Yes," Lyla confirmed pleasingly. "I have been designing jewelry and clothing since your age. I call my line, *Steam*."

"Cool," Celina replied. "And thank you, everything is beautiful." She poured some more juice and asked, "What kind of juice is this? It's really good."

"It's my secret potion," Lyla said as they all laughed. Ritchie had a pleased look on his face.

Lyla liked Danny but she really enjoyed Celina. She told Lyla she read the Bible twice all the way through and she liked to garden. Lyla and Celina had a lot in common and she wanted to spend more time with her in the near future.

Ritchie and Lyla walked away for a minute to talk while the children continued to eat.

"Your children seem very pleasant and stable," Lyla said.

"Because they are, my love," Ritchie replied. "I give them a stable life. Even when my wife and I are going through problems, we never let the kids see that. Our job is to always show stability. If not they will grow up to be insecure."

"You are very wise. They are blessed to have you as their father and I am to have you as my man," Lyla said, wrapping her arms around his neck to give him a kiss.

He pushed Lyla away.

"Not in front of my children," Ritchie reminded.

"Oh yeah," Lyla apologized. "I was just saying I wish my parents showed me stability throughout my childhood. Maybe I would not be so befuddled today."

"Befuddled?" Ritchie questioned.

"Screwed up," Lyla answered. Ritchie did not know what some English words or slang met. He told Lyla he did not know what home wrecker met. Ritchie asked his family and friends the day Lyla said:

"I am a Christian woman, not a potential home wrecker."

They knew what it meant, so asking raised some questions. He almost got himself in trouble.

"The next picnic we have, I want it to be just us," Lyla responded while the both of them walked back towards the area where the kids were eating and playing.

"You don't like my kids?" Ritchie joked, and they chuckled.

"Ooooo," Lyla said. "Look!" Lyla ran to a nearby swing set. No matter what age Lyla was she loved swings. She hopped on the swing and swung high. Ritchie smiled while Lyla jumped off and said, "Okay, I'm done," as she giggled.

"Did you have fun?" Ritchie asked.

"Always," Lyla answered. "And by the way, I love both of your kids, but I have a special picnic basket for just us."

"Oh yeah? What's in it?"

"A little bit of this and a little bit of that," Lyla said in a sensual tone. "But believe me you will be eating...just not food."

"Is it more fun than the swings?" Ritchie asked.

"Nothing is more fun than the swings," Lyla smiled.

"Well this basket sounds interesting," Ritchie said. "Oh it is," Lyla said. "You cannot even imagine what's in it."

"Why wait for the picnic," Ritchie said. "The day is still young. I will take the kids home and we..." Before he could finish his sentence a huge dog charged right towards Lyla. He looked as mean as a rattlesnake. Her long legs sprinted across the grass, leaving Ritchie behind.

The dog was much faster than she thought as she launched across the open area even faster. Not looking she fell over a tree trunk and busted her ass. Lyla looked back at the dog like an actress in a scary movie. She tucked her head down between her knees and cried for help as she thought back to Casmir's phone conversation with her.

"First I would break us up; then patiently wait two years later and send pit bulls after you; no one will suspect it was me."

Lyla continued to scream.

Ritchie grabbed her arm and she hollered, "No! No! Let go!" She pushed and shoved, assuming it was the dog, as Lyla crawled as quickly as possible, tripping over her own hands and knees and screamed, "Get away from me!"

"Stop, Lyla! It's okay! It's me!" Ritchie shouted.

The owner of the dog came rushing over.

"I'm so sorry. My dog likes to chase after squirrels. He got loose, but he's friendly. He is no Cujo." The Chihuahua looked more frightened than Lyla.

The kids came running over to pet the dog, Danny's face was covered in whipped cream from the watermelon. She giggled then cried then giggled and cried again. Poor Lyla.

Ritchie held Lyla and she slowly stopped sobbing and shaking as he said, "What is wrong? You act like the puppy wanted to harm you."

"I thought I saw a huge dog coming after me! It brought back bad memories!" Lyla shouted. She looked Ritchie in the eyes with one of her strong but scared stares. "Will you protect me even if there is someone after me?" Lyla continued.

"Yes," Ritchie said. "Of course, I'm here until the end of the earth with you."

"Why, so you can watch me die?" Lyla said.

"No," Ritchie replied. "I will die for you. Calm down. Who is after you, does this have something to do with your ex-boyfriend?" Lyla did not answer him.

"Your ex is gone. He died a long time ago," Ritchie continued, holding her in his strong arms. "There is something still behind those eyes, a woman of mystery."

She lifted herself off the ground and screamed, "No! I'm an open book now, my love is here and it's true. You are the one who still holds a mystery."

Lyla looked around to only see herself surrounded by a large crowd of people staring.

"Okay, so this completes the entertainment segment of this program," Lyla sneezed. She told the children she was fine. Lyla just wanted to get home and take care of her cold before it got worst.

A rough-looking woman came up to Ritchie and Lyla.

"Why do you want to be with someone like him. He is controlling, why do you want him?" This day could not get any worse. Ignoring the lady, Lyla went to her purse to grab an aspirin and asked, "Ritchie, did you drink the last water?"

Chapter 26

Lyla's super and wife were still looking out for her, but the super pulled away from the idea of managing her. He presumed she wasn't serious about her modeling career anymore. But Lyla figured she would learn as much as she could from Ritchie, and use it in her life, whether it was for modeling or any of her other ideas.

Lyla stayed in the house for a few days to take care of her cold. Later that week, Ritchie showed Lyla his new website and it had the logo idea she discussed with him for her project along with her picture plastered all over the site like she owned it. Every time she attempted to trust Ritchie, something else came up.

Am I just kidding myself about this man? Lyla thought. *This is unbelievable. How much more could I take? Was it really worth me learning business from a guy who steals and lies?* Lyla debated the three years he had mentioned for her to learn everything, but she would hang in there for as long as she could.

Day after day, they worked and worked and worked and, in the midst of his occasional temper tantrums, slept together. Lyla's dreams were still on hold, and he never paid her for working at the office. Sometimes, he would have his watch and sometimes he did not. Lyla didn't know what to do about this guy. She just knew she loved him.

Lyla was scheduled to meet Ritchie at the office. She arrived before him. Roger was there catching up on work. Lyla initiated small talk and, for the first time, she really got to know and like Roger.

He told Lyla a little about his life, how much he loved his wife and some stories about his close friends. Lyla could tell Roger did not like conflict and was not competitive...go figure. Lyla had misjudged him. She thought he was jealous of Ritchie but actually Roger preferred comfortable environments that kept him from taking risks. Roger liked to enjoy life: going fishing, playing his guitar, and teaching singing lessons to young kids at a camp in Staten Island.

But his serene nature made him vulnerable to people who wanted to take advantage of him. Also, his peaceful nature caused him to miss out on good opportunities. If Lyla felt comfortable enough, she would have told him to work on building more self-confidence and self-worth so he could feel more secure. *Something I need to work on more.* Instead she listened and enjoyed their conversation.

Towards the end of their talk, Roger asked, "How do you feel about Ritchie?" He thought Ritchie was a little distrustful and as she mentioned before, she thought so too.

Roger said he was having problems getting the office bills paid. *This all sounds too familiar,* Lyla thought. Ritchie always said he and his family were well off. His kids were in pricey schools. He constantly bragged about his cars and homes; he even claimed to have an apartment in Manhattan but someone was occupying it.

Not too long ago, Ritchie said he wanted to do something nice for Lyla's family. He told her to plan a cruise and her family would stay in his sister's cottage in Florida Keys before returning to Philadelphia. *Wow, he must have a lot of money to do that,* Lyla thought. After she organized the whole trip he told her he never said he was sending her family on any trip.

Upset and mystified, she thought again about the time he attempted to take money from her aunt and super. Lyla went from a two bit hustler to a textbook narcissist and now, under Ritchie's charm, a potential con artist. *I had to let Casmir go when he involved my family, was Ritchie next?* Lyla asked herself.

"I'm going to Google him," Lyla said casually. "You know that is what everyone does these days to find out about people."

"You're right, Google him, Inspector Gadget," Roger replied as they laughed.

"Yeah that's right Roger," Lyla said. She typed in Ritchie Perez and that was when she discovered he was on the run.

Impossible, Lyla thought. *Let me type in his name again, maybe I misspelled it.* Lyla's heart rate became rapid. The same information came up. Ritchie was a fugitive on the most wanted list. *What in the world is going on?* she asked herself.

She skimmed through the article, because she was more interested in finding a photo. But that search soon ended when Roger walked over to her. She quickly minimized the window on the computer monitor. Lyla did not tell Roger about what she just saw.

"What are you looking at?" Roger asked. "Did you find something on Ritchie?" Lyla told Roger things seemed to be okay but some of the stories did not add up and to keep an eye on him.

Lyla failed to mention before she met up with his kids in the park that she had visited Ritchie's house in Connecticut when his wife and family went to Switzerland for a skiing trip. After they made love, he did something strange. He was on the phone with some people he supposedly did business with. He couldn't tell her anything about it because it was highly classified.

"Make sure it's a Mercedes 500 and not 400," Ritchie said during a phone conversation. "I don't care what they tell you. If you want me to do the job, I need push."

Then when he got off the phone he said to Lyla, "Don't listen to anything I said. What you don't know is good so no one can question you." The crazy thing is he was talking to the operator. Lyla heard the recording on the other end saying, "If you like to make a call."

Did he really think I could not hear that? Lyla asked herself. *Well I heard it and it made me wonder why he lied and if this man was completely insane.*

She noticed there was only one Lamborghini in the driveway as she said to Ritchie, "Let's take a ride in your Lamborghini." He said he did not have a driver's license.

This begged the question, "Why doesn't he have a license?" *He said his cars were not insured when we first met. Which one is it?"*

"Well," she said. "I have a license so I can drive." "No," Ritchie replied. "Why?" Lyla asked puzzled. "I have to get it insured," Ritchie answered. *Now it is back to not being insured,* Lyla thought. "Well," she said. "Let's sit down inside of it. I have never been in one before." Ritchie did not even know how to work the car.

She noticed his house was nice inside but worn on the outside. Lyla was expecting a lush manicured lawn and garden with a home gate and security guards to keep his mansion from the outside world. The Picasso paintings looked just as phony as he did. The walk in closet was as small as hers and he was picking up his own clothes from the floor. The only horse and pool Lyla saw was a statue of a horse drinking from a pond.

Did his son lie to me?

Who is this?" Lyla wondered. She reached for a man in a picture frame next to the statue.

"That is my father," Ritchie replied.

"He is handsome," Lyla said. "Now I see where you get your looks from. Where is he?"

"He died of cancer when I was a teenager," Ritchie said sadly.

"Sorry to hear that," Lyla said. She sat the picture back where she found it.

"We were very close," Ritchie responded.

"You will see him again, in heaven."

To get his mind off of his father she changed the subject and asked if she could see the rest of his exotic cars. He said his other cars were in a warehouse and at his main house in the Hamptons. *Funny, he told me his cars were at this house, and now he has another house in the Hamptons,* Lyla thought. Now, Lyla saw what Roger was saying. *This is unacceptable.*

Lyla thought about going to the police to inquiry about Ritchie, but she remembered him saying that he could pass any lie detector test. He also knew she was the type who did not keep in contact with her family like she should.

"Your family wouldn't look for you until two weeks later if you went missing, because they're used to you not calling them. By then your body would be gone." From that point on, Lyla made sure her family heard from her every day and she told her aunt about the situation.

Roger snapped Lyla out of her daydream.

"Are you okay?" Roger asked.

"Yes," she answered. "I'm being a bit melodramatic right now; my mind can get a little creative sometimes." But in the face of the threats and fear of Ritchie, she planned on doing some investigating.

Still thinking about everything she just learned about him, she had to maintain her composure and use some of the techniques he taught her against him to methodically gather clues, to get the full story.

How did I get mixed up with this fool? she asked herself. *He didn't seem foolish at first, but do they ever? I should have left him at Madison Square Garden.*

Ritchie walked in. She told him she had somewhere to be.

"Can you stop by the drug store to get some office supplies?" he asked. "Our shipment was lost."

"Yeah, sure," Lyla answered.

"Thanks," Ritchie replied.

What a liar. The shipment wasn't lost. He doesn't have the money for it. But wait a minute. Isn't he supposed to be the president of this firm? as she pulled out his business card he gave her when they first met.

Chapter 27

For better or worse, Lyla was still with Ritchie despite everything that had happened thus far. And although he may not help her with her dreams like he promised or pay her for the work she did for him, one thing was for sure: he did follow through with sharing his knowledge of business. Lyla was determined to learn all the business expertise she could from this man. Like Lyla said before, she was not leaving another relationship empty handed.

After leaving the store, she went to the police station to find out if it was her Ritchie on the run and if so, why? When she entered the intimidating building she approached a short and overweight detective, and after a brief conversation he pulled up a report on Ritchie Perez.

"Wait here, I'll be right back," the detective ordered. Lyla bit her nails as she waited. Moments later, the detective returned with a much taller and slimmer man. He was easy on the eyes.

"How are you, ma'am?" the detective asked. "I'm okay," Lyla answered.

"I'm leading Detective John Sanchez," he said. "How may I help you?"

Lyla asked the detective, "Can you tell me anything about Ritchie?"

"Sure I can. His real name is Casmir Nowak A.K.A. 'Th...'" She became dizzy before he could finish.

"Wait a minute," Lyla interrupted. "Repeat the name."

"Would you like some water?" Sanchez asked. "Suddenly you look pale."

"No, thank you," Lyla answered. "Please repeat the name again, detective."

"His name is Casmir Nowak A.K.A. 'The Killing Machine.' He is a calculated repeated offender," the detective said. "Nowak has been on the most wanted list for years. He has murdered forty-three people that we know about. His MO is setting his victims' bodies on fire with a torch as he watches them dissolve and melt as they burn. Afterwards, he eats wants left of them for dinner."

"That's impossible!" she exclaimed.

"Why is that impossible? This monster is capable of anything," the detective said.

Lyla corrected the detective and said, "No. I mean he cannot be Casmir Nowak, he is dead. Check the name again."

"Believe me Miss..." Lyla had no intentions on divulging her name so she brushed him off and said, "Never mind my name, but that is my ex-boyfriend's name. He was shot in the back a long time ago. It can't be the same person."

"He has many aliases," the detective responded. "And he told you one of them, Perez, but Nowak is definitely his birth name." He showed Lyla a picture. The face staring back at her was her ex-boyfriend Casmir Nowak.

She dropped the picture and said in a panic, "Ritchie is Spanish with short thick clean-cut black hair, brown eyes, and a sturdy body. Casmir is blonde with blue eyes and he had always been taller than me, and Ritchie is the same height as me so none of this makes sense. There must be a mix up. Casmir is dead!"

The detective disagreed and said, "He is alive."

"So!" Lyla said. "Why not arrest him, Detective, since he is living?"

"We cannot find him. Do you know of his whereabouts?" the detective questioned.

"Yes. Six feet under!" she reminded.

Lyla could not believe her ears. *Who have I've been trusting and sleeping with? I have already traveled down this road before...not being able to trust someone.*

"Are you sure he is died?" the detective asked. "He could have had plastic surgery."

"Very seriously doubt that and yes, I'm sure," Lyla answered. "I have to leave."

"Liar, liar pants on fire," Sanchez said.

"What!" Lyla said. She stood close to the detective and stared up at him with power in her face. "Who are you calling a liar? Do not talk to me like that!"

With anger but concern in his eyes he said, "No. I'm not calling you a liar. Casmir says that before he torches his victims."

She backed up.

"Just making sure," Lyla said calmly.

"Casmir has not done any killings recently that we know of bu-"

"That's because he is dead...I keep telling you that," Lyla interrupted.

"If he's resurfaced from the dead, you may be the person that can help us put this guy away," he continued.

Stunned by the news, Lyla stormed out the door and ran down the hallway. She felt like a hand grenade was thrown at her. The people in the hallway looked as if they were all coming after her in slow motion. She could hear them saying something but the words sounded unclear. Lyla was having a panic attack.

She calmed down to catch her breath while she looked for her phone in her pocket book. Lyla could not find it but she managed to drop the full contents of her purse all over the place; scissors, paper clips, sticky notes from the drug store, and her personal belongings.

Lyla rapidly grabbed her possessions and took a couple of deep breaths to collect herself. When she looked over her shoulder she saw the detective was not too far behind.

"Wait a minute!" the detective hollered. Lyla finished gathering her things. She felt the attack going away so she ran again but faster.

"Stay away!" Lyla screamed back.

"Nowak is incredibly dangerous!" he shouted down the hallway. Lyla was out the door before the detective could catch up with her. She quickly hailed a cab and jumped in.

"Drive!" she said to the cab driver.

I wish my great aunt was still alive and living in New York, Lyla thought, as she told the cab driver an address. *She would know what to do.* Instead, Lyla had no choice but to call Pastor Bill for comfort.

Meanwhile, the detective who first talked to Lyla at the police station rushed to Sanchez.

"I think she had something to do with the drugs being transported on the plane from Mexico," the detective said.

"What?" the detective questioned. "How you figure that, Carpenter?"

"Look what I found."

Chapter 28

Carpenter met Sanchez in his office to talk about what he found on the floor when Lyla dropped all of her belongings. She thought she gathered everything but Lyla forgot one thing.

"We may have a lead," Carpenter said.

"Besides the scissors she left," Sanchez joked. "I hope you have more than that."

"Yeah, what was up with the scissors," Carpenter replied as they both laughed. "I found a round trip plane ticket to Mexico for the same date of the drug trafficking scandal," Carpenter continued. He pulled out a pen from his uniform pocket to take notes as Sanchez pulled out potato chips and a bologna sandwich from a paper bag.

"I'll come back when you're finished lunch," Carpenter said.

"Nonsense, rookie. Let me see that," Sanchez demanded. He took the ticket from Carpenter to review.

"She ran out so fast we couldn't tell her about his drug charges too," Carpenter said.

"Yeah, and that the case was closed due to uncontrollable circumstances," Sanchez replied, as he continued to review the ticket. "But regardless, this is not enough proof. There is no way to tie in her and Casmir; we don't even know if Casmir is involved at all in the Mexico situation. She could have been going to Mexico for a vacation for all we know. We cannot re-open the case based solely on this ticket."

"The guy we spoke with said that the woman in front of him in line was a beautiful tall lady," Carpenter reminded.

"She looked like a supermodel. What do you think that was that just flew out of here, chopped liver?"

"Ha, ha, Carpenter. She looked like Super Woman," the detective replied.

"Super Woman?" Carpenter said.

"Yeah," Sanchez said. "Like a super hero. Isn't that why they are called supermodels - ba dum tsss. Of course I could see she was beautiful, but get me more proof or we can do nothing."

"The witness said he saw something fall out of her dress," Carpenter replied with frustration.

"That could have been anything!" Sanchez said. "Besides he could hardly see. Get me more evidence."

"What about Casmir's business associate?" Carpenter said. "He was in Mexico that day. I have a feeling there is a connection."

"We don't know if that was his business associate at all," Sanchez responded. "And even if he is, we don't want his associate. We want the big dog. We want Casmir." Now he was frustrated.

"Well, maybe she can lead us to him if we play our cards right," Carpenter said without backing down. "I bet Casmir is sending her to do his dirty work."

"Okay, fine, get me the proof," Sanchez repeated, crunching on some potato chips and gobbling down a bologna sandwich.

"I think she knows Casmir Nowak and Ritchie Perez is the same person," Carpenter said. "If she doesn't know yet, she better connect the dots soon before she is sorry."

"Let's hope we connect the dots before she finds out she has been duped," Sanchez replied. "Because love can make you wild, she seems to be under his spell; not in a healthy state of mind. She is scared, flawed, and blinded. We don't know what she might do."

"Yeah," Carpenter smirked. "Because she can't tell the difference between a Spanish guy and a Polish guy."

"It's obvious he had plastic surgery," Sanchez said.

"Why does she think that he could not have had it done?" Carpenter wondered.

"She knows something. She strikes me as a person with many secrets," Sanchez said. "People think they have all the answers about her, but they will never know all of her. She won't allow it."

"You like her, don't you detective?" Carpenter replied.

"What rookie?" Sanchez said. "I'm a professional and you are out of order."

"Well I'm sure you will crack the case wide open, but seriously we need to find out what kind of game Casmir is playing before he has her for dinner," Carpenter responded.

"My guess is that she is his partner, and they work out their killing sprees together," Sanchez theorized. "He sent her here as a spy to see what information we have."

"Isn't that what I said," Carpenter reminded.

"We are both grasping straws, but we have to. Find out everything you can on..." Sanchez looked at the ticket again. "On Ms. Elizabeth Tight. Let's take a trip to the airport to analyze the tapes again.

"We need to not only speak to the security guard who let her go through customs untouched, but we need to bring in that witness as soon as possible. Finding Casmir is like finding a needle in a haystack, but this may be our single link, the common denominator to the recapture of Casmir. We find out who this girl is, we find out where Casmir is. If she is involved, she will go down with Casmir and that's a crying shame."

"Well, don't get too carried away," Carpenter said, writing notes on his pad. "Casmir is well connected especially with law enforcement and the mafia. That's why we had to close the case after he supposedly escaped during that prison transfer in Philly when he was convicted years ago. We know the mob was involved in both the mishandled transfer and tampering with the investigation to find him, even though he killed two special agents."

"True, he is well connected," Sanchez agreed. "But so are we. Besides, according to my source, the mob has a hit out on Casmir for not following through on a business deal. He cost them millions. That's one of the reasons why he uses so many identities."

"So, the mob will not be covering for Casmir anymore," Carpenter concluded.

"You are a smart guy," Sanchez said sarcastically, "and while the case has had some shortcomings, we just need hard evidence. So let's stay focused and put this lunatic away once and for all!"

"I'm ready when you are," Carpenter replied.

"I've been ready," Sanchez said. "I had a feeling Casmir couldn't stop killing after his first victim and won't stop until we stop him."

"Should we contact the victim's families to let them know we are back on the case?" Carpenter asked, naively.

"No! Keep it quiet until we get more proof. We don't want to alert the press."

Chapter 29

Lyla was at a small hole in the wall, in midtown, populated mainly by horse racing bettors. She was having a glass of wine at the bar with her eccentric friend H.L. Unfortunately the pastor was not available, so she left a message for him to call her. She also assigned a special ringtone for Pastor Bill so she knew it was him when he called her back.

H.L. had been the piano player for Frank Sinatra. He wore the same dark brown brimmed hat every time Lyla saw him. *He looks nice in his hat, but I always wonder about guys who wear hats all the time.* But never mind that, this man was a hilarious, colorful character, and fun to hang out with. Lyla needed to laugh after the mind-blowing news she received.

H.L. had a way of messing with everyone at the bar as he placed bids for his favorite horses.

His beloved line was, "I don't like you but I love you...ooooooo." Lyla loved that. Of course H.L.'s goal was to take her home with him, but Lyla found this 70-year-old man amusing, not sexually attractive.

Lyla watched H.L. bet on horses as she thought about her visit with Detective Sanchez. Lyla wondered if it was wise to go see him. Ritchie was not to be played with and Lyla could not trust the law enforcement. Ritchie used to work with the CIA and, according to him allegedly still did from time to time.

He said to Lyla one day, "After a millionaire is finished with his mistress, they may say to her, 'go get me a soda,' and when she leaves there may be someone in the hallway waiting to kill her."

Was Ritchie trying to get rid of me in Mexico? Lyla thought.

She remembered him jokingly saying to her after she returned back from Mexico:

"What do you think I was trying to get you killed or leave your DNA somewhere so you would be thrown in jail forever for something you did not do?"

She thought nothing of the things he says because he was normally drunk, high, or talking nonsense.

On the other hand, he seemed just as creative with killing someone as my Casmir was, Lyla thought.

"I have many ways of killing you and no one will know how I did it."

Ritchie was very clever. The police would never suspect him to be working as an accountant. That job was the perfect cover up if he was actually a killer, but that was impossible. The authorities just wanted her to lose her mind.

But, without a doubt, she knew that if the police did not catch him, or even worse, did catch him but could not keep him in jail, he would come after her if he found out she turned him in.

I will talk to Ritchie myself. Privately.

Lyla's phone rang. She slid her finger across the screen and put her white phone plugs in her ear to free her hands.

"Hello," Lyla said.

"Hey Lyla, where are you?" Roger asked.

"I'm hanging out. What's up," Lyla answered.

"When you left," Roger started, "and Ritchie went to the bathroom, I looked at what you were reading on the computer and it said Ritchie is a fugitive! He is not who he say he is." Lyla was quiet.

"Hello?" Roger said.

"Yes, I'm here," Lyla replied slowly. *Things were already sticky, and they were about to get even stickier*, she said to herself.

Lyla had no choice but to confirm what Roger read. She begged him not to say anything to Ritchie until she found out the whole story. Roger did not listen to Lyla. He wanted to know who the impostor was. He showed Ritchie the website and now he may be on to Lyla.

She wished Roger stayed in his comfort zone, but as of now she had to act like nothing was wrong, and the craziest part was Lyla still wanted to be with Ritchie. Lyla knew she could not have the happily ever after, but they were in love. Why else would he have introduced her to his kids and stayed with her all the time? Like he said, 'his wife was just for show.'

Conversely, Lyla was having mixed feelings again but all-in-all she thought, *There may be some madness to Ritchie's method, but I'm going to stick by my man even if he is wrong, which I know he isn't. I am going to prove to him how strong my love is for him. Ritchie may not be perfect but he almost is.*

Lyla drank one more glass of wine and she told H.L. that she had to leave as she stepped down from her bar stool stumbling. She discerned that she had a bit much to drink.

"How did I get drunk in such a little bar," Lyla giggled. H.L. laughed. "Baby, you are the funniest and prettiest girl I have ever seen. You got that pure, meek, loving personality. You can connect with whomever but you still got that fire in you, that burning touch and you crazy, but you good crazy," as he turned to his friend and said, "True or false?"

"True," his friend replied.

"See, he knows its true too," H.L. said in a playful voice.

"Yes, it's true," his friend repeated while they chuckled.

"We are telling the truth," H.L. said. "There's no one like you and that I can bet."

"Yeah," the bartender said.

"Yes! Even the bartender knows," H.L. said excitedly. "Baby girl if you got it like that then keep it like that...oooooooooooo."

They all laughed and Lyla toddled out the revolving doors of the cloudly bar only to be trampled by a random woman invading her tiny space in between the spinning glass doors just to catch a cab. *How rude!*

Chapter 30

When Lyla arrived home that evening, the worst possible thing happened on the worst possible day: Lyla's super dropped off a new tenant. She recognized the new tenant as Lyla's phone rang.

"Hello," Lyla said.

"Hey babe," Ritchie said with a gentle seduction. "Where are you?"

"I'm home," Lyla replied.

"Are you coming back to the office with the supplies?"

"Yes," Lyla said.

"Can you wear what you wore earlier today?" Ritchie requested. "You looked so nice."

"Thanks, I don't plan on changing my clothes."

"Good," Ritchie said.

"Is everything okay?" Lyla asked.

"Yes," Ritchie answered.

"I will be there soon," Lyla said. "But first, I have to help my new roommate settle in."

"Okay," Ritchie said. "Please come because I have a meeting in a few days I want you to lead. It's time for you to prove yourself."

"Nice!" Lyla said with excitement. "I will be there."

Between what Lyla found out today, Mexico, the lies, her logo being stolen, and the wife and kids situation, she was ready to walk away. But now she was excited about the meeting and if it hadn't been for her new roommate, she probably would have walked away as she said to the girl, "I know you."

"I'm Poison's sister, Rocket," the girl replied.

"Yes, I know," Lyla said. "Your sister is my friend. We used to hang out in Philadelphia before I moved to New York."

"Oh, cool," the girl said.

Lyla had recently introduced Poison to her super, and now her sister, Rocket, was living in New York? *If it wasn't one thing, it was another.*

Rocket told Lyla she was in New York promoting her new shoe line. Lyla had never met Rocket, only heard about her through Poison. Poison described Rocket as entertaining, admirable, creative, and diligent. Her sister also said Rocket was thoughtful, generous, and loved to have a good time. She made every attempt to keep her environment peaceful.

But, according to Rocket, she recently stopped talking to her sister after one betrayed the other, so in short, Poison had no idea Rocket was in New York, using the connection that Lyla set up for Poison.

Rocket told Lyla what happened between the sisters. Lyla knew Poison was wild but she could not believe half of the information Rocket was telling her. Rocket made it seem like Poison was a train wreck with no brakes! Regardless, Poison was always good to Lyla and she wanted to keep it that way.

Lyla changed the subject while Rocket unpacked. It looked like she was into brand name items as well.

"Lovely blouse," Lyla complimented.

"Dolce & Gabbana, my favorite designer. I found this blouse at a sample sale," Rocket said brightly.

"Nice! I wear the perfume," Lyla said, "but Givenchy is my favorite designer."

"Grand taste," Rocket said.

"Always," Lyla replied, nodding with a satisfied smirk.

She asked Rocket about her shoe line, and she showed Lyla her portfolio. Her shoe line was incredible and Lyla wanted to help her become successful, maybe even combine her clothing line with her shoe collection with the help of Ritchie. He always talked about Lyla proving herself, so maybe he can prove himself now.

But one thing Lyla learned while with Nestle was not to have other women around her man. Although Ritchie technically was not her man, he was Lyla's boyfriend; still, Rocket seemed like a nice girl, and she wanted to help her. She figured, if nothing else, she and Rocket could really benefit each other, and she and Ritchie could make some money off of Rocket.

Lyla told Rocket about Ritchie's background, and instantly she was ready to meet him. But, Rocket first had to let Lyla know that her super was also investing in her shoe line so she wanted to keep the meeting hush-hush. She needed all the money she can get as she talked with her hands.

I can understand her hustle, but is this the real reason my super backed out on our deal? Because he saw something new and more promising? What an opportunist.

Rocket and Lyla were eager to work together so Lyla set up a meeting with Ritchie for the following day. She also told Ritchie she would see him tomorrow instead of today.

"I want to go over the proposal with Rocket before we meet; you should receive the proposal shortly," Lyla said. She had given Rocket Ritchie's email address so that he could review the business proposal before they met.

"Okay, captain," Ritchie said. "See you then and don't forget that we also have to go over the details for the meeting we spoke about earlier."

"Not a problem," Lyla replied.

The next afternoon was cloudy and mild when they gathered at Lyla's much-loved sushi spot uptown.

"Man, I should have brought my sweater," Lyla said.

"Yeah, it's a little chilly outside, but even colder in here," Rocket shivered. Lyla took her mind off the chill, ordered a large hot sake, and her favorite volcano roll. Rocket looked at the menu to confirm they sell volcano rolls. "Oh, my eyes have seen the glory. That is the bomb. We order volcanoes all the time in Philly," Rocket said with excitement.

"Yes, girl, they are yummy to the tummy," Lyla said as they both laughed. "I turned Ritchie on to it."

"We share everything but the volcano," Ritchie grinned. *Inappropriate Ritchie.*

Other than Ritchie's inapt comment, so far, the meeting was going well. Rocket was eating excessively and Lyla could tell by her weight she was not very active. What Lyla could also tell was that during the conversation, Lyla was either seeing things or Ritchie and Rocket were on a date, making Lyla feel like a third wheel.

Ritchie had a way of seducing women without really knowing it because he was so attentive. But Rocket had other plans. Ritchie enthralling eyes peered into Rocket's eyes as if she was the most beautiful thing in the world.

"You are married and you hate your job. You are there until you succeed as a shoe designer," he said. Lyla was heated and felt disrespected, but she held her tongue as Rocket gazed back into his eyes and said, "No. I'm not married and I don't have a job, so there is no way I can hate it, Mr. Perez."

Lyla was bubbling inside, but she couldn't afford to lose out on this opportunity, so Lyla stormed into the bathroom and found an empty stall to release her anger.

I don't care what her hustle is, Lyla says in her head. *Why would she think I would let her come from Philly to New York and take over what I worked so hard to get? First she took my super and now Ritchie. I'm the New Yorker, she better recognize.* She returned to the table, but didn't care to hold any conversation with the two of them until Ritchie asked, "What happened?"

"Oh nothing," Lyla answered with a smile. "I just bit my tongue," as she continued to watch them gawk at each other. They didn't even try to be discreet about it. Lyla had no choice, but to nip the situation in the bud.

A young, stylish lady walked by their table wearing a pair of Versace stilettos. Lyla stopped her.

"Excuse me miss," Lyla said. "Are those the new Versace heels?"

"Yes," she said.

"I love those! But I cannot find them anywhere," Lyla said.

"I purchased mine in Paris, but you can order them online," she said.

Lyla smiled.

"Thank you." Lyla then turned to Ritchie. "Please make a note of that, my love." Ritchie looked at Lyla in a way that accused her of not being professional, but neither was he.

Lyla looked into Rocket's unguarded eyes and gave her an undermining look. She understood who was running the show.

"I thought you preferred, Givenchy," Rocket said.

"I said it's my favorite. I did not say I was married to it," Lyla replied. "I'm sure you know about being married to something."

"What is that supposed to mean," Rocket said.

"Never mind," Lyla smirked.

Ritchie and Lyla explained to Rocket that she had to go through Lyla to handle all of her business transactions. Rocket was not to contact Ritchie. They all agreed, and Lyla ordered a glass of wine. The sake was not strong enough.

On their way home, Rocket asked Lyla several questions about Ritchie. From the questions asked it seemed to Lyla, Rocket's priorities have slightly shifted. She wanted to know if Lyla and Ritchie were seeing each other, how much money he had, and his connections. Lyla already saw where this was going.

This conniving woman had a predilection for rich men, and she was on the hunt for a new sugar daddy. Rocket thought Ritchie was her meal ticket, her cash cow. She was nothing but a bona fide gold digger. The complete opposite of what Poison told Lyla.

This was why Lyla does not like other females around her man, especially women like Rocket, with a bottomless pit for money. But Lyla did not care much. Ritchie was not officially her man; he belonged to someone else, neither Lyla nor Rocket.

Besides, her priorities also had slightly changed, once she found out what was going on with him. If Rocket knew what was good for her she would keep her distance. *Damn bitch.*

A few days later, Lyla met Ritchie and three famous NBA players, at a restaurant Ritchie said he owned called *All of It*. Ritchie told them Lyla knew how to organize events. She had never organized an event but today she learned fast in order to prove herself to Ritchie.

Ritchie introduced Lyla to the players. They seemed impressed with her firm handshake, power suit, freshly manicured nails, striking heels, and make-up inspired by Bobbi Brown.

The players wanted to plan a Hawaiian Luau birthday charity event at a new club in Los Angeles called *Heat*. They told her exactly what they wanted as they all sipped on drinks. One of the players said he wanted Chocolate Succumb to host a bikini contest during the event.

"Not a problem," Lyla said. She made a list of items needed on their event forms.

"Okay, I can take it from here," Lyla continued. "Should we order some food?" The players gave her a strange look and one asked, "Aren't you going to ask us about the budget?"

"Well, first I'm going to see who will sponsor the event and then we can discuss money if needed," Lyla answered. Ritchie stared at her with one of his pleased looks as the players seemed shocked. "Who wouldn't want to sponsor your event with hula and fire dancers?" Lyla continued.

One of the other players said, "Yeah but…" Before the player could finish his sentence she said, "Excuse me." There was a well-groomed man walking by their table and Lyla saw an opportunity to prove to the players she knew what she was doing. "Would you like to sponsor a NBA Hawaiian Luau charity event?"

"Absolutely," the gentleman replied. Lyla turned to the players with a sexy confident stare.

"Are you going to be there?" the gentleman asked.

"Of course," Lyla answered nonchalantly.

"She and her fabulous gay friends from the fashion world will be there with bright lights." Everyone strongly and hysterically chuckled. Then Ritchie repeated the joke half-expecting that all would laugh again, but this time no one laughed.

From spending so much time with Ritchie, Lyla noticed he did this every time he said something funny. He was so excited he made someone laugh; he would repeat jokes but the only problem was that it was no longer funny and it made him look desperate and stupid. Ritchie was puzzled to find Lyla staring at him with a staid expression. *I can't believe he just did that at a meeting.*

The well-dressed gentleman told his assistant to give Lyla a blank check.

"Take care of the entire party," the man said. "And here is my business card Ms…"

"Lyla," she said, giving him a firm handshake.

"Like that handshake," the man acknowledged. "Send me the date of the event and depending on how this one goes, I have some events coming up I'd like you to organize."

"Thank you so much," Lyla said. The handsome gentleman walked away. Lyla played it cool until the man was gone. She turned to the players. "We got the money!" She was kissing the check and performing a hilarious dance in her chair. The players thought she was so cute.

"See? I told y'all," Lyla continued.

"We already know people will sponsor us," the player said. "But event planners always want money upfront."

"Why?" Lyla questioned.

All three players looked at her in amazement and they said together, "Will you marry me?" Lyla jumped back and said, "Hold on guys; we just met." They all laughed. "Don't worry, I'll let you know my fee in due time," Lyla said. "And I want it all in singles so I can go to the strip club to find me a man."

Everyone found Lyla's comment funny but Ritchie. *Now he knows how it feels to be the third wheel or to make inappropriate comments at a meeting.* Lyla and Ritchie ended the meeting with the players on a promising note, as Ritchie asked for an autograph from the players and a couple of pictures. *He's acting like he has never been around celebrities before.*

Lyla and Ritchie headed back to the office. Ritchie explained to her that the meeting was a test. It was not real and she should not contact the gentleman nor the players, and he took the forms from her. He also told her she had not done well. Ritchie tore apart the entire meeting.

She was a little disappointed and confused. Lyla got the money before the first meeting was over and the event totally organized. She told Ritchie that she would do better the next time.

When Ritchie and Lyla arrived at the office, she did not see Roger. Ritchie said he was visiting his brother in Texas. Lyla was sitting at the desk with Ritchie while he scrolled through his emails. She happened to glance over at one of his messages.

"Open that message."

"What message," Ritchie said.

"Don't play dumb with me," Lyla replied. "Why is Rocket sending you an email after we told her to contact me only?"

"I didn't see that message," Ritchie said, slumping down in the chair; he knew she had caught him. For the first time, he flinched.

"What do you mean you did not see that message," Lyla said. "It's marked read!"

"I don't know why it would be, because I never saw it," Ritchie replied. Lyla was feeling like the day he told her about his marriage.

"Open it!" Lyla screamed. "And let me see what she sent you!"

Ritchie said with his deep nervous accent, "You know what I love about us," as Lyla read his lips.

"What?" Lyla asked.

"That you are not only my girlfriend but my good friend," Ritchie answered. "I have never had a relationship like this before. I love you so much." Ritchie went on and on and on about how great their relationship was and how much he appreciated her. "How simple my life is now you are here," Ritchie continued.

"Uh?" Lyla said. "Do I look like BooBoo the clown?"

"Who's that," Ritchie replied, irritating Lyla more and more.

"You're only digging yourself deeper and deeper in a hole with all this friendship stuff; you look guiltier. Now open it!"

The email read:

"Thank you for meeting with me. I would be delighted to hear any of your suggestions regarding my shoe line. In the meantime, please follow me on Twitter. Sincerely, Rocket"

"You are full of it," Lyla said to Ritchie. "The truth ain't in you."

"Don't blame me because your friend sent me an email I knew nothing about," Ritchie said.

"I see she left her number!" Lyla said furiously. "So, do you plan on responding to her message, or did you already?"

"No. I did not see it," Ritchie repeated, provoking Lyla even more. *Liar*, she said to herself. *He was definitely hiding something.*

Rocket must not understand English. Clearly she wanted to say thank you, but in another kind of way.

Lyla was so disturbed.

She shouted in her head, *Should I let Rocket burn?* Rocket did not know who Ritchie really was. This man could be very dangerous but Lyla could see Rocket did not know how to listen. Rocket thought she had a gold mine, which confirmed what Lyla believed from the start. *Rocket is a gold digging bitch.*

Lyla called Rocket, and during the heated conversation Rocket had the audacity to say, "So a text message of gratefulness violates our term of agreement."

"Text?" Lyla said confused. "I thought it was an email."

"That is what I meant to say," Rocket retracted.

"For real," Lyla said. "I am not coming out to play with you right now, Rocket. Have you been contacting Ritchie behind my back?"

"What is your problem?" Rocket asked condescendingly.

"I don't like back stabbers," Lyla answered. "You know what you were doing when you contacted him and then you had the nerve to contact him on a gold digging day."

"What?" Rocket said. "What exactly is a gold digging day, Lyla?"

"Fridays," she said, "are a gold digging day...when all gold diggers need money to go shopping over the weekend. It's no coincidence. I know you're a gold digging freak."

"That does not classify me as a gold digger," Rocket said. "And for your information I shop online all day every day."

"Oh," Lyla said. "So you're a gold digging hussy all day every day."

"You know what," Rocket said, "I do not have time for this."

"Whatever!" Lyla said shortly.

"Whatever!" Rocket shouted.

"Whatever!" they screamed simultaneously.

Lyla hung up the phone.

"Whatever money-grabbing BITCH!" Now she saw why Poison left her own sister alone.

The hostile phone conversation sounded like a soap opera, and although Rocket eventually called back to say she was sorry and that her email was innocent, it was too late. Lyla could spot a Jezebel a mile away. Rocket was fired before they got started. But let the truth be told, Lyla should have seen this coming when Rocket went behind her super's back and Poison's.

When Lyla arrived at the apartment she threw Rocket's belongings out the window.

"I dare her go to my super. I'll let him know how she went behind his back to get another investor without consulting him! Lyla threw more of Rocket's things into the streets.

"And if Rocket does not listen to me about Ritchie, well, little does she know she is messing with a potential serial killer!

"There is no room for back stabbing gold diggers. I will not allow her to stop my progress or interfere in what I have worked hard for. Just let her try...Just let her try to stop me!"

Lyla threw the last piece of Rocket's garments on the sidewalk.

Chapter 31

Sanchez and Carpenter arrived at the airport to review the security video. Sanchez looked over the footage first while Carpenter talked to the security guard that had been on duty the day of the drug run. The woman in the video was in full disguise. She had on a penciled black dress, black light-weight jacket, with a long blonde wig, black lipstick, and huge dark round shaped sunglasses like the superstars wear. Absolutely stunning.

He zoomed in the video as the tension in the room grew stronger. His eyes did not leave the video as he moved in closer to the zoomed in screen, the pressure in his shoulders feeling heavy.

Sanchez knew this was his moment, he felt the hair on the back of his neck rise as his sweaty palms turned red.

"Damn it!" Unfortunately, Sanchez could not tell if the woman in the video was Elizabeth.

"Carpenter," Sanchez called.

"Yeah, detective, you called?"

"Take a look. Does that look like Elizabeth?" Sanchez asked.

"No, if it is, she's in a well put-together disguise," Carpenter answered.

"Wait a minute, she's looking into the camera," Sanchez said. Now both detectives were feeling the tension in the room. It felt like the walls were caving in on them and that the temperature in the room had dropped ten degrees. "Man, you still can't tell!" Carpenter huffed, looking away.

"You have video showing Elizabeth coming from Mexico going through customs," Sanchez said to the manager. "Where is the rest of the footage?!"

"This is all we have," the manager replied.

Sanchez shot the manager a displeased look. He then viewed the only footage they had over and over again.

"Why are we looking at this? There was nothing to see the last time," Carpenter said.

"We may have missed something," the detective said.

Sanchez studied the footage carefully, looking for a possible glitch, especially since the manager gave him a hard time. He watched it through at least ten times.

"See - nothing," Carpenter responded.

"You're right," Sanchez agreed. He then turned to the manager and apologized for yelling at him.

"It's okay," the manager replied. "You're doing your job."

The manager brings his pointer finger up to the stop button on the machine and Sanchez yells, "Wait!"

"What," the manager said.

"Come here, Carpenter, and look at this," Sanchez ordered.

Carpenter looked while the manager was instructed to rewind to a certain area.

"The footage jumps. It *has* been tampered with, you troll!" Carpenter blurted to the manager.

"Troll?" the manager said.

"Anyway," Sanchez said. "That's what we missed last time, and I have a feeling that whatever was there would have broken this…"

"Case wide open," Carpenter interrupted.

"There's nothing wrong with it. But now that I think about it, some of the recorded information was erased," the manager said.

"Erased by whom?" Sanchez questioned.

"We don't know," the manager answered.

"Well, we need the rest of the footage. I don't know doesn't help," Sanchez replied.

"I don't know, what to tell you," the manager said.

"Where is the security guard?" Sanchez asked.

"In the manager's office," Carpenter answered.

"We're going to arrest him," Sanchez said, walking towards the office.

"Okay," Carpenter snickered. "But first, wipe that drool off your face. Elizabeth's hot and all, and I know you like her, but we got a job to do, so come out of dream world."

"Funny! If that even is Elizabeth," Sanchez said while he grabbed the security guard.

"Read him his rights, Carpenter." Sanchez puts the security guard's hands behind his back.

"What are you doing?" the security guard asked. "You are under arrest for drug smuggling," Sanchez answered with authority as he handcuffed the guard.

The guard disagreed, "I have nothing to do with drugs."

"You must have erased it from your memory when you erased the footage," Sanchez accused. Carpenter finished reading the security guard his rights. "It's cold outside but the case is getting hot," Sanchez continued.

"It's not cold outside," Carpenter said.

"It's an expression, Carpenter," Sanchez snapped.

The employees watched as the security guard was escorted out the airport. The detectives could not wait to get away from the consuming roar of the airplanes.

"Get back to work, before I dock your pay," the manager said to his employees.

"You ain't docking my pay, mother fucka," one of the security guards muttered.

Chapter 32

Lyla did not see Rocket at the apartment after the phone call. She also saw that her stuff had been removed from the street. For a few months now, Lyla noticed Ritchie disappeared on Thursdays. He left around 10:00 pm, stayed out all night and then came back to Lyla's house at 4:00 am to sleep. One day, he left at 1:00 am and came back around 3:00 am.

First, he said he was working at the New Rochelle location for a special client in need of his accounting services. Then when he finished that, he said he could not tell her anything because it was an extremely classified job, same old story. This was highly irregular behavior, even for Ritchie. *He must think I'm naïve and I do not appreciate the lies. Ritchie is displaying bad character despite teaching me how vital it is to have good character.*

She followed him one day for two hours or so and discovered that her super moved Rocket in his other apartment building, further uptown. This is the same place Ritchie and Lyla used to meet sometimes. *Why is he meeting Rocket here?*

Ritchie looked around and then went inside the three-story building.

Meanwhile, Lyla stood outside the building, talking on the phone with her aunt. After an hour, Lyla grew impatient. She went to the side of the building to see if she could find out some information, and there she stood, lurking behind the wall, like a robber, gazing in the window. Lyla looked through the slightly open curtains and saw what looked to be an arm but heard definite loud indulging thuds of desire, like an animal in heat.

"Ritchie! Don't stop! Oh, yes!"

Lyla's heart tightened like she was having a heart attack, as she came to grips that Ritchie and Rocket were having an affair.

She told her aunt she just heard Rocket and Ritchie having relations. Her aunt could not believe her ears. Lyla's aunt told her to walk away but she could do no such thing. She meant what she wrote in her diary. *I have to fight for what is mine.*

Lyla threw a brick through the window as she ran for cover. Her aunt laughed while Lyla waited for them to come out the front door.

"I know they are wondering what just happened," Lyla said as they laughed. Two minutes later, Ritchie and Rocket came running out the building, like bank robbers looking for their getaway car. With her aunt still on the phone, Lyla approached them both. As all of them stood standing in the middle of the sidewalk, Ritchie could see Lyla darting evil eyes at Rocket.

Ritchie nor Rocket knew what to say. Lyla, on the other hand, had a lot to say.

"Look ah here!" Lyla said in rage. "I thought you were not seeing her!"

"I had a meeting with Rocket," Ritchie said. "Did you throw the brick?"

"Don't worry about it, liar!" she yelled.

"Who are you calling a liar?" Ritchie asked.

"It's not that type of party," Rocket answered, outright insensibly, choosing to stare straight into the distance.

"I heard y'all," Lyla said.

"Heard what?" Ritchie asked.

"Having sex."

"What?" Ritchie chuckled. "I have a cold and I was clearing my throat."

"'Ritchie! Don't stop! Oh yes!'" Lyla reminded. "Don't stop, what Ritchie?

"Don't stop the meeting," Ritchie replied.

"You must think I was born yesterday," Lyla said. "I know what I heard and you go from this to that. She is not hot. I guess she seduced you with her massive emails and luring language."

"How are you going to say I'm not hot? Look at me," Rocket said, turning around in a full circle.

"You're just a girl with a fancy name. And you are drifting away into the deep end of the pool," Lyla responded.

"Well at least I can swim," Rocket said.

"You are treading dangerous water," Lyla said with confidence. "And when you get tired — or should I say 'when he gets tired of you' — we will see who drowns, and who will be by the poolside relaxing with it all."

"Me!" Rocket said.

"Wrong answer!" Lyla smirked. "Now, Ritchie, are you going to subscribe to this classy magazine or that hot piece of trash?" He was about to say something but before he could Lyla interrupted him. "Don't answer, that question was rhetorical. But go ahead. Hoopoe with the bat lashes need love too."

"My lashes cost a lot of money. I take good care of myself," Rocket responded, looking away.

"I just want to say one word to you," Lyla said. "Spanx."

Rocket rolled her eyes and clicked her tongue.

"Whatever, Lyla."

"Why did you and your lashes leave the house today without your Spanx?" Lyla said. "You should know better than that, you flat chested no ass pimple back old biatch! What are you, like 80-years-old?"

"I'm not 80-years-old," Rocket responded.

"Well you look like you 80-years-old," Lyla said. "Still designing shoes with no Spanx. That, she paused, should be against the law."

"You ain't all that," Rocket said. "Your mama, ain't all that," Lyla replied.

"Funny," Rocket said.

"Suck in, girl; just suck in," Lyla said, touching her stomach and demonstrating how to suck in her stomach. "And go home to your five kids and your husband. You know you lied when you said you did not have one."

"We are divorced. And why do I have to go home to a man when I can fuck yours!" Rocket screamed. Lyla grabbed hold of Rocket's hair weave. "You disrespectful bitch!" Lyla shouted. Rocket swung at Lyla like a man, and hit her on the side of her cheek. Lyla swung back, still holding on to Rocket's two-month-old, bird nest of a hair weave.

Ritchie jumped in between them to stop the fighting, but as soon as he stepped out of the middle, Lyla put Rocket in one of her Hapkido holds like she was a Power Ranger dressed in Givenchy. Rocket screamed.

"Lyla let go of her!" Ritchie said.

"What?" Lyla said and wondered why he cared so much about what she was doing to Rocket. Perhaps this was just polite talk. "You care about this bitch now!"

"Do you want to go to jail for seriously hurting her? I don't want to see you throw your life away. It's not worth it," Ritchie said.

Lyla released Rocket from the deadly hold. Rocket backed off, realizing she had some fighting skills.

"What you backing off for, Rocket, come on!" Lyla yelled.

Ignoring what Ritchie just said she lunged to go after her. Lyla and Rocket were swinging again. She was not going to really hurt Rocket like Ritchie thought; Lyla just wanted to humiliate her in front of him.

Ritchie once again attempted to stop the fight, but he stood back and let them rumble. He was not accustomed to this type of behavior.

Lyla realized she was not acting classy, but was hyped when she had snatched a piece of Rocket's weave out of her head. As soon as Ritchie and Rocket thought the fight was over, Lyla grabbed hold of Rocket's weave again and tore out another piece.

Rocket and Lyla were swinging again, but this time, in the middle of the street. By the time Lyla was done with Rocket, there was a trail of European wavy weave all the way to the end of the street. Rocket was as bald as a locust with short pieces of hair sticking up in various places. She was embarrassed as Lyla overturned a can of trash on her head; she then took a picture of Rocket and said, "Since you like for people to follow you online I'll take the initiative and give your customers an update on their shoe designer."

Rocket shook off the trash.

"This is not over! This is not over!"

"Oh, you what some more!" Lyla shouted.

"This is not over!" Rocket repeated, foaming at the mouth. "This is not over! This is not over! This is not over! This is not over!"

Lyla and Ritchie walked away from her. It was quite obvious she was having a nervous breakdown.

"I should have you manage all of my buildings," Ritchie said jokingly to Lyla. He seemed elusive, she hardly considered him as the same person who had been so charming, and she had no time right now to figure him out. Lyla ignored Ritchie as she looked over and glowered at Rocket one last time like she wanted to bleach load her wounds. She then found her phone.

"Damn! My screen is cracked. That's like riding around in a banged up Bentley," Lyla said as she walked away.

Lyla's aunt heard everything on the phone, but before Lyla could speak with her aunt, Ritchie was behind her.

He said to Lyla, "You are too emotional."

"Are you talking to me?" Lyla asked. "Mister, 'don't stop the meeting.' Real clever response, by the way, Ritchie."

"I'm being serious," Ritchie answered.

"So am I," Lyla replied.

"Your attitude flares instantly," Ritchie accused.

"So! What's your point?!" Lyla said.

"My point is, you put yourself on a pedestal," Ritchie said. "And because of that, you react quickly and recklessly and you make bad decisions, like just now."

"So is that a threat?" Lyla asked.

"I'm just saying to slow down and humble yourself," Ritchie answered. "Keep your temper in check, as that's when you'll be at your best."

At this point Lyla was not hearing Ritchie. Normally his wise words would sink right in, but her respect for him was gone.

Instead she said, "Let me give you word of advice, take your mind out of the basement and bring it back to the penthouse if you want to be with me, because you're slipping." Lyla walked away.

"Humble yourself, Lyla," Ritchie said.

"Forget you Ritchie," Lyla replied.

"Hello," Lyla said to her aunt on the phone.

"Why on earth would you put up with him," Lyla's aunt said. "He has a lot of nerve talking to you like that after catching him in bed with Rocket."

"I know right," Lyla agreed. "After all that I've done for him. But regardless, I'm the classy one, so let him read up on some of that yesterday's trash. He'll be back for the new edition. Maybe I'll take him back, maybe I won't."

"You too grown, little girl," her aunt laughed. "Now it is a well-known fact that Ritchie Perez has no respect for you or anyone."

"I know," Lyla replied weakly.

"It seems like when men cheat, they go down instead of up," her aunt said. "Ritchie is doing anything with a vagina. If he keeps this up, in a couple of years, he's going to end up dating a girl from the projects who is going to clean him out, if he really has money like he say he does.

"You are too nice. I would have been taken him for his money and left him in the dust. I don't even think he's really married nor has kids. I think it's all a front."

"I know he's married with kids," Lyla said. "I have met the kids and been to the house."

"Well, okay," her aunt replied. "I don't believe anything he says. His family is probably actors. His house and cars probably belong to friends. I bet if you follow him to Connecticut, he lives in a shack by himself."

"Oh, stop it," Lyla said.

"Ritchie is a straight loony tune just like Casmir," her aunt replied. "Watch what I tell you. But go ahead and learn what you can so you can get yourself together; its way overdue."

"Yes, that's the plan!" Lyla said with excitement.

"But don't let your mother find out about Ritchie because you know my sister will think you are with another crazy one," her aunt said. "You know your mother does not play, she don't care how old you get, little girl, or how many arguments you two get in, you still her baby."

"Yeah okay," Lyla replied. "My mom does not care about me."

"Let me school you on my sister and on mother daughter relationships," her aunt said. "When a daughter is five, she's like a princess. The girl will model in her mom's heels and jewelry; smear her face with her mom's make-up, wanting to be just like mommy. It's like this until about thirteen, and then the game changes. The teenager becomes the mother's worst enemy and somewhere between the twenties and thirties, usually, the daughter becomes the mother's best friend again. Despite how my sister was raised as a child or what has happened between the both of you, you and your mom will be close again."

"Yeah yeah yeah," Lyla responded. "Did she really have to stand on her head and read the bible?"

"What?" her aunt said.

"My mom can make up some stories," Lyla laughed.

"Just watch what I tell you," her aunt said. "You will find out about that Ritchie and you will be close with your mom again little girl."

"I believe you," Lyla replied.

"Well, I can't believe you caught Ritchie and Rocket," Lyla's aunt snickered.

"Even if Ritchie and that bulldog met at the haunted bridge to creep, I would still find them," she said as they both laughed.

"Where is the haunted bridge?" her aunt asked.

"I don't know," Lyla chuckled, "Moon Juice Drive, but wherever it is, I'll be there. They can't hide from me."

They both laughed.

"Where is Moon Juice Drive, little girl?"

"I'll talk to you later," Lyla said still laughing.

Moving on, Lyla knew she could not hate Rocket but given her state of mind, Lyla could not deny that the Rocket and Ritchie situation put a serious dent in Ritchie and Lyla's relationship. Lyla came to the conclusion that he had consumed enough of her personal time. It was hurtful indeed, but her total attention for now on was to learn as much as possible from him for a little while longer, and then leave him for good.

Still, Lyla stopped talking to Ritchie for a while but when he bombarded her phone with literally one hundred phone calls a day for an entire two-week period, her resolves weakened and she finally answered the phone. They made up just before she found out that he signed a country band to his management company.

The lead singer of the band was a woman. *Bastard.*

Chapter 33

At the office, still no Roger. The accountant from across the hall came over looking for Ritchie, and Lyla told him Ritchie wasn't in, he said to tell Ritchie that they needed to talk.

"May I ask why?" Lyla said.

"Well, first I would like to thank him for the referral," he replied. "I made some money but it was not enough to cover what he owes me."

"He owes you money?" Lyla said.

"He owes a lot of people money," he said.

"Really?" Lyla said.

"How can you work in this place concealing such grace? You should not be working for him. He is not a good businessman. Once he gets what he wants, he will leave you hanging," the accountant said. "How would you like to leave with me?"

"Me?" Lyla said.

"Yes," the man responded. "I would love to have your slender model figure and beautiful face in my office."

"I'm flattered. But thank you, no," Lyla said.

So far everything sounded unbelievable, but she still loved Ritchie. To Lyla, love was not a feeling; it was a commitment. It was loyalty. Ritchie never had a person as loyal as Lyla and he admired that. This was why he could not let her go and she could not leave him.

Then again, Lyla felt Ritchie used Roger and her at times. Ritchie talked a good game but he needed to practice what he preached. But in Ritchie's mind, he did not care if he used Lyla or Roger because he knew he was teaching her how to be a great businesswoman, and he brought in lots of clients for the firm.

Regardless, Lyla had to make some decisions, like whether she was going to turn him in to the police or leave it alone. She had to keep in mind that she may not be the only one in danger, but her family's safety could also be at risk if she pushed Ritchie's buttons the wrong way. He was clever but also unpredictable, which made him scary, dangerous, and possibly deadly. She remembered one day, when Ritchie was drunk, he told her that he would take the heads of each of her family members, send them to her house one by one, just to drive her insane, and then throw her out a window.

Lyla may need to leave this one alone.

Luckily she had a great resource to help her decide – her friend Peter, who was good at discerning bullshit. He was coming to New York City soon for a fashion event and Lyla couldn't wait. In the meantime, since Lyla never heard back from Pastor Bill, she went to see him unannounced.

Chapter 34

During Lyla's way overdue morning jog along the Hudson River, she stopped and reminisced about her first photo shoot when she was a teenager. *Those were the easy days,* Lyla thought. *The question is, how did I get from that wonderful moment to this mess?*

Ritchie and I have been through it. *I know it's normal for the person being taught to be like their teacher. The scary part is, I feel like I'm turning into who Ritchie possibly is, which is a con artist instead of a respectful businessperson,* as she cringed. *I'm fooling everyone, just like him. Now both of us are on to another project with this band.*

In a few weeks, Lyla and Ritchie would be meeting the band at the studio in Queens. Meanwhile, she found herself sitting across from Pastor Bill in his office. He had been away on a missionary trip.

The pastor was visibly uncomfortable and Lyla could tell that he had never been around a model before. He was average looking, not really Lyla's type, but he was extremely kind. She could also tell he really loved the Lord by the way he spoke to her. He understood her situation, but could also tell she was holding back during their conversation.

"So, are you going to tell me everything, Lyla?"

"What do you mean?" Lyla asked.

"There is more on your mind. I want you to feel comfortable and tell me what's bothering you," the pastor answered.

"I just feel a little uncomfortable consulting with Mr. Goody Two-Shoes," Lyla said.

"Now that's funny. I'm definitely not Mr. Goody Two-Shoes," the pastor replied.

"You could have fooled me, Pastor," Lyla said.

He stood up and stared at Lyla, as he unbuttoned his shirt one by one.

"Wait a minute pastor!" Lyla said. "I'm not ready for all that, and I'm sure your wife would not appreciate you unbuttoning your shirt in front of me." He continued unbuttoning his shirt. "My wife died two years ago of stomach cancer." *Wow, the same as my great aunt.*

"I'm sorry to hear that," Lyla said.

"No need to be sorry," the pastor said. "She is with the Lord and she left me three wonderful grown sons: Bill Jr., Thomas, and Fred. He showed her family photos on his desk.

"A bachelor pastor. Interesting," Lyla responded.

"Something like that," the pastor chuckled. "Now that we have cleared that up I want to show you something."

He took off his shirt and then moved his sleeveless undershirt over to the side to show the top corner of his chest. The pastor had a tattoo. He had been a member of a well known gang in California.

"I have fallen short of the glory of God, too," Pastor Bill continued. "But God's mercy saved me and he will do the same for you, no matter how many times you have fallen."

Lyla opened up to the pastor. She even told him about Ritchie and the unspeakable chain of events in Mexico. He listened with his eyes and ears and did not judge her. Lyla asked him to keep everything she told him a secret. He reminded her everything is confidential.

Though she typically did not trust authority figures, she trusted him for some reason and after a few more session they became really good friends. She felt like she could now begin the process of letting go of her alter ego by totally getting rid of the anger she held within. He gave her advice and showed her how to think positively and not dwell on what she had done or what had happened to her in her past. The pastor also gave her his cell number and email address so she could easily contact him, and he could return her messages faster.

What a breath of fresh air, Lyla thought, but unfortunately, Lyla knew she had to get back to reality.

With that said, it was time for Lyla to meet the band. She had to make it look as if Ritchie was legit and that he could be trusted. This was hard for her now because of everything that happened with Ritchie and the pastor's positive influence on her life. But nonetheless, Lyla put on her game face hoping the band would eventually see right through him.

Bizzie was the only one that showed up to the first meeting. She said she wanted to talk to Lyla and Ritchie alone. The meeting seemed promising and Lyla took a liking to Bizzie although she could tell Bizzie was already showing signs she was in to Ritchie intimately.

Lyla wanted to warn Bizzie indirectly about him, as she pulled Bizzie aside and said, "You don't know me that well, but trust me when I tell you this - keep it business, and never fall for Ritchie."

"Fuck off! Don't tell me what to do, bitch!" Bizzie shouted.

This band is headed downhill. But whatever, Bizzie looks like a stressed out man with a wig anyways, Lyla said to herself. *I gave her heads up, but now she has to make the right decision for her and the three other people in her band she is responsible for.*

Lyla stood in the bathroom retouching her make-up and brushing through her many tangles that knotted her curls. Moments later, *soft and fluffy again*, she said to herself, as she fixed her hair slightly around her shoulders.

She overheard Ritchie saying to Bizzie in the hallway, "You are as lovely as a dream from heaven." He gave her his credit card to buy some alcohol from the corner store for everyone. *Ritchie won't even let me touch his card,* Lyla thought. *And Bizzie has known him for all of a couple of seconds. He is so backwards and really showing off. The funniest detail is that I know Ritchie has never had any interest in managing a country band, and I suspect he is using this opportunity to get back at me by showering Bizzie, with attention.*

Lyla stepped out into the hallway so they could see her while throwing daggers at Ritchie with her eyes.

Bizzie wasn't sure if Ritchie and Lyla were dating but she could tell something was going on. Lyla walked away without saying anything. Sometimes silence speaks louder than words.

"That bitch is spoiling my fun," Bizzie said to Ritchie.

"Don't worry about her," Ritchie replied.

"She better watch her back," Bizzie said to Ritchie, as she threw a warning glare at him and from a distance at Lyla.

Ritchie's plan was to use Lyla's connections to take the band to the top and leave her hanging. Lyla had already used her connections for Ritchie in a few business ventures that ultimately fell through. She was left looking bad, and now this band. *Not going to happen.*

Ritchie was upset when Lyla said she would not use her connections for the band, and had the nerve to say to her, "What money or connections do you have? You have nothing and you come from nothing." Well, he wasn't saying that when he needed that money or those connections, and this was why she did not like to open up about her life. Now he thought that he knew her, and when he got upset, he could be disrespectful.

Where is his money? The cars? He claims his connections are more important than mine, so he did not use his until it was significant enough. This guy seemed to be phonier as the days went by.

The next day, Ritchie and Lyla had to meet the entire band at the studio in Queens. He worked his charm and now they all trusted him. The band believed Ritchie was going to make them famous. With what connections and with what money Lyla had no idea.

Meanwhile, the studio became Ritchie and Lyla's second home, and as time went on it was obvious Bizzie was falling in love with Ritchie. Poor thing was as blind as a bat. Yeah, Lyla was displeased, but it was only natural. She did not say much about it. Lyla let it play out.

After one of the sessions, they descended down five long flights of a gloomy-looking staircase to go home. One of the band members and Lyla were the first to go while Ritchie and Bizzie lingered behind, slowly catching up. As she stepped down on the fourth set of steps Lyla searched for one of her lifesavers while the band member held a conversation on his phone.

He put the phone on speaker and asked, "Is that Battle?"

"Yes," the person on the other end answered.

"Aww let me speak to her," the band member said.

Lyla assumed it was a dog he was referring to from the barking in the background.

"Ruff, rrrrrruuuu, ruff, ruff, ruff, grouuull, ruff, ruff, rrrruuuuu, ruff, ruff," the band member said to the dog. The dog owner heard the band member and said, "My dog speaks English." Lyla laughed as she felt something at the bottom of her ankles, and before she knew it, she was falling down the stairs. The band member caught her before she reached the bottom, probably saving Lyla's life.

Lyla got up to make sure she did not break any bones. The band member saw a thin piece of wire going across the top of the staircase.

"What the hell is this?" the band member asked, as he looked at Lyla.

"How should I know?!" Lyla answered. "But I know one thing, Bizzie tripped me!"

"What?" he said as he hung up from his call.

Lyla ran upstairs looking for Bizzie, but she was nowhere to be found.

She called out her name and shouted at the top of her lungs, "I know you tripped me! You think you are so slick!" Still no answer, so Lyla proceeded to say, "Bizzie where are you, you busy little bee!"

In response, Lyla heard gunshots and then felt a blow to her head. Everything went black.

She laid there, unconscious, in the middle of the hallway with part of her leg hanging in the bathroom, and after a few moments, regained consciousness. Lyla swayed her head slowly right then left then right then left then right and then stopped. She realized that a gun with a small dent had been placed in her hand.

Where did this gun come from? she asked herself.

Bizzie came running around the corner like a butcher's dog. She took note of the gun in Lyla's hand.

"You shot at me!" Bizzie shouted.

"No, I did not," Lyla replied as she sat up to rub her head. "But you tripped me, so maybe I should shoot you." Bizzie was mischievous to be a country singer, she acted and dressed more like a rock star. She was known to be playful and thought everything was a joke. No one knew what she'd do next.

"I did not trip you," Bizzie said.

"And I did not shoot you," Lyla responded. "I don't know where this gun came from."

"Yeah, okay," Bizzie said. "I'm calling the cops."

"Call them," Lyla said derisively.

Ritchie reappeared rushing over to Lyla to help her off the ground and asked, "What happened?" Lyla and Bizzie yelled simultaneously.

"She tripped me!"

"She shot at me!"

Ritchie looked bamboozled; he attempted to assuage the situation.

"Where were you, Ritchie?" Lyla asked. "How did I get a gun in my hand?"

"I have no idea," he answered. Ritchie reached for the envelope that was hanging halfway out her purse.

"Give me that," Lyla snapped.

"Sorry," Ritchie said. "I was helping you put it back."

"I got it," Lyla responded.

"This is bullshit!" Bizzie blurted. "The truth will come out when the police arrive." They waited for about thirty minutes. The police never showed. In New York, a person had to be shot five times before the police show up, especially in Queens.

The justice system was imperfect at times.

Lyla couldn't believe Ritchie was in Queens, anyway. He would always tell her that the top-secret associates he worked for did not allow him to leave the city, but for Bizzie, it was okay to go where he wanted. *Men.*

Lyla told Bizzie if she wanted to press charges then come find her. She was not letting Ritchie or the band take her down. Lyla left the studio.

When she arrived home, Lyla placed the gun with the dent under her pillow to sleep with from now on. Believe or not, Lyla hated guns, considering everything she had been through involving them, but it did provide her with some sense of security. It was fully loaded, safety off.

Chapter 35

Lyla received an urgent message from her modeling agency in Chicago. Her agency said she was requested to be the lead girl in a rap video for a known artist in Los Angeles.

First of all, I do not care much for rap videos, Lyla thought, as she associated rappers with Casmir throwing his hands up in the air to his gangsta music, at the park, shortly followed by her face being slapped and her stomach kicked in. *No, thank you.*

Furthermore, I did not know I had an agency in Chicago until now.

Her agency in New York explained to her they submitted her pictures to their Chicago division, and they loved her look. *It would have been nice if I knew,* Lyla thought. *But that is how the modeling world works sometimes.*

Lyla's agency said she did not have to be the lead girl. She will be in the party scene. After a bit more convincing, she did not think about the incident with Casmir anymore and agreed to do the shoot as long as she was not the main girl. Lyla needed a break anyways, from the chaos in New York and now she could get a natural tan. *Ha, ha.*

The next morning she was on a plane to the city of endless summers. Her friend Sean met her at the airport, an hour late.

"Were you busy with your morning errands," Lyla said jokingly to Sean as they hugged each other.

"No, I was just sitting around waiting for your arrival, Buckle Duck," Sean laughed. *I hate when he calls me that,* she said to herself.

"Okay, Butter Buns," Lyla said.

"You know I hate when you call me that," Sean said.

"Well don't call me Buckle Duck," Lyla insisted.

"Okay, Buckle Duck," Sean replied. They both chuckled.

"Okay, Butter Buns."

She had not seen him since he left New York a few years ago, so they were on an expedition of hitting the clubs. Lyla stayed at the place he shared with their friend Social instead of the model's apartment. This was her first time in LA, and she wanted to be around people she knew.

When Lyla arrived, Social was wearing an adorable baby blue short set showing off her beautiful long thin legs. Her hair was in two long ponytails shaping her appealing apple pie face, and her perfect bow lips were filled in with Barbie doll pink lipstick. She was a beautiful 30-year-old model, straight country Caucasian from Kansas City. Even past her prime years, her beautiful sun tanned skin, unique features, and body kept her in the modeling game.

She had the car she faithfully rented three days a week parked out front, but was saving her modeling money for a traitor trailer to ride the streets of LA. Social was sawing wood in her backyard with a cigarette hanging out the side of her mouth. Lyla laughed.

"She is off the chain. I do not understand why Social does not move to Sanguine Land, A.K.A. New York City, because she is non-stop."

"Do you want me to let Social know you are here?" Sean asked.

"Nahyesh," Lyla answered.

"Uh?" Sean laughed. "What does Nahyesh mean?"

"It just came out that way. It's no and yes put together with a twist," Lyla giggled. "I did not know what to say so it came out Nahyesh."

"You want to wait, don't you?" Sean asked.

"Yes. Let me rest. They don't call her Social for nothing and I want to be well rested for tonight," Lyla answered.

"Gotcha," Sean said.

Lyla missed breakfast in LA but she was not going to miss LA brunch. She took a couple of pictures of the three of them with her phone's camera while they were eating.

"Awww, picture perfect. Love your almost-Italian nose Sean," Lyla joked. Social pulled out her rolling paper to make herself a cigarette. It looked like she was puffing weed, and she loved watching people's reaction.

After brunch, they went shopping on Belair Road.

"This is an awesome spot to promote my Steam line," Lyla continued.

"What is that?" Social asked.

"My clothing line," Lyla answered.

"Look at you! Not lying down. You never told me," Social responded.

"I know. I want to get something going before I tell anyone, because I'm always starting things and not finishing them," Lyla said.

"Well, join the club, I'm the same way," Social replied.

"She already has, you guys are friends, birds of a feather flock together. How is your book coming along, Social?" Sean chuckled.

"I sold six books. I'm rich bitch!" Social laughed.

"Yeah right," Sean replied.

"Don't be jealous!" Social shouted.

"You did not finish writing it, so how in the hell did you sell six books," Sean said.

"Sean you can be a real pain in my 'you know what' sometimes," Social said. "Now shut up!"

Lyla happened to look across the road and saw a famous actor talking to someone in an ice cream parking lot.

"I love you," he mouthed to her from across the street. *Whatever...he's married*, she said to herself and kept walking. She did not dare tell Social because she would have forced Lyla across the street to get his number. Lyla did not want any more married men around her.

That whisper will be my secret of endearment, she thought.

Social and Lyla made their way to Venice Beach after a long day of hanging out and shopping while Sean headed back to the apartment.

"Dag it, my flip-flop broke. I done worn these things out," Lyla said.

"Call Sean and ask him to bring some from the house," Social suggested.

"Good idea," Lyla said. "I'll have him bring my nude ones, but I got to get a new pair of black ones. Man, there are no fat traps on this beach."

"What are fat traps?" Social asked.

"Cellulite, fat traps, it's all the same," Lyla answered.

While watching the wild waves of the sea shedding the foam of their own shame and fine beach-bodied men, Lyla received a text from her old manager, Sugar: "You are always missing your blessing, you are a dumb ass." One of the many reasons that Lyla dropped Sugar was because he did not know how to respectfully communicate to her. Lyla had no idea what he was talking about and could not care less. If anything, her life was looking up again.

"He is so rude," Lyla murmured.

"Who's that, Lyla?" Social wondered.

"Just my old manager getting on my nerves," Lyla said.

"I thought you guys were tight," Social replied.

"We were," Lyla said. "But he's rude and he gives me terrible advice all the time. The straw that broke the camel's back is when he messed up my shot at becoming a Sports Illustrated model through a contest they had."

"What?!"

"Yes," Lyla continued. "I did my part, staying small by walking a hundred blocks a day in New York, showing personality, so on and so forth. I was in the top ten out of five thousand girls and I asked him to do some public relations for that and he slept on it. He blamed it on politics when I didn't win."

"So why didn't he politically promote you!" Social laughed. "You could have gotten some kind of acknowledgment from it if he had of done some PR. He sounds lazy to me."

"Exactly," Lyla agreed.

"All that hard work, down the drain," Social said.

"So what did I need him for?" Lyla said. "I cannot even continue to be his friend because of his disrespectful and insensitive attitude, always bringing up my past from when I was a teenager only to have him turn around and mess up the biggest client in the industry."

"Yeah, that's crazy," Social replied.

"Not only that, he moved me back to Manhattan, which was cool but I had to hide from my superintendant when it was time to pay for that expensive rent, that he promised to pay," Lyla said. "It was a mess, and it's a good thing my super and his wife took me under their wing. But, for real, I was just fine in Jersey City. I could afford the rent and I had enough to take care of myself."

"I hear you," Social responded.

"I fired him through a text message," Lyla laughed. "It would have taken too much energy to call and argue."

"Yeah! You already wasted enough time so why waste your breath. You have to drawn the line somewhere," Social said, as they both laughed.

"And that was not the only thing he slept on," Lyla said. "He used to fall asleep while doing clients hair."

"What!" Social screamed.

"Yeah," Lyla giggled. "He fell asleep doing my hair one day, burning me and stuff."

"Ouch!" Social laughed.

"And to top it all off he has the nerve to be upset with me," Lyla said.

"What?!" Social replied.

"Yelp, he started a 'Hate Lyla Campaign,'" Lyla laughed.

"That's insane," Social said. "He can put all of his energy in to a 'Hate Lyla Campaign,' but too lazy to start a PR campaign for something that would have helped the both of you."

"Exactly!" Lyla replied. "Backwards, right?"

"Yes, girl," Social said. "Haters love to hate me and I can see they love to hate you too, Lyla."

"They love it! Lyla laughed. "Love it, you hear me girl?! Love to hate me!"

Regardless of the hate, I know Sugar means well, and I still love him and will forever be grateful for what he did do, but I will love him and be thankful from afar, as she erased and ignored Sugar's text.

"If I'm not mistaken," Social said. "Didn't you try out for the Miss USA pageant?"

"Yes, but I bailed," Lyla said.

"Why?"

"Nerves," Lyla admitted. "But I entered another contest and won!"

"Nice!" Social said with excitement.

Lyla was relaxing on her beach towel, soaking in the sun, while tourist watched Social, sunbathing topless to avoid tan lines.

Sean finally showed up with the flip-flops.

"Whose are these?" Lyla questioned.

"I bought you some new ones from Calvin Klein," he answered.

"Nice, but they don't match what I'm wearing Sean," she said as she slipped them on. "And they don't fit silly willy," Lyla laughed. "They're two sizes two small, I look like a beach bum! Who does that?"

"I can't help you got big feet, now wear them," Sean demanded.

"Well," Lyla said. "I don't have a choice now, do I? Don't you know you're not supposed to buy woman shoes because they will walk right out of your life."

"You ain't going anywhere," Sean laughed hysterically. "Especially in those...big foot."

"You set me up," Lyla giggled. "And in the future I only buy J. Crew flip flops."

"That's funny," Sean said.

"Y'all laughing about my hair," a girl on the next towel over while eating an apple said. "Y'all laughing about my hair," the girl repeated.

"What," Lyla said.

"Is she talking to us?" Social asked.

"Y'all laughing about my hair," the girl said again and again.

"No one is laughing about your hair," Lyla said.

"We didn't see your hair," Sean responded.

Now that they'd seen the girl's hair, though, she looked like she was the sister of Edward Scissor Hands if Beetle Juice was their dad. Lyla, Social, and Sean did not know whether or not to laugh about what she was saying or her hair.

"It's time to go," Sean said.

"We are not laughing about your hair," Lyla replied. "But you need to cut your apple before eating it. Your front teeth are made for smiling only and, in your case, laughing." The girl spit at Lyla and missed. She was obviously a joke because she ran for her life when Lyla leaned forward, getting ready to strangle her.

Sean grabbed Lyla pushing her forward to get her off the beach.

"This is not New York," Sean said. "Keep it moving."

"Venice Beach has got some weirdos," Lyla said. "'Y'all laughing about my hair,'" as they laughed and continued to walk away.

Social received a text.

"There is a Hawaiian Luau party tonight at some new club," Social announced. "It doesn't give the name but I got the address. Everyone has to wear their swim suits."

"Alright," Sean said.

"Yeah, I can show off my tan," Lyla smiled.

"Yes," Sean said. "You look exotic when you are tanned...yum."

"Let me find out," Social said, looking at Sean and Lyla.

"There is nothing to find out, Social," Lyla said.

"Yeah, okay but oooo," Social said. "You can wear that nice bathing suit you bought today."

"Ah, no," Lyla said. "Not before I take it to the dry cleaners."

"What? It's brand new," Social said.

"Yeah," Lyla said. "But I don't know who was wearing it before me. Yuck, that thing has DNA and sweat and everything. I dry clean all of my new clothes especially bathing suits."

"Okay, I'm wearing my new Gucci bikini tonight," Social replied.

While they were getting dressed back at the apartment, Lyla was singing her favorite old school Al B Sure song in opera, "Waiting by the Phone," while thinking about the Hawaiian Luau party. *Is this the same party I was supposed to organize with Ritchie?* Lyla asked herself.

Lyla continued singing. Social saw Sean dunking.

"What are you doing, Sean?" Social asked.

"Don't you hear that? It sounds like an exotic bird," Sean answered.

"That is Lyla singing. It goes along with her exotic tan," Social replied."

"Oh man. I thought a bird flew in here," Sean said.

Sean and Social could not stop laughing.

"There you go with your orgasm laugh," Social said.

"Fuck you," he replied.

Sean walked into the bedroom where Lyla was getting ready.

"Get out of here!" Lyla yelled, while hiding her naked body and her special make-up concealer.

"Man, why you tripping, I seen it before," Sean said while Social peaked from behind Sean's shoulder.

"Oh really," Social said, pushing Sean out the way. "I knew there was something going on between you two! You kept this dirty little secret from me."

"There is nothing dirty about it," Lyla said. "And you need to stop your lying, Sean. You wish you saw this, now get out!"

"You always so damn bossy. Just stop the singing," Sean said.

"When I get famous, don't ask me for some money," she laughed. "Now get out!"

"You look so beautiful and radiant when you mad," Sean said, sarcastically.

"Shut up!" Lyla replied sternly. "And I'm not mad yet. But I will be if you do not leave!"

"Stop being immature," Sean said.

Lyla pushed Sean out the door and yelled, "You are agitating me!"

After freshening up her Chanel eyeliner and applying a second coat of Givenchy mascara, she examined her suitcase for the perfect bathing suit and decided on a leopard print two piece. It wasn't her favorite, but it made her feel wild and daring. Lyla shortly grabbed her magic concealer she had specially made by a make-up artist friend. Lyla called it magic because it hid the stab and bullet scars so well it was like they didn't exist.

She filed what little bit of nails she had left so she could polish them plum purple. Then, Lyla threw on her bathing suit, open toed pumps, black shawl, and a few squirts of her favorite sun splash mist and then in walked Sean again eyeing her like an animal in heat.

He closed the door behind him.

"So, what's up?"

"Look, Sean. The last person I want knowing that you're my LA fling is Social," Lyla replied.

"Fling? You know I love you," Sean said.

"Yeah, okay. You love these," Lyla smiled, cupping her breasts in her hands. "Love is sexy."

He walked towards Lyla.

"Yes, it is."

"So you want to be that unwritten chapter in Social's book," Lyla laughed.

"Yeah," Sean said. "The love of your life you never speak about." He held Lyla in his arms.

"Not while Social is around," Lyla said.

"She's in the kitchen smoking weed," Sean replied.

"Just stop!" Lyla screamed. She pushed him away. "Get out of here Sean."

"Man, whatever," Sean said. He grabbed Lyla again and slowly kissed her. Lyla simply couldn't resist any more until she finally pushed him away again.

"You tease," he accused.

"I'm not the one who came looking for you," Lyla reminded. "I was in here minding my business." Lyla's phone rang, displaying Ritchie's name across the screen.

"Don't answer the phone for that old man," Sean demanded.

"He is not old," Lyla said.

"Dating that old married man."

"You think you know everything, don't you Sean," Lyla said as she answered the phone while Sean kissed on her neck. *He just won't give up.*

"I'm glad you called, because I got a question," Lyla said, Sean continuing to kiss her.

"Ask me," Ritchie said.

"Get off the phone Lyla," Sean blurted.

"Who is that?" Ritchie asked angrily. "I thought you were staying with your friend Social. You fucking him!"

"I am with Social and I'm not fucking anyone but you," Lyla answered.

Ritchie did not want to hear anymore and told Lyla to never call him again. Lyla was devastated, especially because Sean was just a friend, and Lyla was not doing anything. Ritchie refused to take her back after telling him over and over again there was nothing going on between her and Sean. Lyla had no choice but to use her ace card to get Ritchie back.

Lyla told Sean she'd have sex with him if he called Ritchie and tell him they did not have sex.

"Say that again," Sean said. "You heard me," Lyla replied.

As tempted as Sean was he did not want to talk to Ritchie, so he declined. She took her bikini and shawl off and stood there in front of him, completely naked, wearing only high heels.

Sean walked towards Lyla, gently wrapped his arms around her waist, and kissed her forehead.

"So, you're seriously going to let me in that juice box if I call Bitchie?"

"It's Ritchie," Lyla corrected as she paused and then looked him in the eyes. She then proceeded to kiss and suck on his chest and said, "What you think? Now make that phone call." Lyla continued to kiss him while she told him what to say to Ritchie. He finally gave in and made the call for Lyla, as she suckled on Sean's available earlobe while speaking with Ritchie.

After Sean convinced Ritchie that he and Lyla did not have sex, Sean threw Lyla on the bed and she rode his huge bologna pony, doggy style, like there was no tomorrow. Social and Ritchie had no clue, and Lyla wanted to keep it that way.

They drove to the club while Lyla admired the beautiful hills and valleys framing the city of California, music blasting in the car. When they pulled up in front of the club, they took note of the people in line.

"I thought everyone had to wear a bathing suit," Lyla said.

"Yeah," Social said. "That is what my friend told me."

"Well, everyone is fully clothed. But whatever, let's still go in," Lyla responded.

"It doesn't matter to me," Sean shrugged. "Yeah that's because you did not wear your bright pink Speedo's," Lyla said.

"Fuck you, I don't wear no damn Speedos," Sean said.

Social turned down the music and turned to Sean.

"The point is you did not put on your swimwear Sean!" Sean laughed and said to Social, "You got a big mouth. You know that, right?"

"You just need to take off your pants and wear your boxers," Social suggested. "You silly!" Sean said as he pointed out a parking space.

Social parked the car and walked up to the front door of the club, handing Lyla weed to hide in her clutch bag. Lyla thought nothing of it since she was the only one with a purse. When they entered the club, security was checking everyone's bags. Distracted and checking out the club Lyla forgot she had the weed in her clutch.

The guard was about to throw her out the club until Social told him that Lyla was going to be in a music video tomorrow for Silk.

"Who?" the guard asked, "Snoop?"

"Yeah, Snoop," Social answered. He took the weed from Lyla and told them to go in the club. Lyla was relieved.

Sean and Social ordered their drinks from the drink tickets Social's friend gave her. The drink tickets didn't cover wine, so Lyla had to purchase her own. They walked around, checking out the new three-level club. Lyla saw someone on the second floor holding a silent auction for a charity.

This better not be the event Ritchie said was a fake, Lyla thought.

"Lyla!" Social yelled.

"What's up? Are you drunk already?" Lyla asked.

"I'm not drunk," Social answered. "I was trying to get your attention. You look like you were daydreaming."

"I'm not daydreaming and don't drink too much, Social," Lyla said. "You know the last time you got drunk, you were hanging off my chandeliers."

"Ha, ha. I got this," Social said.

Social found out there was going to be a bikini contest and the prize was fifteen hundred dollars.

"We are the only ones in bikinis. This is going to be easy money," Lyla said.

"Like taking candy from a baby," Social replied, high-fiving Lyla, as she continued to say, "Yah!"

Lyla's first night in LA, and she was about to do a bikini contest, something she had never done before in her life. *Whoo Hoo!* Social and Lyla agreed to split the money when they win.

"Let's go to the bar and have a shot before we go backstage," Social suggested.

"Okay," Lyla agreed. "But I want a shot of wine."

"I never heard of a shot of wine," Social said.

"I just made it up."

"Forget about wine for the night," Social said. "Live a little!"

"I drink other stuff," Lyla replied.

"Here, Lyla," Sean said as he handed Lyla a glass. "Taste this." Lyla took a sip and then downed the full shot.

"That tasted like juice," Lyla said. "This is not going to get me tipsy for the night; give me another one please." Shot after shot after shot after shot after shot they drank Patron.

Sean stood in the crowd while Social and Lyla went backstage to get ready. Lyla's felt her cell phone vibrating.

"Hello! Ritchie, I have to call you back!" Lyla shouted over the music, her finger hovering over the end button.

"Are you out?" Ritchie asked.

"Yes, I'm having beers with the boys!" Lyla answered. "What?!" Ritchie shouted...Lyla chuckled.

"What are you doing out? Did you ask me?" Ritchie questioned. Ritchie must be losing his mind, talking to her like that. She hung up on him.

The announcer, LA's finest talk show host was on stage. She was a fiery character as she pumped the crowd up while the music switched over to a selected tune for the contest.

"Social, the show is starting," Lyla said excitedly, drinking more Patron.

The host was wearing a chocolate bikini drenched in chocolate diamonds on top of her chocolate skin. She announced her name as "Chocolate Succumb," and then revealed the name of the club as she pointed at the flashing sign to her left. It read, "Heat." Lyla swallowed her liquor hard. She knew for sure this was the event she was supposed to organize.

I will deal with Ritchie later.

"I have never seen anything like her before," Lyla continued. "We have to go to one of Chocolate's shows, Social."

"I've been. And she's awesome," Social said.

Lyla was first in line pumping herself up.

"We are about to get this money, girl!" Lyla laughed.

"Yes, biatch!" Social replied.

Lyla felt her phone vibrating again and it was Ritchie, but this time he was listening to her voice mail saying, "Hello you reached L-Y-L-A leave a message and I will call you back...maybe." She turned around to drop her bathing suit shawl on the ground and saw a line of girls in the most sluttish G-string bikinis.

"Ah, Social, look behind you," Lyla said. Social turned her head and was startled.

"Whatever," Social said. "They are video girls. We are models, real models. We will win."

Meanwhile, Lyla's heart raced slightly as she scrutinized the girls, and it didn't help when she saw Peter's ex-girlfriend, Mad Love. She was the sluttish looking of the bunch. Lyla could see why Peter broke up with her. Mad Love had to be at least seven months pregnant and was about to dance. Lyla kept her distance because Mad Love did Peter wrong, but she couldn't help wondering who the father was.

Lyla pushed the red velvet curtains to the side to sneak a look into the crowd, now she was nervous and thank goodness it's a short runway. Nonetheless, Social went before her. She pleased the crowd in her own way as they whistled and cheered. Lyla then decided to let the girl behind her go next while the other girls rubbed themselves down with baby oil.

The girl went out on stage and did some splits and flips and some sexy dance moves. The crowd went wild. Lyla had to go behind this girl. *How was I going to out stage her?* Regardless, Lyla was going to make her big splash!

"Go ahead Lyla," Social said.

"I'm going Social," Lyla said.

"Alright. I have to pee. I will be right back," Social responded.

Goodness when is the juice going to kick in, Lyla thought. *I knew I should have stuck with wine.*

"It's your turn to go, hoe!" a girl shouted from behind Lyla. Lyla turned around and saw a familiar face with a headset, holding a clipboard.

"Look ah here. If it ain't Puddin' Pop," Lyla said. Lyla crossed her arms by her chest. "What are you supposed to be?"

"The stage manager," Puddin' Pop said. "What are you waiting for?"

Lyla took a nearby glass and threw it on the ground.

"Well, it looks like you have a mess to clean up, housekeeper," Lyla said.

"I'm a stage manager not your maid," Puddin' Pop replied. "Now stop acting like a child, and get out there!"

It seemed that Lyla letting go of her alter ego was short lived. All of the pastor's hard work went out the window, as she punched Puddin' Pop in the face. She was on her back, knocked out as Lyla stood over her helpless body on the ground.

"Don't ever bark at me like that again with your chicken wrist frail looking self."

Lyla got herself together and was about to go out on stage until Mad Love stopped Lyla with her hand on her shoulder, as if sensing Lyla was too nervous to walk the runway.

"Let me show you how it's done," Mad Love said. "I can tell you nervous," Lyla looked at her shoulder where Mad Love's hand was resting and then caught Mad Love's eye. Lyla face turned into a look that read, 'you better get your hand off my shoulder right now' and Mad Love took her hand away to acknowledge Lyla's blatant cold expression.

Lyla continued to give a cold expression as the drink finally kicked in. She was feeling a little woozy but still coherent and said to Mad Love, "Oh? Because you're so brilliant?"

"Please," Mad Love said.

"I'm not coming out to play with you right now Mad Love. I'll spare you since you're pregnant," Lyla said. "And for your information, I'm not nervous!"

"Yeah, okay," Mad Love responded as she stepped out on stage with her glow in the dark G-string bikini. The crowd went crazy before she shook a leg as men of all ages dashed towards the front of the stage. It was like they knew she was going to give them an unforgettable show. Mad Love did a couple of sexy dance moves and then laid on the stage and opened her legs wide.

Her hole was exposed.

Lyla peeped from behind stage. She saw a guy leap in front of another guy to shine his flash light from his key ring down her gap. Lyla could not believe her eyes as another guy held up his tattooed arm motioning Lyla to come out. It was definitely not cute – for a professional model to be caught peeping from behind stage. What would her agency say of such unprofessional behavior?

She quickly closed the curtain, but could still see the stage as she said, "What a raunchy girl. I'm so glad my friend got rid of her."

One of the guys poured alcohol in Mad Love's coochie and she squirted it back out like a water fountain. The guys drank the contaminated alcohol falling back down.

"That is repulsive," Lyla said as Mad Love disappeared from of the stage, but not before giving the audience a tantalizing look. The crowd got even wilder as they shouted for more.

Lyla was not nervous anymore; thank goodness. The "juice" fully kicked in.

"You don't know who your baby's daddy is, do you, Mad Love?" Lyla laughed as Mad Love walked passed her.

"Nope, I love dick," Mad Love said shockingly.

"You've definitely got that Wow Factor," Lyla laughed.

"Thank you," she said. "That's why they call me Mad Love."

"Ugh, that was not a compliment," Lyla laughed.

"It's your turn. Let's see what you can do," Mad Love challenged.

Lyla took a deep breath and stumbled out on stage. She was so drunk and disgusted about Mad Love that she walked the runway with her heels on the wrong feet. She did her runway walk pigeon toed. Lyla saw Sean laughing as if she was pathetic. *Asshole.*

The rest of the girls did their thing, and Social and Lyla knew they did not have a chance of winning.

They all went out on stage and Chocolate Succumb announced, "Give it up for Precious." The crowd leaped up in excitement and shouted out.

"And now give it up for Star," Chocolate Succumb continued as the crowd whistled and clapped.

"Now what about our girl Serina?" the announcer continued as the crowd slowed their clapping and whistling down. "Dreamz," Chocolate Succumb said, as the claps and whistles got louder again.

"Lyla and Social..." The girls got much love from the crowd but when Chocolate Succumb announced, "Mad Love" the crowd roared like thunder. Mad Love won and as it turned out, most of those girls were strippers.

Social noticed Lyla wasn't paying attention to anything, except for the girls on stage.

"We never had a chance," Lyla said to Social. "Those girls have so much body, especially boobs."

Lyla told Social if she gets breast implants; that would be her golden ticket. Social told her that was extravagant but Lyla didn't care until Social told her breast surgery cost seventy five hundred dollars.

"Never mind," Lyla said as she rubbed her stomach. "Let's get Sean and leave, I'm about to throw up. But not before I redeem myself." She took her sexy butt up on the bar and danced.

"That's my girl!" Social said.

Lyla felt like she was on Mount Everest, and everyone was watching her shake her tail feather until Puddin' Pop pushed Lyla off the bar. She went through the alcohol bottles and was suddenly on her back behind the bar, surrounded by broken shattered glass. Social was upset. She ran over to her, but Lyla was already on her feet with a bottle of Alize.

Social asked Lyla, "What're you about to do with that?"

Lyla saw Puddin' Pop, Mad Love, and Jell-O tittering together. *So they all know each other, eh? Let the party begin!* Lyla walked slowly to Puddin' Pop and clouted her in the head with the bottle. She never saw it coming.

Jell-O was in a fighting stance as Mad Love shouted, "Beat that pigeon toed bitch up!" Lyla circled her with the broken bottle, ready to cut her at any second. Jell-O came closer and Lyla leaped forward to stab her, but she wobbled from the alcohol. She did it again and missed. Jell-O attempted to attack, but the bodyguard finally stepped in and stopped the possible ugly altercation.

"That's why Nestle lives with me now," Jell-O boasted.

"Who cares! When he looks at you he thinks of me!" Lyla screams.

"'You're just mad because the guy that every girl wants wants me,' isn't that what you told me? Now stand to the side."

Lyla's face was twisted with rage.

"Now you want to use my own words to twist the knife?" Lyla said. "I'm over him and I got a real man now." The bodyguard continued to hold Lyla back from Jell-O.

"Get off of me," Lyla demanded as she turned around and notice the bodyguard was actually one of the NBA players she had the meeting with. Lyla was too drunk to feel embarrassed or say anything. She stumbled away.

Sean finally reappeared, fixing his pants, his zipper down and all. Social and Lyla already knew what Sean was doing with his Herman the one-eyed German.

"Let's get out of here. I'm feeling sicker," Lyla said.

They left the club and Social's rental car was being towed. She charged after the guy as he drove off. Social kicked and screamed, cursing the air. Lyla knew how Social felt from the countless times the same had happened to her in New York.

Two dudes they saw at the club asked if they needed a ride.

"Three against two if something does happen," Social said as she calmed down. "Let's go!" This wasn't the ideal way to get home, especially since Lyla was not in any shape to perform her kung fu if needed.

"Fasten your seat belts," the driver said, speeding off. The guy driving was speeding aimlessly around a winding dark California road. To the left was a cliff and closely on the right, the side of a mountain. Lyla put her arms up in the air like she was on a roller coaster.

The driver went faster and faster, cutting off his headlights while his spinning wheels continued to accelerate around the twisted roads. Lyla could not see the hand in front of her face.

"Stop!" Lyla and Social screamed. The driver continued flicking his headlamps on and off.

"This is not funny," Lyla said. "Turn the car to the left now!" The driver was going straight, and according to his navigator, if he did not turn the car to the left, they would go over the cliff. At least that's what Lyla thought, because as of now she was seeing double.

Lyla jumped over the seat and turned the wheel to a hazardous hard left, swerving towards the mountain.

"Shit, are you trying to kill us!" the guy shouted.

"You are trying to kill us, you idiot!" Lyla screamed.

"Sit your drunk ass down and chill out. I know these roads. We are just having some fun."

The guy in the passenger seat asked them, "Where y'all from?"

"Don't worry about it," Lyla answered.

"Damn I got to get some gas," the driver said.

On the way to the gas station, everyone got a little bit more acquainted. Coincidentally, the guys were from New York, and actually knew some of the people Lyla knew. They finally felt comfortable and relaxed. The guy in the passenger seat asked Social if he could see her necklace.

Social was very classy in her own way but she loved the ghetto necklaces the rappers wore in the eighties. She made it look chic and elegant.

"Yeah," Social said. "It was specially made for me; I'm into the chains..."

"And whips," the driver laughed.

"Ha, ha," Social replied.

"What is hanging off of it?" the guy in the passenger seat asked. "It looks like it says sin..."

"Sin Sick," Social interrupted. She took the long necklace from around her neck and let him take a closer look.

"This necklace is hot," the guy said. The driver took a look too.

While they were discussing Social's necklace, Lyla received a text from another friend of hers in LA: "Are you coming to see me and my niggas? Bring your girls."

Lyla wrote back and asked, "How old are the niggas?"

"LOL," he wrote back. She laughed to herself as she noticed the time. Lyla was not going anywhere else. It was 3:20 am. "Tonight is not good," Lyla responded. "Will catch up with you before I leave." Her screen went black; dead battery.

They all arrived at the gas station. As soon as Lyla opened her door, she threw up.

"Social!" Sean shouted. "Lyla is throwing up blood."

"No I'm not, silly," Lyla slurred. "It's red wine mixed with Patron." She stumbled to the bathroom. Social went into the store, and Sean followed.

A few moments later, Sean, Lyla, and Social were all back in front of the gas station store.

"Rock on Lyla, Rock on," Sean laughed.

"What," Lyla said.

"Your hair is all over your head," Social said. "Like the girl on the beach."

"'Y'all laughing about my hair,'" Lyla said. They all laughed.

The driver just finished pumping his gas while the passenger stood near a parked car. Social forgot to get something from the store. She went back in while Sean and Lyla stood talking and drinking water. Lyla also ate a beef hot dog with chili and cheese to even out the alcohol.

Suddenly, the gas attendant came running out of the store and stood in the middle of the gas station lot.

"Stop!" The attendant swiftly leaped over to get out of the way of the guys speeding off abandoning Lyla, Social, and Sean. The car missed the attendant by a hair.

Lyla and Sean were in shock, as Social came running out the store.

"My necklace! They have my necklace! Call the police!" She ran to the end of the curb, but the thieves were long gone.

"Girl, they are out with your necklace," Lyla said.

"Why would you let them hold your necklace anyway? You must be drunk," Sean said. That was an understatement: they were all drunk.

"Do you know them?" the attendant asked. "That was my car they drove off in."

"Your car?" Sean answered. "It was different from the first one they had, now that I think about it. We met them tonight, sir."

"Yeah," Social said. "I think the first car they had was stolen, too. We were driving around in a stolen car!"

"Wow," Sean said. "Stealing gas in a stolen car."

"This is all your fault, Sean!" Social accused.

"How is it my fault Social?!"

They all fumed back and forth, back and forth, back and forth, BOOM! They all fell to the ground. The car the criminals left behind blew up. The attendant used the store's fire extinguisher to put out the small fire. *Are we in the Bronx or LA?* Lyla thought as she lifted herself off the ground to sit on the curb.

Lyla grabbed her phone to see if she could call the police to help Social and the gas attendant but she forgot her phone was dead and honestly, she was ready to go home. Lyla had a video shoot to do in a few hours, she should have been in the bed. Sean called 9-1-1, and then a cab for them. Which they should have done in the first place.

What a night.

Chapter 36

Lyla dosed off in the backseat of the cab, until they arrived in front of Sean and Social's place. As soon as the cab door opened, Lyla threw up again as her stomach churned. The cab driver was disgusted. Lyla told Sean she was staying in the cab and going straight to the shoot while holding her stomach. It was already 4:30 am and Lyla had to be on set by 5:00 sharp.

She closed the door and the driver cautiously and slowly drove off.

"I have no idea why I have to be there so early," Lyla slurred. "I already know they are not going to use me until late afternoon...hurry up and wait. Goodness."

Social accompanied her to the shoot, hoping to get a part in the video as she told the driver the address and said, "Faster please...We are running late."

"I do not want her throwing up in my cab so I drive slowly," the man said with an Arabic accent.

"Floor it!" Social said. "I'm paying you and my girl will hold her liquor. Thank you very much!"

"I hope so," the driver replied.

"Shut the fuck up!" Social shouted.

Forty five minutes later they arrived at their destination. When they left the cab, it was daylight. Social paid the driver, minus a tip. The driver sighed and sped off.

Social turned her head and saw Lyla walking the wrong way. Lyla was late and sleepwalking.

"Wait a minute, Lyla," Social said as she ran over to help her friend. "It's this way and let me fix your hair, you need some eye drops too. Your eyes look dim."

"Who cares, girl. I just want to sleep," Lyla replied.

"You have to look good," Social said.

"I'm not going to be seen in the video," Lyla reminded.

"Silk may want to marry you or something," Social laughed. "Now get it together."

She and Social finally made it inside the building. They signed in and headed to the snack table. They both needed to absorb the rest of the alcohol to stay up for a long workday.

While eating, Lyla pulled her phone from her charger and saw it was powered up, as she turned on her ringer. She also saw seventy-five text messages from Ritchie, asking where she was. Lyla bent over and shoved her phone and charger in her bag, but just as she lifted up, the shrill ringing of her phone, stopped her movement. She bent back over, digging in her bag to take her phone back out.

Ritchie.

She still was not in any condition to talk to him right now especially considering the way he was talking to her last night at the club. *That definitely brought back bad memories of Casmir, not to mention the party he organized behind my back.*

She shoved her phone back in her bag. Lyla continued to eat and chat with Social and the other girls at the table getting their grub on. Social was yapping away.

All Lyla could hear is, "Wop wop wop wop." The alcohol was still in her system. Social grabbed some potato chips and when she turned around, Lyla was under the food table asleep. She slept for three hours straight.

When Lyla woke up, she was in full hair and make-up.

"Who did my hair and make-up?" Lyla asked. She checked herself out in the mirror. "This make-up looks good! They used the number two and number seven eyelashes."

"The make-up artist could not wake you, so he did your make-up under the table, followed by the hair stylist. You were out," Social laughed.

"For real," Lyla said. "Were they mad?"

"For what? You're the star!" Social said stroking her ego, "but I guess Patron is much stronger than juice."

"Well it tasted like juice," Lyla cackled. "And I felt like it wasn't strong enough to get me drunk, but it snuck up on me later."

"I'm fine. Patron does not do anything to me," Social said. "Well, you are used to it girl. Anyway, I feel a little better," Lyla said, performing backstretches. "My back is killing me."

Now that the alcohol had worn off, Lyla felt back pains.

"Don't you remember what happened at the club?" Social questioned.

"Nope," Lyla answered. "I mean, I remember fussing Puddin' Pop out backstage and some of the contest - stuff like that, but that is it."

"Wow, and you talk about me hanging off chandeliers," Social laughed. "Get your back checked out if it keeps hurting."

"Why?" Lyla wondered.

"You was pushed off the bar, girl! And we got robbed!" Social yelled as Lyla shushed her and asked, "Are you serious?"

"Yes," Social confirmed.

"To tell you the truth I don't know how I got here this morning," Lyla admitted.

"Well Patron is known to cause a mental fog," Social laughed while she told Lyla the whole story.

As she told the story, the director of the video approached Lyla; she asked her if she would like to be the lead girl in the video.

"What is the role?" Lyla asked curiously.

"I need you to play the S&M girl," the director answered. *That was out of the question.*

"I'm sorry I cannot play that part," Lyla rebuffed. "I'm here to be in the background and to collect my coins, but maybe my girlfriend Social can do it."

Social was asked by the director, if she was scheduled to be on set today. Before Social could answer, Lyla interrupted.

"No, but she came with me hoping to get a part." The director politely asked Social to leave. Production couldn't afford to add extra girls.

Meanwhile, the director practically begged Lyla to do the scene. Lyla compromised and said she would like to see the clothes. If the clothes were not too vulgar, she might consider doing it.

Lyla went to the wardrobe area. To her surprise, the stylist was a famous singer. Lyla tried on a number of outfits and each seemed to get sluttier and sluttier. She was so upset, Lyla wanted to go home.

"Why are you acting like that?" the director asked. "Look at the photo shoot you did for this fashion magazine." Lyla looked at the photo shoot in question. It was a bathing suit shot. The director thought, if Lyla did that shoot, then why not the lead role?

Lyla called her best-kept secret, her producer friend. She was like a big sister. Lyla asked for some advice.

"What is wrong? Are you cranky?" her friend asked.

"Why do you say that?" Lyla answered with a question.

"Because you only act like this when you are sleepy or hungry," her friend answered.

"Well I am sleepy but I'm serious about this," Lyla said. "Out of all people you know how I feel about stuff like this." Her friend told her if she did not want to do it, walk off set.

Social rushed over to Lyla and the director in full hair, make-up, and wardrobe.

"I will do it." The director was disconcerted and Lyla was so embarrassed. The director decisively told her to leave immediately before she called security.

"Well I'm leaving too," Lyla said.

"Why?" the director asked.

"Because I'm not interested in being the lead girl," Lyla answered as she gathered her things to walk off set.

"We will pay you way more than what you were booked for," the director replied. Social looked at Lyla and said, "You better take that offer."

Lyla said to Social, "I cannot be sold. Now, let's go!"

"You will be paid ten thousand dollars," the director said.

"Where do I get dressed?" Lyla asked.

"Follow me," the director answered.

"Alright Social, I will catch up with you later, girl."

"Okay, have fun," Social said. "Say hi to Silk for me."

"I will, love you," Lyla replied, throwing Silk's signature hand sign in the air.

"You are beautiful. We will use you the next time," the director said to Social.

"Thanks," Social said. Social left the building.

Lyla headed back to wardrobe feeling confident about her decision. *Ten thousand dollars is enough for me to get my boob job and some Victoria Secret bras.* She entered the room scanning every piece of clothing again to see what she would be comfortable in, but obviously S&M garments were all risqué.

Eventually, Lyla walked on set in a dress shorter than her underwear. She saw all of the video girls standing in a circle.

Silk, the rapper, was testing them out, as each one danced for him so he could pick who is doing what.

The director said to Silk, "This is our S&M girl. Her name is Lyla."

"Okay, but let me see what Lyla can do," Silk said.

"I'll save it for when the director says go," Lyla replied.

"Girl, you better throw your leg around his neck or something," one of the video girls snickered.

The director whispered something in Silk's ear. Silk looked at Lyla and went on to the next girl. After Silk's cheap thrill show was over, the director signed for Lyla to go on the heavily dimmed fully furnished living room set. It looked like a New Orleans whorehouse with burgundy everything including an old time sofa, phone, wooden table, throw rug, television set, and velvet curtains.

"Wait!" Lyla said. Lyla ran back to her dressing room, and pulled out a small bag of cocaine she bought from one of the girls at the club. She scooped the stuff up her nose and went back on set. After the director explained the scene to Lyla, she placed her and Silk. She motioned for them to get ready for taping.

As Silk's song was played he stroked Lyla's cheek and then kissed her lips. Their mouths moved in time with each other and Silk touched Lyla's hair and tangled his fingers in it as he lip synced the words of his song. His other hand slowly moved up to her face and cupped her cheek in the palm of his hand.

Lyla pushed up his shirt and slowly felt on Silk's body. She moved from his lips to his neck while Silk forced her onto his thighs. Silk placed his hands on Lyla's lower back slipping one hand up her patent leather dress.

"Cut!" the director yelled.

"Perfect. Now do it again." After twenty takes of the same shot, it was finally time to go to the bedroom scene.

"Bedroom scene?" Lyla said.

"Don't worry, its fake sex," the director replied. Lyla stepped into a room filled with candles, sex toys, and a huge bed with berry red silk sheets and a black mosquito looking net covering over it. After Silk and Lyla, were positioned they did not waste any time getting back into character. Silk hard-kissed and touched Lyla. She felt like this was not for daytime television but for the underground video world.

Lyla went along with it, peeled off her dress, and pressed her chest against Silk's while slowly running her hand all over his built body. Silk kissed Lyla's jaw line to her throat, down to her collar, and then kissed between her breasts. He turned her over to lean over her ass.

The arousal made her moan as he touched her body so aggressively. Silk then kissed and licked her down her back. He dropped down one strap from her bra and then off came his shirt, grabbing the nipple clamps for her tits. Lyla sat up and unbuckled Silk's belt with one hand, using the other to run her fingers over his stomach. She turned it up a notch and slapped the hell out of him and then bit repeatedly all over his upper body.

The intensity grew more and more as she pushed and he pulled and she shoved and he pulled again, bringing her closer to him biting his neck and all over his chest. He grabbed her ass, pulling her soft pretty hair and sucked on her breast, while placing one of the nipple clamps on her tit. She threw the clamp and moved away.

"Come here girl," Silk said. "Let me get some of that." He pulled her again and grabbed her neck and she slapped him, as he continued to say, "You slap me all you want as long as I can slap that ass with my dick."

"This is not for real," Lyla reminded. "It is a video shoot and you are going too far."

"I don't give a fuck," Silk said disrespectfully.

"I think you have been popping too many pills," she assumed. "Now stop it...you ain't DMX. I don't even know who you are. My agency lied to me. You are no one famous. You wanna be Ol' Dirty Bastard."

"Shut the fuck up!" Silk said, "I'm putting my porn flick together and guess what? You're in it. So you better pull up."

"Not me. You are sadly mistaken," Lyla said.

"You biting me and shit. You gonna get fucked," Silk said.

"Why are you guys talking I need action," the director said. "What is going on?"

"Nothing," Silk said, looking at Lyla. "Right?"

Lyla looked at the director and then looked at Silk like she wanted to drop kick him in his neck.

She looked back at the director.

"Right, let's just get this over with."

Silk climbed on top of Lyla and turned her head to the side, slowly licking her. He then lied on his back while she poured candle wax down his chest. Silk flipped her back over, lifted her, and walked her over while kissing her roughly to the sex swing nearby, locking her in. He then took the whip and hit her with it again and again.

At first, Lyla was okay with the beating, until she saw images of Casmir tying her to the bedposts, choking and beating her with his belt. She tried so hard to clear the images from her mind. Lyla even thought about the advice Pastor Bill had given her, but she could not stop thinking about the images. She went into panic mode.

Silk could tell something was wrong so he took advantage of her uncomfortable state and attempted to have sex with her again.

"Stop," Lyla commanded.

The director thought Lyla was getting into it so she kept rolling. Silk took the whip and beat her again and he then slapped her. She thought she was in a nightmare.

"Stop! Please!" Lyla cried. The unexpected visions of Casmir slapping her in the park, her abortion and rapes taunted her over and over again in her head.

"Stop!" Lyla commanded again, smacking him in the face, kicking, and pounding him hard on the chest. In defense she would not have attacked Silk if the director listened to her command the first time as Lyla shouted, "I'm not playing! Take the cuffs off of me now!"

The director yelled cut and the production assistant took the cuffs of her strangled wrist. Lyla hurried and made her exit.

"What's up? She's a weird one," the director said with a mean spirit.

"Let that bitch run. We got what we need," Silk said.

"That was explicit footage Silk," the director smiled.

"Yea!" he said, throwing his signature sign in the air. "Silk!"

Lyla realized bondage sex is pleasurable for people, who like to indulge in that type of thing, but for Lyla, it reminded her of her depraved abuse as a teenager and not to mention the recent tragedies she thought she buried but now knew could be damaging.

Who would have thought LA would be so exciting – throwing up from partying all night, getting into bar fights, riding in a sex swing, almost getting raped by a knock-off Method Man, robbed, and all of that good stuff. But on a serious note, thankfully, some good things happened for Lyla during her trip to LA.

Lyla made the appointment to have her breasts done and this "B" model became the new "it" girl. She booked numerous gigs crushin' the pavements nationally and was on the cusp of going international. Lyla hated being labeled as the video girl, but she was finally making a name for herself in the industry. Even her sparkling Veneers became a big hit.

Everyone wanted them.

Her video girl success also landed her some interviews on popular networks. This was a triumphant moment in her life, but Lyla declined due to the situation with Ritchie. Lyla had to clean that up first. *This is what distractions can do to a person.*

Chapter 37

After Lyla returned to New York City from another video shoot in Jamaica looking fresh and beautiful, with a natural sun kissed tan, Ritchie asked her to meet him at the movie theatre in Times Square. He said he had a surprise for her. As usual, whenever he felt like he messed up or the relationship was headed in the wrong direction, he came up with something Lyla would want to hear. On the other hand, it had been a long time since Ritchie and Lyla were out and about just to have a nice time.

Lyla accepted the invite and told him she had a surprise for him too. Ritchie had yet to see her new boob job up close and personal.

She met Ritchie at the movie theatre. When they finally saw each other they were so excited. It was like they just met for the first time, as he handed her a bouquet of beautiful, exotic flowers and said, "I missed that sparkle in your eyes." She was pleasantly surprised as she breathlessly said, "You remembered."

"Of course I did, my love," Ritchie said. "I have come to realize I cannot live without you, even for one day."

Ritchie and Lyla decided to put everything that had happened behind them and not think about anything negative. They wanted to enjoy themselves, so she did not say anything about the break-up or the party he organized behind her back.

"Why did you get your breast enlarged? They were nice the way they were."

"Yeah, but I wanted to improve them," she said.

"Can I test them out?"

"Maybe," Lyla smiled brightly.

"You look well," Ritchie said cheerily. "Did you have a good time while you were away from me?"

"Why you asking me? You are the one who invented the satellite. You can see everything! Remember?" Lyla giggled.

Ritchie walked to a nearby magazine stand on the sidewalk and yelled, "Oh my goodness, that's her!" He turned the pages of a magazine layout Lyla recently posed in.

"Stop it Ritchie!" Lyla said.

"You stop being shy, my love," he replied. "I'm having some fun with your newfound fame."

"Don't patronize me Ritchie," she said.

Ritchie laughed as she signed an autograph for a young girl who admired her.

"Whoa," a hulking man who looked to be a football player said. "The legendary Lyla Tight. You look better in person." Lyla turned her head to see who was making all the fuss about her.

"I don't know about legendary," Lyla said, "but thank you."

"Can you shake it for me?" the fellow asked.

"Excuse me," Lyla answered.

"I said can you shake it for me?" the man said. "Or is that only for Hollywood?"

"Whatever," Lyla said.

She smiled and gives the little girl a wave goodbye. Lyla walked past the rude man to grab hold of Ritchie. The man slapped Lyla on her ass. She was stunned, but before she could react to the insane motion, he was laid out on the ground from two swift punches from Ritchie. *That dude towered over Ritchie.*

Ritchie pulled her away from the passed out lunatic, as she gaped over her shoulder, her untamed hair flinging wildly from the wind.

Lyla finally asked, "Where did you learn that from?"

"Oh," he said. "That was just a lucky punch." Lyla did not ask any more questions but thought to herself, *What else is Ritchie capable of?*

After watching a good movie…well, actually making love on the floor in the back row of a fairly empty movie theatre, Lyla's stomach was screaming for food so they went to eat something delicious at one of her favorite chain restaurants in the middle of Times Square. While they were at the table waiting for the waitress, Ritchie whispered urgent, sweet nothings in her ear. His love was so essential, so wild, and so vivid. Kiss by kiss, touch by touch, Lyla was being drawn back into his arms.

"Let's try something different tonight," Ritchie said.

"Like what?" Lyla asked.

"Let's have dessert before dinner," Ritchie answered.

"Nice," Lyla said.

"A hot brownie with ice-cream," Ritchie said as the waitress brought it to the table.

"I see you have everything planned for tonight," Lyla smiled.

"Yes, my love," Ritchie said.

Lyla leaned back to eat some of the dessert placed on the table when she smelled something burning.

"Are my flowers on fire?" Lyla joked. "Oh goodness, my hair is on fire!" Her hair got caught in the candle on the table. She did not panic as Lyla took her hand and soothingly patted the fire out. Lyla was more discomforted than anything else.

They both acted like nothing happened until the scent from the burned hair was overwhelming, so they left the restaurant.

As they left he said, "You really handled that fire situation well my love. You did not flinch. I must be teaching you well."

Lyla remembered her mom telling her the same thing happened to her cousin Ryland so she knew what to do. *See, my cousin saved my life, and she doesn't even know it because we still don't speak,* Lyla said to herself as she swished her hair in a messy bun to deal with it later.

"Thank you, I got skills Ritchie," Lyla said as they both laughed.

"Somehow the bun makes you look a few years younger," Ritchie said. Lyla took that as a compliment and said, "The younger...the prettier in my line of work, right?"

"I love you," Ritchie whispered by her ear.

Lyla slowly backed away from Ritchie and gave him an odd look and murmured, "I-love-you too."

"What's wrong?" he asked.

"I love you," Casmir whispered by her ear. "I – love – you too," Elizabeth murmured."

"Nothing," she said. "So, where is my surprise?"

"Yes," Ritchie said. "I have some making up to do, don't I?" He danced a little. For a person that was in the music business, he had no rhythm whatsoever, but she enjoyed watching him dance as if he had two left feet.

Ritchie paused for a second and then held Lyla. He breathed in her opened mouth as she breathed in his, their breathe connecting like they were destined to walk down the aisle together. Ritchie stepped back a little and danced again and said, "I'm proposing..."

"What?" Lyla interrupted. Her heart fluttered as she thought this was unreal.

"I'm proposing a dance," he said.

"Oh," she said, a little disappointed, but still content.

Ritchie and Lyla laughed and danced in the wind, as he whisked her through the street sheathed in slumber, her soft eyes reflecting the dark velvet sky, the full moon shining bright above their heads. A few moments later she noticed at least two hundred people surrounding her and Ritchie.

"Now this is cool," Lyla smiled, realizing they were flash mob dancers. Ritchie put this all together. They continued to dance and dance. *I'm having a good old time,* Lyla thought.

She had forgotten all of their happy memories, but this occasion reminded her of why she loved being in love with this man as they locked lips and kissed in the middle of Times Square to make new memories.

"So lovely, so grand," Lyla said. "You put everything together just the way I like it. You can't imagine how pleasant this feels."

"I was highly motivated, Mademoiselle," he said as they continued kissing and Ritchie proceeded to say, "We fought lions and tigers and bears."

"Oh my," Lyla giggled.

"And have been torn from each other's arms, yet our love prevailed," Ritchie said. "We are meant to be."

With a huge smile on his face he gave Lyla a big hug, but in a matter of seconds, his smile turned to a frown; there were gunshots going off and the honeymoon was over. Everyone screamed and ran. Both got trampled as if they were in the center of a tornado. Ritchie managed to get up off the ground to help Lyla and he said to follow him.

The gunshots were still going off and they seem to be following Ritchie and Lyla. After dodging several bullets, they finally made their getaway. With no cabs in sight, Ritchie waved down a limo one avenue over. The driver hesitated about letting them in but Lyla tossed him a fifty dollar bill through his window to change his mind.

As they rode off, Lyla and Ritchie sat quietly until Lyla turned all of her frustration on Ritchie and screamed, "What the hell was that?!"

"How should I know?" Ritchie replied.

"Ever since you have been seeing these women, I have been shot at, tripped down the stairs, and who knows what else there is to come!" Lyla exclaimed. "I had myself a good time in LA and Jamaica, and now I have to come back to this mess. I'm finally making something of myself. You are supposed to be helping me, not ruining me!"

"How am I ruining you?" Ritchie asked. "You are thriving because of me and I thought you felt the same way, my love."

"Is this coming from the same person who had the nerve to break up with me in LA!" Lyla reminded.

"You were messing around," Ritchie said.

"That was after you and I got back together," Lyla smirked.

"What do you mean, 'after you and I got back together?'" Ritchie questioned.

"Don't worry about it," Lyla answered. "I do not have to explain myself to you. We are not married!" She told the limo to stop.

"If it wasn't for me you would not be traveling," he said. "I'm the one who is grooming you."

"Grooming me?" Lyla laughed. "Don't kid yourself Ritchie, my jobs have been through my agency. If anything my resources don't trust me anymore because the business deals have not gone through. Nothing has yet come through you but talk. And the first job I could have gotten through you you said was a fake!"

"What?" Ritchie asked.

"I was at the party for the NBA players that you said was fake!" Lyla hissed before reaching for the door handle.

"I don't know what you're talking about," Ritchie said.

"You love playing dumb, don't you!" Lyla shouted.

"I have taught you everything you know," Ritchie reminded.

"What? So, you are proud because you taught me how not to flinch," Lyla replied sarcastically.

"Don't talk to me like that," Ritchie said. "What happened to putting the negative things behind us tonight?"

"You are a joke," Lyla said boldly. "And since this day has been hijacked from me once again, watch me flinch now because I'm walking away from you. And add some money to the tip I gave the driver. Can you manage that?!"

The livid Lyla left the limo and ran down the street to catch a cab, but she heard someone calling her name. Lyla turned around and saw Detective Sanchez from the police station. She was nervous. The last time Lyla saw the detective, she was running from him.

Lyla threw her purse over her shoulder and swiftly walked away.

"Wait!" the detective said.

"Are you following me, Detective?" Lyla asked, continuing to walk away.

"No," the detective answered.

"Are you here to ask me if Casmir is alive?"

"No," the detective said. "Please stop, I need to talk to you, that's all."

She stopped and asked, "What do you want, Detective?"

He looked at her like he really had something personal to say to that question, but instead he asked about the shooting in Times Square.

"I don't know anything about it," she answered.

"Are you sure?" Detective Sanchez questioned.

"Yes," Lyla says. He could tell Lyla was lying but he said okay and gave her his business card.

"If you find out anything, please give me a call," the detective said.

She looked at the detective, then the business card, and smirked, but she could tell he was serious. Lyla could care less how serious he was, so she made a joke out of the business card by kissing the back of it, leaving a flirty fuchsia kiss print of her lips in the upper right hand corner. She wrote her number next to her lips and handed back the card with a smile.

"You call me."

He did not take the card back, but he did say to her, "This is not a joke. If you find out anything let me know. Help us do our job, Ms. Elizabeth Tight."

"How do you know my name?" she asked while putting the card away and searching for a cab.

"I'm a detective, remember? We know a lot more than you think."

"Taxi!" Lyla shouted through the streets of Manhattan, waving her hand. "Man, someone is in there."

She noticed there was a crowd leaving Madison Square Garden. An event just ended.

"Dag it, it's going to be impossible to catch a cab now." She signaled a taxi to stop one last time, but still no taxi. "I'm going to try the next avenue over," Lyla muttered.

Lyla walked away, but before she could, the detective said, "Remember, if you find out anything, let me know."

"I heard you the first time," Lyla said harshly.

The detective picked up Lyla's scarf she did not realize fell from around her neck and walked towards her.

"If you need anything, I mean anything, let me know that too. I can take good care of you."

Lyla stopped walking, looked at the detective and asked herself, *Is the detective coming on to me?* as she said, "I have everything I need. Goodbye, Detective Sanchez." She yanked the scarf from his hand and swished her booty side to side as she stomped away.

The Detective murmured, "Her ass is a sensation," as he whistled down a cab.

"Here is your taxi!" the detective hollered, opening the cab door for her.

Lyla stopped swishing her ass and turned around. She stood there for a few seconds, looked at the detective again.

"Just like that, uh?! Just snap your fingers and you get a taxi?!"

"Just like that, Elizabeth!" the detective said, watching her from a distance as pedestrians asked a stupid question, "Is this cab taken?"

Her never ending legs stride back towards the detective's direction, and with a watchful eye he enjoyed every moment. It was obvious why the detective was enamored by her, as she stopped in front of him.

"I did not think you were coming at first," Sanchez said quietly. "Get in."

Lyla was silent for a moment as she observed his face, glinting in the moonlight. The detective stepped towards her.

She did not want him to get the wrong idea so she stepped back as she finally replied, "So demanding."

The detective gently roused Lyla, touching his hand to her waist waiting for Lyla to step in. She finally lifted her dress to climb in, showing enough leg for the detective to stare at, as if it was her way of saying 'thank you.'

Although the detective was persistent about proving Lyla wrong about Ritchie, he wasn't bad looking for a detective nor crazy acting, like most cops out there. As the cab drove off, she looked at Sanchez from the back window shield, the tall city buildings and shining bright lights outlining his handsome face and body.

The detective knew he acted inappropriately, but he could not resist her wholesome and captivating beauty as he stared back at her.

Lyla turned around and said to the driver, "Take me to Hell's Kitchen. Fifty-Seventh Street and Tenth Avenue and make it quick please."

This was too much for me on a Monday. But then she had a change of heart. Lyla was up to something.

Chapter 38

Bizzie and Ritchie were officially seeing each other on a consistent basis, even after Bizzie allegedly tripped Lyla down the stairs. While Lyla spent time with her family in Philly for the holiday, Bizzie and another band member went to Ritchie's home in Connecticut for a fourth of July cookout. It took Lyla almost a year to meet the kids. He did not waste anytime letting her meet the whole family.

His wife had no idea her husband was seeing Bizzie and she better watch out because Bizzie was hard to satisfy and her gluttony could allow her to take him from his family and leave his wife husbandless and the children fatherless. Lyla was nothing like that. But now Lyla wondered if his wife knows about Bizzie and Ritchie and did not care or she was just like him.

I wonder if his wife knows about the information the police have. She should know if her husband is a fugitive or not, Lyla thought.

Moreover, Lyla used to think she was special because he introduced him to his children, but now she saw he used them to get woman to give in to him. In his mind, he and Lyla were going to be a family in the city while he kept his family in Connecticut and his mistresses on the side. This whole relationship was sloppy and pitiable, and Lyla was done with him. But until she was able to let it go, and regardless of what she said to him before leaving the limo, she was still his girlfriend.

Meanwhile, Lyla took full advantage of the detective's flirty advance to see what he knew. She phoned and asked him to meet her in Philadelphia. At first he did not think it was a good idea. He would have rather waited until she returned to

New York City, but Lyla had a convincing way about her. She also reminded him if he wanted to know more about Ritchie, he must play by her rules.

Sanchez said, "Meet me at the restaurant on…"

Lyla interrupted, "No, I will pick the place, and text you the address."

Sanchez was on the train to Philly.

He received a text from Carpenter stating, "The witness in the video was found dead. Without the witness or Ms. Tight's identity revealed, we have no case against the security guard. We had to drop the charges. Call me when you arrive in Philly."

The detective caught a cab to his hotel while speaking with Carpenter on his cell phone.

"Did you get my text?" Carpenter asked.

"Yep, I got your book," Sanchez answered.

"Funny," Carpenter said.

"I'm still going to talk to this girl," Sanchez replied, "but without the witness, I really have to get her to talk. That's not going to be easy."

"It may be easier than what you think," Carpenter said. "I found out some information on Ms. Tight."

"How?" Sanchez asked.

"I talked to some of her friends and family, against the lieutenant's orders," Carpenter answered.

"What do you mean?" Sanchez questioned.

"The lieutenant gave strict orders to leave the Nowak case alone."

"Why am I not surprised. We are staying on the case," Sanchez said.

"I'm glad you said that," Carpenter replied.

"So, what did you find out?" Sanchez wondered.

"Elizabeth seems to be a head case; although her mom tried to keep her from her dad because she was jealous of their relationship. She is close to him and her aunt. Elizabeth has lots of friends, well respected, educated, and is a good person but she and her mom have had lots of quarrels..."

"All daughters have fights with their moms," Sanchez interrupted.

"Let me finish," Carpenter said. "In the early part of Elizabeth's life she had to go back home after things did not work out for her as a model. She felt like a failure and her mom, along with her younger cousin, kicked her while she was down, directly and indirectly sabotaging everything she wanted to do."

"That is all jealousy," Sanchez said.

"Exactly," Carpenter replied. "This girl was on her way to success numerous times but there was one small problem; now she sabotages herself. Every time she was on her way to the top she found a way to destroy it which means she normally ruined her chances of closing a deal or going to the next level in her career. She is her worst enemy."

"Well it's been done to her so many times she can't help but do it to herself," Sanchez said.

"Yes, she has developed and mastered the 'Art of Sabotaging,'" Carpenter said. "As a result, she became afraid of success, but this Ritchie dude, who is a hoax, has helped her with her confidence and self-esteem."

"Sounds about right," Sanchez said.

"This explains why she picks feminine guys like models to replace what her mom did not give her and abusive men to replace what she could not receive from her dad because of her mom's interference. Nowak is taking advantage of her while she is vulnerable," Carpenter continued.

Sanchez agreed and then corrected Carpenter by saying, "All-in-all, Elizabeth's a good person, but you are wrong about one thing, she is not a head case. She did not get want she needed growing up and now she has to rely on her experiences to teach her about life."

"That is what I was about to say," Carpenter said. "In turn she is always helping people or rescuing..."

"Hoping someone will rescue her," Sanchez interrupted.

"Exactly," Carpenter agreed. "Elizabeth had a revelation during the time spent at home. So, that is when she got a second win and moved back to New York."

"Yeah," Sanchez said. "Now she has some fame from being a video girl."

"Yeah, but Elizabeth does not like what video girls represent," Carpenter said, "she has goals that no one cannot even imagine; but get this, she has a problem with trusting authority, maybe you can play on that."

The next day, Sanchez met up with Lyla in Fairmount Park. They sat near the boating dock drinking a smoothie and enjoying the summer weather.

"Have you ever been to Philly, Detective?" Lyla asked while watching squirrels chasing each other up and down trees.

"No," the detective answered, "but I rode through Philly once to get to Maryland."

"Oh yeah? What part?"

"Cockeysville, Lutherville one of those villes," Sanchez said.

"Nice," Lyla smiled. "I use to live there."

"You know I could lose my job meeting you here, Ms. Tight," Sanchez said.

"Why? Don't you have permission?"

"You didn't give me much time to make arrangements. And not to mention, it's the weekend and I'm supposed to be playing soccer with the boys," Sanchez said, watching passing families and friends walking through the green grass, playing Frisbee games, and flying kites, enjoying their weekend outing.

"So, why are you here?" Lyla asked.

"I want to get to know you," Sanchez answered.

"Get to know me," Lyla smiled. "Now that's interesting. You have no case, do you, Detective? And call me Lyla, please."

"Is that your stage name?" Sanchez asked.

"My stage name?" Lyla smiled.

"You shine when you smile," the detective noted.

"Yes, I do," Lyla said.

"I know Lyla is your middle name, by the way," the detective said.

"You know everything Detective," Lyla replied with a smile again.

The detective and Lyla caught themselves as she realized they were passively flirting with each other.

"But enough about me; have you found information on Ritchie?"

"I found out some new information," the detective said. "I know you went to Mexico the same day that a drug smuggling investigation occurred." He thought back to the video footage at the airport to see if he could remember if she smiled; that would definitely put her at the scene.

Lyla was not fazed. She learned that from Ritchie, of course. Lyla also knew she would have been arrested already, but he could not tell who the woman in the video was due to her disguise including her fake front teeth. They also hadn't figured out if Ritchie was connected to the drug deal. It was obvious he had no new leads, solid suspects, or information on Ritchie that might be useful to her.

He was fishing.

She kept her composure and changed the subject.

"I chose to meet you here, because this is where my parents used to bring me when I was a little girl."

"It's a nice place," the detective replied.

"Yeah, they loved to come here during cherry blossom season to watch them drop like snowflakes," Lyla said. "This is my special haven no one knows about unless I tell them. I only bring people here I trust."

She looked at the detective's cerulean eyes, as he looked into the hue of her eyes magnifying control but definitely seduction. It was obvious they were attracted to each other and the flirting was out the window.

Despite what Officer Carpenter told Sanchez about Lyla he asked, "Are you saying you trust me?"

"Why do you ask?" Lyla said as he sipped on his blueberry and banana smoothie.

He held his head.

"Oooooo."

"Brain freeze? You better slow down," Lyla recommended.

"Yeah," the detective chuckled.

Lyla and the detective spent the rest of the day together eating one of Philadelphia's famous cheese steaks, visiting nearby shops, and later had dinner. During the dinner, the detective sat and pondered while darting furtive glances at Lyla who was peacefully drinking her red wine, remaining a silent spectator of the restaurant's discussions and chatter.

As if sensing her thoughts, he instantly noticed a change in her attitude as she touched her beautiful curly hair inelegantly, looking at her watch angrily.

It was 11:19 pm and Lyla was ready to go home, but before she could tell the detective she stormed out in a huff. The detective chased after her as she stopped under a canopy, realizing it was raining. She turned her head, looked at the detective and blurted out, "You had no right to look at my plane ticket." She ran out into the rain to catch a cab, the streetlights beaming down on her.

"Lyla, wait," the detective said. "You had that on your mind all day? How did you know I had your ticket?"

"How else would you know my first name?" Lyla said. "Besides, my ticket was gone. Do you think I'm a stupid model, Detective?"

To appease the situation he said, "No, not at all, Lyla. You are actually very smart. And beautiful. But this is a murder and drug investigation. I have to do what I have to do, even if it means picking up your dropped ticket at the police station."

"Is that right," Lyla said with an unexpected twinkle in her eye.

"Yes," Sanchez said detecting the twinkle. He touched her cheek and his adoration showered down on her like the rain; suddenly Lyla calmed down, and all of the odds and pains drowned. Quietly, provocatively heaving her new chest, she asked, "What do you want from me?"

The detective did not immediately answer her nor did he notice her breast enhancement, but she continued to use her powers of seduction. He gazed at her perfection and beauty with rapturous admiration, and when, at those rare moments his magnificent eyes met hers, she could tell the detective could not contain his desire.

He proceeded to touch her drenched hair softly, still so perfect in the rain. Sanchez knew this girl was not going to break, so why not have some fun — off the record.

The detective kissed her, from bare shoulder down to the palm of her hand that caught the rain falling from the sky. Lyla watched him, eventually closing her eyes rubbing her fingers through his wet hair, enjoying every wet kiss. Lights strung over the building reflected in the water covering everything, and shining in her eyes as he lifted her wet silk dress and touched her soaked body.

Sanchez kissed from her neck to her bottom lip, touching her waist to her bursting chest as he pinned her to the tree on the sidewalk. She gripped onto his shirt and pulled him next to her, and while the sounds of the rain pounded the ground and the roof of parked cars reverberated down the narrow street – Sanchez was fucking her.

As they continued, a few walkers speedily glanced at the forbidden thrill. Lyla moaned as she saw, from the corner of her eye, one passerby with a dark blue umbrella, sticking around to check her out, turning Lyla on. She performed as if on stage at a local theatre.

The detective saw nothing, so he had no idea why he was getting torn up. He sucked her breast as she held her head against the bark of the tree, allowing the rain to fall on her face. She stuck her tongue out to taste the rain as she moaned for more.

Lyla then noticed people were watching from their apartment windows; one couple having sex between their curtains, while another one watched in awe. She could not tell the detective because if he knew, he would stop due to his profession, so she sustained the naughty performance.

The booming sounds of lightning, thunder and, "AH! Fuck it, baby! AH! AH! AH!" now filled the skies followed by police sirens ending the wondrous union.

The patrol car announced over the intercom to leave the area.

Sanchez straightened his pants, gently grabbed Lyla by the arm and shouted, "Let's go!"

Lyla laughed.

"This is not funny," the detective said. The thunder was stronger and the breeze skipped over the water. "I can get in serious trouble."

If he only knew he was being secretly gawked at by the entire neighborhood.

All of a sudden, Lyla did not feel the detective's hand holding her arm anymore. She turned around and the detective was holding on to a tree for dear life, from the strong winds.

"You can't get enough of trees, uh? Lyla laughed, the rain hitting her face. "Come on. Take my hand." The detective laughed. I thought you would find that hilarious. "You are fun in the rain," Lyla joked. *Much better than a bucket of water being dumped on me and Ritchie,* Lyla thought.

After departing from the pleasing and provocative extracurricular activities, they headed back to the detective's hotel instead of parting ways. As soon as they entered the room, Lyla instantly kicked off her heels and yanked off her sopping clothes. She could not get them off fast enough. The detective shortly did the same thing. For the first time she saw his naked muscular body.

Needless to say, they were back in each other arms, elation keeping them warm.

He cooed and she wooed as he sank into Lyla's eyes again and asked, "Did someone make you in their basement?"

"What," Lyla said.

"You are so perfectly made, both inside and out, from head to toe," Sanchez said. Lyla smiled.

The sex they had throughout the first part of the night was like wicked fireworks.

364

After fantastic sex, she climbed on the detective's chest and lied there comfortably. He rubbed her hair slowly and softly. Lyla stared at him like she had something to confess.

The detective stared at her breasts and asked, "Do you have something to get off your chest?"

"Funny," Lyla said. *So, I was wrong*, Lyla thought. "So you noticed."

"I'm a detective Lyla. I notice everything," Sanchez reminded.

"Right," Lyla said. "I keep forgetting that."

"You know what else I noticed?" Sanchez said.

She kissed his chest.

"What?"

"From 1 to 10, that loving was a 20."

"We made a fire in the middle of August," she said.

Lyla touched the tip of his nose.

"You are so cute, you know that?"

"Cute?" Sanchez laughed.

"Yes, cute," Lyla giggled. "Cute and fun."

"Lyla," the detective said.

She felt a soft blow to her head. Lyla laughed and laughed as she grabbed a pillow. He hit her again with his pillow, and she hit him over and over again. They had a pillow fight until the feathers busted through one of the pillows and they tired themselves out.

Lyla curled up next to Sanchez, not thinking about Ritchie at all as they drifted off to sleep.

The next morning while the detective was still sleeping, Lyla slowly moved Sanchez's arm from around her. She gathered her clothes and quietly put them on as she felt her bare feet sinking into the soft carpet underneath her. Lyla peeped at the detective one last time as she quickly and quietly left the room, but not before tripping over his shoe.

Shortly after, the detective's cell phone rang. He popped up, looking around for Lyla. From the disturbed lamp hanging off the dresser, the broken alarm clock on the floor, and the sheets and blankets scattered throughout the room, Lyla and the detective had a wild night.

"Lyla, Lyla, LYLA!" he called out, searching for his phone. She bluffed him. Sanchez realized she became a con to catch a con. The only problem was Ritchie was not just an unstable con artist; he was also a criminal mastermind, a killer, and a sociopath. On top of that, this man thought he was above the law and that he cannot be touched.

Lyla was in grave danger.

Sanchez found his phone and answered after the sixth or seventh ring.

"Come home, now!" Sanchez's wife exclaimed. "There was a head delivered to the house!"

Chapter 39

Lyla returned to the city. She was exhausted from the train ride. *Man, I miss my car. I loved driving back and forth to Philly. That's when I came up with my best ideas.*

Peter was finally in New York. *Thank goodness for that.* Peter and Lyla met Ritchie in the lobby of his office building. Peter was well traveled, always well dressed, and fun to be around.

All of the girls wanted him.

She introduced Peter to Ritchie. Though only a brief encounter, it was enough for Peter to see what type of person Ritchie was.

Before they left, Lyla said she was going to the bathroom. Instead, she took the elevator to Ritchie's office and looked through his desk drawers and coat pockets. She had to be proactive to see if she could find Ritchie's wallet with his personal information, like a passport, social security number, anything, since the detective still had nothing.

I'm not stupid. I did not believe the detective's excuse of why he could lose his job. The detective was fishing because he was told to leave the case alone. Now, I'm left stranded still with no answers. I'm on my own.

"Hopefully I can find out Ritchie's real name or something," she said softly out loud.

She located his wallet in his briefcase, but she did not find anything useful except for a couple of credit cards that had the name Julian on it. *Who's that?* Lyla put the wallet away, but she saw something laying there she happened to overlook, his license. She thought he didn't have one. Lyla examined the ID and it said his name was Ritchie Perez and had the street address she visited in Connecticut.

She felt relieved until she saw his age.

"He is really 55-years- old," Lyla murmured. "He told me he was 45-years-old. He shaved off ten years. Wow, he looks good." She put the license back where she found it.

Lyla proceeded to hunt for information, looking in his cabinets, but something told her to feel around the top part of the cabinet and that was when she felt a folder, which piqued her interest. She looked through it quickly; peeping out into the hallway making sure Ritchie was not around. Lyla read through the information and the information before her was of off shore accounts. The accounts were not in Ritchie's name but his wife's; money laundering on a grand scale through real estate.

"So, it looks like his wife is the one with the millions," Lyla continued to murmur.

She then read through the paper work and saw the forms she filled out during the NBA meeting. It showed completed. Ritchie and an assistant he hired made almost $25,000 organizing the event.

"He lied to me! I knew I proved myself!" Lyla exclaimed. "And the party was never a fake, because I attended it!"

Lyla continued to look and she also saw papers to his restaurant and the paperwork was not in his name either. The only thing in his name was a prescription for dick enhancement pills. *Well he must not be taking them because it ain't working*! as she jammed the papers back in the folder and slammed it on top of the high cabinet to head out the door, but she could not leave. Ritchie was standing in the doorway, as Lyla hastily jerked.

"Hey," Lyla said nervously, wondering how long he had been standing there. "You scared me."

"Hey," Peter said.

"I wanted to show your friend the office," Ritchie said.

"Oh, cool," Lyla replied.

"I thought you had to use the bathroom," Ritchie said.

"I do," Lyla responded. "I was looking for the bathroom key."

"The key is where it always is." Ritchie nodded towards the key holder.

"You are right," Lyla smiled. "There is the key hanging there, as usual."

Peter looked confused.

"What is going on?"

"Nothing, we should go now," Lyla said, grabbing Peter by the arm pushing him out the door.

"Aren't you going to use the bathroom?" Ritchie reminded.

"Oh yeah," Lyla said. "I'll use it later. I don't have to go now."

Lyla and Peter left, but not before Peter and Ritchie exchanged phone numbers. Lyla was not sure if that was a good idea. Anyway, Peter told her Ritchie was as fake as his Ferrari watch he was wearing.

"Yeah right," Lyla said. "Then why did you take his number?"

"Just politicking," Peter chuckled.

"Well, he told me designers were sending him limited edition merchandise."

"Yeah okay," Peter laughed.

He also had lead Lyla to believe that he was spending thousands of dollars on his watches. Maybe his license was a fake, too, though it looked real to her.

Lyla reached in her Givenchy bag and pulled out the diamond ring and the loose diamond Ritchie gave her. She showed it to Peter.

He held the ring and diamond up to the sun and said, "This is nice, but the ring and diamond are as phony as that Louis Vuitton man purse he was wearing."

"Are you serious?" she asked.

"Yes."

"He had the nerve to tell me to watch where I wear the ring because someone may hurt me and take it," Lyla said.

"Where did you find this dude?" Peter asked. "You always find the crazy ones, Lyla."

"Ha, ha, ha," she answered. "But I trust you know what you're talking about, since you are the number one stylist in the world."

"I am the best in the world, my friend," Peter bragged.

"And don't talk about who I meet," Lyla said. "You may be focused on your career as a fashion stylist, but you definitely put in the time for girlfriends."

He popped his collar.

"Yeah, that's right."

"But you need to watch who you meet, like that nasty girl, Mad Love."

Lyla almost forgot to tell Peter about LA.

"Where did that come from?" Peter questioned.

"She is pregnant," Lyla answered. "I saw her in LA." Peter did not seem surprised.

"I know she is pregnant and my baby is due soon," Peter sighed. "I'm the father and I don't want to hear your mouth, Lyla."

"It's your life, Peter," Lyla said. "But I remember when you called and told me you caught her cheating because you could still smell the condom on her from whoever she was with the night before. I'm just saying, that could be anybody's baby." Peter walked ahead of Lyla.

"Well at least she is using protected sex!" Peter yelled.

"So, you took her back because she used a condom?!" Lyla screamed. "That's crazy! It doesn't mean she used one with every guy she cheated on you with! I just saw her opening up her legs to everyone! No privacy for your baby!"

Peter walked back towards her.

"Just let the whole world know Lyla! Scream it louder, why don't you!"

"I'm not yelling! You are!" Lyla screamed. "I'm talking!"

"Look! Don't worry about Mad Love and me, let's deal with your issue right now," Peter said.

"Don't come crying to me when you find out you are not the father, call Maury Povich," Lyla replied.

Then again, Peter was right. She had her own problems, like finding out about her Rolex. Before Ritchie gave Lyla the diamond ring, he surprised her with a platinum Rolex packaged so elegant and nice when she attended his music event in Union Square.

I'm not a superficial person, Lyla said to herself, *but I hope the Rolex is real, he made me believe he valued his watches which met he valued me.*

Furthermore, when a man gives a piece of jewelry to a woman that is supposed to be symbolic. It means he wants to keep that woman and for that woman to think about him all day while wearing it. If my watch is a counterfeit, it meant the foundation of our relationship is a lie, and from the beginning, he never planned on keeping me around, and that the guy at the office was right when he said that after he got what he wanted he would leave me hanging.

Chapter 40

Regardless of whether or not the gifts or Ritchie were a fake, love was officially jilted. Lyla left Ritchie alone instead of turning him over to the police; mainly, because there was no smoking gun to convict him and Ritchie had once told Lyla about a woman who sued him. He put a large amount of heroin in the woman's bag. The woman was caught and went to jail. He justified it by saying it served her right because she was wanted for murder.

He could have easily done that to me when I went to Mexico or worse, have had me killed, Lyla thought. *But whether or not he wanted me dead in Mexico, I cannot imagine what he might to do to me if he found out I turned him in. Let the law find him!*

Besides, except for her pastor, she still did not trust or respect authority. The one night love affair with Detective Sanchez had not changed her mind. But thank goodness Lyla broke it off with Ritchie because she would soon realize that though he came in sheep's clothing, Ritchie was neither the sheep nor the Christian he claimed to be, but a ravenous wolf in a nice suit, making him immeasurably worse than Casmir and Nestle combined.

Nevertheless, Lyla sent her lawyer an email with all of Ritchie's information. She asked him to only read the email if something happened to her and give it to Detective John Sanchez. Lyla was not sure how much good it would do, but she had to feel like she was doing something.

When Lyla officially dropped Ritchie, she thought she would be heartbroken but she wasn't; she actually felt like a weight had been lifted off her shoulders and just like the old saying goes, there are more fish in the sea. *But for now on I have to keep in mind there are two types of fishing,* Lyla thought. *One type is when you catch a fish and then it is thrown back into the water, called catch-and-release. The other type of fishing is when you catch a fish and take it home, called fishing. Too many women take home the fish they should have thrown back into the sea.*

On the other hand, Ritchie did not understand why she wanted to break it off. Ritchie acted like the world was coming to an end. He told Lyla he would miss her yellow brick road questions and her sparkled smile. Ritchie pleaded for Lyla to stay with him. He would have done anything to stay present in her life.

Ritchie also mentioned how loyal Lyla was to him. But he did not understand there was too much disloyalty happening on his end and her loyalty was being taking advantage of, and ultimately Lyla hated being lied too.

Lyla told him, "Love me enough to let me go babe." She made him believe it was her and not him, and after a little bit more of convincing, reminding him he was married to a beautiful woman, and had great kids, he finally calmed down. Lyla hoped he got the point, because she prayed to God he would not hurt her or her family, as she remembered Ritchie telling her he was good with disguises.

Lyla already knew Ritchie could change his eye color, teeth, and hair, but he later said he could have plastic surgery done. He claimed he already had his face altered to do one of those secret jobs. Ritchie was supposed to let Lyla see pictures of his old face, but he never brought them to her. He said he may be going back to his old look soon so she could see it in person.

His comment planted a seed in her head. *Could he be Casmir?* Lyla wanted to tell the detective all of this, but first she wanted to get to the bottom of it all. She did not want to be in jail accused of something she did not do because of Ritchie.

But to think that Casmir had surgery done to become Ritchie was crazy thinking. He may have been good with changing eye color and a wig here and there like he did with me before leaving for Mexico, but it would take large amounts of money and a drastic change in order for him to look like Casmir. Besides, Ritchie looked way older than my Casmir. And on top of that, their cocks were way different in size.

Lyla refused to believe Ritchie was a monster, and though there were no more expensive dinners and going to the movies she continued to work with him sometimes. At moments he would talk like they were still together, but she reminded him they were not.

Later that week, Lyla was at the office alone waiting for Ritchie, still no sign of Roger.

While going over some accounts at the office, Lyla thought about telling Ritchie's wife everything. Lyla knew she shouldn't have wasted her time with a married man who was better paired with his wife. In other words, Lyla knew she had no chance against her, and most importantly his kids' happiness mattered more to her than anything else, so she stayed out of it. But Lyla had no choice about approaching Ritchie's wife; *I guess my aunt was wrong after all, here she is in the flesh,* Lyla said to herself.

"Are you looking for Ritchie?" Lyla asked, staring at Mrs. Perez thinking about what was next.

"Yes," Mrs. Perez answered with her Australian accent. "I'm looking for Julian."

Lyla thought about the paperwork signed under the name Julian at his office and asked, "Julian? Who is Julian?"

"I call my husband, Julian," Mrs. Perez answered.

"Well that is one way to separate yourself from the latent mistresses," Lyla joked. *I can't believe I just said that.*

"Are you one of them?" Mrs. Perez said, sarcastically.

"I'm not going to justify that with an answer," Lyla said, snobbish.

I could tell she knew about our affair. She probably isn't certain, but she knew the signs, Lyla thought. *And just like how I felt awkward about being with his children at the park like they were mine, I felt the same way in front of his wife.*

"Ritchie is not here. Can I help you?" Lyla asked.

"No, I will wait. I have heard so much about you," his wife answered.

"Likewise. Ritchie talks about you all the time," Lyla said.

"So! What are doing with my husband?" Mrs. Perez questioned.

"Working," Lyla answered.

"Let me just cut to the point," Mrs. Perez snapped. "Why involve my children with your affair with my husband?"

Lyla was troubled, but she kept her serenity.

"Ask your husband. Now, excuse me, I have some work to do," Lyla said.

"I know your type," his wife replied. "I'm a model and actress, too, as are my children, but I'm getting a little extra from the back end for my dedication and years of experience."

"That's nice. We have to pay the bills the best way we can," Lyla said.

"Sweetie, we don't need the money," his wife boasted, "but I like to help my husband out as much as I can. If you know what I mean."

"No, I don't," Lyla said.

"You'll figure it out one day. I just hope it's not too late for you," his wife warned.

Lyla looked at her. *She should be discussing this matter with Ritchie, not me so now I have no choice but agitate the bitch.*

"You have family Bible night on Fridays, no?" Lyla replied.

"Yes," his wife said.

"I hear you on the phone with him when you call," Lyla said. "Making him feel guilty if he does not show up for Bible night, it's a shame he never calls you. You get the kids to call and I'm sitting right there knowing he's telling you and your children lies, and I also know he is going home with me. Why do you stay?"

"It takes two to tango," his wife said.

"I'm not the one encouraging it," Lyla smiled. "He seduces me, and the frightening part is that he's good at it. And for your information, it is over between us. I'm no longer his girlfriend, so don't judge me for your husband's sins. Now, like I said, I have work to do."

"You know nothing," his wife said. "Let me give you a word of advice: a man has to be scared of losing a woman, he has to feel like he cannot live without that woman. Julian literally cannot live without me."

"So you think," Lyla replied.

"Oh, believe me, I know," Mrs. Perez said.

"Well, I'm loyal to Ritchie, even as his friend," Lyla said, "so I'm sure we will see each other again. Now please, I have to work."

"Don't count on it darling," his wife responded. "You must know that playing the woman of the manor takes a lot of work. Now, you have work to do, and so do I. You know the boss doesn't like it when things aren't at their best." Mrs. Perez walked away.

Silly woman. She had to make me go there, Lyla thought. But on the other hand, *I understand how she feels. I too was cheated on, by Nestle, but sometimes you can't help who you love. Speaking of love, I'm sure Ritchie is somewhere with Bizzie while I was stuck at the office with his wife.*

About an hour later, Ritchie arrived. Lyla did not acknowledge him right away. She was too busy looking pissed while staring at the computer. Evidently Lyla was in a bad mood.

"What is wrong with you?" Ritchie asked.

"Nothing," Lyla answered.

"Sure there is," Ritchie said.

"Your little wifey stopped by," Lyla snapped.

"That's all you had to say," Ritchie said. "Did you argue with her?"

"Now, why would I do that?" Lyla said, sarcastically.

"So what happened?" Ritchie asked.

"She is beautiful," Lyla answered.

"Well that is positive," Ritchie replied.

"But I don't like her," Lyla said.

"I'm sure she likes you," Ritchie grinned.

During a relative period of harmony Ritchie said softly in her ear, "Let's do something daring that will get your heart racing."

"My heart is already racing. From stress!" Lyla said.

"You know what I mean, Elizabeth," Ritchie said.

"What did you just call me?"

"Lyla," he lied.

"No," she said. "You called me by my first name, Elizabeth." This would be the first time he called her by her name, let alone her first name. "Have you been snooping through my things?" Lyla continued.

"Have you been snooping in *my* things," Ritchie said.

Lyla did not answer as Ritchie directed Lyla into their secret hallway to have a cigarette. *This is crazy. We normally sneak and smoke at night when we work late. But what the hell.*

"You know I only smoke around you," Lyla said.

"I only smoke around me too," Ritchie joked.

"Ha, ha," Lyla replied.

"So, when did my wife stop by?"

"Not too long ago," Lyla said. "At least you did not arrive when she was here. It would have pained me to see you two making goo goo eyes at each other. Not that I'm experiencing feelings for you again." He gave Lyla an odd look.

"Mademoiselle. You still love me."

"Puh-leeze," Lyla responded. "And it's a pity she is still deliriously in love with you."

"What did you say to my wife?"

"Don't worry, I didn't tell her anything."

"What is there to tell?" Ritchie asked condescendingly.

"Funny. Where is your watch?" Lyla questioned. "That seems to be missing quite often, and it's not at my house. So whose house is it at?"

Ritchie dropped his cigarette on the ground and crushed it until the fire faded out. He laughed at Lyla brush ashes off her dress pants, as she forgot to ash again. She looked at him and walked away.

"Wait a minute," he said, gently pulling her to him. "I said, 'let's do something daring that will get your heart racing.'"

"I thought that is what we just did," Lyla said.

"That is not what I was talking about," he smiled, pulling her into the men's bathroom. *My heart is racing. Anyone could walk in and catch us!* He pulled her pants down, touching and kissing her in the lightest, most sensitive parts of her body, playing with her new tits like he was at an adult playground. They made love that was so deep, nothing else existed around them.

As they came to the end of their passionate moment Ritchie muttered, "You still love me."

"Why?" Lyla questioned as she lifted up her pants. "Because this is déjà vu...having sex in the bathroom. I could have better articulated my lingering feelings for you, but the sex between us is overrated. This was just a meaningless office quickie. Got it!"

"Say what you want, but it was definitely enjoyable and meaningful for me," Ritchie answered fastening his belt.

"Hello, are you hearing me. This was goodbye sex, don't get it twisted. Now fix your shirt so we can get out of here." Lyla said as she continued to fix her clothing."

"I meant it when I said I love you," he replied, "and I will love you today, tomorrow and forever."

"Sounds nice Ritchie," Lyla said sarcastically.

"What happened to you being with me through thick and thin?" Ritchie asked. "Through all that life throws our way. You were so loyal to me."

"That was before you slept with my girlfriend's sister and..." Lyla slowed down before she said something she would regret.

"And what?" Ritchie wondered.

"Nothing," Lyla said. "Fix your tie and let's go."

"Those women mean nothing to me," Ritchie replied, assuming that is what she was still referring to.

"You and Rocket had sex in the same bed we did," Lyla reminded.

"I told you. I was not having sex." Ritchie denied. "I was clearing my throat."

"Whatever," Lyla said. "And when are you coming to get your things from my place."

"Never mind that," Ritchie said. "So, that's what's been bothering you? You think I had sex with Rocket?"

"Yes, but there's more," Lyla replied.

"Like?" Ritchie said.

"Let's talk about it later," Lyla said. "No," Ritchie demanded. "Talk to me now."

Lyla had an itching question.

"You're a spy, right?"

"What? Where is this coming from?" Ritchie asked.

Would you rather me ask you if you are a con artist or a serial killer, Lyla said to herself.

"Just answer me," Lyla answered. "Are you a spy?"

"Sort of," Ritchie said.

"Have you killed someone?"

"You are right. We should talk later."

"That's what I thought." *You asshole.*

"Let's go!" Lyla continued.

"Why are you rushing me?" Ritchie asked.

"I'm not rushing you, now hurry up." Lyla answered.

Ritchie and Lyla hurried to get themselves together, and as they left, Lyla saw a purse. Someone was watching them.

Chapter 41

A few days later Ritchie said to Lyla, "I have to leave the country. I'm getting a liver operation," as he bent his body to the side from the constant pain. "The pain is getting worse."

"Serves him right," Lyla blurted.

"What was that?" Ritchie asked.

"You're hearing things," Lyla answered.

"I leave tomorrow evening," Ritchie said. "I'll be back in a couple of weeks. Can you watch over things while I'm gone?" Lyla told him yes.

Ritchie has to leave, how convenient. Just leave me here to figure out whose purse was left behind. Now that I think about it, everything he does is convenient for him. Everyone else is a mere prop in his world.

Nonetheless, she was happy he was leaving town, because she had enough. While he was out of the country, Lyla thought it would be a good time to find out if the Rolex was real or not, as she dashed up Fifth Avenue like someone was after her. The anticipation grew stronger as she drew closer to the Rolex store. At last, she was in front of the store pacing back and forth, fiddling with her phone and biting her nails.

Okay, I'm going to do this, she said to herself, as she ignored the pulling in her gut. Lyla slowly opened the glass door and silently entered. The crowd was not too big, but big enough to be embarrassed if the watch was fake.

Lyla stood in line studying everyone around her. She normally would not care what people thought about her but for some reason she did not want anyone to think she was wearing a fake Rolex. Lyla would rather not wear anything unless it was the real thing. She was not a knock off kind of gal. Ritchie had no right to make her one.

Lyla was next in line but she did not like the clerk. She seemed snooty so Lyla waited patiently for the other clerk who was available in a matter of seconds. Lyla pulled out the watch and held it in front of the clerk.

"Is this real?" Lyla asked, lowering her head.

He took one quick look at the watch and said, "No."

Lyla's head snapped up.

"What do you mean no?" she croaked out, clearing her throat, as the world she knew bottomed out and came crumbling down around her.

"Are you sure?" she questioned.

He looked at her with stern eyes.

"Yes, I'm sure. It's a fake."

Armed with this new information, Lyla ran out the store. She wanted to go to another watch store just to double check, but she knew it was a knock off. Lyla knew it was counterfeit when he gave it to her, but she was in denial. She was in denial about everything.

"I'm starting to believe my whole life is a sham," Lyla said as she screamed without screaming and cried without crying. The people around watched her like she was crazy. "This guy is a fraud. He's the biggest manipulator I know and is very good at it.

"Ritchie preys on genuinely kind people who are vulnerable. He uses them so his businesses soars and throws business knowledge around so he thinks he is doing some good but yet he takes all the glory. But what did I expect from a man who wears sunglasses in the dark?"

Lyla caught a cab to head home and as she rode in the cab, she saw posters along the streets in bus stands and large billboards on the side of buildings.

The billboards read, "Heavenly Secrets." She thought it was awesome they had their advertisements up, until Lyla realized something. *Ritchie used the sister of the model I was working with at the Garden instead of me for the make-up campaign. I knew he was asking about her, because he liked her.* Lyla totally lost it.

"Stop! Wait here!" Lyla shouted to the cab driver.

She grabbed paint from a nearby painter and threw the paint on the posters.

The angry painter came running after her. Lyla apologized after she realized what she had done.

"Here." She handed him a lump sum of money. "Wow," the guy said, "I can retire."

Lyla was having another panic attack. She took a couple of breaths to calm down.

"Are you okay?" the painter asked.

"I'm fine. Don't worry about me, go and buy some more paint." She made her way into the cab.

Lyla was headed towards her apartment the sun was dipping low but it seemed like Ritchie had the sunrise in his pocket. *I trusted, respected, and was loyal to Ritchie,* Lyla said to herself, *but not anymore!* She pulled out the mystery envelope and although her mind was in a million different places, she felt like it was time to find out what was inside.

"When do I open it?"

"You will know when."

Finally at her building, she paid her fare, jumped out of the cab, tore open the envelope, looked for her keys to get in the large steel gate, opened the envelope some more, and out of nowhere, a slew of reporters approached her.

Lyla said, "What the…"

"Do you know where Ritchie Perez is, or should we say Casmir Nowak?" one reporter asked, as the cameras rudely flickered in her face. Normally Lyla only had to smile and wave to the press but now it was a whole different story. She ended up fielding a bevy of hardball questions. Lyla was so confused. She shouted, "Get away from my home!"

"Do you know he is on the run and that there is a $50,000 reward on his head?" another reporter said. *This is what I dreaded; my newfound success destroyed because of Ritchie.* She did not believe that any press was good press, she wanted good press, even as a video girl. "You don't know what you're talking about," Lyla said.

"Don't you read the blogs?" the reporter replied. "We heard you were his mistress and that you help him with his business deals. You're all over his website. Do you care to comment?" Lyla stopped and stared angrily at the reporter for a moment and then boldly faced the media frenzy.

"First of all, I am no one's mistress. Furthermore, check your resources," Lyla said. "Blogs are full of careless research."

"Oh really," the same reporter responded. "So what about the nude pictures that are on the internet, would that be careless research too?"

"Nonsense, what nude pictures?" Lyla asked.

386

"The naked pictures online," the reporter answered. "Did you take them for one of your video girl shoots?"

Lyla disregarded the reporter and marched upstairs to her apartment.

"Dag it!" Lyla said, tripping over her neighbor's package. "There is always a package in front of her door. I hope I'm not living next door to some terrorist. She's probably building a bomb in there; dag on neighbor."

Lyla picked up her dropped keys, the envelope, and her newspaper she saw laying in front of her door. The headline said, "The Fugitive's Girlfriend," with a photograph of Lyla and Ritchie kissing in the office bathroom. *Great, the goal was to keep the relationship a secret. And although I broke it off with him, it doesn't matter now, the whole world knows about us.*

She knew what the reporter was talking about when he asked her about the naked pictures. The nude photos from years ago had surfaced. Lyla was sure Casmir had given those pictures to a friend before he died, and his boy must have put them on the Internet. She was afraid that once she became a known model, those pictures would show up.

Casmir continued to haunt her even after his death.

Lyla also understood why Ritchie posted her photos all over his website; if something went wrong, Lyla would be the fall guy for it and not him.

She wept as she slammed the envelope down on the counter. Then she swiftly walked towards the bathroom, grabbing a ponytail holder along the way. Lyla flipped on the light switch and stopped in front of the bathroom mirror. Her normally tamed curly hair was messy from the wind. She pulled it off her face with her ponytail holder, some short curls escaping while splashing a handful of ice-cold water over her angry face.

After the rinse, she opened the medicine cabinet to grab a couple of band aids for the backs of her ankles made sore by walking in heels all day.

"I can't believe I forgot my flats." She closed the medicine cabinet and she used her reflection in the smudged up mirror to ask herself, *What have I become?* Lyla looked harder and harder in the mirror and for the first time her sad brown eyes frightened her and then they made her mad again. She squinted her eyes and shoved everything out of the medicine cabinet.

Lyla was pissed at life.

She contemplated whether she should make sense of her thoughts and face them head on, or shut her thoughts up and move back to Philadelphia. But Lyla knew she could not keep running home every time something happened, and things weren't any better there anyways. Lyla contacted her pastor for a pep talk, but he was nowhere to be found.

She sat on her couch to put her feet up and thought to herself, *I am a crazy man magnet and I would remain an arm piece or sex toy, forever, always missing out on true love and never being appreciated.*

From now on I'm going to pussy fart on guys! as she thought about what one of her Asian friends told her, "I do more for woman who have sex with me than the ones that don't."

"Why?" Lyla asked.

"Because the woman who has had sex with me has given me her all, so in return, I give her my all," he answered.

"Not that I'm condoning sex before marriage," Lyla said. "But I wish all guys thought like that, but it's always been the opposite for me and for most women. Once you give it up, they treat you like crap or leave you."

"That is because you pick low-lifes," he said. "They just want to get in your pants. You have so much more to offer. You're gorgeous, talented with lots of potential. You need a nice, regular guy.

"Stop going after these wannabe rock stars who look in the mirror all day, date the mailman for heaven sakes! He will appreciate you and worship the ground you walk on. So far the guys you've come across have played you. You got played girl."

Lyla laughed at the ending of her friend's preaching.

"Yes, I will obey you my sensei, so I will not be played. Chinky chinky chang chang chang chang chang."

"Shut the hell up," her friend laughed.

Regardless of her playful personality and teasing her friend, she had to agree with him as she thought about her pastor.

My pastor is a very friendly and special man. Someone I could count on for the rest of my life. I'm so grateful for his pep talks. He's a good friend and I'm glad he has all of his teeth. Lyla giggled.

The pastor had taken her to dinners and shown her a great time, treated her like a queen. But she figured he would not want to be in a serious relationship, due to the drama in her life. *Nice thought though.*

In turn, the story was written and Lyla saw no end. She could not take any more disappointments. Lyla asked God for forgiveness, but sometimes she wished she followed through with slitting her wrist with the razor blade, so she could rush her death to feel life again.

But anyway, Lyla searched the Internet for naked pictures of herself and found nothing. She was relieved, and thought the reporter was lying, until she realized that Casmir's friend would not know her by Lyla Tight, and typed in Elizabeth Tight. *There they are!*

She jumped up.

"Who did this?!"

Lyla looked different now than when she was a teenager, but one could still tell it was her. What devastated Lyla the most were the visible scars and bruises in some of the pictures, evidence of Casmir's beatings.

One of the captions read, "She likes it rough."

"People can be so cruel! If only they knew I was a victim of teenage abuse!" Lyla screamed, feeling a little lightheaded.

Lyla went to the kitchen to get some water only to find her kitchen filled with dirty dishes, not a clean glass in sight. She attempted to wash out a cup, but the sponge was old. Lyla wrote "sponge" on her grocery list posted on the huge stainless steel refrigerator as she held her head with her other hand. She then cupped some water in her hands to drink. Lyla headed back to her room hoping her head would eventually feel better.

She took a look at one of her social networking pages she had abandoned a while back, making sure there were no tags on her page.

"I don't know why I'm looking at this crap," Lyla said. "No one uses this stupid stuff anymore." Lyla did not find anything, thank goodness, but she did want to see if others are still using this silly mess and see what they were up to. *It cannot be as bad as my life.*

Lyla looked around. *Oh wow,* she said to herself, *Casmir's brother is friending me?* She hesitated but saw nothing wrong with accepting his request. His brother did not do anything to her. He actually treated her kindly when she dated Casmir. She added his brother as a friend, and she read his status update, **Revenge is served on a cold platter.**

"Goodness," Lyla said, "lighten up. The whole family is insane." Lyla changed her mind and deleted him as a friend. *I think the best thing to do is to stay away from the whole family.*

Lyla looked on her producer friend's page who she phoned while in LA. She looked under some of her photos. All of her pictures were so nice. Lyla's friend said so many wonderful things about people. She kept looking and saw a picture they took together. Lyla smiled.

"Wow, I forgot all about this picture. Look at my big sister." She read the caption, "Crazy."

"Well, I know I'm crazy, but I have learned how to control it," Lyla said jokingly.

Lyla understands her girlfriend does not like some of the decisions she had made but she thought that it was insensitive to put something like that on her social networking page.

She wanted to call and talk to her about it, but Lyla came to realize that she and her friend were equally crazy, and if that made her feel better about herself, then so be it. Two crazy people fighting over something like that was, well, crazy.

Lyla logged out of her account, hoping she misinterpreted her friends comment. She felt light headed again. Lyla stood up and walked to her bed to rest. As she approached her bed, everything bad that happened in her life raced in her head, and she collapsed on the floor from too much stress.

Her head turned to the side as if she was looking for something under the bed, then suddenly, her body shook with a force she could not stop. Lyla's eyes rolled back into her head while her hands tightened into fists, spit sliding down the side of her mouth. After a few moments, she slipped away into a deep abyss.

The beautiful Lyla was a hot mess.

Chapter 42

The next day, Lyla woke up with blurred vision. She could only see shapes and colors. Lyla thought she was in the Promised Land. *Pastor,* she thought. Lyla's focus came back and she realized she had tubes glued to her body and the people dressed in white standing around her were not angels, they were physicians.

"I'm Dr. Burt Petrulo," the doctor said. "How are you feeling, Ms. Tight?"

"Why am I in the hospital?" Lyla asked.

"You had a seizure," the doctor answered. "Your friend called the ambulance for you. Have you been under a lot of stress?"

"Friend?" Lyla said. "Yes, I have been under a lot of stress, but I can handle it. I want to leave, this is nonsense."

"Well," Dr. Petrulo said. "From the looks of things, I would like for you to stay for a few days to keep you under observation."

"Don't worry," Lyla replied. "I'm not so upset to kill myself if that is what you are insinuating."

"Not at all," the doctor said. "Is there anyone you'd like me to contact for you?"

"NO!" Lyla said. "I mean, no thank you, I'll be fine. But please find out who brought me here."

"That person left," the doctor said. "I'll send them in if she returns. I'll be back in a few to check on you."

"I'm sorry," Lyla replied. "What name do you go by again?"

"Dr. Petrulo."

"Dr. Friendly," Lyla smiled.

Lyla is such a flirt at times, as I chuckle.

"Get some rest," the doctor said.

For days, she sat in the room, angry at the world. She did not eat or speak.

This is when I need a man to hold me. Women want to feel secure and I have never felt that from any guy. When I love, I love hard, but I feel like love does not love me. She continued to not eat or speak for days until one day, Lyla woke up and saw someone unexpected sitting at her bedside, looking like she was born to lead.

The beautiful woman was wearing a pair of nude Manolo Blahnik heels with a white and black long cashmere shawl, covering a slightly sheer midnight black Prada dress complimenting her voluptuous figure. No dame could afford an outfit like that. She had no job and when she had one, she didn't stay long. But no matter what, she landed on her feet, always finding a way to live in extraordinary apartments and always dressed to kill. Lyla knew she was a champion eBay shopper but with her lifestyle, rumors were rampant that she sold her body.

There was only one thing wrong with her outfit. The Dolce & Gabbana nude handbag she carried was the same bag left behind in the office bathroom where Ritchie and Lyla fucked.

"Hey hey hey hey. How are you, sweetie?" Poison asked. She walked over to Lyla with her freshly colored long honey blonde hair and a tan bringing out her sweet dimples and hazel eyes. Poison glowed in the light. She gave Lyla a tight hug.

"What a surprise," Lyla answered.

"I wanted to come and surprise you, and that is when I found you on the floor. I called the ambulance," Poison pouted.

"Well as you can see, I'm not doing so great," Lyla replied sadly. "But I'm glad you're here, Poison," Lyla continued with a smile. "Oh gosh, I remember reporters! Did you see reporters?!"

"Calm down, girl. I did," Poison said. "Don't worry I told them you slipped and fell and to mind their business."

"Nice," Lyla said as they both laughed. That moment brought back the old days, as Lyla went from laughing to looking sad again.

"Lyla, talk to me," Poison said.

"You should have left me on the floor," Lyla said. A teardrop fell. "Why does it matter if there is one less Lyla Tight on earth?"

"It matters to me. You know I'm there for people I love." Poison reached in her purse to grab a tissue for Lyla.

"You have always been there for me. Nice purse, by the way."

"This ol' thing," Poison said. "I borrowed it from my sister this morning. It matches my nude heels but I have to get it back before she notices it's gone. She's generous but she can be stingy with her designer bags. Especially this one, since apparently the designer only made one."

Lyla now could believe Rocket was watching her and Ritchie like a stalker at the office and sold the photo to the press.

"So," Lyla said, "you and Rocket are speaking?"

"Of course," Poison replied. "She's my sister, why? And don't think I didn't notice the twin girls, Oodles and Noodles."

"Oodles and Noodles?" Lyla lightly laughed.

"I don't know girl; it rhymes," Poison said. They laughed as Lyla shook her breasts.

Lyla told her everything. She related the details of the nightmare, including why the reporters were outside her front door. Lyla told her who Ritchie was. She even told her what Rocket did.

Poison was on full alert when she talked about her sister.

"This story sounds all too familiar," Poison said.

"Why?" Lyla asked.

"Rocket told Sugar about Ritchie and you," Poison answered. "She also told him something about your superintendent."

"Rocket knows Sugar? And what did she say about my super?" Lyla wondered.

"Yes, she knows Sugar," Poison said. "I introduced them to help her with her shoe line and I'm not sure what she told Sugar about your super. You will have to ask her that question."

So that explains Sugar's text. I guess he thought the same thing I was thinking. That Rocket and I could work together.

"I can only imagine the story Rocket told Sugar about Ritchie and me," Lyla responded. "Rocket probably told Sugar I stole Ritchie from her and I screwed up the shoe deal. The crazy part is, whatever she told him, Sugar believed her over me. That's why I got rid of him because of stuff like this." *Fuck this shit.*

"Well the joke was that you thought Ritchie and Rocket were having sex and you over reacted, because they claimed to be having a meeting and Ritchie was 'clearing his throat,'" Poison laughed.

"Yeah okay," Lyla said.

"We know that's not true," Poison replied. "So, I guess Rocket joined Sugar's 'Hate Lyla Campaign.'"

"What's that?" Poison asked.

"Never mind," Lyla answered.

"Well, now I'm upset with Rocket. Doing you wrong like this," Poison said.

"Don't be," Lyla said. "I'm just giving you the 4-1-1. Besides, I left Ritchie alone."

"Well, good. Because now that I think about it, he was playing both of you."

"You seem to know something I don't, Poison."

"Rocket showed me some love letters between them two," Poison said.

"What were the letters about? 'Why Ritchie should be her sugar daddy?'" Lyla giggled...Poison laughed.

"Rocket was in New York for business, but still spending most of her time in Philly," Poison continued. "They came up with this idea of getting a journal to write the letters in. She would write him a letter and leave it with him when she left town, and then Ritchie would write one right behind hers in the same journal, and when they met he would give it to her. They wrote back and forth for months like love birds."

"Wow," Lyla said.

"Girl, you could not have predicted what was going to happen," Poison replied. "So don't beat yourself up over it. You followed your instincts and you let him go. It's Ritchie's loss, not yours."

"That's the problem," Lyla said as she turned on the TV and channeled surfed. "I wasted my life away with no good guys and people period. And what is wrong with this remote control?" Lyla banged the remote against the wall.

"I'm sure if you deposit a quarter it will work," Poison jested. Lyla laughed. "Yeah. I think they bought the demo version," Lyla joked as she stopped banging the remote control and finally landed on a news channel. The news reporter announced, "Today, 'The Fugitive's Girlfriend,' was taken to the hospital because of a nervous breakdown and..." Lyla flipped off the TV with a grunt.

"Goodness, Lyla, your story is getting a lot of media coverage," Poison said.

"It's got all of the elements of a great story," Lyla said.

"What?" Poison asked. "Sex, money, and drugs?"

"No," Lyla answered. "Betrayal, Poison. But for real, people are just people. Nothing more, nothing less. So it does not matter to me what they say because they are just people. People put too much emphasizes on people when they are just people, and I have to remind myself of that when people want to act up. On another note, as long as "people" don't touch me, she paused, it's all good."

"If you look at it that way, then yeah, who gives a fuck," Poison laughed. "But as far as love is concerned. Love is like this and love is like that, and this situation is going to make you a stronger person, Lyla."

"I hope so, because right now, I do not feel so strong, not because of people, of course, but because of the choices I have made," Lyla said.

"You're trying to find your way," Poison replied while putting on some of her red lipstick.

"Love that," Lyla smiled.

"It's yours," Poison said. "You can have it. I have plenty more."

"Thanks babe," Lyla said. "You are the only one I know who can pull off wearing red lips in the middle of the day."

"You know me," Poison laughed.

Lyla asked Poison not to say anything to anybody about the situation, especially her parents.

"Ah," Poison said. "I have something to tell you."

From the look on her face, Lyla had to brace herself because she knew how Poison was.

"What? Just tell me," Lyla said with a sad look on her face.

"Well..." Before Poison could get it out, she noticed Lyla needed some more consoling. She gave her another hug. This embrace actually felt more affectionate. "It's going to be okay, I promise you," she continued, dropping her shawl. The top part of her dressed dipped low allowing her cleavage to explode from her dress as she gazed into Lyla eyes.

Lyla knew where this was going.

Poison was bisexual and she always used her charm to come on to Lyla. Poison's stubbornness finally paid off and for the first time, at Lyla's lowest point, she gave in.

Poison slowly kissed Lyla and Lyla kissed her back. They teased and giggled and giggled and teased, playing with each other's hair until Poison felt comfortable enough to pull up her dress, climbing on top of Lyla like a naughty pussycat.

Lyla lied back onto her hospital bed while one leg was straight up in the air, Poison rubbing and kissing it, leaving a trail of cherry red lips up and down her thigh.

She whispered to Lyla, "Don't worry. This is our little secret."

In a matter of moments, Poison's chest was out showing the rose tattoo wrapped around her one breast. She definitely did not need a breast enhancement, if anything she needed to deflate them. Poison softly rubbed her hands over Lyla's seventy five hundred dollar tits and grabbed hold of her neck as she lifted Lyla's gown to lick and tug at her perky nipples. Their bodies were glued together, moving in slow motion, stimulating each other's clitorises.

From the sounds of it, Poison was already climaxing.

"Lyla," Poison moaned.

"Poison," Lyla moaned.

They continued kissing as Lyla sucked and tugged on Poison's boobs with one hand, and rubbed the pubic hair on her kitty cat with the other.

"AH! AH! AH!" Poison said. She placed her finger inside of Lyla as they moaned some more. Poison released her wet finger from Lyla's pussy, both licking and sucking her finger like it was a hard dick as they continued to ride each other, this time, faster. Poison could not help but let the animal in her take control as she repeatedly bit Lyla on her neck, in between her breast, heading downtown, only to stop at that precise moment.

Rocket swung the door wide open like a witch with bad news written in her crystal ball. Poison jumped up like a cat on a hot tin roof and Lyla looked as red as a beet.

"Damn!" Poison said. "Can't you knock?" I was giving Lyla a massage to calm her nerves." Lyla and Poison didn't think Rocket saw anything, but behind Lyla's naughty little eyes, she couldn't hide much the fact that she wanted to repeat that delicious route of kissing and licking with Poison.

Lyla noticed Rocket had a new-fangled weave she wanted to pull out again, but Lyla's main concern was finding out what Rocket was up to.

"So yeah," Poison said. "I already told Rocket you were here. If I knew what she did, I would not have told her." Poison hid the purse from Rocket, fixed her clothes, and spun on her heels, as Lyla defiantly stared at Rocket.

"It's okay, Poison. I need to talk to her anyways, woman to woman. I like your weave."

Rocket sharply corrected Lyla.

"It's a wig."

"Oh, forgive me," Lyla said. "So, it looks like you and your sister are not mad at each other."

"So sue me," Rocket said.

"Sue you? You know now that I think about it, I should sue you," Lyla threatened.

"What ever for," Rocket sassed.

"I heard you've been talking about me to my old manager and whoever else," Lyla reminded.

"So?" Rocket said.

"Oh," Lyla said. "So you are not denying it."

"I say what I want. I'm not afraid of you."

"Maybe not," Lyla replied. "But you will be scared of the law after I sue you for slander and defamation of character. People do get sued for that. If I hear you're spreading lies about me again, you will pay the consequences for it."

"Whatever," Rocket said, clearly bored.

"I'm not coming out to play with you, Rocket," Lyla said.

"Like I said...whatever!" Rocket shouted.

"I have a feeling you had this planned from the start, huh, Rocket?"

"What do you want me to say, Lyla," Rocket responded.

"You know what," Lyla said. "I'm going to give you a heads up about Ritchie, and quite frankly, I don't care how you take it." She explained to Rocket who Ritchie was and Rocket did not believe her. Rocket claimed Lyla was jealous and that she was the one Ritchie wanted to be with. "So you think," Lyla chuckled.

"Yes," Rocket replied.

"In your dreams," Lyla said.

"Don't hate me because I'm beautiful," Rocket said.

"You're just easy pickings," Lyla said. The bottom-line was Rocket did not understand Lyla's and Ritchie's relationship and she never will.

"What about his wife and Bizzie?" Lyla asked.

"Who and Who?" Rocket said. *She was clearly delusional.*

"You are giving it up to a man you don't know," Lyla said.

"Just stop talking! You don't know what you are talking about," Rocket replied.

"Who are you telling to stop talking?! I am not your child!" Lyla said.

"Stop talking!" Rocket repeated.

"Have you gotten anything from your sugar daddy yet? Has he invested in your shoe line?" Lyla questioned.

"You are the user! Not me!" Rocket said.

"How am I the user when you were using me to get to my contacts," Lyla reminded. "You were never a sincere person."

"Was I supposed to be?" Rocket asked sarcastically.

"You are right Rocket," Lyla answered. "So, I guess that is why you slept with Ritchie in my bed! That's dirty! Were you going to change the sheets before I returned?"

"You were not staying there at the time, Lyla!" Rocket responded. "And we were not sleeping together."

"Yeah, okay!" Lyla shouted.

"So anyway, what have you received, Ms. Lyla from Ritchie?"

"I'm not in it for the money," Lyla said. "But if you must know, I got a ring."

"A ring? Go ahead girl," Poison said.

"I'm not finish," Lyla said. "And a Rolex."

"Get it get it," Poison replied.

"You want it, Rocket," Lyla laughed. "It's all real. You could probably pawn it if Ritchie hasn't given you any money yet."

Rocket said to Lyla, "Ritchie and I are the perfect power couple. I don't need anything from you."

"Ritchie belonged to me," Lyla said. "And I belonged to him and you tried to take that away from me. Ritchie and I are through, not because of you, but because I know what kind of person he is and I'm warning you. But the $50,000 question is, who do you belong to?"

"$50,000?" Rocket said.

"I heard that is what criminals are going for these days," Lyla laughed.

Rocket boldly glanced at Poison and then glanced over at Lyla. It was clear Rocket was blinded by selfishness.

"I used to think love was just an illusion of the mind," Rocket said. "Something unreal and impossible to find, but the day I met Ritchie I began to see that love is real, and it lives in me for him."

Lyla approached Rocket, standing firmly in front of her face.

"I'm so deeply touched, but you're forgetting one thing: he was mine!"

"Is that why you got those fake breasts?" Rocket said. "Were they the yin and yang of his life? Seems a little desperate to me."

"You are just mad because my tits are the same size as your stomach," Lyla pointed out. Rocket sputtered. She was shocked Lyla said that to her. "Now suck in like I taught you."

"You are evil!" Rocket shouted, putting her finger in Lyla's face.

"Spanx!"

"Whatever!"

"Spanx!" Lyla screamed, "And get your hand out of my face, Rocket!

"Evil!" Rocket yelled. Poison pulled Lyla away.

"Love is blind, sweetie!" Lyla screamed. "You are blind!" Rocket shouted.

"Stop being a sore LOSER, Rocket," Poison said.

"Whose side are you on, sis?"

"Just drop it," Poison replied. "There are plenty of men out there, and to tell you both the truth, it seems to me, Ritchie has walked all over the both of you." Rocket's jealousy agitated like a smoldering furnace.

"Lyla! You leave Ritchie alone completely," Rocket demanded. "Don't call him or ever see him again and your secret will be safe with me!"

Lyla shouted to Rocket, "What secret, bitch?! You have nothing on me, silly little girl."

Rocket showed Lyla the video she just recorded from her phone of her and Poison making out. *I can definitely see my face in this video. Unlike the elevator fight debut.* Although Lyla was devastated, she did not show any emotion.

"You like watching people have sex, huh?" Lyla continued. "First me and Ritchie in the bathroom and now me and Poison. Get a life!" Rocket hastily retreated, stomping down the hall in a fury with her Dolce & Gabbana stilettos. *This girl was way past keeping the peace.*

Poison was up to any challenge and knew she could handle Rocket later, but Lyla had to get out of the hospital room. Believe or not, she did not want to leave again on bad terms with Rocket, and she needed that recording erased immediately.

Lyla reached the main entrance to the hospital and spotted Rocket crossing the street. As she crossed, Rocket reminded Lyla of how Kermit the Frog crossed the street in the movie, *The Muppets Go to Manhattan*. She could not help but laugh.

On top of that, Rocket was so upset that she did not notice the wind had tilted her wig to the side. She looked so silly.

Rocket stopped in the middle of the street to wait for a car to pass. She saw Lyla crossing the street to meet her.

"Wait, Rocket!" Lyla hollered.

She put her middle finger up at Lyla.

"Stay away from me, Ritchie, and our unborn twins, or this recording will be on YouTube."

"Twins?!" Lyla shouted. "You pregnant by Ritchie?"

When Rocket turned around to finish crossing the street she tripped in her heel. BAM! A car hit Rocket and she went flying. The force made her literally fly like a rocket while her wig and one Dolce & Gabbana heel went flying in the opposite direction. She hit head first on the uneven sidewalk.

Lyla ran over to her. Her sister came running behind Lyla. Lyla elevated Rocket's bloody head on top of her arm. She was still conscious but Rocket couldn't move. Lyla could see in Rocket's eyes she was scared, but she wanted to tell Lyla something.

"Rocket, what is it?" Lyla asked. Her sister was crying, sitting in a puddle of blood.

"No!" Poison answered. "Don't talk, someone get some help!" Rocket's head was bleeding pretty badly but she said, "I was..."

"Huh?" Lyla said, lowering her ear down to Rocket's mouth. Rocket whispered, "I was the one who tripped you in the stairway at the studio, I put the gun in your hand, and I shot at you in Times Square, I also..." Rocket was drifting away quickly.

"Rocket!" Lyla screamed. "What are you saying? Tell me!"

"They won't open the door," Rocket responded softly, blood gushing out the top of her head. "They won't open the door." Rocket put her hand over her stomach.

The physicians came running over. It was too late – Rocket was gone. She wanted to tell Lyla something, but Rocket could not get it out. Poison bawled uncontrollably as Lyla held her.

"What did she mean?" Poison asked. "They won't open the door."

Chapter 43

Still traumatized over Rocket's unforeseen death, Lyla had someone to call, and that person was Ritchie.

Ritchie was still overseas, so she contacted him through Skype, but not before calling Ritchie's college to find out if he really had a PhD. She wasn't surprised that they had never heard of him, but nonetheless, Lyla was even more furious at Ritchie after uncovering that lie, as Lyla thought about Rocket.

I cannot believe Rocket wanted to kill me over Ritchie. In spite of our differences, I would not wish death on any one, not even my worst enemy. Ritchie had lead Rocket down a sinister road with no return.

I got into the modeling business to travel, be a light for God, meet new people, and have some excitement in my life, but I got more than what I bargained for when I met Ritchie. I lost track of what I wanted. I already ended my relationship as Ritchie's girlfriend but now it was time to make changes - permanent changes, like ending our friendship and business relationships too.

Lyla spoke to Ritchie. She did not tell him about her visit to the hospital. The conversation did end up leading to a horrific argument that her pastor had advised against ever having with him, because he may sabotage her.

Pastor Bill also said that he does not know what it is, but God had something huge for her to do in life, bigger than being a video girl. But first God needs her to leave low-life men alone once and for all because He is not going to take Lyla to the top with the bad boys. The only thing they will do is spend the money God blessed her with, and bring her down mentally like before.

Lastly, just like he had to warn her about Nestle, Pastor Bill told Lyla that Ritchie is not good for her either. Lyla thanked the pastor for that prophetic information.

During the horrific argument, Lyla dressed down Ritchie, telling him he was to blame for everything: their personal and business relationships going downhill and the death of Rocket.

Lyla asked Ritchie about Rocket's pregnancy and he denied it and said, "You and Rocket are both foolish. She was never pregnant by me." Ritchie laughed.

"According to the doctors, Ritchie, Rocket was two months pregnant with twins and, of course, they could not save them when she passed away. What? Did you think I was going to be the stepmom?" Lyla said as she thought back to what Nestle told her.

Ritchie was dead silent.

"Hello?" Lyla called. "Hello...hello?" For the first time he lost control and raised his voice more than normal.

"You can paint whatever picture you want of me!" Ritchie shouted. "But I will not supply you the paint. You have a sharp tongue you ungrateful little..." He stopped himself as she said to herself, *The nerve of him! I leave an impression on everyone I meet, so I know Ritchie will miss me when I'm gone for good.*

He proceeded to lie right through his teeth about the pregnancy, but she knew he was not telling the truth.

Lyla also said something to him about cheating on her with Bizzie and about the fake Rolex. She also brought up the Heavenly Secrets make-up ads. The excuse he told Lyla was that the novice model was blacklisted for almost five years because of a well-known fashion designer dragging her name in the mud. Ritchie believed himself to have saved her from all of this by offering her the make-up campaign. *A Black Blondie, eh?* Lyla said to herself. Whatever the excuse was for using the girl over Lyla, she was not pleased.

Shortly after the phone conversation, Lyla sent Ritchie an email reminding him about his things at her apartment. She wanted it out as soon as possible. From his email reply, his temper had gone from simmer to boil, again. He asked for his ring and diamond back.

"So now you're an Indian giver! Why do you want the ring and diamond back? So you can use the same phony ring, diamond, and your bogus PhD to trick another woman? You want it back, come and get it!" she replied as she flushed the ring and diamond down the toilet.

Lyla hated when she got hostile and she had no idea what Ritchie was going to do, but God would protect Lyla and her family from him.

He responded, "This is why I also gave the other model your event planning job, you bitch."

Chapter 44

Lyla always had warnings about Ritchie, as she remembered a number of red flags she should have not ignored.

"This is a very nice girl; you have a really nice girl."

"Why do you want to be with someone like him, he is controlling, why do you want him?"

She also remembered a tall, middle-aged guy walking by Lyla and Ritchie one day and he said, "You need to get rid of that shit." Lyla turned her head and he kept walking.

Then, one time while she was walking with Ritchie, one of two guys talking to each other said, "He's just using her for work and sex." None of these people knew Lyla or Ritchie.

Most of all, now that she thought about it, Lyla remembered the time she auditioned for a big movie role. She was not an actress, but Ritchie claimed he was an expert at training actresses and he could get her ready for the part. Before Lyla went to the audition, he went over the lines with her. When she read the script, it sounded like it was a conversation between two girlfriends talking about a man she thought was bad news and that her girlfriend should leave him alone.

The lines sounded like the girl was mad, but because Lyla was a woman, she knew the girl wasn't mad; they were joking around with each other. He insisted the girl was being a bitch, so Lyla listened to Ritchie. They practiced and practiced to the point where she went to her audition in character, which means Lyla was a bitch walking in. It was her turn to audition and the casting director said just what Lyla said to Ritchie. The two girls were best friends and they were joking around about the guy.

Lyla felt like an idiot. First, she came in the building being mean to people and then she ended up screwing up the entire audition because she could not get out of the character Lyla practiced for almost a month. This part could have changed her life and she lost the role.

Ritchie called the casting director he supposedly knew to make up for what he had done but nothing came out of it.

Why didn't I have enough strength and courage to leave Ritchie alone sooner? Lyla asked herself as she checked out of the hospital.

Chapter 45

Lyla was relaxing at her place blasting her opera through her entire apartment building. She picked up the solitary dried out blue rose sitting on her bedside table, the only rose she kept.

"The blue rose represents mystery and attaining the impossible."

She sat the rose back down on the stand, next to the newspaper with the famous headline, "The Fugitive's Girlfriend."

Ritchie was coming home today. She told him when he arrived to come to her place to get his things. Lyla walked to the kitchen to turn off the teakettle she heard going off. She was in the mood for some hot green tea.

Lyla poured the water in a cup but she suddenly stopped.

"Oh my gosh, I forgot, hot! hot! ho-" Lyla burned her hand with the scalding hot water she was pouring into a mug while thinking about what she forgot. *That's what I get for not keeping my mind on one thing.* She dumped the blistering hot water in the sink. *I don't want it anymore.*

Lyla was saying she forgot about the envelope. She had not seen it since she passed out.

Lyla blindly searched for the envelope, ripping her place apart while thinking about Ritchie and how much time she wasted. She stepped out of the situation so she could see everything from a different view.

Another summer, Lyla thought. *It's been almost two years now. How time flies when a person is being mentally abused. Nothing good happened between Ritchie and me, yet he promised me the world. He said everything was going to be different for my family. Everything sounded so wonderful, and I believed in him.*

He taught me business to keep me around, along with creating this mystery man to make him more appealing. But Ritchie's intentions were never to help me, but for me to help him become successful. I was basically his slave, just like I was to Nestle, both are predators.

But never mind that, now I have the answer to my question, "Where did I go wrong in my life?" It has nothing to do with my family, Nestle, Ritchie, or anything else; it's me. I had to stop making wrong choices and take responsibility for myself. This is how I was able to get my career back on track without Ritchie.

Lyla rinsed her wine glass with tap water and soap to pour some wine instead of tea as her favorite opera singer hit his high tenor note in the background. She stopped and absorbed the fine music.

"Oh, how I love opera," she said. Lyla went back to rinsing out her glass but forgot she threw away her sponge, and hadn't picked up another one from the store yet, so she watched the water fill the hollow glass a few more times, and used a new dish cloth she remembered she purchased a little while ago. *I need to hire a cleaning lady to help me out around here.*

She poured the wine, turned down the music a little, and phoned Poison to see if she saw the envelope when she found her on the floor, but there was no answer. Lyla continued to look for the envelope and a few minutes later, she heard a knock on her front door. She turned off the music completely and set the glass of wine down on the kitchen counter.

Lyla opened the door and did not see anyone until she looked down. There was a package with the word fragile stamped on it. *I'm not expecting a package,* Lyla thought. *Does this belong to that neighbor?* The neighbor in question was actually leaving when Lyla saw the package.

"Hello," the neighbor said to Lyla.

"How are you?" Lyla asked.

"Good," the neighbor replied.

"Is this yours?" Lyla asked.

"It doesn't look like mine," the neighbor answered.

"I'm not expecting anything," Lyla said. "And I don't see a sender's name or return address."

Her neighbor checked out the box.

"Nope, it's not mine. But it's nice to receive gifts."

"Yeah, that's true," Lyla smiled.

"Enjoy, see you later," the neighbor said, waving goodbye. *Um, I knew she was building a bomb,* Lyla joked to herself as she sat the mystery box on the counter.

Lyla put her dirty dishes in the dish washer and then sipped her wine as she admired the snow globes she collected as trophies through her many travels as a model. She was very pleased. During her long, hot shower, she thanked God for her many blessings and then she dressed in a pair of black skinny jeans and gray tank top.

As Lyla walked back to the kitchen to drink the rest of her wine, she saw the package.

"Oh, yeah," Lyla said. "Who is this from, anyway?" Lyla examined the outside of the box one last time to make sure she did not miss anything. She then shook the box and heard nothing. Lyla opened the box and almost jumped out of her skin.

She remembered what the doctor said to do when she felt like she was under stress, but no technique could prepare a person for what was now in front of her. It was the surreal face of a man; the head of Roger!

She dropped the box on the ground and screamed, "Who sent this?!"

Lyla saw something sticking out the top of the box. At a snail's pace she bent over the package to see what's inside. There were photos, and a DVD. Lyla could hardly stand on her feet let alone reaching inside to grab the material. But she had no choice. She gradually reached inside and quickly pulled out the photos, holding her stomach in disgust.

As the blood slowly dripped off the images in her hand, it revealed her and Sanchez hanging out at the park and having sex in the rain. Lyla released the pictures. They fell to the ground while her hand covered her mouth in distress. One of the images was flipped on its back. Attached was a black rose.

"Is Ritchie on to me?!"

She pulled the DVD out of the box to put it in the DVD player and Silk appeared, saying, "What's up mami? I guess you're wondering what this is all about. Well, little mama, I told you I wanted to make my porn flick, right?"

Lyla struggled for breath.

"Well, thanks to your boy I got what I needed. I didn't know you was into fucking cops and all. Loved the sex in the rain up against the tree, very original I must say. You played with me and you called me fake, well, this is real, ma."

Lyla watched some of the footage as she heard more knocks at her front door. The sex tape showed both the footage from the video shoot in LA with her and Silk, and her and the detective in Philly.

'My boy,' Lyla thought. *He had to be talking about Ritchie, but he wasn't in LA or Philly, unless he had someone spying on me. No, wait a minute...*

"How did you know where to send the roses?"

"Oh, I invented the technology for the satellite, of course. I can see everything and take pictures or video, so don't be surprised if I send you material of you and the guy you cheated on me with."

Lyla reached under her pillow to grab her gun. The gun was missing.

There was another knock on Lyla's door. She paused.

Keys rattled and then her super called her name, "Lyla!" She ran to the door and opened it.

"Hey," Lyla said.

"Is everything okay?" the super asked. "I heard a loud scream. Hold up, who did that to you?" He stared at her chest.

"My breast surgeon of course," Lyla answered sarcastically.

"Your tittie surgeon did that to you?" he said. "You need to sue. Then maybe you can afford to pay me some rent."

"Excuse me," Lyla replied. "What is wrong with my breast?"

"Uh?" her super said. "I'm talking about the marks on your chest." Lyla reddened as she looked down. She forgot to cover her love marks from Poison as she covered them quickly. "It's nothing," Lyla said, embarrassed. "I thought you were referring to my new breast."

"I already saw those double d's in your music video," he responded. "Who could miss them?" Lyla deeply sighed.

"I'm not trying to be disrespectful," he said, as he saw she was uncomfortable.

"I know. I'm being overly sensitive at the moment, and you are right. I do need to pay you some rent money, eventually."

Still distraught, Lyla really did not care about rent money or love marks, she had bigger things on her mind. Lyla was not sure if she should tell her super about what she just discovered, but then she thought he would tell her what to do. But before she could get it out her super said he heard about Ritchie. Lyla gave him a strange stare.

"What do you mean?" Lyla questioned. He saw the reporters and Poison told her super about Lyla passing out, Ritchie attempting to steal his ten thousand dollars, and Rocket's shoe deal from him. But Poison was always absent minded and told her side of the story, which was usually 90% wrong. Lyla told her super some of the story was true.

"Poison told me to give you this," the super said, handing Lyla the envelope she was searching for. "It was lying next to you when she found you. She forgot to give it to you at the hospital."

"Oh man. Thank you so much," Lyla said.

Her super now gave her an odd stare.

"You don't look so well."

"I have something to show you," Lyla said. "But please don't panic. I really need to know what to do about this because there was one nagging "fact" Poison was right about, and that is, Ritchie is crazy."

She showed him Roger's head. Her super was flabbergasted and the room was silent for a split second, the screeching ceiling fan Ritchie never replaced making the only sound.

The super continued to look at the head.

"Call the police." There was another knock on the door and without thinking Lyla ran to the door, and her super shouted, "No, wait!" Too late! She answered the door, and there stood Ritchie and, to her surprise, a rail-thin, bugged out Bizzie.

Considering her hollowed cheeks and dark eyes, she was obviously out of her brain on drugs. Ritchie's face was hidden. He was wearing a huge brimmed hat with a long tan trench coat, and sunglasses.

Lyla's super pulled out his 357 magnum. He threatened Ritchie to stay away from Lyla. As fanatical as Lyla's super was he had no idea who he was dealing with.

"Wait, put that gun away!" Lyla shouted to her super while turning to Ritchie. "What is going on? Why is Bizzie here?"

"Bizzie went with me to be by my side for the operation," Ritchie said.

"I should have been there by your side," Lyla replied.

"You broke up with me," Ritchie reminded.

"Yeah," Bizzie responded. "You're not his girlfriend and you have no right to say anything; you shot at me!"

"No Bizzie," Lyla said. "That was Rocket, she set me up."

"Who is Rocket," Bizzie said. "Anyway, blame it on anybody else but you, right Lyla."

"Believe what you want to believe," Lyla replied. "Just like I told Rocket, you have no idea what he is capable of."

"Look! We're here to pick up his things!" Bizzie yelled. "He's done with you!" Ritchie gave Bizzie a deceitful look. He was up to something. Her super looked at everyone like they had all lost it and said, "Why are you worried about this drugged out he-she."

"Who are you calling a he-she," Bizzie said. "And I'm on prescribed pills through my doctor."

"So you are addicted to prescription pills. Just as bad!" Lyla said.

"Don't put words in my mouth," Bizzie growled.

"She is not popping pills," her super said. "Look at her. She is a drugged out man."

"Fuck you!" Bizzie said.

"Anyway, show Ritchie and he-she the head Lyla! Did you send Lyla a human head, Ritchie?!" Her super walked towards the head. Ritchie pulled out a gun from his coat pocket and held it up like a hunter who shoots for fun.

Ritchie then squeezed the trigger and shot at her super while bending to the side from the pain of his liver; apparently he did not get the operation. He missed the super.

Lyla ran down to the lower level and stopped in the hallway. She saw her super's wife. Lyla heard more gunshots go off but she was thinking she would be safe with the wife.

The super's wife had a huge twelve-gauge shotgun, almost longer than she was tall. Lyla thought the super's wife was on her way to find and help her husband but instead, she had the gun pointed at Lyla.

Come to find out, Rocket told the wife, Lyla was sleeping with her husband and this was obviously what she had told Sugar, suggesting this is Rocket's way of getting Lyla back for not going through with the shoe deal and humiliating her in front of Ritchie when Lyla kicked her ass.

Oh wow! This is what Rocket was warning me about before she died. Rocket is the one who sounded this alarm; she was toxic.

The wife came closer to Lyla and Lyla told her she did not sleep with her husband. At the same time she was telling her this, the super's wife pulled back the pump of the gun to eject the spent shell from the magazine tube to load into the chamber.

While her finger was on the trigger she told Lyla, "I don't believe you you slut!"

"Wait!" Ritchie shouted. The super's wife turned around and saw Ritchie standing in her doorway. "That's my job."

He shot the super's wife in the stomach, causing the gun to fall, sliding to Lyla's area of the floor. Ritchie then aimed his gun at Lyla, bringing back bad memories, like the time Casmir pointed his gun at her.

The conversation escalated, and as Bizzie came running through the door, Lyla asked, "What do you mean, 'that is my job,' Casmir Nowak? I know your real name and it's not Ritchie Perez. Who are you?"

"You always told me you would love me and you would not leave me," Ritchie answered.

"Like I said before" Lyla said. "That's before you slept with Rocket and Bizzie."

"You still don't get it, do you," Ritchie said. "I left the mother of my child to be with you. And you left me. Why didn't you visit my grave?"

"What?" Lyla said with a puzzled look on her face.

"Uh?" Bizzie said.

"The both of you shut up! I'm talking now," Ritchie said angrily.

"You telling me to shut up?" Bizzie replied.

"I told you I would find a way to kill you and no one would know it was me," Ritchie said to Lyla, circling her. Little by little Lyla stepped away, causing her to be further away from the gun on the floor she needed to grab. Bizzie was scared stiff and her subtle movements showed panic.

Meanwhile, tears from fear and pain dropped like a waterfall on Lyla's exotic face, as she said, "I love you. Don't do this, Ritchie. I don't care what your name is; we are destined to be together. Remember our dance in Times Square?"

"No, I love you," Bizzie said.

"You've been brain washed," Lyla said to Bizzie. "You're just as delusional and confused as Rocket."

"You are out of line," Bizzie said.

"No! You are out of control!" Lyla shouted.

She turned back to Ritchie.

"We shared so much together," Lyla reminded. "Please put down the gun." She moved seductively closer to him.

"Don't listen to her, babe," Bizzie said. "I'm the one who's there for you." Bizzie was adding more fuel to the fire.

"Please, Ritchie, I'm begging you," Lyla replied.

"We are way past please," Ritchie said. "Do you know how many people I had to rob, kill, and scam to get enough money to pay for my surgeries?" Lyla stopped crying, but her rosy cheeks showed she was experiencing anxiety.

"What surgeries?" Lyla wondered. "Your liver operation?"

"The face surgery he just had done. You didn't know?" Bizzie questioned.

All of a sudden, Ritchie, still holding the gun pulled off his hat. Lyla glared at him, anticipating.

He looked like...

Ritchie then took off his sunglasses to reveal his face.

"I win, Elizabeth."

"Elizabeth?" Bizzie said bewildered. "Who is Elizabeth?"

Chapter 46

Finding the right man can take almost your entire life but Lyla had no idea it could potentially lead to her death. Ritchie laid his charm on so thick it was hard for woman to see through him, and even Lyla was deceived. People were not always who they seem to be.

Paralyzed with terror, the truth emerged like the lingering teardrops left on Lyla's face, her body feeling like it turned to stone as time froze. Everything came to a head and Lyla thought she saw three of them simultaneously in front of her. The baby in her dream with the hat and trench coat was not her child. It represented her abusive ex-boyfriend from when she was 15-years-old.

You mean to tell me he has been under my nose this whole time, having sex with me, teaching me business, Lyla thought. *Is he a ghost? He's got to be a ghost.*

She continued to stare. His aged skin was young again. His hair was shorter. He went from Spanish to Polish, blue eyes, accent gone, and all. I don't understand.

"I may be going back to my old look soon."

He felt the pain in his side again which made him tilt the gun. Lyla saw a dent, which told her it was the gun that was under her pillow. He was not a ghost. She gathered enough strength from within to stand up against Casmir and not be afraid of him.

"You took my gun," Lyla said with eyes of rage. "Bizzie, this man is a killer!"

"What!" Bizzie shouted.

"He's my ex-boyfriend from years ago! Run, Bizzie, run!" Lyla exclaimed.

"No way, you're insane," Bizzie said.

"Psycho," Lyla said to Casmir.

"Funny," Casmir replied.

"And psycho girl," Lyla said to Bizzie.

"I'm with your man," Bizzie smirked.

"Exactly my point and I'm so happy for you, Bizzie," Lyla said sarcastically.

"You said you would find a way to kill me," Lyla said to Casmir. "And no one would see it coming. You are my pit bull."

Casmir said with a straight, evil face, "I told you I was coming after you and I could have killed you as Ritchie Perez, but I wanted to see the look on your face when you saw it was me. Absolutely priceless. Your family, my family, they don't know I'm alive so they will never suspect me, not even your lawyer." Lyla looked surprised.

"Yeah I know about your lawyer," he continued.

"If you touched him, I will..."

"Don't worry, I spared his life. He has the wrong information anyways," Casmir laughed an evil laugh.

"You take it as far as faking your death," Lyla said, "and then coming to New York to act like my boyfriend."

"Far," Casmir said. "You don't know how far I can take it. I usually freeze my killings until I have an appetite for them, but I heard that Detective Sanchez was on to me so I unfroze one particular person just for you and him. That meat you ate at dinner on my birthday? That was a cooked heart of the witness in Mexico, marinated in my special blood sauce. I remembered you said, 'that hit the spot.'"

Lyla threw up in the nearby trashcan and screamed, "That's sick! There are no words for what you have done."

"I'm not finished. I sent the head of the witness to Sanchez's house," Casmir laughed.

"Pathetic. You are not human," Lyla said. "So you wanted me to die in Mexico?"

"That was the plan," Casmir replied. "But Trigger got a little softhearted on me and saved your life."

I knew he looked familiar. Mexico was all a part of his twisted plan.

Lyla was in a deep whirlwind. He continued to tell her how he pulled this off.

What shocked Lyla the most was that he was not married with kids. The wife and children were all fake except Celina. She was his real daughter. Lyla thought back to what her aunt told her.

"Well, okay. I don't believe anything he says. His family is probably actors."

Ritchie hired the wife, Danny, and Sarah to seem normal.

"Let me give you a word of advice, a man has to be scared of losing a woman, he has to feel like he cannot live without that woman. Julian literally cannot live without me."

Lyla's aunt was right after all, and that was what his "son" wanted to tell Lyla that day at the park. Even the dog from under the table ate the children's crumbs. Now she knew what his wife meant when she said:

"I'm a model and actress too and so are my children, but I'm getting a little extra from the back end for my dedication and years of experience."

"The way you walk, your body structure," Lyla said. "I had a feeling it was you and I even entertained that reincarnation could be true. I thought you were shot."

"I was shot," Casmir confirmed. "But no one knew I survived, so I took advantage of the opportunity. The first attempt on your life at the hospital was impulsive, so I was not successful, but I got my creative juices flowing again. It took me years to fine tune my momentous plan to come after you and finish the job!"

"That's why you have the pain," Lyla said with anger. "It's from the gunshot wound and you didn't leave the country for a liver transplant, you were getting your old face back. Lies! Lies! Lies! The truth ain't in you!"

"Now you got it," Casmir laughed. "You look so beautiful when you are mad."

"Who cares," Bizzie said. "You're no longer his girlfriend!"

He flapped his trench coat; turned towards Bizzie and with a deep low confident voice said, "Neither are you." Casmir shot Bizzie in her upper frail forearm.

Bizzie looked at her arm and looked back at Casmir and screamed, "You shot me!" *Now she's thinking about running the other way but she knew it was too late; Bizzie was played.*

"I have no more use for you," Casmir said.

She unzipped her pants.

"Fuck you! And suck on this!"

Lyla was in shock.

"Oh my goodness, you have a..."

"I'm a MAN bitches!" Bizzie interrupted.

"You're transgendered?" Lyla said. Casmir and Ritchie were improbably prepared for this unveiling. "You sure know how to pick'em, don't you Casmir?"

"A woman there...a man here," Casmir said.

"Like father, like son," Lyla responded.

"It doesn't matter; I just wanted to get your ass. Speaking of ass, how did you like the anal sex?" Casmir grinned, looking at Lyla while shooting Bizzie again and again and again like a piece of raw meat at a slaughterhouse. Bizzie had dug her own grave, but that was definitely overkill.

He continued to look at Lyla like nothing had happened.

"I don't know if you are sick or just mean," Lyla said.

"Consider me both, Mademoiselle," Casmir said.

"I'm not your Mademoiselle, you sociopath!"

"Mademoiselle, my love, Elizabeth, Lyla, it doesn't matter what I call you. But I have to say I almost didn't find you. I had no idea you were going by your middle name. But all that matters is that I did. I was determined to find you. You know my best friend died because of you."

"How so?" Lyla questioned.

"When me, Trigger, and Franky came to your school to fight those guys, he went into a coma that same day and six months later, he died. Trigger's teardrop tattoo is his memorial."

"Don't blame me Casmir," Lyla replied. "You were always in fight mode, I never told you to come to my school to beat up that guy, I never told you to steal my pictures from the agency, you did it all on your own because of your bad temper!"

"That's funny," Casmir said. "Because you never told me to do that stuff but what you should have told me about you did not."

"What are you talking about?" Lyla asked.

"Our baby!" Casmir answered. "I should have had some say in that. He was my baby boy too."

"How do you know it was a he?" Lyla asked. "How did you know I was pregnant or getting an abortion?"

"The sonographer was a friend of mine," Casmir answered, grinning. "She called me the day your dad set up the appointment at the hospital."

"So!" Lyla said. "That explains why she treated me so badly! She also told you when I was leaving the hospital."

"Ding, ding, ding by golly she got it now," Casmir said.

"I was going to keep our baby Casmir, but my dad would not allow it," Lyla replied.

"Well, you still should have come to me."

"I said I was going to keep our baby, but not with you," Lyla said. "You were beating on me. I couldn't raise our baby in those conditions."

"Say what you want, today's is our baby's birthday, or do you even care? I named and nicknamed him. And on top of that, you killed my twins."

"Oh," Lyla said. "So you do admit you had sex with Rocket."

"My son, my twins, and Franky's blood are on your hands," Casmir said vindictively, preparing to shoot Lyla.

"Wait!" she said hysterically.

"Goodbye bitch!" Casmir shouted.

"No," Lyla said. "I knew it was you the whole time. I could tell when we kissed. My heart sung so loudly. I'm still your girlfriend."

"You're lying," Casmir said. "You left me for a Jewish boy."

"My parents made me do it," Lyla said. "I always wanted to be with you, Casmir. I thought you were gone forever."

"I don't believe you, Elizabeth," Casmir responded.

"When your grandmother told me you were shot that was an emotional experience for me, but now that you're alive, you and I can raise your daughter just like if we kept our son. We can be a family, Casmir. Hold my hand as we start this journey."

"You sound so phony," Casmir said.

"I'm being real, the mystery has unfolded," Lyla said. "That's what the blue rose represents, right? A mystery uncovered one can only wish. You are my everything."

Casmir was deep in thought. The grey began to fade. Had the lost boy found direction? Did he believe Lyla? After a few seconds, he lowered his gun while Lyla looked at the gun behind him on the floor that the super's wife dropped. She was ready to grab the gun to shoot Casmir.

"Please Casmir," she said. "Let's try and work this out, you and me...together."

Casmir was still deep in thought. Astonished, he took off his trench coat and put his gun on his hip, underneath his famous white nylon sweat suit he had always worn. Lyla thought she was in the clear but, like a snake that sheds its skin to grow another one, Casmir pulled out his fire torch that the detective had told Lyla about.

"Liar, liar pants on fire," he said, lighting the torch. "Now I'm going to have you for dinner." Lyla did not know what to do as he drew closer to her, the sweat suit material making a swishing sound along the way.

Then it dawned on Lyla why Casmir was acting this way. Love can cut deep enough to make a person do crazy things, but this went way deeper than her. Lyla knew this was her time to really get in his mind, and she knew just where to start.

"Casmir!" Lyla said.

"Come here!" Casmir yelled.

"Your dad, Casmir!" Lyla said. Casmir stopped walking towards her.

"What about my dad?"

"I know he hurt you. Your father said, he was born gay, when in fact he only turned gay after you were born."

"You know nothing about my family, especially my dad," Casmir said.

"You know I know your family, and especially your dad. You think that because your dad turned gay after you were born, you felt like you were nothing. You think you caused your dad to become gay."

"Shut up!" Casmir yelled.

"This is why you change your identity: because you hate yourself," Lyla said.

"No," Casmir groaned.

"The fire represents your pain; you eat the people you kill to get rid of the pain and I reminded you of that pain when I left you. You think everyone is out to hurt you. You see this goes way deeper than me," Lyla continued.

"That's not true," Casmir roared. "Don't interfere in something you know nothing about, you think you know the whole story but you have no idea."

"Yes, it is true," Lyla said as she saw something peeling on Casmir's neck. "Your father did this to you and you hate me because I remind you of your neglect, but your dad loves you and I do too. Don't let your dad take over your life anymore. Let's build a real family together."

It looked like Lyla might have gotten through to him from the lowered torch, but then he raised it again.

"No! I'm in control!"

Casmir charged at Lyla with the torch, but her super came rushing through the opened door. He noticed Bizzie laying dead on the floor, but had not yet seen his wife laying there as dark red blood ran slowly out of her body. Lyla's super shot Casmir in the arm. Casmir dropped the torch, but it did not stop him from reaching for his gun on his hip and pointing it at her super.

The super leaped out of the way to escape the gunfire but one caught him in the shoulder and he fell, right next to his wife, who was struggling to breathe.

Lyla grabbed the gun she saw on the floor earlier. Casmir turned around and aimed the gun at her, but then winced and lowered it; he was finally feeling pain from the gunshot.

He ran after Lyla, holding his arm. When he caught up with her, he hit Lyla fast and he hit her hard. She fell to the ground and her gun went flying across the tiled floor.

Lyla grabbed a nearby chair. She hit him on his arm as hard as she could as his gun skimmed the floor. Lyla found herself in a sparring match with Casmir, and she was time enough for him. He ripped her shirt and punched her face while she kicked him in the liver. There was no reaction. *That's was weird.*

Instead, Lyla kicked him where the sun didn't shine. She was able to drop this monster down to his knees. The only thing Lyla needed was a phone cord to wrap around his neck and something to stick up his ass like he did to her.

In a pool of his own blood, Casmir slowly but surely crawled towards his gun as she followed behind him. Her super slid Lyla his gun. She grabbed it. Casmir and Lyla knew that he was on his way to meet Rocket in hell as she thought about Rocket's last words:

"They won't open the door."

Lyla knew that was a spiritual thing between God and Rocket. And Lyla also knew she was referring to God not opening the gates of heaven to her. Lyla could never tell Poison that.

"You're a weak, demonic, conniving human being. No compassion for humanity," Lyla said to Casmir as she noticed his neck peeling more and more. "You murdered Roger, he was an innocent victim!" Casmir and the gun finally met up like old friends as she heard loud banging coming from the front gate downstairs.

Lyla ignored the sound as she faced the moment of truth. She stood over Casmir and held the gun with both hands. Would she take her chance and set herself free?

She was ready to shoot him but then she began to cry. Lyla realized she could not bring herself to kill him. She heard her phone ringing. Lyla did not know where it was, but she knew it was Pastor Bill based on the ringtone she assigned him.

"An eye for an eye. There's got to be another way."

Lyla silently prayed for help and said, "Repent and save your soul Casmir." His gloom of utter darkness was reserved as she lowered her gun.

Casmir lifted his gun towards her; she huffed. *Click, click, click,* there were no more bullets. He looked like a blown out tire with no spare. Casmir gave her a heartless and uncaring blank stare. Lyla realized there was no rehabilitation for this creep and he needed to be taken off the streets.

"The devil has been sinning from the beginning and so have you," Lyla said. Forgetting to breathe, she held the gun again towards him with no particular direction, still hesitating.

"Lyla, shoot him!" her super shouted.

"She can't, she still loves me," Casmir laughed.

"Wrong," Lyla corrected, fighting her alter ego. "I don't want to be like you. Your father took over your life, but I'm no longer letting you take over mine."

"Maybe this will help you rethink that," her super said to Lyla, as he grabbed a rolled up envelope from his back pants pocket. She noticed it was the mysterious envelope. "This is the real reason why he hates you," the super continued, tossing the envelope towards her. She picked up the envelope to observe the information.

Lyla stood there pondering, and then dropped the envelope on the floor.

"I told you," Lyla said. "Your dad did this to you. I knew this went way deeper than me but it goes even way deeper than what I would have ever imagined. I was wrong about one thing, why you like fire, why you like to torture people. I gave you my fragile heart to cherish and love, but you are a little boy in a man's world."

"What is in that envelope?" Casmir questioned.

"You know what it is," Lyla answered. She grabbed the gun with both of her hands again attempting to hold it steady. Lyla tightly closed her eyes so that she did not have to watch herself shoot him, when seconds later, a lady appeared in her mind. It was the high lady at the condiment table in the café.

"May the Lord bless you."

"Jesus," Lyla whispered in the air. A gunshot went off. Lyla opened her eyes. Casmir laid there with a fatal gunshot to the back. "Forgive me, Lord," Lyla continued.

She looked at the gun and then threw it down. Lyla turned her head and her super's assistant was there with the shotgun in his hand pointed at Casmir. In the end, the 'gentle giant' killed Casmir. *I guess the assistant skipped his medication today*, Lyla thought.

She hugged him while crying and then ran to her super. Lyla's super made painful sounds as he held his shoulder.

She embraced him.

"Someone call an ambulance! "Don't die! Don't die! Stay with us!" The people in the building who heard all the commotion had presumably already called authorities.

The superintendant's assistant cautioned Lyla not to move her super until the paramedics arrived, but the super said he was okay.

As Lyla continued to hold her super, she could see Casmir's body jerking, but in a matter of seconds, it stopped. She stared at the blood-saturated walls and furniture surrounding Casmir, and then glanced over at him again.

"This whole time, I thought I was doing something to Casmir," Lyla said. "But the information in the envelope said it all."

Cops in uniforms filled the room, releasing Lyla from the horror. She was pleasantly shocked to see that one of the authorities was Detective Sanchez.

Lyla approached him after the ambulance rolled her super away and asked, "How is it you knew to come here?" as the EMT gave Lyla a large blanket to cover her bloody body.

"This place is a mess. The clean-up crew has got their work cut out for them," Sanchez said as the investigators processed the crime scene.

"You are going to ignore me now," Lyla said.

"Hello stranger," Sanchez replied.

"Answer my question," Lyla demanded.

"Despite your trickery in Philly," Sanchez said, "we looked into that Times Square shooting and we saw you and Casmir. He planned the dance routine for you. I could see it was not the same guy we had a picture of, but being a seasoned detective, I rolled the dice on a hutch and I went with it. We put up surveillance in his house."

"I'm sorry I left the room," Lyla said. "I was scared."

"I understand, you like to keep secrets," Sanchez said.

"Ha, ha, ha detective," Lyla said. "I could not tell you everything, at the time, but I will not deceive you anymore."

"Okay, we will see, but seriously," Sanchez replied, "we followed Casmir when he returned from his trip. We tracked him to this location and waited outside. It's hard to hear anything in this building, but then we saw the tenants running and screaming. By the time we got to the front door downstairs, we couldn't find anyone to let us in, so we busted in."

"Thank you detective," Lyla said. "So, are you going to cuff me?"

"Not this time," the detective smiled. "We are sorry we could not catch Casmir sooner, but this man was of many faces; a true artist. He used all kinds of identities to rob, steal, and kill people." The detective grabbed his laptop.

"Really?" Lyla said.

"Casmir was not only disguising himself as a loving person to swindle you," Sanchez said, showing Lyla the photos from his laptop. "But as a landscaper, pizza man, maintenance guy, and even a woman."

I wonder what would have happened if I never asked him at Madison Square Garden, where he was from? Would he have secretly followed me this whole time with his selected cast of characters to kill me?

She glanced again at the photo with the woman.

"I know this lady. Where do I know her from?" She stared, then glared, at the image. "Oh yeah, she was the lady from Elite Modeling Agency. She was one of the judges at my contest in Virginia back in the day.

Wow he has been following me longer than I thought, since way before I moved to New York.

"He did enough damage in Philly," Sanchez said. "But the thing that most puzzled the department for years was why he came to New York. Now we know why."

"Anyway, now the speculation is over," Lyla said. "Well, actually..."

"We thought he was getting surgeries done, but he used other skillful techniques that looked real to the human eye," Sanchez interrupted, "and unfortunately there is one more thing I have to tell you. When we got the warrant to search his house there was..."

"I already know," Lyla interrupted.

"Uh?" Sanchez said. "Know what?"

She handed him the envelope and walked over to Casmir. Lyla then searched for the area where she saw something peeling on Casmir's neck.

"Hey, wait!" Carpenter said. "Here are some gloves."

Lyla took the gloves.

"So you know this is *not* Casmir," Sanchez said, as Lyla put the gloves on.

"Yes," Lyla said, "but I don't know who it is."

"When did you find out?" Sanchez questioned.

"Today," Lyla answered.

She found the peeling area and ripped off a mask. Underneath the mask was Casmir's brother.

"I'm sorry, Lyla," the detective said.

"Sorry for what?" Lyla asked. "There is nothing to be sorry about. He never had plastic surgeries done. He used masks."

"Straight from the movie, *Mission Impossible*, type masks," Carpenter replied.

She studied the mask and said, "Exactly. The masks were to make us think he had surgeries done to carry out Casmir's mission to murder me."

"Casmir and his brother were fugitive's," the detective informed.

"I had no idea his brother was a fugitive," Lyla said. "I thought he was the nice one in the family." *But, like I said before, the whole family is crazy as far as I'm concerned.*

"Casmir's brother is the oldest and more dangerous than Casmir," the detective said. "He taught Casmir everything he knows. That is how he was able to fool you."

"Wow," Lyla replied.

"So, where is Casmir?" Sanchez asked.

"Well, detective, Philly will be happy to know they are both dead," Lyla answered sharply. "I keep telling you Casmir is dead!"

"Okay!" Sanchez said. "I believe you."

"Good!" Lyla responded.

"You are lucky to be alive," Sanchez said, handing back the envelope.

"No," Lyla said. "I'm blessed to be alive, and I know you thought this impostor was walking all over me, like he had me whipped or something."

"Well, at first," he admitted.

"Detective," Lyla said. "Casmir's brother figured out what I wanted and appeared to be smarter than everyone else. I was his supposedly girlfriend, plus he had his mistresses and supposedly wife and kids, a New York City playboy. The mansions were all a fantasy, an unreal world of money and glamour..."

"Yelp," the detective interrupted. "That is why it was hard to tell fact from fiction, Lyla."

"But everything that happens in the dark eventually comes out into the light," Lyla continued. "And whatever ditch someone digs for someone else, they dig for themselves, and they fall right in it, just ask Rocket and Bizzie."

"And Casmir and his brother," the detective added.

"Yes. And on another note, I used to let men take over my mind and use and abuse me but now I make them think they can control me while I'm always a step ahead." She looked at Sanchez like he knew she got over on him too.

"Good for you," Sanchez said. "Casmir's brother mailed some pictures of you and me to my wife."

Maybe I'm not a step ahead.

"Who is keeping secrets now, detective?" Lyla asked.

"I failed to mention I'm married," the detective answered, "but don't be mad at me."

"You men can't help but be deceitful, why be mad," she replied, seductively gazing into his eyes. "You deserve a good guy, someone who will treat you like a queen, but until that happens we can continue to have some fun. No one has to know about us."

"Love is naughty Sanchez," Lyla smiled, as she looked away. "But I will know about us and those days are over for me. I'm practicing abstinence until I meet my husband and I mean it this time. Lyla pondered. Or maybe I already met my husband?"

"Really?" Sanchez said.

"Yes."

"Okay, Ms. Tight," he said, as they were interrupted by a media hurricane outside the super's apartment door.

"Are you happy Casmir is dead?!" a reporter asked. "What was in the envelope?!" another reporter shouted. "Is that really Casmir? What are you going to do about the sex tape between you and the detective?"

The authorities pushed the media away and Detective Sanchez bellowed, "Lyla is not answering any of your questions!" The media was escorted out of the area.

The detective quickly turned to Lyla and asked, "What sex tape?"

"Don't worry, you cannot see our faces," she answered.

"It's obvious they can," the detective said.

"The media is only assuming it's us because we are so cute together," she said, as she touches the tip of his nose. "And fun."

"This is not a joke," the detective said. "Where is this tape?"

"Have a nice life, detective," Lyla smiled.

She swayed her dips and grooves like a tigress walking into a Burmese asylum. He stared subtly at her feline grace as her long legs walked right out of his life forever.

Chapter 47

Months Later

Lyla's superintendent survived the gunshot wound. The bullet only grazed his shoulder. His wife also made it through her gunshot but sadly she was thrown in jail to await her trail for attempted murder on Lyla's life. Later, she would reach out from behind bars to ask Lyla to drop the charges. Lyla dropped them for her super and their children. She figured the gunshot wound was enough punishment, and she knew Rocket was the one who filled her head with shattered lies.

Unfortunately, the prosecution re-opened the case and charged her with a lower charge of attempted manslaughter. *Very ambitious.*

On a lighter note, the dream of becoming a model came true for Casmir's daughter! Lyla decided to manage Celina's career with the help of her super.

Lyla had no idea Casmir was a father. Now his daughter was a beautiful 15-year-old young lady, and Lyla also discovered who the mother of the child was: Binga, her best friend at the time when Lyla met Casmir at the mall. *I must have died a thousand deaths when I found out,* Lyla said to herself.

But I should have known, because Celina is a Polish name and Binga and Casmir are Polish. Furthermore, Lyla had always wondered why her friend became distant and basically turned on Lyla out of nowhere...*unbelievable.*

Lyla also found out how Casmir's brother gained sole custody of Casmir's daughter. Binga gave full custody to

Casmir because she could not handle the guilt. Then after Casmir's death his brother gained full custody.

At the time, no one knew how crazy Casmir's brother was.

It's funny how life worked out. Eventually, Lyla became more than just a manager to Celina she ended up adopting her. She was happy because she wasn't sure if she could have children. Now Lyla knew why the doctor was calling her Celina. It was a sign from God, and she knew at the picnic that she and Celina had a connection.

Lyla did pretty well with her career but she hung up her wigs and stilettos and retired as a video girl. Instead, Lyla choose to use her name and MBA to focus on her daughter's career and promote Steam. The first modeling gig they booked for Celina was a $250,000 contract with a reputable make-up company. Russian lady, eat your heart out.

The shoot was in South Africa.

"See? At the end of the day," her superintendant said.

"Yes," Lyla smiled. "God works in mysterious ways and you got your rent money plus more."

It was like God started Lyla's life back at the beginning but through someone else – her daughter. *Literally starting over.* Those pictures surfing the Internet were taken down because Lyla was a minor and anyone that had them would be thrown in jail for child pornography.

Right before they boarded the plane to South Africa, her phone rang. It was Lyla's mom. She was actually really happy to hear her voice. In spite of everything that happened between them, she loved her mom and she knew her mom adored her.

Lyla recognized that her mom could not do any better. She was brought up in an abusive environment, and it caused her mind to be misguided. Lyla's mom thought fighting was normal, so when someone showed her love and kindness, that wasn't normal.

In turn, Lyla's mom had to attack whoever showed her love in order to feel love, but she had freed her mind of what happened in her past. And Lyla can say with confidence that she was happy to have a praying mother.

Lyla told her mom she was on her way to South Africa. She knew Lyla to be spontaneous.

"Didn't you just come from a honeymoon for two with your special someone?" her mom asked.

"Yes," Lyla answered, giggling. "The island was beautiful but shhhh, no one knows about that yet."

"Okay, sweetie," her mom said.

They prayed and her mom apologized for how she treated her. She explained to her how upset she was about the relationship Lyla had with Casmir. Her mom also told Lyla she knew about the abortion and how she found out.

Lyla's mom was shocked to know that the sonographer was Casmir's friend.

"I should have been there for you more, especially when choosing the right man instead of preaching to you." Then it dawned on Lyla why she picked reckless guys.

"Mom," Lyla said. "Let me tell you a little secret. The best way to help a teenager in an abusive relationship is to figure out the root of the problem."

"How is that?" her mom asked.

"If a young girl is dating an abusive boyfriend, it is obvious she has low self-esteem," Lyla answered. "Instead of telling me to stay away from Casmir it would have been better if you had of help me build my self-esteem by indirectly doing self-esteem exercises with me. Because when you told me to leave Casmir alone, it only pushed me into his arms and farther away from you."

"Okay, I'm listening," her mom said.

"Once that self-esteem is built, introduce me to a good guy. But don't tell me that is what you are going to do. Invite me to a gathering where you know guys are going to be."

"That makes sense."

"I bet you I would have left Casmir alone and went with the nice guy, because now I feel good about myself, and in turn, my relationship with you will still be strong because you're not fighting me about the bad dude."

"Wow, you are right," her mom smiled. "But what if during the process you are harmed while I'm teaching you about self-esteem?"

"Either way, it's a process," Lyla said. "So if I get hurt, it was going to happen anyway but at least you know you did your best and took a responsible and effective approach. And if I did need to talk to someone, I would have felt comfortable coming to you to talk because our relationship is still strong during this process.

"In other words, mom, if parents do not nip it in the bud, any teenage girl will continue to date the wrong guy for the rest of her life and end up marrying that wrong guy."

"Well, it looks like I did something right when I raised you. You are very wise," her mom said.

"Yes mom, you did," Lyla smiled. "It took me some time to learn this and I still have more learning to do."

"I love you," her mom said.

"I love you too," Lyla replied.

My aunt was right, once again.

Lyla told her mom she would call her when she arrived. On the plane, she thought about her and her mom's conversation, everything that happened in the past year, and Casmir.

Although Casmir was a messed up individual, Lyla will always love him with all of her heart. That was her first love and a person can only experience that once in a lifetime.

Lyla stared out the window with delight as the pleasant memories of the Casmir she fell in love with flowed back to her in a rush...

"For the first time, I began to see and understand the taste and texture of love."

"His rich and radiant diamond like eyes made contact with mine, captivating every nerve in my body as if our spirits had known each other forever."

"He held up a bag to hand to me. I accepted the gesture and looked inside; it was red coated popcorn, the only kind I ate."

"He was undeniably a true gentleman with a pleasant and respectable persona."

"I'm a sucker for her love," he said to my dad."

"All of my good morals and values went out the window as I gave Casmir my virginity that night."

And with a silent tear, Lyla forgave Casmir and his brother. Her anger was released and ultimately, she finally had closure.

But Lyla still couldn't believe she missed or ignored the signs and didn't realize what kind of danger she was in. One of the things she did do to move forward was change her number. Nestle sent her an email asking for her new number. He also owned up to being a jerk and he wanted to get back together.

Sometimes love the second time around was good, but not with Nestle Crunch.

"Knockem Out Lil Nestle...Knockem Out...Knockem Out Lil Nestle...Crunch!"

Lyla ignored the message only to receive another one asking if she could help him with his career.

What for? Lyla thought. *He is on Showtime and HBO. What does he need me for? This is just another trick to ruin my life. Besides, he should have appreciated me when he had me.* Lyla just wanted to move on, rebuild her life, and enjoy it. She replied back.

"I'm not on the market anymore."

Lyla scrolled through the Internet on her phone. She Googled Casmir, to see what came up this time.

Lyla saw an article that read, "Fugitive, Bogdan Nowak, brother of killer Casmir Nowak is dead. He was found in New York City. We would like to thank Lyla Tight for helping us uncover the crime mystery." Lyla showed her super and after he read it he asked, "What about me? I saved the day as well."

"Yes you did and 'the gentle giant,'" Lyla smiled.

"God please protect me," Lyla prayed. "No one has the right to hurt someone else. Thank you for getting me through all of this. I'm so grateful you protected me even though I disobeyed you so many times, but because of your mercy I'm still here. And thank you for the opportunity to break the family curse by giving me a daughter that I can love. Amen."

The Lord never said it was going to be easy once you become a Christian. He never said we would be free of sin and wouldn't make mistakes. The difference is, Lyla knew to go to God when she was in trouble and not to sex, drugs, or alcohol anymore. But she was happy to know he would never judge her for what she did. God forgave Lyla just like she forgave Casmir and his brother.

On another note, *I dated thugs with missing teeth, GQ pretty boys, and every type in between,* she said to herself, *but I have come to the conclusion that although bad boys are more exciting and fun, it is time for me to leave them alone with an exclamation mark at the end of that sentence.*

It's never worth fighting or dying over a man, as she thought back to what the pastor told her during one of their sessions, "Lyla you have grown by leaps and bounds and it's amazing you haven't been fully scared by any of your life tragedies. Do you realize God has been spoiling you by not causing your past to permanently damage you?"

"Yeah," Lyla smiled with her eyes. "God has finally pulled me out of the lion's den without a serious scratch. And the funny part is I haven't even told you the whole story, but the important thing is I'm a reborn virgin and I'm alive.

"You want to know a secret? That 15-year-old lost girl is me; I'm Elizabeth 'Lyla' Tight. Now I'm strong and wise enough to tell my story," as she cut out the new headline from her newspaper, "The Fugitive's (Ex) Girlfriend." She placed it in her diary and wrote:

Dear God,

I find myself looking back at the chapters of my life and wondering why I had to relive the events that happened to me. Now, I realize why.

Looking back made me see where I came from and how far you have brought me. I still have a lot to face and it took a great deal of real courage to come out okay on this end.

Before I left for South Africa, I was able come from behind the shadows to hold a way overdue press conference. I spoke about my career, the teenage abuse I went through with Casmir, the abuse I went through as an adult, and how Casmir's brother wanted to finish the job of murdering me. I shared how my life has evolved and how I have become a better person, no matter how painful my experiences have been. Like Poison said in so many words, my experiences will only make me stronger!

A woman from my church told me about five years ago I would have a testimony. I looked at her like she was foolish but she was right.

Most people think that a testimony is supposed to be happy and positive but some testimonies are not, like mine. Some testimonies are meant to shine a light down on your sin and to show you where you may need to ask God for forgiveness.

I remember when a few of my girlfriends from church said, "I can't believe you were in music videos, you are supposed to be a Christian."

"What are you doing watching the videos?" I said.

Some other church friends asked, "Why did you have sex out of marriage?"

"Why do you have five kids out of wedlock?" I said.

People are quick to point the finger but they have to understand we all have sinned and have come short of the glory of God.

Thank you God again for listening. Oh and thanks for my monster truck!

"What are you writing?" her super asked.

I safely tucked my diary away and said, "Just a little something."

"Probably writing about her new man," Celina laughed.

"Ha, ha," I said.

The super looked at Celina.

"You know you are supposed to be studying for a test. No matter, how much money you make in modeling, you have to keep up with your studies, right Lyla?"

"Oh, please, she already knows all of that stuff she is studying. Celina will be teaching the test, instead of the test teaching her." We all laughed as I thought about my purpose in life.

I know why God kept me alive when Casmir wanted me dead, He wants me to help other abusive teens and women. But first, He had me humbly expose myself to not only me, but to the world.

In turn, I use my platform to passionately teach young adults about self-esteem through my modeling and Read –n-

Style workshops. I'm like their mom. They actually call me mom, as I smile.

I think what I love the most is, regardless of my retirement from modeling, magazines want to interview and shoot me for the covers about the workshops. This, to me, is success, and I did not have to sell my soul to get here.

The questions I'm always asked during an interview are, "What was in the envelope? And is this a true story?" The questions are simple, right? Well, I sit back and think about those questions, and I tell them to mind their freakin' business, as I giggle. All that matters is that a woman named Lyla Tight put her life on the line to help all women who want to be helped. It's up to the reader to figure out what secrets are true and which ones are fantasies.

But whether this story is true or not, I would not change a thing. The conclusion during my interviews is that we all fall down; what counts is how we get back up.

YCliff told me one secret I could never tell, but I can tell you something else he told me, "Life is like a cycle and when it's your turn no one can stop it!"

Honestly, you want to know one more secret? I always thought modeling was my desire but in the end, it was my stepping-stone to lead me in the direction of something bigger, just like Pastor Bill told me. I have succeeded and overcame! I feel like my life is just beginning and I'm so spiritually, mentally, and physically strong. No one can knock down my castle!

While relaxing by the pool drinking lemonade at the beautiful resort in South Africa, I looked at my real Rolex watch to see what time it was. I can afford it now. The money that was supposedly forgotten in Mexico, well, I got that cash and gave it to an organization fighting against sex trafficking. But the reward money for Casmir's brother is mine. As a bonus, I received a nice huge settlement for my burned hair and negotiated a fifty million dollar deal to sell off my 101 ideas.

The buyers entitled it, "The Fifty Million Dollar Gold Mine."

I once said to Rocket, "We will see who is by the poolside with it all." I smirk at the memory while I glance down at my wedding band, enjoying my charmed life.

Ryland and I made up just in time for her to help plan my wedding. She even moved to New York on the upper eastside near us.

Oh, wow it's time for my daughter's photo shoot. I turned around and saw an average looking guy with a very kind personality who definitely felt comfortable around me now.

"How is my wife today?" he said so graciously.

I responded with a bright sparkling 'Peppermint' smile...

"Wealthy," as my husband and I held hands, and he replied, "This extended honeymoon just gets better and better..."

"As if the island wasn't enough," I said, completing his sentence.

He smiled and kissed my bottom lip softly, as I thought how lovely it feels to finally be with a proper gentleman.

"I love you," he said.

"I love you more," she said.

"I love you more," he said.

"I love you more," she giggled.

"I love you more," he said.

Okay you win this one, Pastor Bill.

The End!

Domestic Violence Hotline

There is a light at the end of this story and there can be one for you too. If anyone is involved in domestic violence please contact House of Ruth at 1-888-880-7884.

Romans Road

Lyla repented and asked God for forgiveness and because He is a merciful God he forgave her regardless of what she did. If you would like that same kind of forgiveness follow the information below and be blessed!

Romans Road to Salvation – It's Simple

Read:

- Romans 3:23
- Romans 3:10-18
- Romans 6:23
- Romans 5:8
- Romans 10:9
- Romans 10:13
- Romans 5:1
- Romans 8:1
- Romans 8:38-39

Say this Prayer:

"God, I know that I have sinned against you and am deserving of punishment. But Jesus Christ took the punishment that I deserve so that through faith in Him I could be forgiven. With your help, I place my trust in You for salvation. Thank You for Your wonderful grace and forgiveness - the gift of eternal life! Amen!"

This prayer has now declared you to God and that you are relying on Jesus Christ for your salvation. The words themselves will not save you. Only faith in Jesus Christ can provide salvation!

34238445R00255

Made in the USA
Middletown, DE
14 August 2016